DUDLEY PUBLIC LIBRARIES

The loan of this book may be renewed if not required by other readers, by contacting the library from which it was borrowed.

D1464040

4

Italian Playboys

June 2021	September 2021
Temptations	**Proposals**
July 2021	October 2021
Nights	**Innocence**
August 2021	November 2021
Tycoons	**Seduction**

Italian Playboys: Tycoons

CATHY WILLIAMS

JENNIFER FAYE

CHANTELLE SHAW

MILLS & BOON

First Published in Great Britain 2021
by Mills & Boon, an imprint of HarperCollins*Publishers* Ltd,
1 London Bridge Street, London, SE1 9GF

www.harpercollins.co.uk

HarperCollins*Publishers*
1st Floor, Watermarque Building,
Ringsend Road, Dublin 4, Ireland

ITALIAN PLAYBOYS: TYCOONS © 2021 Harlequin Books S.A.

The Uncompromising Italian © 2014 Cathy Williams
Return of the Italian Tycoon © 2015 Harlequin Books S.A.
A Bride Worth Millions © 2015 Chantelle Shaw

Special thanks and acknowledgement are given to Jennifer Faye for her contribution to *The Vineyards of Calanetti* series.

ISBN: 978-0-263-30250-9

MIX
Paper from
responsible sources
FSC® C007454

This book is produced from independently certified FSC™ paper to ensure responsible forest management.

For more information visit: www.harpercollins.co.uk/green

Printed and bound in Spain
by CPI, Barcelona

THE UNCOMPROMISING ITALIAN

CATHY WILLIAMS

To my wonderful daughters.

CHAPTER ONE

LESLEY FOX SLOWLY drew to a stop in front of the most imposing house she had ever seen.

The journey out of London had taken barely any time at all. It was Monday, it was the middle of August and she had been heading against the traffic. In all it had taken her under an hour to leave her flat in crowded Ladbroke Grove and arrive at a place that looked as though it should be plastered on the cover of a *House Beautiful* magazine.

The wrought-iron gates announced its splendour, as had the tree-lined avenue and acres of manicured lawns through which she had driven.

The guy was beyond wealthy. Of course, she had known that. The first thing she had done when she had been asked to do this job had been to look him up online.

Alessio Baldini—Italian, but resident in the UK for a long time. The list of his various companies was vast and she had skipped over all of that. What he did for a living was none of her business. She had just wanted to make sure that the man existed and was who Stan said he was.

Commissions via friends of friends were not always to be recommended, least of all in her niche sideline business. A girl couldn't be too careful, as her father liked to say.

She stepped out of her little Mini, which was dwarfed in the vast courtyard, and took a few minutes to look around her.

The brilliance of a perfect summer's day made the sprawling green lawns, the dense copse to one side lush with lavender and the clambering roses against the stone of the mansion facing her seem almost too breathtakingly beautiful to be entirely real.

This country estate was in a league of its own.

There had been a bit of information on the Internet about where the man lived, but no pictures, and she had been ill-prepared for this concrete display of wealth.

A gentle breeze ruffled her short brown hair and for once she felt a little awkward in her routine garb of lightweight combat trousers, espadrilles and one of her less faded tee-shirts advertising the rock band she had gone to see five years ago.

This didn't seem the sort of place where dressing down would be tolerated.

For the first time, she wished she had paid a little more attention to the details of the guy she was going to see.

There had been long articles about him but few pictures and she had skimmed over those, barely noting which one he was amidst the groups of boring men in business suits who'd all seemed to wear the identical smug smiles of people who had made far too much money for their own good.

She grabbed her laptop from the passenger seat and slammed the door shut.

If it weren't for Stan, she wouldn't be here now. She didn't need the money. She could afford the mortgage on her one-bedroom flat, had little interest in buying pointless girly clothes for a figure she didn't possess to attract men in whom she had scant interest—or who, she amended with scrupulous honesty to herself, had scant interest in *her*—and she wasn't into expensive, long-haul holidays.

With that in mind, she had more than enough to be going on with. Her full-time job as a website designer paid well and, as far as she was concerned, she lacked for nothing.

But Stan was her dad's long-time friend from Ireland. They had grown up together. He had taken her under his wing when she had moved down to London after university and she owed him.

With any luck, she would be in and out of the man's place in no time at all.

She breathed in deeply and stared at the mansion in front of her.

It seemed a never-ending edifice of elegant cream stone, a dream of a house, with ivy climbing in all the right places and windows that looked as though they dated back to the turn of the century.

This was just the sort of ostentatious wealth that should have held little appeal, but in fact she was reluctantly charmed by its beauty.

Of course, the man would be a lot less charming than his house. It was always the way. Rich guys always thought they were God's gift to women even when they obviously weren't. She had met one or two in her line of work and it had been a struggle to keep a smile pinned to her face.

There was no doorbell but an impressive knocker. She could hear it reverberating through the bowels of the house as she banged it hard on the front door and then stood back to wait for however long it would take for the man's butler or servant, or whoever he employed to answer doors for him, to arrive on the scene and let her in.

She wondered what he would look like. Rich and Italian, so probably dark-haired with a heavy accent. Possibly short, which would be a bit embarrassing, because she was five-eleven and a half and likely to tower over him—never a good thing. She knew from experience that men hated women who towered over them. He would probably be quite dapper, kitted out in expensive Italian gear and wearing expensive Italian footwear. She had no idea what either might look like but it was safe to say that trainers and old clothes would not feature on the sartorial menu.

She was fully occupied amusing herself with a variety of mental pictures when the door was pulled open without warning.

For a few seconds, Lesley Fox lost the ability to speak. Her lips parted and she stared. Stared in a way she had never stared at any man in her life before.

The guy standing in front of her was, quite simply, beautiful. Taller than her by a few inches, and wearing faded jeans and a navy-blue polo shirt, he was barefoot. Raven-black hair was combed back from a sinfully sexy face. His eyes were as black as his hair and lazily returned her stare, until she felt the blood rush to her face and she returned to Planet Earth with a feeling of sickening embarrassment.

'Who are you?'

His cool, rich, velvety voice galvanised her senses back into working order and she cleared her throat and reminded herself that she wasn't the type of girl who had ever been daunted by a guy, however good-looking he was. She came from a family of six and she was the only girl. She had been brought up going to rugby matches, watching the football on television, climbing trees and exploring the glorious countryside of wild Ireland with brothers who hadn't always appreciated their younger sister tagging along.

She had always been able to handle the opposite sex. She had lived her life being one of the lads, for God's sake!

'I'm here about your… Er…my name's Lesley Fox.' As an afterthought, she stuck out her hand and then dropped it when he failed to respond with a return gesture.

'I wasn't expecting a girl.' Alessio looked at her narrowly. That, he thought, had to be the understatement of the year. He had been expecting a Les Fox—Les, as in a man. Les, as in a man who was a contemporary of Rob Dawson, his IT guy. Rob Dawson was in his forties and resembled a beach ball. He had been expecting a forty-something-year-old man of similar build.

Instead, he was looking at a girl with cropped dark hair, eyes the colour of milk chocolate and a lanky, boyish physique, wearing…

Alessio took in the baggy sludge-green trousers with awkward pockets and the faded tee-shirt.

He couldn't quite recall the last time he had seen a woman dressed with such obvious, scathing disregard for fashion.

Women always tried their very hardest when around him to show their best side. Their hair was always perfect, make-up always flawless, clothes always the height of fashion and shoes always high and sexy.

His eyes drifted down to her feet. She was wearing cloth shoes.

'I'm so sorry to have disappointed you, Mr Baldini. I

take it you *are* Mr Baldini and not his manservant, sent to chase away callers by being rude to them?'

'I didn't think anyone used that term any more...'

'What term?'

'*Manservant*. When I asked Dawson to provide me with the name of someone who could help me with my current little...problem, I assumed he would have recommended someone a bit older. More experienced.'

'I happen to be very good at what I do.'

'As this isn't a job interview, I can't very well ask for references.' He stood aside, inviting her to enter. 'But, considering you look as though you're barely out of school, I'll want to know a little bit about you before I explain the situation.'

Lesley held on to her temper. She didn't need the money. Even though the hourly rate that she had been told about was staggering, she really didn't have to stand here and listen to this perfect stranger quiz her about her experience for a job she hadn't applied for. But then she thought of Stan and all he had done for her and she gritted back the temptation to turn on her heel, climb back into her car and head down to London without a backward glance.

'Come on in,' Alessio threw over his shoulder as she remained hovering on the doorstep and, after a few seconds, Lesley took a step into the house.

She was surrounded by pale marble only broken by the richness of a Persian rug. The walls were adorned with the sort of modern masterpieces that should have looked out of place in a house of this age but somehow didn't. The vast hall was dominated by a staircase that swept upwards before branching out in opposite directions, and doors indicated that there was a multitude of rooms winging on either side, not that she wouldn't have guessed.

More than ever, she felt inappropriately dressed. He might be casual, but he was casual in the sort of elegant, expensive way of the very wealthy.

'Big place for one person,' she said, staring around her, openly impressed.

'How do you know I haven't got a sprawling family lurking somewhere out of sight?'

'Because I looked you up,' Lesley answered truthfully. Her eyes finally returned to him and once again she was struck by his dark, saturnine good looks. And once again she had to drag her eyes away reluctantly, desperate to return her gaze to him, to drink him in. 'I don't usually travel into unknown territory when I do my freelance jobs. Usually the computer comes to me, I don't go to the computer.'

'Always illuminating to get out of one's comfort zone,' Alessio drawled. He watched as she ran her fingers through her short hair, spiking it up. She had very dark eyebrows, as dark as her hair, which emphasised the peculiar shade of brown of her eyes. And she was pale, with satiny skin that should have been freckled but wasn't. 'Follow me. We can sit out in the garden and I'll get Violet to bring us something to drink… Have you had lunch?'

Lesley frowned. Had she? She was careless with her eating habits, something she daily promised herself to rectify. If she ate more, she knew she'd stand a fighting chance of not looking like a gawky runner bean. 'A sandwich before I left,' she returned politely. 'But a cup of tea would be wonderful.'

'It never fails to amuse me that on a hot summer's

day you English will still opt for a cup of tea instead of something cold.'

'I'm not English. I'm Irish.'

Alessio cocked his head to one side and looked at her, consideringly. 'Now that you mention it, I do detect a certain twang…'

'But I'm still partial to a cup of tea.'

He smiled and she was knocked sideways. The man oozed sex appeal. He'd had it when he'd been unsmiling, but now…it was enough to throw her into a state of confusion and she blinked, driving away the unaccustomed sensation.

'This isn't my preferred place of residence,' he took up easily as he led the way out of the magnificent hall and towards sprawling doors that led towards the back of the house. 'I come here to give it an airing every so often but most of my time is spent either in London or abroad on business.'

'And who looks after this place when you're not in it?'

'I have people who do that for me.'

'Bit of a waste, isn't it?'

Alessio spun round and looked at her with a mixture of irritation and amusement. 'From whose point of view?' he asked politely and Lesley shrugged and folded her arms.

'There are such extreme housing problems in this country that it seems crazy for one person to have a place of this size.'

'You mean, when I could subdivide the whole house and turn it into a million rabbit hutches to cater for down and outs?' He laughed drily. 'Did my guy explain to you what the situation was?'

Lesley frowned. She had thought he might have been

offended by her remark, but she was here on business of sorts, and her opinions were of little consequence.

'Your guy got in touch with Stan who's a friend of my dad and he... Well, he just said that you had a sensitive situation that needed sorting. No details.'

'None were given. I was just curious to find out whether idle speculation had entered the equation.' He pushed open some doors and they emerged into a magnificent back garden.

Tall trees bordered pristine, sprawling lawns. To one side was a tennis court and beyond that she could see a swimming pool with a low, modern outbuilding which she assumed was changing rooms. The patio on which they were standing was as broad as the entire little communal garden she shared with the other residents in her block of flats and stretched the length of the house. If a hundred people were to stand side by side, they wouldn't be jostling for space.

Low wooden chairs were arranged around a glass-topped table and as she sat down a middle-aged woman bustled into her line of vision, as though summoned by some kind of whistle audible only to her.

Tea, Alessio instructed; something cold for him, a few things to eat.

Orders given, he sat down on one of the chairs facing her and leaned forward with his elbows resting on his knees.

'So the man my guy went to is a friend of your father's?'

'That's right. Stan grew up with my dad and when I moved down to London after university... Well, he and his wife took me under their wing. Made room for me in their house until I was settled—even paid the three months' deposit on my first rental property because they knew that it would be a struggle for my dad to afford it. So, yeah, I owe Stan a lot and it's why I took this job, Mr Baldini.'

'Alessio, please. And you work as…?'

'I design websites but occasionally I work as a freelance hacker. Companies employ me to see if their firewalls are intact and secure. If something can be hacked, then I can do it.'

'Not a job I immediately associate with a woman,' he murmured and raised his eyebrows as she bristled. 'That's not meant as an insult. It's purely a statement of fact. There are a couple of women in my IT department, but largely they're guys.'

'Why didn't you get one of your own employees to sort out your problem?'

'Because it's a sensitive issue and, the less my private life is discussed within the walls of my offices, the better. So you design websites. You freelance and you claim you can get into anything.'

'That's right. Despite not being a man.'

Alessio heard the defensive edge to her voice and his curiosity was piqued. His life had settled into a predictable routine when it came to members of the opposite sex. His one mistake, made when he was eighteen, had been enough for him to develop a very healthy scepticism when it came to women. The fairer sex, he had concluded, was a misconception of stunning magnitude.

'So if you could explain the situation…' Lesley looked at him levelly, her mind already flying ahead to the thrill of solving whatever problem lay in store for her. She barely noticed his housekeeper placing a pot of tea in front of her and a plate crammed with pastries, produced from heaven only knew where.

'I've been getting anonymous emails.' Alessio

flushed as he grappled with the unaccustomed sensation of admitting to having his hands tied when it came to sorting out his own dilemma. 'They started a few weeks ago.'

'At regular intervals?'

'No.' He raked his fingers through his hair and looked at her earnest face tilted to one side... A small crease indented her forehead and he could almost hear her thinking, her mind working as methodically as one of the computers she dealt with. 'I ignored them to start with but the last couple have been...how shall I describe them?...a little *forceful*.' He reached for the pitcher of homemade lemonade to pour himself a glass. 'If you looked me up, you probably know that I own several IT companies. Despite that, I confess that my knowledge of the ins and outs of computers is scant.'

'Actually, I have no idea what companies you own or don't own. I looked you up because I wanted to make sure that there was nothing dodgy about you. I've done this sort of thing before. I'm not looking for background detail, I'm generally looking for any articles that might point a suspicious finger.'

'Dodgy? You thought I might be *dodgy*?'

He looked so genuinely shocked and insulted that she couldn't help laughing. 'You might have had newspaper cuttings about suspect dealings, mafia connections...you know the sort of thing. I'd have been able to find even the most obscure article within minutes if there had been anything untoward about you. You came up clean.'

Alessio nearly choked on his lemonade. 'Mafia dealings...because I'm Italian? That's the most ridiculous thing I've ever heard.'

Lesley shrugged sheepishly. 'I don't like taking chances.'

'I've never done a crooked thing in my entire life.' He flung his arms wide in a gesture that was peculiarly foreign. 'I even buck the trend of the super-rich and am a fully paid-up member of the honest, no-offshore-scams, tax-paying club! To suggest that I might be linked to the Mafia because I happen to be Italian...'

He sat forward and stared at her and she had to fight off the very feminine and girlish response to wonder what he thought of her, as a woman, as opposed to a talented computer whizz-kid there at his bidding. Suddenly flustered, she gulped back a mouthful of hot tea and grimaced.

Wondering what men thought of her wasn't her style. She pretty much *knew* what they thought of her. She had lived her whole life knowing that she was one of the lads. Even her job helped to advance that conclusion.

No, she was too tall, too angular and too mouthy to hold any appeal when it came to the whole sexual attraction thing. Least of all when the guy in question looked like Alessio Baldini. She cringed just thinking about it.

'No, you've been watching too many gangster movies. Surely you must have heard of me?' He was always in the newspapers. Usually in connection with big business deals—occasionally in the gossip columns with a woman hanging onto his arm.

He wasn't sure why he had inserted that irrelevant question but, now that he had, he found that he was awaiting her answer with keen curiosity.

'Nope.'

'No?'

'I guess you probably think that everyone's heard of you, but in actual fact I don't read the newspapers.'

'You don't read the newspapers…not even the gossip columns?'

'Especially not the gossip columns,' she said scathingly. 'Not all girls are interested in what celebs get up to.' She tried to reconnect with the familiar feeling of satisfaction that she wasn't one of those simpering females who became embroiled in silly gossip about the rich and famous, but for once the feeling eluded her.

For once, she longed to be one of those giggly, coy girls who knew how to bat their eyelashes and attract the cute guys; she wanted to be part of the prom set instead of the clever, boyish one lurking on the sidelines; she wanted to be a member of that invisible club from which she had always been excluded because she just never seemed to have the right code words to get in.

She fought back a surge of dissatisfaction with herself and had to stifle a sense of anger that the man sitting opposite her had been the one to have generated the emotion. She had conquered whatever insecurities she had about her looks a long time ago and was perfectly content with her appearance. She might not be to everyone's taste, and she certainly wouldn't be to *his*, but her time would come and she would find someone. At the age of twenty-seven, she was hardly over the hill and, besides, her career was taking off. The last thing she needed or wanted was to be side-tracked by a guy.

She wondered how they had ended up talking about something that had nothing at all to do with the job for which she had been hired.

Was this part of his 'getting to know her' exercise? Was he quietly vetting her the way she had vetted him, when she had skimmed over all that information about him on the computer, making sure that there was nothing worrying about him?

'You were telling me about the emails you received…' She brought the conversation back to the business in hand.

Alessio sighed heavily and gave her a long, considering look from under his lashes.

'The first few were innocuous enough—a couple of one-liners hinting that they had information I might be interested in. Nothing worrying.'

'You get emails like that all the time?'

'I'm a rich man. I get a lot of emails that have little or nothing to do with work.' He smiled wryly and Lesley felt that odd tingling feeling in her body once again. 'I have several email accounts and my secretary is excellent when it comes to weeding out the dross.'

'But these managed to slip through?'

'These went to my personal email address. Very few people have that.'

'Okay.' She frowned and stared off into the distance. 'So you say that the first few were innocuous enough and then the tenor of the emails changed?'

'A few days ago, the first request for money came. Don't get me wrong, I get a lot of requests for money, but they usually take a more straightforward route. Someone wants a sponsor for something; charities asking for hand-outs; small businesses angling for investment…and then the usual assortment of nut cases who need money for dying relatives or to pay lawyers before they can claim their inheritance, which they would happily share with me.'

'And your secretary deals with all of that?'

'She does. It's usually called pressing the delete button on the computer. Some get through to me but, in general, we have established charities to which we give healthy sums of money, and all requests for business investment are automatically referred to my corporate finance division.'

'But this slipped through the net because it came to your personal address. Any idea how he or she could have accessed that information?' She was beginning to think that this sounded a little out of her area of expertise. Hackers usually went for information or, in some cases tried to attack the accounts, but this was clearly... personal. 'And don't you think that this might be better referred to the police?' she inserted, before he could answer.

Alessio laughed drily. He took a long mouthful of his drink and looked at her over the rim of the glass as he drank.

'If you read the papers,' he drawled, 'you might discover that the police have been having a few off-months when it comes to safeguarding the privacy of the rich and famous. I'm a very private man. The less of my life is splashed across the news, the better.'

'So my job is to find out who is behind these emails.'

'Correct.'

'At which point you'll...?'

'Deal with the matter myself.'

He was still smiling, with that suggestion of amusement on his lips, but she could see the steel behind the lazy, watchful dark eyes. 'I should tell you from the offset that I cannot accept this commission if there's any suggestion that you might turn...err...*violent* when it comes to sorting out whoever is behind this.'

Alessio laughed and relaxed back in his chair, stretching out his long legs to cross them at the ankle and loosely linking his fingers on his stomach. 'You have my word that I won't turn, as you say, violent.'

'I hope you're not making fun of me, Mr Baldini,' Lesley said stiffly. 'I'm being perfectly serious.'

'Alessio. The name's Alessio. And you aren't still under the impression that I'm a member of the Mafia, are you? With a stash of guns under the bed and henchmen to do my bidding?'

Lesley flushed. Where had her easy, sassy manner gone? She was seldom lost for words but she was now, especially when those dark, dark eyes were lingering on her flushed cheeks, making her feel even more uncomfortable than she already felt. A burst of shameful heat exploded somewhere deep inside her, her body's acknowledgment of his sexual magnetism, chemistry that was wrapping itself around her like a web, confusing her thoughts and making her pulses race.

'Do I strike you as a violent man, Lesley?'

'I never said that. I'm just being…cautious.'

'Have you had awkward situations before?' The soft pink of her cheeks when she blushed was curiously appealing, maybe because she was at such pains to project herself as a tough woman with no time for frivolity.

'What do you mean?'

'You intimated that you checked me out to make sure that I wasn't *dodgy*…and I think I'm quoting you here. So are you cautious in situations like these… when the computer doesn't go to you but you're forced to go to the computer…because of bad experiences?'

'I'm a careful person.' Why did that make her sound like such a bore, when she wasn't? Once again weirdly conscious of the image she must present to a guy like him, Lesley inhaled deeply and ploughed on. 'And yes,' she asserted matter-of-factly, 'I *have* had a number of poor experiences in the past. A few months ago, I was asked to do a favour for a friend's friend only to find that what he wanted was for me to hack into his ex-wife's bank account and see where her money was being spent. When I refused, he turned ugly.'

'Turned ugly?'

'He'd had a bit too much to drink. He thought that if he pushed me around a bit I'd do what he wanted.' And just in case her awkward responses had been letting her down, maybe giving him the mistaken impression that she was anything but one hundred per cent professional, she concluded crisply, 'Of course, it's annoying, but nothing I can't handle.'

'You can handle men who turn ugly.' Fascinating. He was in the company of someone from another planet. She might have the creamiest complexion he had ever seen, and a heart-shaped face that insisted on looking ridiculously feminine despite the aggressive get-up, but she was certainly nothing like any woman he had ever met. 'Tell me how you do that,' he said with genuine curiosity.

Absently, he noticed that she had depleted the plate of pastries by half its contents. A hearty appetite; his eyes flicked to her body which, despite being well hidden beneath her anti-fashion-statement clothing, was long and slender.

On some subliminal level, Lesley was aware of the shift in his attention, away from her face and onto her body. Her instinct was to squirm. Instead, she clasped her hands tightly together on her lap and tried to force her uncooperative body into a position of relaxed ease.

'I have a black belt in karate.'

Alessio was stunned into silence. 'You do?'

'I do.' She shrugged and held his confounded gaze. 'And it's not that shocking,' she continued into the lengthening silence. 'There were loads of girls in my class when I did it. 'Course, a few of them fell by the wayside when we began moving up the levels.'

'And you did these classes…when, exactly?'

In passing, Lesley wondered what this had to do with her qualifications for doing the job she had come to do. On the other hand, it never hurt to let someone know that you weren't the sort of woman to be messed with.

'I started when I was ten and the classes continued into my teens with a couple of breaks in between.'

'So, when other girls were experimenting with make-up, you were learning the valuable art of self-defence.'

Lesley felt the sharp jab of discomfort as he yet again unwittingly hit the soft spot inside her, the place where her insecurities lay, neatly parcelled up but always ready to be unwrapped at a moment's notice.

'I think every woman should know how to physically defend herself.'

'That's an extremely laudable ambition,' Alessio murmured. He noticed that his long, cold drink was finished. 'Let's go inside. I'll show you to my office and we can continue our conversation there. It's getting a little oppressive out here.' He stood up, squinted towards his gardens and half-smiled when he saw her automatically reach for the plate of pastries and whatever else she could manage to take in with her.

'No need.' He briefly rested one finger on her outstretched hand and Lesley shot back as though she had been scalded. 'Violet will tidy all this away.'

Lesley bit back an automatic retort that it was illuminating to see how the other half lived. She was no inverted snob, even though she might have no time for outward trappings and the importance other people sometimes placed on them, but he made her feel defensive. Worse, he made her feel gauche and awkward, sixteen all over again, cringing at the prospect of having to wear a frock to go to the school leaving dance, knowing that she just couldn't pull it off.

'I'm thinking that your mother must be a strong woman to instil such priorities in her daughter,' he said neutrally.

'My mother died when I was three—a hit-and-run accident when she was cycling back from doing the shopping.'

Alessio stopped in his tracks and stared down at her until she was forced uncomfortably to return his stare.

'Please don't say something trite like *I'm sorry to hear that*.' She tilted her chin and looked at him unblinkingly. 'It happened a long time ago.'

'No. I wasn't going to say that,' Alessio said in a low, musing voice that made her skin tingle.

'My father was the strong influence in my life,' she pressed on in a high voice. 'My father and my five brothers. They all gave me the confidence to know that I could do whatever I chose to do, that my gender did not have to stand in the way of my ambition. I got my degree in maths—the world was my oyster.'

Heart beating as fast as if she had run a marathon, she stared up at him, their eyes tangling until her defensiveness subsided and gave way to something else, something she could barely comprehend, something that made her say quickly, with a tight smile, 'But I don't see how any of this is relevant. If you lead the way to your computer, it shouldn't take long for me to figure out who your problem pest is.'

CHAPTER TWO

THE OFFICE TO which she was led allowed her a good opportunity to really take in the splendour of her surroundings.

Really big country estates devoured money and consequently were rarely in the finest of conditions. Imposing exteriors were often let down by run-down, sad interiors in want of attention.

This house was as magnificent inside as it was out. The pristine gardens, the splendid ivy-clad walls, were replicated inside by a glorious attention to detail. From the cool elegance of the hall, she bypassed a series of rooms, each magnificently decorated. Of course, she could only peek through slightly open doors, because she had to half-run to keep up with him, but she saw enough to convince her that serious money had been thrown at the place—which was incredible, considering it was not used on a regular basis.

Eventually they ended up in an office with book-lined walls and a massive antique desk housing a computer, a lap-top and a small stack of legal tomes. She looked around at the rich burgundy drapes pooling to the ground, the pin-striped sober wallpaper, the deep sofa and chairs.

It was a decor she would not have associated with

him and, as though reading her mind, he said wryly, 'It makes a change from what I'm used to in London. I'm more of a modern man myself but I find there's something soothing about working in a turn-of-the-century gentleman's den.' He moved smoothly round to the chair at the desk and powered up his computer. 'When I bought this house several years ago, it was practically derelict. I paid over the odds for it because of its history and because I wanted to make sure the owner and her daughter could be rehoused in the manner to which they had clearly once been accustomed. Before, that is, the money ran out. They were immensely grateful and only suggested one thing—that I try and keep a couple of the rooms as close as possible to the original format. This was one.'

'It's beautiful.' Lesley hovered by the door and looked around her. Through the French doors, the lawns outside stretched away to an impossibly distant horizon. The sun turned everything into dazzling technicolour. The greens of the grass and the trees seemed greener than possible and the sky was blindingly turquoise. Inside the office, though, the dark colours threw everything into muted relief. He was right; the space was soothing.

She looked at him frowning in front of the computer, sitting forward slightly, his long, powerful body still managing to emanate force even though he wasn't moving.

'There's no need to remain by the door,' he said without looking at her. 'You'll actually need to venture into the room and sit next to me if you're to work on this problem. Ah. Right. Here we go.' He stood up, vacating the chair for her.

The leather was warm from where he had been sitting, and the heat seemed to infiltrate her entire body as she took his place in front of the computer screen. When he leaned over to tap on the keyboard, she felt her breathing become rapid and shallow and she had to stop herself from gasping out loud.

His forearm was inches away from her breasts and never had the proximity of one person's body proved so rattling. She willed herself to focus on what he was calling up on the screen in front of her and to remember that she was here in a professional capacity.

Why was he getting to her? Perhaps she had been too long without a guy in her life. Friends and family were all very good, but maybe her life of pleasant celibacy had made her unexpectedly vulnerable to a spot of swarthy good looks and a wicked smile.

'So...'

Lesley blinked herself back into the present to find herself staring directly into dark, dark eyes that were far too close to her for comfort.

'So?'

'Email one—a little too familiar, a little too chatty, but nothing that couldn't be easily ignored.'

Lesley looked thoughtfully at the computer screen and read through the email. Her surroundings faded away as she began studying the series of emails posted to him, looking for clues, asking him questions, her fingers moving swiftly and confidently across the key board.

She could understand why he had decided to farm out this little problem to an outside source.

If he valued his privacy, then he would not want his IT division to have access to what appeared to be vaguely menacing threats, suggestions of something that could harm his business or ruin his reputation. It would be fodder for any over-imaginative employee, of which there were always a few in any office environment.

Alessio pushed himself away from the desk and strolled towards one of the comfortable, deep chairs facing her.

She was utterly absorbed in what she was doing. He took time out to study her and he was amused and a little surprised to discover that he enjoyed the view.

It wasn't simply the arrangement of her features that he found curiously captivating.

There was a lively intelligence to her that made a refreshing change from the beautiful but intellectually challenged women he dated. He looked at the way her short chocolate-brown hair spiked up, as though too feisty and too wilful to be controlled. Her eyelashes were long and thick; her mouth, as he now saw, was full and, yes, sexy.

A sexy mouth, especially just at this very moment, when her lips were slightly parted.

She frowned and ran her tongue thoughtfully along her upper lip and, on cue, Alessio's body jerked into startling life. His libido, which had been unusually quiet since he'd ended his relationship with a blonde with a penchant for diamonds two months ago, fired up.

It was so unexpected a reaction that he nearly groaned in shock.

Instead, he shifted on the chair and smiled politely as her eyes briefly skittered across to him before resuming their intent concentration on the computer screen.

'Whoever's sent this knows what they're doing.'

'Come again?' Alessio crossed his legs, trying to maintain the illusion that he was in complete control of himself.

'They've been careful to make themselves as untraceable as possible.' Lesley stretched, then slumped back into the chair and swivelled it round so that she was facing him.

She stuck out her legs and gazed at her espadrilles. 'That first email may have been chatty and friendly but he or she knew that they didn't want to be traced. Why didn't you delete them, at least the earlier ones?'

'I had an instinct that they might be worth hanging onto.' He stood up and strolled towards the French doors. He had intended this meeting to be brief and functional, a blip that needed sorting out in his hectic life. Now, he found that his mind was stubbornly refusing to return to the matter in hand. Instead, it was relentlessly pulled back to the image he had of her sitting in front of his computer concentrating ferociously. He wondered what she would look like out of the unappealing ensemble. He wondered whether she would be any different from all the other naked women who had lain across his bed in readiness for him.

He knew she would—instinct again. Somehow he couldn't envisage her lying provocatively for him to take her, passive and willing to please.

No. That wasn't what girls with black belts in karate and a sideline in computer hacking did.

He played with the suddenly tempting notion of prolonging her task. Who knew what might happen between them if she were to be around longer than originally envisaged?

'What would you suggest my next step should be? Because I'm taking from the expression on your face that it's not going to be as straightforward as you first thought.'

'Usually it's pretty easy to sort something like this

out,' Lesley confessed, linking her hands on her stomach and staring off at nothing in particular. The weird, edgy tension she had felt earlier on had dissipated. Work had that effect on her. It occupied her whole mind and left no room for anything else. 'People are predictable when it comes to leaving tracks behind them, but obviously whoever is behind this hasn't used his own computer. He's gone to an Internet café. In fact, I wouldn't be surprised if he goes to a variety of Internet cafés, because we certainly would be able to trace the café he uses if he sticks there. And it wouldn't be too much of a headache finding out which terminal is his and then it would be a short step to identifying the person... I keep saying *he* but it might very well be a *she.*'

'How so? No, we'll get to that over something to drink—and I insist you forfeit the tea in favour of something a little more exciting. My housekeeper makes a very good Pimm's.'

'I couldn't,' Lesley said awkwardly. 'I'm not much of a drinker and I'm...err...driving anyway.'

'Fresh lemonade, in that case.' Alessio strolled towards her and held out his hand to tug her up from the chair to which she seemed to be glued.

For a few seconds, Lesley froze. When she grasped his hand—because frankly she couldn't think of what else to do without appearing ridiculous and childish—she felt a spurt of red-hot electricity zap through her body until every inch of her was galvanised into shrieking, heightened awareness of the dangerously sexy man standing in front of her.

'That would be nice,' she said a little breathlessly. As soon as she could she retrieved her scorching hand and resisted the urge to rub it against her trousers.

Alessio didn't miss a thing. She was a different person when she was concentrating on a computer. Looking at a screen, analysing what was in front of her, working out how to solve the problem he had presented, she oozed self-confidence. He idly wondered what her websites looked like.

But without a computer to absorb her attention she was prickly and defensive, a weird, intriguing mix of independent and vulnerable.

He smiled, turning her insides to liquid, and stood aside to allow her to pass by him out of the office.

'So we have a he or a she who goes to a certain Internet café, or more likely a variety of Internet cafés, for the sole reason of emailing me to, well, purpose as yet slightly unclear, but if I'm any reader of human motivation I'm smelling a lead-up to asking for money for information he or she may or may not know. There seem to be a lot of imponderables in this case.'

They had arrived at the kitchen without her being aware of having padded through the house at all, and she found a glass of fresh lemonade in her hands while he helped himself to a bottle of mineral water.

He motioned to the kitchen table and they sat facing one another on opposite sides.

'Generally,' Lesley said, sipping the lemonade, 'This should be a straightforward case of sourcing the computer in question, paying a visit to the Internet café—and usually these places have CCTV cameras. You would be able to find the culprit without too much bother.'

'But if he's clever enough to hop from café to café...'

'Then it'll take a bit longer but I'll get there. Of course, if you have no skeletons in the cupboard, Mr Baldini, then you could just walk away from this situation.'

'Is there such a thing as an adult without one or two skeletons in the cupboard?'

'Well, then.'

'Although,' Alessio continued thoughtfully, 'Skeletons imply something…wrong, in need of concealment. I can't think of any dark secrets I have under lock or key but there are certain things I would rather not have revealed.'

'Do you honestly care what the public thinks of you? Or maybe it's to do with your company? Sorry, but I don't really know how the big, bad world of business operates, but I'm just assuming that if something gets out that could affect your share prices then you mightn't be too happy.'

'I have a daughter.'

'You *have a daughter*?'

'Surely you got that from your search of me on the Internet?' Alessio said drily.

'I told you, I just skimmed through the stuff. There's an awful lot written up about you and I honestly just wanted to cut to the chase—any articles that could have suggested that I needed to be careful about getting involved. Like I said, I've fine-tuned my search engine when it comes to picking out relevant stuff or else I'd be swamped underneath useless speculation.' *A daughter?*

'Yes. I forgot—the "bodies under the motorway" scenario.' He raised his eyebrows and once again Lesley felt herself in danger of losing touch with common sense.

'I never imagined anything so dramatic, at least not really,' she returned truthfully, which had the effect of making that sexy smile on his face even broader. Flustered, she continued, 'But you were telling me that you have a daughter.'

'You still can't erase the incredulity from your voice,' he remarked, amused. 'Surely you've bumped into people who have had kids?'

'Yes! Of course! But…'

'But?'

Lesley stared at him. 'Why do I get the feeling that you're making fun of me?' she asked, ruffled and red-faced.

'My apologies.' But there was the echo of a smile still lingering in his voice, even though his expression was serious and contrite. 'But you blush so prettily.'

'That's the most ridiculous thing I've ever heard in my life!' And it was. Ridiculous. 'Pretty' was something she most definitely was *not*. Nor was she going to let this guy, this *sex God* of a man—who could have any woman he wanted, if you happened to like that kind of thing—get under her skin.

'Why is it ridiculous?' Alessio allowed himself to be temporarily side-tracked.

'I know you're probably one of these guys who slips into flattery mode with any woman you happen to find yourself confined with, but I'm afraid that I don't go into meltdown at empty compliments.' *What on earth was she going on about?* Why was she jumping into heated self-defence over nonsense like this?

When it came to business, Alessio rarely lost sight of the goal. Right now, not only had he lost sight of it, but he didn't mind. 'Do you go into meltdown at compliments you think are genuine?'

'I…I…'

'You're stammering,' he needlessly pointed out. 'I don't mean to make you feel uncomfortable.'

'I don't…err…feel uncomfortable.'

'Well, that's good.'

Lesley stared helplessly at him. He wasn't just sinfully sexy. The man was beautiful. He hadn't looked beautiful in those pictures, but then she had barely taken them in—a couple of grainy black-and-white shots of a load of businessmen had barely registered on her consciousness. Now, she wished she had paid attention so that she at least could have been prepared for the sort of effect he might have had on her.

Except, she admitted truthfully to herself, she would still have considered herself above and beyond being affected by any man, however good-looking he might happen to be. When it came to matters of the heart, she had always prided herself on her practicality. She knew her limitations and had accepted them. When and if the time came that she wanted a relationship, then she had always known that the man for her would not be the sort who was into looks but the sort who enjoyed intelligence, personality—a meeting of minds as much as anything else.

'You were telling me about your daughter...'

'My daughter.' Alessio sighed heavily and raked his fingers through his dark hair.

It was a gesture of hesitancy that seemed so at odds with his forceful personality that Lesley sat up and stared at him with narrowed eyes.

'Where is she?' Lesley looked past him, as though half-expecting this unexpected addition to his life suddenly to materialise out of nowhere. 'I thought you mentioned that you had no family. Where is your wife?'

'No *sprawling* family,' Alessio amended. 'And no wife. My wife died two years ago.'

'I'm so sorry.'

'There's no need for tears and sympathy.' He waved aside her interruption, although he was startled at how easily a softer nature shone through. 'When I say *wife,* it might be more accurate to say *ex-wife.* Bianca and I were divorced a long time ago.'

'How old is your daughter?'

'Sixteen. And, to save you the hassle of doing the maths, she was, shall we say, an unexpected arrival when I was eighteen.'

'You were a *father* at eighteen?'

'Bianca and I had been seeing each other in a fairly loose fashion for a matter of three months when she announced that her contraceptive pill had failed and I was going to be a father.' His lips thinned. The past was rarely raked up and when it was, as now, it still brought a sour taste to his mouth.

Unfortunately, he could see no way around a certain amount of confidential information exchanging hands because he had a gut feeling that, whatever his uninvited email correspondent wanted, it involved his daughter.

'And you weren't happy about that.' Lesley groped her way to understanding the darkening of his expression.

'A family was not something high on my agenda at the time,' Alessio imparted grimly. 'In fact, I would go so far as to say that it hadn't even crossed my radar. But, naturally, I did the honourable thing and married her. It was a match approved by both sides of the family until, that is, it became apparent that her family's wealth was an illusion. Her parents were up to their eyes in debt and I was a convenient match because of the financial rewards I brought with me.'

'She married you for your *money*?'

'It occurred to no one to do a background check.' He shrugged elegantly. 'You're looking at me as though I've suddenly landed from another planet.'

His slow smile knocked her sideways and she cleared her throat nervously. 'I'm not familiar with people marrying for no better reason than money,' she answered honestly.

Alessio raised his eyebrows. 'In that case, we really *do* come from different planets. My family is extremely wealthy, as am I. Believe me, I am extremely well versed in the tactics women will employ to gain entry to my bank balance.' He crossed his legs, relaxing. 'But you might say that, once bitten, twice shy.'

She made an exceptionally good listener. Was this why he had expanded on the skeleton brief he could have given her? Had gone into details that were irrelevant in the grand scheme of things? He hadn't been lying when he had told her that his unfortunate experience with his ex had left him jaded about women and the lengths they would go to in order to secure themselves a piece of the pie. He was rich and women liked money. It was therefore a given that he employed a healthy amount of caution in his dealings with the opposite sex.

But the woman sitting in front of him couldn't have been less interested in his earnings.

His little problem intrigued her far more than *he* did. It was a situation that Alessio had never encountered in his life before and there was something sexy and challenging about that.

'You mean you don't intend to marry again? I can understand that. And I guess you have your daughter. She must mean the world to you.'

'Naturally.' Alessio's voice cooled. 'Although I'll be the first to admit that things have not been easy between us. I had relatively little contact with Rachel when she was growing up, thanks to my ex-wife's talent for vindictiveness. She lived in Italy but travelled extensively, and usually when she knew that I had arranged a visit.

She was quite happy to whip our daughter out of school at a moment's notice if only to make sure that my trip to Italy to visit would be a waste of time.'

'How awful.'

'At any rate, when Bianca died Rachel naturally came to me, but at the age of fourteen she was virtually a stranger and a fairly hostile one. Frankly, a nightmare.'

'She would have been grieving for her mother.' Lesley could barely remember her own mother and yet *she* still grieved at the lack of one in her life. How much more traumatic to have lost one at the age of fourteen, a time in life when a maternal, guiding hand could not have been more needed.

'She was behind in her schoolwork thanks to my ex-wife's antics, and refused to speak English in the classroom, so the whole business of teaching her was practically impossible. In the end, boarding school seemed the only option and, thankfully, she appears to have settled in there with somewhat more success. At least, there have been no phone calls threatening expulsion.'

'Boarding school…'

Alessio frowned. 'You say that as though it ranks alongside "prison cell".'

'I can't imagine the horror of being separated from my family. My brothers could be little devils when I was growing up but we were a family. Dad, the boys and me.'

Alessio tilted his head and looked at her, considering, tempted to ask her if that was why she had opted for a male-dominated profession, and why she wore clothes better suited to a boy. But the conversation had already drifted too far from the matter at hand. When he glanced down at his watch, it was to find that more time had passed than he might have expected.

'My gut feeling tells me that these emails are in some way connected to my daughter,' Alessio admitted. 'Reason should dictate that they're to do with work but I can't imagine why anyone wouldn't approach me directly about anything to do with my business concerns.'

'No. And if you're as above board as you say you are…'

'You doubt my word?'

Lesley shrugged. 'I don't think that's really my business; the only reason I mention it is because it might be pertinent to finding out who is behind this. 'Course, I shall continue working at the problem, but if it's established that the threat is to do with your work then you might actually be able to pinpoint the culprit yourself.'

'How many people do you imagine work for me?' Alessio asked curiously, and Lesley shrugged and gave the matter some thought.

'No idea.' The company she worked for was small, although prominent in its field, employing only a handful of people on the creative side and slightly fewer on the admin side. 'A hundred or so?'

'You really skimmed through those articles you called up on your computer, didn't you?'

'Big business doesn't interest me,' she informed him airily. 'I may have a talent for numbers, and can do the maths without any trouble at all, but those numbers only matter when it comes to my work. I can work things out precisely but it's really the artistic side of my job that I love. In fact, I only did maths at university because Shane, one of my brothers, told me that it was a man's subject.'

'Thousands.'

Lesley looked at him blankly for a few seconds. 'What are you talking about?'

'Thousands. In various countries. I own several companies and I employ thousands, not hundreds. But that's by the by. This isn't to do with work. This is to do with my daughter. The only problem is that we don't have a great relationship and if I approach her with my suspicions, if I quiz her about her friends, about whether anyone's been acting strangely, asking too many questions…well, I don't anticipate a good outcome to any such conversation. So what would you have done if you hadn't done maths?'

Time had slipped past and they were no nearer to solving the problem, yet he was drawn to asking her yet more questions about herself.

Lesley—following his lead and envisaging the sort of awkward, maybe even downright incendiary conversation that might ensue in the face of Alessio's concerns, should he confront a hostile teenager with them—was taken aback by his abrupt change of topic.

'You said that you only did maths because your brother told you that you couldn't.'

'He never said that I *couldn't*.' She smiled, remembering their war of words. Shane was two years older than her and she always swore that his main purpose in life was to annoy her. He was now a barrister working in Dublin but he still teased her as though they were still kids in primary school. 'He said that it was a man's field, which immediately made me decide to do it.'

'Because, growing up as the only girl in a family of all males, it would have been taken as a given that, whatever your brothers could do, you could as well.'

'I'm wondering what this has to do with the reason I've come here.' She pulled out her mobile phone, checked the time on it and was surprised to discover how much of the day had flown by. 'I'm sorry I haven't been able to sort things out for you immediately. I'd understand perfectly if you want to take the matter to someone else, someone who can devote concentrated time to working on it. It shouldn't take too long, but longer than an hour or two.'

'Would you have done art?' He overrode her interjection as though he hadn't heard any of it and she flung him an exasperated look.

'I did, actually—courses in the town once a week. It was a good decision. It may have clinched me my job.'

'I have no interest in farming out this problem to someone else.'

'I can't give it my full-time attention.'

'Why not?'

'Because,' she said patiently, 'I have a nine-to-five job. And I live in London. And by the time I get back to my place—usually after seven, what with working overtime and then the travel—I'm exhausted. The last thing I need is to start trying to sort your problem out remotely.'

'Who said anything about doing it remotely? Take time off and come here.'

'I beg your pardon?'

'A week. You must be able to take some holiday time? Take it off and come here instead. Trying to sort this out remotely isn't the answer. You won't have sufficient time to do it consistently and also, while this may be to do with unearthing something about my own past, it may also have to do with something in my daughter's life. Something this person thinks poses a risk, should it be exposed. Have you considered that?'

'It had crossed my mind,' Lesley admitted.

'In which case, there could be a double-pronged attack on this problem if you moved in here.'

'What do you mean?'

'My daughter occupies several rooms in the house, by which I mean she has spread herself thin. She has a million books, items of clothing, at least one desktop computer, tablets… If this has to do with anything Rachel has got up to, then you could be on hand to go through her stuff.'

'You want me to *invade her privacy* by searching through her private things?'

'It's all for the greater good.' Their eyes locked and she was suddenly seduced by the temptation to take him up on his offer, to step right out of her comfort zone.

'What's the point of having misplaced scruples? Frankly, I don't see the problem.'

In that single sentence, she glimpsed the man whose natural assumption was that the world would fall in line with what he wanted. And then he smiled, as if he had read her mind, and guessed exactly what was going through it. 'Wouldn't your company allow you a week off? Holiday?'

'That's not the point.'

'Then what is? Possessive boyfriend, perhaps? Won't let you out of his sight for longer than five minutes?'

Lesley looked at him scornfully. 'I would never get involved with anyone who wouldn't let me out of his sight for longer than five minutes! I'm not one of those pathetic, clingy females who craves protection from a big, strong man.' She had a fleeting image of the man sitting opposite her, big, strong, powerful, protecting his woman, making her feel small, fragile and delicate. She had never thought of herself as delicate—too tall, too boyish, too independent. It was ridiculous to have that squirmy sensation in the pit of her stomach now and she thanked the Lord that he really couldn't read her mind.

'So, no boyfriend,' Alessio murmured, cocking his head to one side. 'Then explain to me why you're finding reasons not to do this. I don't want to source anyone else to work on this for me. You might not have been what I expected, but you're good and I trust you, and if my daughter's possessions are to be searched it's essential they be searched by a woman.'

'It wouldn't be ethical to go through someone else's stuff.'

'What if by doing that you spared her a far worse situation? Rachel, I feel, would not be equipped to deal with unpleasant revelations that could damage the foundations of her young life. Furthermore, I won't be looking over your shoulder. You'll be able to work to your own timetable. In fact, I shall be in London most of the time, only returning here some evenings.'

Lesley opened her mouth to formulate a half-hearted protest, because this was all so sudden and so out of the ordinary, but with a slash of his hand he cut her off before any words could leave her mouth.

'She also returns in a few days' time. This is a job that has a very definite deadline; piecemeal when you get a chance isn't going to cut it. You have reservations—I see that—but I need this to be sorted out and I think you're the one to do it. So, please.'

Lesley heard the dark uncertainty in his voice and gritted her teeth with frustration. In a lot of ways, what he said made sense. Even if this job were to take a day or two, she would not be able to give it anything like her full attention if she worked on it remotely for half an hour every evening. And, if she needed to see whether his daughter had logged on to other computer devices, then she would need to be at his house where the equipment was to hand. It wasn't something she relished doing—everyone deserved their privacy—but sometimes privacy had to be invaded as a means of protection.

But moving in, sharing the same space as him? He did something disturbing to her pulse rate, so how was she supposed to live under the same roof?

But the thought drew her with the force of the forbidden.

Watching, Alessio smelled his advantage and lowered his eyes. 'If you won't do this for me…and I realise it would be inconvenient for you…then do it for my daughter, Lesley. She's sixteen and vulnerable.'

CHAPTER THREE

'THIS IS IT…'

Alessio flung back the door to the suite of rooms and stood to one side, allowing Lesley to brush past him.

It was a mere matter of hours since he had pressed home his advantage and persuaded her to take up his offer to move into the house.

She had her misgivings, he could see that, but he wanted her there at hand and he was a man who was accustomed to getting what he wanted, whatever the cost.

As far as he was concerned, his proposition made sense. If she needed to try and hunt down clues from his daughter's possessions, then the only way she could do that would be here, in his house. There was no other way.

He hadn't anticipated this eventuality. He had thought that it would be a simple matter of following a trail of clues on his computer which would lead him straight to whoever was responsible for the emails.

Given that it was not going to be as straightforward as he first thought, it was a stroke of luck that the person working on the case was a woman. She would understand the workings of the female mind and would know where to locate whatever information she might find useful.

Added to that…

He looked at Lesley with lazy, brooding eyes as she stepped into the room.

There was something about the woman. She didn't pull her punches and, whilst a part of him was grimly disapproving of her forthright manner, another part of him was intrigued.

When was the last time he had been in the company of a woman who didn't say what she wanted him to hear?

When had he *ever* been in the company of any woman who didn't say what she wanted him to hear?

He was the product of a life of privilege. He had grown up accustomed to servants and chauffeurs and then, barely into adulthood, had found himself an expectant father. In a heartbeat, his world had changed. He'd no longer had the freedom to make youthful mistakes and to learn from them over time. Responsibility had landed on his doorstep without an invitation and then, on top of that, had come the grim realisation that he had been used for his money.

Not even out of his teens, he had discovered the bitter truth that his fortune would always be targeted. He would never be able to relax in the company of any woman without suspecting that she had her eye to the main chance. He would always have to be on his guard, always watchful, always making sure that no one got too close.

He was a generous lover, and had no problem splashing out on whatever woman happened to be sharing his bed, but he knew where to draw the line and was ruthless when it came to making sure that no woman got too close, certainly not close enough ever to harbour notions of longevity.

It was unusual to find himself in a situation such as

this. It was unusual to be in close personal confines with a woman where sex wasn't on the menu.

It was even more unusual to find himself in this situation with a woman who made no effort to try and please him in any way.

'I was expecting a bedroom.' Lesley turned to look at him. 'Posters on the walls, cuddly toys, that sort of thing.'

'Rachel occupies one wing of the house. There are actually three bedrooms, along with a sitting room, a study, two bathrooms and an exercise room.' He strolled towards her and looked around him, hands shoved in the pockets of his cream trousers. 'This is the first time I've stepped foot into this section of the house since my daughter returned from boarding school for the holidays. When I saw the state it was in, I immediately got in touch with Violet, who informed me that she, along with her assistants, were barred from entry.'

Disapproval was stamped all over his face and Lesley could understand why. The place looked as though a bomb had been detonated in it. The tiled, marble floor of the small hallway was barely visible under discarded clothes and books and, through the open doors, she could see the other rooms appeared to be in a similar state of chaos.

Magazines were strewn everywhere. Shoes, kicked off, had landed randomly and then had been left there. School books lay open on various surfaces.

Going through all of this would be a full-time job.

'Teenagers can be very private creatures,' Lesley said dubiously. 'They hate having their space invaded.' She picked her way into bedroom number one and then continued to explore the various rooms, all the time conscious of Alessio lounging indolently against the wall and watching her progress.

She had the uneasy feeling of having been manipulated. How had she managed to end up here? Now she felt *involved.* She was no longer doing a quick job to help her father's pal out. She was ensconced in the middle of a family saga and wasn't quite sure where to begin.

'I will get Violet to make sure that these rooms are tidied first thing in the morning,' Alessio said as she finally walked towards him. 'At least then you will have something of a clean slate to start on.'

'Probably not such a good idea.' Lesley looked up at him. He was one of the few men with whom she could do that and, as she had quickly discovered, her breathing quickened as their eyes met. 'Adolescents are fond of writing stuff down on bits of paper. If there is anything to be found, that's probably where I'll find it, and that's just the sort of thing a cleaner would stick in the bin.' She hesitated. 'Don't you communicate with your daughter *at all*? I mean, how could she get away with keeping her room—her *rooms*—as messy as this?'

Alessio took one final glance around him and then headed for the door. 'Rachel has spent most of the summer here while I have been in London, only popping back now and again. She's clearly intimidated the cleaners into not going anywhere near her rooms and they've obeyed.'

'You've just *popped back here now and again* to see how she's doing?'

Alessio stopped in his tracks and looked at her coolly. 'You're here to try and sort out a situation involving computers and emails. You're not here to pass judgement on my parenting skills.'

Lesley sighed with obvious exasperation. She had been hustled here with unholy speed. He had even come with her to her office, on the pretext of having a look at what her company did, and had so impressed her boss that Jake had had no trouble in giving her the week off.

And now, having found herself in a situation that somehow didn't seem to be of her own choosing, she wasn't about to be lectured to in that patronising tone of voice.

'I'm not passing opinions on your parenting skills,' she said with restraint. 'I'm trying to make sense of a picture. If I can see the whole picture, then I might have an idea of how and where to proceed.' She had not yet had time since arriving to get down to the business of working her way through the emails and trying to trace the culprit responsible for them.

That was a job for the following day. Right now, she would barely have time to have dinner, run a bath and then hit the sack. It had been a long day.

'I mean,' she said into an unresponsive silence, 'If and when I do find out who is responsible for those emails, we still won't know why he's sending them. He could clam up, refuse to say anything, and then you may still be left with a problem on your hands in connection with your daughter.'

They had reached the kitchen, which was a vast space dominated by a massive oak table big enough to seat ten. Everything in the house was larger than life, including all the furnishings.

'They may have nothing to do with Rachel. That's just another possibility.' He took a bottle of wine from the fridge and two wine glasses from one of the cupboards. There was a rich smell of food and Lesley looked around for Violet, who seemed to be an invisible but constant presence in the house.

'Where's Violet?' she asked, hovering.

'Gone for the evening. I try and not keep the hired help chained to the walls at night.' He proffered the glass of wine. 'And you can come inside, Lesley. You're not entering a lion's den.'

It felt like it, however. In ways she couldn't put her finger on, Alessio Baldini felt exciting and dangerous at the same time. Especially so at night, here, in his house with no one around.

'She's kindly prepared a casserole for us. Beef. It's in the oven. We can have it with bread, if that suits you.'

'Of course,' Lesley said faintly. 'Is that how it works when you're here? Meals are prepared for you so that all you have to do is switch the oven on?'

'One of the housekeepers tends to stick around when Rachel's here.' Alessio flushed and turned away.

In that fleeting window, she glimpsed the situation with far more clarity than if she had had it spelled out for her.

He was so awkward with his own daughter that he preferred to have a third party to dilute the atmosphere. Rachel probably felt the same way. Two people, father and daughter, were circling one another like strangers in a ring.

He had been pushed to the background during her formative years, had found his efforts at bonding repelled and dismantled by a vengeful wife, and now found himself with a teenager he didn't know. Nor was he, by nature, a people person—the sort of man who could joke his way back into a relationship.

Into that vacuum, any number of gremlins could have entered.

'So you're *never* on your own with your daughter? Okay. In that case you really wouldn't have a clue what was happening in her life, especially as she spends most of the year away from home. But you were saying that this may not have anything directly to do with Rachel. What did you mean by that?'

She watched him bring the food to the table and re-fill their glasses with more wine.

Alessio gave her a long, considered look from under his lashes.

'What I am about to tell you stays within the walls of this house, is that clear?'

Lesley paused with her glass halfway to her mouth and looked at him over the rim with astonishment.

'And you laugh at me for thinking that you might have links to the Mafia?'

Alessio stared at her and then shook his head and slowly grinned. 'Okay, maybe that sounded a little melodramatic.'

Lesley was knocked sideways by that smile. It was so full of charm, so lacking in the controlled cool she had seen in him before. It felt as though, the more time she spent in his company, the more intriguing and complex he became. He was not simply a mega-rich guy employ-ing her to do a job for him, but a man with so many fac-ets to his personality that it made her head spin.

Worse than that, she could feel herself being sucked in, and that scared her.

'I don't do melodrama,' Alessio was saying with the remnants of his smile. 'Do you?'

'Never.' Lesley licked her lips nervously. 'What are you going to tell me that has to stay here?'

His dark eyes lingered on her flushed face. 'It's un-likely that our guy would have got hold of this informa-tion but, just in case, it's information I would want to protect my daughter from knowing. I certainly would not want it in the public arena.' He swigged the remainder of his wine and did the honours by dishing food onto the plates which had already been put on the table, along with glasses and cutlery.

Mesmerised by the economic elegance of his movements, and lulled by the wine and the creeping darkness outside, Lesley cupped her chin in her hand and stared at him.

He wasn't looking at her. He was concentrating on not spilling any food. He had the expression of someone unaccustomed to doing anything of a culinary nature for themselves—focused yet awkward at the same time.

'You don't look comfortable with a serving spoon,' she remarked idly and Alessio glanced across to where she was sitting, staring at him. She wore a thin gold chain with a tiny pendant around her neck and she was playing with the pendant, rolling it between her fingers as she looked at him.

Suddenly and for no reason, his breathing thickened and heat surged through his body with unexpected force. His libido, that had not seen the light of day for the past couple of months, reared up with such urgency that he felt his sharp intake of breath.

She was not trying to be seductive but somehow he could feel her seducing him.

'I bet you don't do much cooking for yourself.'

'Come again?' Alessio did his best to get his thoughts back in order. An erection was jamming against the zipper of his trousers, rock-hard and painful, and it was a relief to sit down.

'I said, you don't look as though handling pots and pans comes as second nature to you.' She tucked into the casserole, which was mouth-wateringly fragrant. They should be discussing work but the wine had made her feel relaxed and mellow and had allowed her curiosity about him to come out of hiding and to take centre stage.

Sober, she would have chased that curiosity away, because she could feel its danger. But pleasantly tipsy, she wanted to know more about him.

'I don't do much cooking, no.'

'I guess you can always get someone else to do it for you. Top chefs or housekeepers, or maybe just your girlfriends.' She wondered what his girlfriends looked like. He might have had a rocky marriage that had ended in divorce, but he would have lots of girlfriends.

'I don't let women near my kitchen.' Alessio was amused at her disingenuous curiosity. He swirled his wine around in the glass and swallowed a mouthful.

With a bit of alcohol in her system, she looked more relaxed, softer, less defensive.

His erection was still throbbing and his eyes dropped to her mouth, then lower to where the loose neckline of her tee-shirt allowed a glimpse of her shoulder blades and the soft hint of a cleavage. She wasn't big breasted and the little she had was never on show.

'Why? Don't you ever go out with women who like to cook?'

'I've never asked whether they like to cook or not,' he said wryly, finishing his wine, pouring himself another glass and keeping his eyes safely away from her loose-limbed body. 'I've found that, the minute a woman starts eulogising about the joys of home-cooked food, it usually marks the end of the relationship.'

'What do you mean?' Lesley looked at him, surprised.

'It means that the last thing I need is someone trying to prove that they're a domestic goddess in my kitchen. I prefer that the women I date don't get too settled.'

'In case they get ideas of permanence?'

'Which brings me neatly back to what I wanted to say.' That disturbing moment of intense sexual attraction began to ebb away and he wondered how it had arisen in the first place.

She was nothing like the women he dated. Could it be that her intelligence, the strange role she occupied as receiver of information no other woman had ever had, the sheer difference of her body, had all those things conspired against him?

There was a certain intimacy to their conversation. Had that entered the mix and worked some kind of passing, peculiar magic?

More to the point, a little voice inside him asked, what did he intend to do about it?

'I have a certain amount of correspondence locked away that could be very damaging.'

'Correspondence?'

'Of the non-silicon-chip variety,' Alessio elaborated drily. 'Correspondence of the old-fashioned sort— namely, letters.'

'To do with business?' She felt a sudden stab of intense disappointment that she had actually believed him when he had told her that he was an honest guy in all his business dealings.

'No, not to do with business, so you can stop thinking that you've opened a can of worms and you need to clear off as fast as you can. I told you I'm perfectly straight when it comes to my financial dealings and I wasn't lying.'

Lesley released a long sigh of relief. Of course, it was because she would have been in a very awkward situation had he confessed to anything shady, especially considering she was alone with him in his house.

It definitely wasn't because she would have been disappointed in him as a man had he been party to anything crooked.

'Then what? And what is the relevance to the case?'

'This could hurt my daughter. It would certainly be annoying for me should it hit the press. If I fill you in, then you might be able to join some dots and discover if this is the subject of his emails.'

'You have far too much confidence in my abilities, Mr Baldini.' She smiled. 'I may be good at what I do but I'm not a miracle worker.'

'I think we've reached the point where you can call me Alessio. It occurred to me that there may have been stray references in the course of the emails that might point in a certain direction.'

'And you feel that I need to know the direction they may point in so that I can pick them up if they're there?'

'Something like that.'

'Wouldn't you have seen them for yourself?'

'I only began paying attention to those emails the day you were hired. Before that, I had kept them, but hadn't examined them in any depth and I haven't had the opportunity to do so since. It's a slim chance but we can cover all bases.'

'And what if I do find a link?'

'Then I shall know what options to take when it comes to dealing with the perpetrator.'

Lesley sighed and fluffed her short hair up with her fingers. 'Do you know, I have never been in this sort of situation before.'

'But you've had a couple of tricky occasions.'

'Not as complicated as this. The tricky ones have usually involved friends of friends imagining that I can unearth marital affairs by bugging computers, and then

I have to let them down. If I can even be bothered to see what they want in the first place.'

'And this?'

'This feels as though it's got layers.' And she wasn't sure that she wanted to peel them back to see what was lying underneath. It bothered her that he had such an effect on her that he had been able to entice her into taking time off work to help him in the first place.

And it bothered her even more that she couldn't seem to stop wanting to stare at him. Of course he was good-looking, but she was sensible when it came to guys, and this one was definitely off-limits. The gulf between them was so great that they could be living on different planets.

And yet her eyes still sought him out, and that was worrying.

'I had more than one reason for divorcing my wife,' he said heavily, after a while. He hesitated, at a loss as to where to go from there, because sharing confidences was not something he ever did. From the age of eighteen, he had learnt how to keep his opinions to himself—first through a sense of shame that he had been hoodwinked by a girl he had been seeing for a handful of months, a girl who had conned him into thinking she had been on the pill. Later, when his marriage had predictably collapsed, he had developed a forbidding ability to keep his emotions and his thoughts under tight rein. It was what he had always seen as protection against ever making another mistake when it came to the opposite sex.

But now...

Her intelligent eyes were fixed on his face. He reminded himself that this was a woman against whom he needed no protection because she had no ulterior agenda.

'Not only did Bianca lie her way into a marriage but she also managed to lie her way into making me believe that she was in love with me.'

'You were a kid,' Lesley pointed out, when he failed to elaborate on that remark. 'It happens.'

'And you know because…?'

'I don't,' she said abruptly. 'I wasn't one of those girls anyone lied to about being in love with. Carry on.'

Alessio tilted his head and looked at her enquiringly, tempted to take her up on that enigmatic statement, even though he knew he wouldn't get anywhere with it.

'We married and, very shortly after Rachel was born, my wife began fooling around. Discreetly at first, but that didn't last very long. We moved in certain circles and it became a bore to try and work out who she wanted to sleep with and when she would make a move.'

'How awful for you.'

Alessio opened his mouth to brush that show of sympathy to one side but instead stared at her for a few moments in silence. 'It wasn't great,' he admitted heavily.

'It can't have been. Not at any age, but particularly not when you were practically a child yourself and not equipped to deal with that kind of disillusionment.'

'No.' His voice was rough but he gave a little shrug, dismissing that episode in his life.

'I can understand why you would want to protect your daughter from knowing that her mother was… promiscuous.'

'There's rather more.' His voice was steady and matter-of-fact. 'When our marriage was at its lowest ebb, Bianca implied, during one of our rows, that I wasn't Rachel's father at all. Afterwards she retracted her words and said that she hadn't been thinking straight. God knows, she probably realised that Rachel was her lifeline to money, and the last thing she should do was to jeopardise that lifeline, but the words were out and as far as I was concerned couldn't be taken back.'

'No, I can understand that.' Whoever said that money could buy happiness? she thought, feeling her heart constrict for the young boy he must have been then—deceived, betrayed, cheated on; forced to become a man when he was still in his teens.

'One day when she was out shopping, I returned early from work and decided, on impulse, to go through her drawers. By this time, we were sleeping in separate rooms. I found a stash of letters, all from the same guy, someone she had known when she was sixteen. Met him on holiday somewhere in Majorca. Young love. Touching, don't you think? They kept in contact and she was seeing him when she was married to me. I gathered from reading between the lines that he was the son of a poor fisherman, someone her parents would certainly not have welcomed with open arms.'

'No.'

'The lifestyles of the rich and famous,' he mocked wryly. 'I bet you're glad you weren't one of the privileged crowd.'

'I never gave it much thought, but now that you mention it…' She smiled and he grudgingly returned the smile.

'I have no idea whether the affair ended when her behaviour became more out of control but it certainly made me wonder whether she was right about our daughter not being biologically mine. Not that it would have made a scrap of difference but…'

'You'd have to find out that sort of thing.'

'Tests proved conclusively that Rachel is my child but you can see why this information could be highly destructive if it came to light, especially considering the poor relationship I have with my daughter. It could be catastrophic. She would always doubt my love for her if she thought that I had taken a paternity test to prove she was mine in the first place. It would certainly destroy the happy memories she has of her mother and, much as Bianca appalled me, I wouldn't want to deprive Rachel of her memories.'

'But if this information was always private and historic, and only contained in letter form, then I don't see how anyone else could have got hold of it.' But there were always links to links to links; it just took one person to start delving and who knew what could come out in the wash? 'I'll see if I can spot any names or hints that this might be the basis of the threats.'

And at the same time, she would have her work cut out going through his daughter's things, a job which still didn't sit well with her, even though a part of her know that it was probably essential.

'I should be heading up to bed now,' she said, rising to her feet.

'It's not yet nine-thirty.'

'I'm an early-to-bed kind of person,' she said awkwardly, not knowing whether to leave the kitchen or remain where she was, then realising that she was behaving like an employee waiting for her boss to dismiss her. But her feet remained nailed to the spot.

'I have never talked so much about myself,' Alessio murmured, which got her attention, and she looked at him quizzically. 'It's not in my nature. I'm a very private man, hence what I've told you goes no further than this room.'

'Of course it won't,' Lesley assured him vigorously. 'Who would I tell?'

'If someone could consider blackmailing me over this information, then it might occur to you that you could do the same. You would certainly have unrivalled proof of whatever you wanted to glean about my private life in the palm of your hand.'

It was a perfectly logical argument and he was, if nothing else, an extremely logical man. But Alessio still felt an uncustomary twinge of discomfort at having spelled it out so clearly.

He noticed the patches of angry colour that flooded her cheeks and bit back the temptation to apologise for being more blunt than strictly necessary.

She worked with computers; she would know the value of logic and reason.

'You're telling me that you don't trust me.'

'I'm telling you that you keep all of this to yourself. No girly gossip in the toilets at work, or over a glass of wine with your friends, and certainly no pillow talk with whoever you end up sharing your bed with.'

'Thank you for spelling it out so clearly,' Lesley said coldly. 'But I know how to keep a confidence and I fully understand that it's important that none of this gets out. If you have a piece of paper, you can draft something up right here and I'll sign it!'

'Draft something up?' Under normal circumstances, he certainly would have had that in place before hiring her for the job, but for some reason it simply hadn't occurred to him.

Perhaps it had been the surprise of opening the front door to a girl instead of the man he had been expecting.

Perhaps there was something about her that had worked its way past his normal defences so that he had failed to go down the predicted route.

'I'm happy to sign whatever silence clause you want.

One word of what we've spoken about here, and you will have my full permission to fling me into jail and throw away the key.'

'I thought you said that you weren't melodramatic.'

'I'm insulted that you think I'd break the confidence you have in me to do my job and keep the details of it to myself.'

'You may be insulted, but are you surprised?' He rose to his feet, towering over her, and she fell back a couple of steps and held onto the back of the kitchen chair.

Alessio, on his way to make them some coffee, sensed the change in the atmosphere the way a big cat can sense the presence of prey in the shift of the wind. Their eyes met and something inside him, something that operated on an instinctual level, understood that, however scathing and derisive her tone of voice had been, she was tuned in to him in ways that matched his.

Tuned in to him in ways that were sexual.

The realisation struck him from out of nowhere and yet, as he held her gaze a few seconds longer than was necessary, he actually doubted himself because her expression was so tight, straightforward and openly annoyed.

'I am a man who is accustomed to taking precautions,' he murmured huskily.

'I get that.' Especially after everything he had told her. Of course he would want to make sure that he didn't leave himself open to exploitation of any kind. That was probably one of the rules by which he lived his life.

So he was right; why should she be surprised that he had taken her to task?

Except she had been lulled into a false sense of confidences shared, had warmed to the fact that he had

opened up to her, and in the process had chosen to ignore the reality, which was that he had decided that he
had no choice. He hadn't opened up to her because she
was special. He had opened up to her because it was
necessary to make her task a little easier.

'Do you?'

'Of course I do,' she said on a sigh. 'I'm just not used
to people distrusting me. I'm one of the most reliable
people I know when it comes to keeping a secret.'

'Really?' Mere inches separated them. He could feel
the warmth radiating from her body out towards his and
he wondered again whether his instincts had been right
when they had told him that she was not as unaffected
by him as she would have liked to pretend.

'Yes!' She relaxed with a laugh. 'When I was a teenager, I was the one person all the lads turned to when it
came to confidences. They knew I would never breathe
a word when they told me that they fancied someone,
or asked me what I thought it would take to impress
someone else...'

And all the while, Alessio thought to himself, you
were taking lessons in self-defence.

Never one to do much prying into female motiva-
tions, he was surprised to find that he quite wanted to
know more about her. 'You've won your argument,' he
said with a slow smile.

'You mean, you won't be asking me to sign something?'

'No. So there will be no need for you to live in fear
that you will be flung into prison and the key thrown
away if the mood takes me.' His eyes dipped down to
the barely visible swell of her small breasts under the
baggy tee-shirt.

'I appreciate that,' Lesley told him sincerely. 'I don't
know how easy I would have found it, working for some-

one who didn't trust me. So I shall start first thing in the morning.' She suddenly realised just how close their bodies were to one another and she shuffled a couple of discreet inches back. 'If it's all the same to you, you can point me in the direction of your computer and I'll spend the morning there, and the afternoon going through your daughter's rooms just in case I find anything of interest. And you needn't worry about asking your housekeeper to prepare any lunch for me. I usually just eat on the run. I can fill you in when you return from London or else I can call you if you decide to stay in London overnight.'

Alessio inclined his head in agreeable assent—except, maybe there would be no need for that.

Maybe he would stay here in the country—so much more restful than London and so much easier were he to be at hand.

CHAPTER FOUR

LESLEY WAS NOT finding life particularly restful. Having been under the impression that Alessio would be commuting to and from London, with a high possibility of remaining in London for at least part of the time, she'd been dismayed when, two days previously, he'd informed her that there had been a change of plan.

'I'll be staying here,' he had said the morning after she had arrived. 'Makes sense.'

Lesley had no idea how he had reached that conclusion. How did it make sense for him to be around: bothering her; getting under her skin; just *being* within her line of vision and therefore compelling her to look at him?

'You'll probably have a lot of questions and it'll be easier if I'm here to answer them.'

'I could always phone you,' she had said, staring at him with rising panic, because she'd been able to see just how the week was going to play out.

'And then,' he had continued, steamrollering over her interruption, 'I would feel guilty were I to leave you here on your own. The house is very big. My conscience wouldn't be able to live with the thought that you might find it quite unsettling being here with no one around.'

He had directed her to where she would be working

and she'd been appalled to find that she would be sharing office space with him.

'Of course, if you find it uncomfortable working in such close proximity to me, then naturally I can set up camp somewhere else. The house has enough rooms to accommodate one of them being turned into a makeshift work place.'

She had closed her mouth and said nothing, because what had there been to say? That, yes, she *would* find it uncomfortable working in such close proximity to him, because she was just too *aware* of him for her own good; because he made her nervous and tense; because her skin tingled the second he got too close?

She had moved from acknowledging that the man was sexy to accepting that she was attracted to him. She had no idea how that could be the case, given that he just wasn't the sort of person she had ever envisaged herself taking an interest in, but she had given up fighting it. There was just something too demanding about his physicality for her to ignore.

So she had spent her mornings in a state of rigid, hyper-sensitive awareness. She had been conscious of his every small move as he'd peered at his computer screen, reached across his desk to get something or swivelled his chair so that he could find a more comfortable position for his long legs.

She had not been able to block out the timbre of his deep voice whenever he was on the phone. She wouldn't have been able to recall any of the conversations he had had, but she could recall exactly what that voice did to her.

The range of unwanted physical sensations he evoked in her was frankly exhausting.

So she had contrived to have a simple routine of disappearing outside to communicate with her office on the pretext that she didn't want to disturb him.

Besides, she had added, making sure to forestall any objections, she never got the chance to leave London. She had never been to stay at a country estate in her life before. It would be marvellous if she could take advantage of the wonderful opportunity he had given her by working outdoors so that she could enjoy being in the countryside, especially given that the weather was so brilliant.

He had acquiesced although when he had looked at her she had been sure that she could detect a certain amount of amusement.

Now, in a break with this routine, Lesley had decided to start on Rachel's rooms.

She had gone over all of the emails with a fine toothcomb and had found no evidence that the mystery writer was aware of Bianca's past.

She looked around room number one and wondered where to begin.

As per specific instructions, Violet had left everything as it was and Lesley, by no means a neat freak, was not looking forward to going through the stacks of dispersed clothes, books, magazines and random bits of paper that littered the ground.

But she dug in, working her way steadily through the chaos, flinging clothes in the stainless-steel hamper she had dragged from the massive bathroom and marvelling that a child of sixteen could possess so much designer clothing.

This was what money bought: expensive clothes and jewellery. But no amount of expensive clothes and jewellery could fix a broken relationship and, over the past two days, she had seen for herself just how broken the relationship between father and daughter was.

He kept his emotions under tight control but every so often there were glimpses of the man underneath who was confused at his inability to communicate with his daughter and despairing of what the future held for them.

And yet, he wanted to protect her, and would do anything to that end.

She began rifling through the pockets of a pair of jeans, her mind playing with the memory of just how weirdly close the past couple of days had brought them.

Or, at least, *her.*

But then, she thought ruefully, she was handicapped by the fact that she found him attractive. She was therefore primed to analyse everything he said, to be superattentive to every stray remark, to hang onto his every word with breathless intensity.

Thank God he didn't know what was going through her head.

It took her a couple of seconds before the piece of paper she extracted from the jeans pocket made sense and then a couple more seconds before the links she had begun to see in the emails began to tie up in front of her.

More carefully now, she began feeling her way through the mess, inspecting everything in her path. She went over the clothes she had carelessly chucked into the hamper just in case she had missed something.

Had she expected to find anything at all like this, searching through a few rooms? No; maybe when she got to the computer or the tablet, or whatever other computer gadgets might be lying around.

But scribbles on a bit of paper? No. She thought that teenagers were way beyond using pens and paper by way of communication.

What else might she find?

She had lost that initial feeling of intruding in some-one else's space. Something about the messiness made her search more acceptable.

No attempts had been made to hide anything and nothing was under lock and key.

Did that make a difference? In a strange way it did, as did the little things lying about that showed Rachel for the child she still was, even if she had entered the teenage battleground of rebellion and disobedience.

Her art book was wonderful. There were cute little doodles in the margins of her exercise books. Her stationery was very cute, with lots of puppy motifs on the pencil cases and folders. It was at odds with the rest of what was to be found in the room.

An hour and a half into the search, Lesley opened the first of the wardrobes and gasped at the racks of clothes confronting her.

You didn't need to be a connoisseur of fine clothing to know that these were the finest money could buy. She ran her hands through the dresses, skirts and tops and felt silk, cashmere and pure cotton. Some of them were youthful and brightly coloured, others looked far too grown-up for a sixteen-year-old child. Quite a few things still had tags attached because they had yet to be used.

As she pushed the clothes at the front aside, she came across some dresses at the back that were clearly too old for a sixteen-year-old; they must have belonged to Rachel's mother. Lesley gently pulled a demure black dress from the selection and admired the fine material and elegant cut of the design. She knew that it was wrong to try on someone else's clothes but she lost her head for a moment and suddenly found herself slipping into the gorgeous creation. As she turned to look at herself in the mirror, she gasped.

Usually she was awkward, one of the lads, at her most comfortable when she was exchanging banter; yet the creature staring back at her wasn't that person at all. The creature staring back at her was a leggy, attractive young woman with a good figure, good legs and a long neck.

She spun away from the mirror suddenly as she heard the door open and saw Alessio look at her in shock.

'What are you doing here?' She felt naked as his eyes slowly raked over her, from the top of her head, along her body and then all the way back again.

Alessio couldn't stop looking at her. He had left the office to stretch his legs and had decided to check on how Lesley's search was coming along. He hadn't expected to find her in a stunning cocktail dress, her legs seeming to go on for ever.

'Well?' Lesley folded her arms defensively, although what she really wanted to do was somehow reach down and cover her exposed thighs. The skirt should have been a couple of inches above the knee but, because she was obviously taller than Rachel's mother had been, it was obscenely short on her.

'I've interrupted a catwalk session,' he murmured, walking slowly towards her. 'My apologies.'

'I was… I thought…'

'It suits you, just in case you're interested in what I think. The dress, I mean. You should reveal your legs more often.'

'If you would please just go, I'll get changed. I apologise for having tried on the dress. It was totally out of order, and if you want to give me my marching orders then I would completely understand.' She had never felt so mortified in her entire life. What must he be thinking? She had taken something that didn't belong to her and put it on, an especially unforgivable offence, considering she was under his roof in the capacity of a paid employee.

His 'catwalk' comment struck her as an offensive insult but there was no way she was going to call him out on that. She just wanted him to leave the room but he showed no signs of going.

'Why would I give you your marching orders?' She was bright red and as stiff as a plank of wood.

Any other woman would have been overjoyed to be the centre of his attention, as she now was, but instead she was staring straight ahead, unblinking, doing her utmost to shut him out of her line of vision.

He had never wanted a woman as much as he wanted this one right now. Mind and body fused. This wasn't just another of his glamorous, sex-kitten women. This thinking, questioning, irreverent creature was in a different league.

The attraction he had felt for her, which had been there from the second they had met, clarified into the absolute certainty that he wanted her in his bed. It was a thought he had flirted with, dwelled on; rejected because she'd challenged him on too many levels and he liked his women unchallenging.

But, hell…

'Please leave.'

'You don't have to take off the dress,' he said in a lazy drawl. 'I'd quite like to see you working in that outfit.'

'You're making fun of me and I don't like it.' She had managed to blank him out, so that she was just aware of him on the periphery of her vision, but she could still feel his power radiating outwards, wrapping around her like something thick, suffocating and tangible.

She felt like something small and helpless being circled by a beautiful, dangerous predator.

Except he would never hurt her. No; his capacity for destruction lay in his ability to make her hurt herself by believing what he was saying, by allowing her feelings for him get the better of her. She had never realised that lust could be so overwhelming. Nothing had prepared her for the crazy, inappropriate emotions that rode roughshod over her prized and treasured common sense.

'I'll pretend I didn't hear that,' Alessio said softly. Then he reached out and ran his hand along her arm, feeling its soft, silky smoothness. She was so slender. For a few seconds, Lesley didn't react, then the feel of his warm hand on her skin made her stumble backwards with a yelp.

His instincts had been right. How could he have doubted himself? The electricity between them flowed both ways. He stepped back and looked at her lazily. Her eyes were huge and she looked very young and very vulnerable. And she was still wobbling in the high stilettos; that was how uncomfortable she was in a pair of heels. He was struck with a pressing desire to see her dolled up to the nines and, with an even more contradictory one, to have her naked in his arms.

'I'll leave you to get back into your clothes,' he said with the gentleness of someone trying to calm a panicked, highly strung thoroughbred. 'And, to answer your question as to what I'm doing here, I thought I would just pop in and see if your search up here was being fruitful.'

Relieved to have the focus off her and onto work, Lesley allowed some of the tension to ooze out of her body.

'I *have* found one or two things you might be interested in,' she said with staccato jerkiness. 'And I'll come right down to the office.'

'Better still, meet me outside. I'll get Violet to bring us out some tea.' He smiled, encouraging her to relax further. It was all he could do not to let his eyes wander over her, drink her in. He lowered his eyes and reluctantly spun round, walking towards the door and knowing that she wouldn't move a muscle until he was well and truly out of the suite of rooms and heading down the staircase.

Once outside, he couldn't wait for her to join him. He was oblivious to his surroundings as he stared off into the distance, thinking of how she had looked in that outfit. She had incredible legs, an incredible body and it was all the more enhanced by the fact that she was so unaware of her charms.

Five brothers; no mother; karate lessons when the rest of her friends were practising the feminine skills that would serve them well in later life. Was that why she was so skittish around him? Was she skittish around *all* men, or was it just him? Was that why she chose to dress the way she did, why she projected such a capable image, why she deliberately seemed to spurn feminine clothes?

He found himself idly trying to work out what made her tick and he was enjoying the game when he saw her walking towards him with a sheaf of papers in her hand, all business as usual.

'Thank you.' Lesley sat down, taking the glass that was offered to her. She had been so hot and bothered after he had left that she had taken time out to wash her face in cold water and gather herself. 'First of all—and I'm almost one-hundred-per-cent sure about this—our emailing friend has no idea about your wife or the sort of person she was.'

Alessio leant closer, forearms resting on his thighs. 'And you've reached that conclusion because…?'

'Because I've been through each and every email very carefully, looking for clues. I've also found a couple of earlier emails which arrived in your junk box and for some reason weren't deleted. They weren't significant. Perhaps our friend was just having a bit of fun.'

'So you think this isn't about a blackmail plot to do with revelations about Bianca?'

'Yes, partly from reading through the emails and partly common sense. I think if they involved your ex-wife there would have been some sort of guarded reference made that would have warned you of what was to come. And, whilst he or she knew what they were doing and were careful to leave as few tracks behind them as they could, some of those emails are definitely more rushed than others.'

'Woman's intuition?' There was genuine curiosity in his voice and Lesley nodded slowly.

'I think so. What's really significant, though, is that the Internet cafés used were all in roughly the same area, within a radius of a dozen miles or so, and they are all in the general vicinity of where Rachel goes to school. Which leads me to think that she is at the centre of this in some way, shape or form because the person responsible probably knows her or knows of her.'

Alessio sat back and rubbed his eyes wearily. Lesley could see the strain visible beneath the cool, collected exterior when he next looked at her. He might have approached this problem with pragmatism and detachment, as a job to be done—but his daughter was involved and that showed on his face now, in the worry and the stress.

'Any idea of what could be going on? It could still

be that our friend, as you call him, has information on Bianca and wants me to pay him for not sharing that information with Rachel.'

'Does Rachel know anything about what her mother was like as…err…a young girl? I mean, when she was still married to you? I know your daughter would have been a toddler with no memories of that time, but you know how it is: overheard conversations between adults, bits and pieces of gossip from friends or family or whatever.'

Alessio leaned back in the chair and closed his eyes.

'As far as I am aware, Rachel is completely in the dark about Bianca, but who knows? We haven't talked about it. We've barely got past the stage of polite pleasantries.'

Lesley stared at his averted profile. Seeing them in repose, as now, she felt the full impact of his devastating good looks. His sensual mouth lost its stern contours; she could appreciate the length and thickness of his eyelashes, the strong angle of his jaw, the tousled blackness of his slightly too-long hair. His fingers were linked loosely on his stomach; she took in the dark hair on his forearms and then burned when she wondered where that dark hair was replicated.

She wondered whether she should tell him about those random scribbles she had found and decided against it. They formed part of the jigsaw puzzle but she would hang on until more of the pieces came together. It was only fair. He was a desperately concerned father, worried about a daughter he barely knew; to add yet more stress to his situation, when she wasn't even one-hundred per cent sure whether what she had found would prove significant in the end, seemed downright selfish.

The lingering embarrassment she had brought with her after the mini-skirt-wearing episode faded as the silence lengthened between them, a telling indication of his state of mind.

It would have cost him dearly to confide the personal details of his situation with his ex-wife. No matter that he had been practically a child at the time. No one enjoyed being used and Alessio, in particular, was a proud man today and would have been a proud boy all those years ago.

Her heart softened and she resisted the temptation to reach out and stroke the side of his cheek.

'I'm making you feel awkward,' Alessio murmured, breaking the silence, but not opening his eyes or turning in her direction.

Lesley buried the wickedly tantalising thought of touching his cheek. 'Of course not!'

'I don't suppose you banked on this sort of situation when you agreed to the job.'

'I don't suppose you banked on it either when you decided to hire me.'

'True,' he admitted with a ghost of a smile. 'So, where do you suggest we go from here? Quiz Rachel when she gets home day after tomorrow? Try and find out if she has any idea what's going on?' He listened as she ran through some options. He liked hearing her talk. He liked the soft but decisive tone of her voice. He liked the way she could talk to him like this, on his level, with no coy intonations and no irritating indications that she wanted the conversation to take any personal detours.

Mind you, she had so much information about him that personal detours were pretty much an irrelevance:

there really weren't that many nooks and crannies left to discover.

His mind swung back to when he had caught her wearing that dress and his body began to stir into life.

'Talk to me about something else,' he ordered huskily when there was a pause in the conversation. This was as close to relaxation he had come in a long time, despite the grim nature of what was going on. He had his eyes closed, the sun was on his face and his body felt lazy and nicely lethargic.

'What do you want me to talk about?' She could understand why he might not want to dwell ad infinitum on a painful subject, even one that needed to be discussed.

'You. I want you to talk about you.'

Even though he wasn't looking at her, Lesley still reddened. That voice of his; had he any idea how sexy it was? No, of course not.

'I'm a very boring person,' she half-laughed with embarrassment. 'Besides, you know all the basic stuff: my brothers; my dad bringing us all up on his own.'

'So let's skip the basics. Tell me what drove you to try on that dress.'

'I don't want to talk about that.' Lesley's skin prickled with acute discomfort. The mortification she had felt assailed her all over again and she clenched her fists on her lap. 'I've already apologised and I'd really rather we drop the subject and pretend it never happened. It was a mistake.'

'You're embarrassed.'

'Of course I am.'

'No need to be, and I'm not prying. I'm really just trying to grasp anything that might take my mind off what's happening right now with Rachel.'

Suddenly Lesley felt herself deflate. While she was on her high horse, defending her position and beating back his very natural curiosity, he was in the unenviable position of having had to open the door to his past and let her in.

Was it any wonder that he was desperate to take his mind off his situation? Talking relentlessly about something worrying only magnified the worry and anxiety.

'I—I don't know why I tried it,' Lesley offered haltingly. 'Actually, I do know why I tried it on. I was never one for dresses and frocks when I was a teenager. That was stuff meant for other girls but not for me.'

'Because you lacked a mother's guiding hand,' Alessio contributed astutely. 'And even more influential was the fact that you had five brothers.' He grinned and some of the worry that had been etched on his face lifted. 'I remember what I was like and what my friends were like when we were fourteen—not sensitive. I bet they gave you a hard time.'

Lesley laughed. 'And the rest of it. At any rate, I had one embarrassing encounter with a mini-skirt and I decided after that that I was probably better off not going down that road. Besides, at the age of fourteen I was already taller than all the other girls in my class. Downplaying my height didn't involve wearing dresses and short skirts.'

Alessio slowly opened his eyes and then inclined his head so that he was looking directly at her.

Her skin was like satin. As far as he knew, she had yet to make use of the swimming pool, but sitting outside for the past couple of afternoons in the blazing sun had lent a golden tint to her complexion. It suited her.

'But you're not fourteen any longer,' he said huskily.

Lesley was lost for words. Drowning in his eyes, her

throat suddenly went dry and her body turned to lead. She couldn't move a muscle. She could just watch him, watching her.

He would physically have to get out of his chair if he were to come any closer, and he made no move to do anything of the sort, but she was still overwhelmed by the feeling that he was going to kiss her. It was written in the dark depths of his eyes, a certain intent that made her quiver and tremble inside.

'No, I don't suppose I am,' she choked out.

'But you still don't wear short skirts…'

'Old habits die hard.' She gave up trying to look away. She didn't care what he thought—not at this moment in time, at any rate. 'I… There's no need to dress up for the sort of job that I do. Jeans and jumpers are what we all wear.'

'You don't do justice to your body.' He glanced at his watch. He had broken off working in part, as he had said, to check on Lesley and see whether she had managed to find anything in Rachel's quarters; but also in part because he was due in London for a meeting.

The time had run away. It was much later than he had imagined…something about the sun, the slight breeze, the company of the woman sitting next to him, the way she had frozen to the spot… He wondered whether any man had ever complimented her about the way she looked or whether she had spent a lifetime assuming that no one would, therefore making sure that she carved her own niche through her intelligence and ambition.

He wondered what she would do if he touched her, kissed her.

More than ever, he wanted to have her. In fact, he was tempted to abandon the meeting in London and spend the rest of this lazy afternoon playing the game of seduction.

Already she was standing up, all of a fluster, telling him that she was feeling a little hot and wanted to get back into the shade. With an inward, rueful sigh of resignation, he followed suit.

'You're doing a brilliant job, trying to unravel what the hell is going on with these emails,' he said, uncomfortably aware of his body demanding a certain type of attention that was probably going to make his drive down to London a bit uncomfortable.

Lesley put some much-needed physical distance between them.

What had happened just then? He seemed normal enough now. Had it been her imagination playing tricks on her, making her think that he was going to kiss her? Or was it her own forbidden attraction trying to find a way to become a reality?

It absolutely terrified her that she might encourage him to think that she was attracted to him. It was even more terrifying that she might be reading all sorts of nonsense into his throwaway remarks. The guy was the last word in eligible. He was charming, highly intelligent and sophisticated, and he probably had that sexy, ever so slightly flirty manner with every woman he spoke to. It was just the kind of person he was and misinterpreting anything he said in her favour would be something she did at her own peril.

'Thank you. You're paying me handsomely to do just that.'

Alessio frowned. He didn't like money being brought into the conversation. It lowered the tone.

'Well, carry on the good work,' he said with equal politeness. 'And you'll have the house all to yourself until tomorrow to do it. I have an important meeting in London and I'll be spending the night there in my apartment.' He scowled at her immediate look of relief. Hell, she was attracted to him, but she was determined to fight it, despite the clear signals he had sent that the feeling was reciprocated. Didn't she know that for a man like him, a man who could snap his fingers and have any woman he wanted, her reticence was a challenge?

And yet, was he the type to set off in pursuit of someone who was reluctant—even though she might be as hot for him as he was for her?

A night away might cool him down a bit.

He left her dithering in the hall, seeing him off, but with a look of impatience on her face for him to be gone.

She needed this. Her nerves were getting progressively more shot by the minute; she couldn't wait for him to leave. She went to see him off, half-expecting him suddenly to decide that he wasn't going anywhere after all, and sagged with relief when the front door slammed behind him and she heard the roar of his car diminishing as he cleared the courtyard and disappeared down the long drive.

She couldn't stay. Certainly, she wanted to be out by the time his daughter arrived. She just couldn't bear the tension of being around him: she couldn't bear the loss of self-control, the way her eyes wanted to seek him out, the constant roller-coaster ride of her emotions. She felt vulnerable and confused.

Well, she had found rather more searching through Rachel's room than she had told him. Not quite enough, but just a little bit more information and she would have sufficient to present to him and leave with the case closed.

She had seen the desk-top computer and was sure

that there would be a certain amount of helpful information there.

She had an afternoon, a night and hopefully part of the day tomorrow, and during that time she would make sure that everything was sorted, because she desperately needed to return to the safety of her comfort zone...

CHAPTER FIVE

LESLEY FLEXED HER fingers, which were stiff from working solidly on Rachel's desk-top for the past two and a half hours.

Alessio had given her the green light to look through anything and everything in his daughter's room and she knew that he was right to allow her to do so. If Rachel was under some sort of threat, whatever that threat was, then everything had to be done to neutralise the situation, even if it meant an invasion of her privacy.

However, Lesley had still felt guilty and nervous when she had sat down in front of the computer to begin opening files.

She had expected to find lots of personal teenage stuff. She had never been one of those girls who had sat around giggling and pouring her heart out to all her friends. She and her friends had mostly belonged to the sporting set, and the sporting set had only occasionally crossed over into the cheerleader set, which was where most of the giggling about boys and confiding had taken place.

However, the computer seemed largely to store school work. Lesley had assumed that the more personal information was probably carried on Rachel's tablet, or else her mobile phone, neither of which were in the house.

But she had found a couple of little strands that added to the building jigsaw puzzle.

Most of the really important information, however, had been gathered the old-fashioned way: pockets of jeans; scraps of paper; old exercise books; margins of text books; letters tossed carelessly in the drawer by the bed.

There had been no attempt to hide any of the stuff Lesley had gathered, and that made her feel much better.

Rachel might have given orders to a very pliant housekeeper not to go anywhere near her rooms, but had there been a little part of her that maybe wanted the information to be found? Was that why she had not destroyed notes that were definitely incriminating?

Lesley could only speculate.

By six that evening, she was exhausted. She ached all over, but she knew that she would be able to hand everything she had found over to Alessio and be on her way.

She felt a little panicky when she thought about getting into her little car and driving away from him for ever, then she told herself that it was just as well she was going to do that, because panicking at the prospect of not seeing him was a very dangerous place to be.

How had he managed to get under her skin so thoroughly and so fast?

When it came to men, she was a girl who had always taken things slowly. Friendships were built over a reasonable period of time. Generally speaking, during that protracted build-up any prospect of the friendship developing into something more serious was apt to fizzle out, which always reassured her that the relationship had not been destined.

But the speed with which Alessio had succeeded in filling her head was scary.

She found that even being alone in his house for a few hours was an unsettling business because she missed his presence!

In the space of only a couple of days, she had become accustomed to living life in the emotional fast lane; had become used to a heightened state of awareness, knowing that he was *around*. When she sat outside in the garden—working on her lap-top, enjoying the peace of the countryside, telling herself what a relief it was that she was not in the same room as him—she was still *conscious* of the fact that he was in the house. Somewhere.

With a little sigh of frustration, she decided that she would have a swim.

She hadn't been near the pool since she had arrived. She hadn't been able to deal with the prospect of him suggesting that he join her, even less with the prospect of him seeing just how angular, flat-chested and boyish her figure was.

He might have made the occasional flirty remark, but she had seen the sort of women he was attracted to. He had handed over his computer files to her and within them were photos of him with various busty, curvaceous, five-foot-two blonde bombshells. They all looked like clones of Marilyn Monroe.

But he wasn't here now, and it was still so hot and muggy, even at this hour of the evening.

When she looked at herself in the mirror, she was startled at how much it changed her appearance. However, she had seen herself in her navy-blue bikini sufficient times to be reassured that she was the same lanky Lesley she had always been.

Without bothering to glance at her reflection, she grabbed a towel from the bathroom and headed downstairs for the pool.

She should have felt wary venturing out with no one around, and just acres upon acres of fields and open land stretching away into the distance, but she didn't. In fact, she felt far more cautious in London, where she was constantly surrounded by people and where there was no such thing as complete darkness even in the dead of night in the middle of winter.

She dived cleanly into the water, gasping at the temperature, but then her body acclimatised as she began swimming.

She was a good swimmer. After being cooped up in front of a computer for several hours, it felt good to be exercising, and she swam without stopping, cutting through the water length after length after length.

She wasn't sure exactly how long she swam; maybe forty-five minutes. She could feel the beginning of that pleasant burn in her body that indicated that her muscles were being stretched to their limit.

At this point, she pulled herself up out of the pool, water sluicing down her body, her short, dark hair plastered down...and it was only then that she noticed Alessio standing to one side, half-concealed in the shadow of one of the trees fringing the side of the veranda.

It took a few seconds for her brain to register his presence there at all because she hadn't been expecting him.

And it took a few seconds more for her to realise that, not only was he standing there, but she wasn't even sure how long he had been standing there looking at her.

With an outraged yelp she walked quickly over to where she had dumped her towel on one of the chairs by the pool and, by the time she had secured it around her, he had walked lazily to where she was standing.

'I hope I didn't interrupt your workout,' he murmured without a hint of an apology in his voice.

'You're not supposed to be here!'

'There was a slight change of plan.'

'You should have warned me that you were going to be coming back!'

'I didn't think I needed to inform you that I would be returning to my own home.'

'How long have you been standing there?' She couldn't bring herself to meet those amused dark eyes. She was horribly conscious of what she must look like, with her wet hair like a cap on her head and her face completely bare of make-up—not that she ever wore much, but still.

'Long enough to realise that it's been a while since I used that pool. In fact, I can't remember the last time I stepped foot in it.' Water droplets were like tiny diamonds on her eyelashes and he wished she would look at him so that he could read the expression in her eyes. Was she genuinely annoyed that he had disturbed her, shown up unexpectedly? Or was she all of a dither because she had been caught off-guard, because he was seeing her for the first time without her armour of jeans, flats and faded tee-shirts? Clothes that neutralised her femininity.

He wondered what she would say if he told her just how delicious she looked, standing there dripping wet with only a towel that barely covered her.

He also wondered what she would say if he told her that he had been standing there for the better part of fifteen minutes, mesmerised as he'd watched her swimming, as at home in the water as a seal. He had been so wrapped up in the sight that he had completely forgotten why he had been obliged to drive back from London.

'Wait right here,' he urged suddenly. 'I'm going to join you. Give me ten minutes. It'll do me good to get rid of the London grime.'

'Join me?' Lesley was frankly horrified.

'You don't have a problem with that, do you?'

'No…err…'

'Good. I'll be back before you can get back in the water.'

Lesley was frozen to the spot as she watched him disappear back through the sprawling triple-fronted French doors that led into the conservatory.

Then, galvanised into action—because diving in while he watched was just out of the question—she hurried back into the water. What choice did she have? To have told him that she was fed up swimming and wanted to go inside, just as he was about to join her in the pool, would have been tantamount to confessing just how awkward he made her feel. The last thing she wanted was for him to know the effect he had on her. He might have some idea that she wasn't as impartial to his presence as she liked to pretend but her feelings were more confused than that and ran a lot deeper.

That was something she was desperate to keep to herself. She could just about cope if he thought that she fancied him; half the female population in the country between the ages of eighteen and eighty would have fancied the man, so it would be no big deal were he to include her in that category.

But it was more than that. Not only was she not the type to randomly fancy guys because of the way they looked, but her reactions to him pointed to something a lot more complex than a simple case of lust which could easily be cured by putting some distance between them.

She had just reached the shallow end of the pool

when Alessio emerged back out in the mellow evening sunshine.

Lesley thought that she might faint. Only now did she fully comprehend how much time she had spent daydreaming about him, about what he might look like under those expensive, casual designer clothes he was fond of wearing.

What would his body look like?

Now she knew: lean, bronzed and utterly beautiful. His shoulders were broad and muscled and his torso tapered to a narrow waist and hips.

He was at home with his body, that much was evident from the way he moved with an easy, casual grace.

Lesley sat on one of the steps at the shallow end of the pool, so that she was levered into a half-sitting position on her elbows while her long legs and most of her body remained under the surface of the water. She felt safer that way.

He dived into the water, as straight as an arrow, and swam steadily and powerfully towards her. It took every ounce of will power not to flinch back as he reared up out of the water and joined her on the step.

'Nice,' he said appreciatively, wiping his face with the palm of his hand, then leaning back just as she did.

'You haven't explained what you're doing here.' Lesley eyed the proximity of his body nervously.

'And I shall do that as soon as we're inside. For the moment, I just want to enjoy being out here. I don't get much by way of time out. I don't want to spoil it by launching into the unexpected little problem that's cropped up.' He glanced across to her. 'You're a good swimmer.'

'Thank you.'

'Been swimming a long time?'

'Since I was four.' She paused and then continued, because talking seemed a bit less stressful than remaining silent and concentrating all her energies on what he was doing to her. 'My father had always been a good swimmer. All my brothers were as well. After my mother died, he got it into his head that he would channel all his energy into getting me into competitive swimming. The boys were all a bit older and had their own hobbies, but he's fond of telling me that I was fertile ground for him to work on.' Lesley laughed and relaxed a little. 'So he made sure to take me down to the local swimming baths at least twice a week. I was out of arm bands and swimming by the time I was five.'

'But you didn't end up becoming a professional swimmer.'

'I didn't,' Lesley admitted. 'Although I entered lots of competitions right up until I went to secondary school, then once I was in secondary school I began to play lots of different types of sport and the swimming was put on the back burner.'

'What sport did you play?' Alessio thought of his last girlfriend, whose only stab at anything energetic had involved the ski slope. He had once made the mistake of trying to get her to play a game of squash with him and had been irritated when she had shrieked with horror at the thought of getting too sweaty. Her hair, apparently, would not have been able to cope. He wondered whether she would have submerged herself in the pool the way Lesley had or whether she would have spent her time lying on a sun lounger and only dipping her feet in when the heat became unbearable.

Any wonder he had broken up with her after a couple of months?

'Squash, tennis, hockey, and of course in between I had my self-defence classes.'

'Energetic.'

'Very.'

'And in between all of that vigorous exercise you still had time for studying.'

Hence no time at all for what every other teenage girl would have been doing. Lesley read behind that mild observation. 'How else would I have ever been able to have a career?' Lesley responded tartly. 'Playing sport is all well and good but it doesn't get you jobs at the end of the day.' She stood up. 'I've been out here for long enough. I should really get back inside, have a shower. Please don't let me keep you from enjoying the pool. It's a shame to have this and not make use of it, especially when you think that it's so rare for the weather to be as good as it has been recently.' She didn't give him time to answer. Instead, she headed for her towel and breathed a sigh of relief when she had wrapped it around her.

When she turned around, it was to find him standing so close to her that she gave a little stumble back, almost crashing into the sun lounger behind her.

'Steady.' Alessio reached out and gripped her arms, then left his hands on her arms. 'I should really talk to you about what's brought me back here. I've got quite a bit of work to catch up on and I'll probably work through the night.'

Lesley found that she couldn't focus on anything while he was still holding her.

'Of course,' she eventually managed to croak. 'I'll go and have a shower, and then shall I meet you in the office?' She could smell him—the clean, chlorinated scent of the swimming pool combined with the heady aroma of the sun drying him as he stood there, practically naked.

'Meet me in the kitchen instead.' Alessio released her abruptly. Just then every instinct inside him wanted to pull her towards him and kiss her, taste her, see whether she would be as delectable as his imagination told him she would be. The intensity of what had shot through him was disturbing.

'I…I didn't expect you to return; I told Violet that there was no need to prepare anything for me before she left. In fact, I let her go early. I do hope you don't mind but I'm accustomed to cooking for myself. I was only going to do myself a plate of pasta.'

'Sounds good to me.'

'Right, then,' Lesley said faintly. She pushed her fingers through her hair, spiking it up.

She left him watching her and dashed upstairs for a very quick shower.

She should have found his unexpected arrival intensely annoying. It had thrown her whole evening out of sync. But there was a dark excitement swirling around inside her and she found that she was looking forward to having dinner with him, stupidly thrilled that he was back at the house.

She told herself that it was simply because she would be able to fill him in on all sorts of discoveries she had made and, the faster she filled him in, the sooner she would be able to leave and the quicker her life would return to normal. Normality seemed like a lifetime away.

He wasn't in the kitchen when she got there half an hour later, with all her paperwork in a folder, so she poured herself a glass of wine and waited for him.

She couldn't think what might have brought him back to his country estate. Something to do with his daughter, she was sure, but what? Might he have discovered something independently? Something that would make it easier for her to tell him what she thought this whole situation was about?

He strolled in when she was halfway through her glass of wine and proceeded to pour himself a whisky and soda.

'I need this,' Alessio said heavily, sinking onto the chair at the head of the table and angling it so that he could stretch his legs out whilst still facing her. 'My mother-in-law called when I was in the middle of my meetings.'

'Is that unusual?'

'Extremely. We may well be on cordial terms but not so cordial that she telephones out of the blue. There's still that ugly residue of their manipulation, although I will concede that Bianca's mother was not the one behind it. And it has to be said that, for the duration of our divorce, it was only thanks to Claudia that I ever got to see Rachel at all. I can count the number of times that happened on the fingers of one hand, but then Claudia never was a match for her daughter.' He caught himself in the act of wanting to talk more about the destructive marriage that had made him the cynical man he was today. How had that happened?

'What did she want?' Lesley eventually asked.

'Rachel has been staying with her for the past four weeks. Pretty much as soon as her school ended, she decided that she wanted to go over there. She doesn't know a great deal of people around here and only a handful in London. The down side of a boarding school out in the country, I suppose.' He sighed heavily and tipped the remainder of his drink down before resting the empty glass on the table and staring at it in brooding silence.

'Yes,' Lesley contributed vaguely. 'It must be difficult.'

'At any rate, the upshot appears to be that my daughter is refusing to return to the UK.'

Lesley's mouth fell open and Alessio smiled crookedly at her. 'She's refusing to speak to me on the telephone. She's dug her heels in and has decided to set up camp with Claudia and, Claudia being Claudia, she lacks the strength to stand up to my daughter.'

'You must be a little put out.'

'That's the understatement of the hour.' He stood up and signalled to her that they should start preparing something to eat. He needed to move around. For a small window, he had been so preoccupied with her, with arriving back and surprising her in the swimming pool, that he had actually put the gravity of the situation to the back of his mind, but now it had returned in full force.

Strangely, he was thankful that Lesley was there.

As if knowing that he would return to the topic in his own time, Lesley began preparing their meal. She had earlier piled all the ingredients she would need on the counter and now she began chopping mushrooms, tomatoes, onions and garlic.

For once, his silence didn't send her into instant meltdown. Rather, she began chatting easily and pleasantly. She told him about her lack of cooking experience. She joked that her brothers were all better cooks than she was and that two of them had even offered to show her the basics. She could sense him begin to unwind, even though she wasn't looking at him at all and he wasn't saying anything, just listening to her rabbit on aimlessly about nothing in particular.

It was soothing, Alessio thought as he watched her

prepare the vegetables slowly and with the painstaking care of someone who wasn't comfortable in the arena of the kitchen.

Nor was he feeling trapped at the thought of a woman busying herself in his kitchen. He cleared as she cooked. It was a picture-perfect snapshot of just the sort of domesticity he avoided at all costs.

'So…' They were sitting at the kitchen table with bowls of pasta in front of them. She had maintained a steady flow of non-threatening conversation, and it had been surprisingly easy, considering she was always a bundle of nervous tension whenever she was in his presence. 'When you say that Rachel is digging her heels in and doesn't want to return to the UK, are you saying *for ever*, or just for the remainder of the summer holidays?'

'I'm saying that she's decided that she hates it over here and doesn't want to return at all.'

'And your mother-in-law can't talk her out of that?'

'Claudia has always been the pushover in the family. Between her bullying husband and Bianca, she was the one who got dragged into their plot and now, in this situation, well, it's probably a mixture of not wanting to hurt or offend her only grandchild and wanting to go down the path of least resistance.'

'So what are you going to do about that?'

'Well, there's simply no question of Rachel staying out there and going to school.' He pushed his empty plate to one side and sat back to look at her. 'I could have waited until tomorrow to come back here and tell you this but…'

'But…?' Lesley rested her chin in the palm of her hand and looked at him. The kitchen lights hadn't been switched on. It had still been bright when they had started preparing dinner, but the sun had suddenly faded, giving way to a violet twilight that cast shadows and angles across his face.

'I have a favour to ask of you.'

'What is it?' Lesley asked cautiously. She began standing to clear the table and he circled her wrist with his hand.

'Sit. Tidying can come later, or not at all. Violet will do it in the morning. I need to ask you something and I will need your undivided attention when I do so.'

She subsided back into the chair, heart beating madly.

'I want you to accompany me to Italy,' Alessio said heavily. 'It's a big ask, I know, but my fear is that, short of dragging Rachel to the plane and forcibly strapping her to the seat, she will simply refuse to listen to a word I have to say.'

'But I don't even know your daughter, Alessio!'

'If I cannot persuade my daughter to return to the UK, this will spell the end of any chance of a relationship I will ever have with her.' He rubbed his eyes wearily and then leaned back and stared blankly up at the ceiling.

Lesley's heart went out to him. Was that how it would be? Most likely. And yet…

'There's something you should see.' She stood up and went to the folder which she had brought down with her. This was the point at which she should now point out that she had gathered as much information as she could and it was up to him to do what needed to be done. In the end, it had been fiddly, but not impossible.

'You've found something?' Alessio was suddenly alert. He sat forward and pulled his chair towards her as she began smoothing out the various bits of paper she had found and the pages she had printed out over the past couple of days she had been at the house.

She had only given him a rough, skeleton idea of her findings before, not wanting to build any pictures that might be incorrect.

'I collated all of this and, well, okay, so I told you that I didn't think that this had anything to do with your wife…'

'Ex-wife.'

'Ex-wife. Well, I was right. I managed to trace our friend. He jumped around a bit, used a few different Internet cafés to cover his tracks, but the cafés, as I told you, were all in the vicinity of your daughter's school. It took a bit of time, but I eventually identified the one he used most frequently. Most importantly, though, in one of the very early emails—one of the emails you never identified as coming from him—he used his own computer. It was a little bit tougher than I thought but I got through to the identity of the person.'

Alessio was listening intently. 'You know who he is?'

'It would have been a bit more difficult to piece together conclusively if I hadn't discovered those very early emails when he'd obviously just been testing the ground. They were very innocuous, which is why he probably thought that they would have been deleted. I guess he didn't figure that they would still be uncovered and brought out of hiding.' She shoved the stack of printed emails across to Alessio and watched as he read them one by one. She had highlighted important bits, phrases, certain ways of saying things that pointed to the same writer behind them.

'You're brilliant.'

Lesley flushed with pleasure. 'I was only doing what you paid me to do.'

'So, build me the picture,' he said softly.

She did and, as she did so, she watched his expression darken and change.

'So now you pretty much have the complete story,' she finished. 'I gathered all this so that I could actually present it to you tomorrow when you returned. I was going to tell you that there's really nothing left for me to do now.'

'I still want you to come with me to Italy.'

'I can't,' Lesley said quickly, with a note of desperation in her voice.

'You've sorted all of this out, but there is still the problem of my daughter. Bringing her back over here with this information, it's going to be even more difficult.'

That was something Lesley had not taken into account when she had worked out her plan to present him with her findings and leave while common sense and her instinct for self-preservation were still intact.

'Yes, but it all remains the same. She's going to be—I can't imagine—certainly not warm and welcoming to the person who brought the whole thing to light.'

'But you have no personal axe to grind with her.' Would she come? It suddenly seemed very important that she was at his side. He was uneasily aware that there was an element of need there. How and why had that happened? He swept aside his discomfort.

'I also have my job, Alessio.' She was certain that she should be feeling horrified and indignant at his nerve in asking her to go way beyond the bounds of what she had been paid to do. Especially when she had made such a big effort to wrap everything up so that she could escape the suffocating, dangerous effect he had on her.

'You can leave that to me,' he murmured.

'Leave that to you? How do you work that one out?'

'I've just concluded a deal to buy a string of luxury boutique hotels in Italy. Failing business, mismanagement, feuding amongst the board members; that's what the trip to London was all about. I needed to be there to finalise the details with lawyers.'

'How exciting,' Lesley said politely.

'More so than you might imagine. It's the first time I shall be dabbling in the leisure industry and, naturally, I will want a comprehensive website designed.'

'You have your own people to do that.'

'They're remarkably busy at the moment. This will be a job that will definitely have to be outsourced. Not only could it be worth a great deal of money to the company lucky enough to get the job, but there's no telling how many other jobs will come in its wake.'

'Are you *coercing* me?'

'I prefer to call it *persuasion*.'

'I don't believe it.'

'I usually get what I want,' Alessio said with utter truth. 'And what I want is for you to come with me to Italy and, if this proves a helpful lever, then that's all to the good. I'm sure when I explain to your boss the size and scale of the job, and the fact that it would be extremely useful to have you over there so that you can soak up the atmosphere and get a handle on how best to pitch the project…' He gave an elegant shrug and a smile of utter devastation; both relayed the message that she was more or less trapped.

Naturally she could turn down his offer but her boss might be a little miffed should he get to hear that. They were a thriving company but, with the current economic climate, potential setbacks lurked round every corner.

Whatever work came their way was not to be sniffed

at, especially when the work in question could be highly lucrative and extensive.

'And if you're concerned about your pay,' he continued, 'Rest assured that you will be earning exactly the same rate as you were for the job you just so successfully completed.'

'I'm not concerned about the money!'

'Why don't you want to come? It'll be a holiday.'

'You don't need me there, not really.'

'You have no idea what I need or don't need,' Alessio murmured softly.

'You might change your mind when you see what else I have to show you.' But already she was trying to staunch the wave of anticipation at the thought of going abroad with him, having a few more days in his company, feeding her silly addiction.

She rescued papers from the bottom of the folder, pushed them across to him and watched carefully as he rifled through them.

But then, the moment felt too private, and she stood up and began getting them both a couple of cups of coffee.

What would he be thinking? she wondered as he looked at the little collection of articles about him which she had found in a scrap book in Rachel's room. Again, no attempt had been made to conceal them. Rachel had collected bits and pieces about her father over the years; there were photographs as well, which she must have taken from an album somewhere. Photos of him as a young man.

Eventually, when she could no longer pretend to be taking her time with the coffee, she handed a mug to him and sat back down.

'You found these…' Alessio cleared his throat but he couldn't look her in the eyes.

'I found them,' Lesley said gently. 'So, you see, your daughter isn't quite as indifferent to you as you might believe. Having the conversation you need to have with her might not be quite so difficult as you imagine.'

CHAPTER SIX

'This is quite a surprise.' This was all Alessio could find to say and he knew that it was inadequate. His daughter had been collecting a scrap book about him. That reached deep down to a part of him he'd thought no longer existed. He stared down at the most recent cutting of him printed off the Internet. He had had an article written in the business section of the *Financial Times* following the acquisition of a small, independent bank in Spain. It was a poor picture but she had still printed it off and shoved it inside the scrap book.

What was he to think?

He rested his forehead against his clenched fist and drew in a long breath.

A wave of compassion washed over Lesley. Alessio Baldini was tough, cool, controlled. If he hadn't already told her, his entire manner was indicative of someone who knew that they could get what he wanted simply by snapping his fingers. It was a trait she couldn't abide in anyone.

She hated rich men who acted as though they owned the world and everything in it.

She hated men who felt that they could fling money at any problem and, lo and behold, a solution would be forthcoming.

And she hated anyone who didn't value the importance of family life. Family was what grounded you, made you put everything into perspective; stopped you from ever taking yourself too seriously or sacrificing too much in pursuit of your goals.

Alessio acted as he if he owned the world and he certainly acted as though money was the root of solving all problems. If he was a victim of circumstances when it came to an unfortunate family life, then he definitely did not behave as though now was the time when he could begin sorting it out.

So why was she now reaching out to place her hand on his arm? Why had she pulled her chair just that little bit nearer to his so that she could feel the heat radiating from his body?

Was it because the vulnerability she had always sensed in him whenever the subject of his daughter came up was now so glaringly obvious?

Rachel was his Achilles heel; in a flash of comprehension, Lesley saw that. In every other area, Alessio was in complete control of his surroundings, of his *life*, but when it came to his daughter he floundered.

The women he had dated in the past had been kept at a distance. Once bitten, twice shy, and after his experiences with Bianca he had made sure never to let any other woman get past the steel walls that surrounded him. They would never have glimpsed the man who was at a loss when it came to his daughter. She wondered how many of them even *knew* that he had a daughter.

But here she was. She had seen him at his most naked, emotionally.

That was a good thing, she thought, and a bad thing. It was good insofar as everyone needed a sounding board when it came to dark thoughts and emotions.

Those were burdens that could not be carried single-handed. He might have passed the years with his deepest thoughts locked away, but there was no way he would ever have been able to eradicate them, and letting them out could only be a good thing.

With this situation, he had been forced to reveal more about those thoughts to her than he ever had to anyone else. She was certain of that.

The down side was that, for a proud man, the necessity of having to confide thoughts normally hidden would eventually be seen as a sign of weakness.

The sympathetic, listening ear would only work for so long before it turned into a source of resentment.

But did that matter? Really? They wouldn't be around one another for much longer and right here, right now, in some weird, unspoken way, he needed her. She *felt* it, even though it was something he would never, ever articulate.

Those cuttings had moved him beyond words. He was trying hard to control his reaction in front of an audience; that was evident in the thickness of the silence.

'You'll have to return that scrap book to where you found it,' he said gruffly when the silence had been stretched to breaking point. 'Leave it with me overnight and I'll give it to you in the morning.'

Lesley nodded. Her hand was still on his arm and he hadn't shrugged it away. She allowed it to travel so that she was stroking upwards, feeling the strength of his muscles straining under the shirt and the definition of his shoulders and collarbone.

Alessio's eyes narrowed on her.

'Are you feeling sorry for me?' His voice was less cold than it should have been. 'Is that a pity caress?'

He had never confided in anyone. He certainly had

never been an object of pity to anyone, any woman, ever. The thought alone was laughable. Women had always hung onto his every word, longed for some small indication that they occupied a more special role in his life than he was willing to admit to them.

Naturally, they hadn't.

Lesley, though…

She was in a different category. The pity caress did not evoke the expected feelings of contempt, impatience and anger that he would have expected.

He caught her hand in his and held on to it.

'It's not a *pity caress*.' Lesley breathed. Her skin burned where he was touching it, a blaze that was stoked by the expression in his eyes: dark, thoughtful, insightful, amused. 'But I know it must be disconcerting, looking through Rachel's scrap book, seeing pictures of yourself there, articles cut out or printed off from the Internet.' He still wasn't saying anything. He was still just staring at her, his head slightly to one side, his expression brooding and intent.

Her voice petered out and she stared right back at him, eyes wide. She could barely breathe. The moment seemed as fragile as a droplet of water balancing on the tip of a leaf, ready to fall and splinter apart.

She didn't want the moment to end. It was wrong, she knew that, but still she wanted to touch his face and smooth away those very human, very uncertain feelings she knew he would be having; feelings he would be taking great care of to conceal.

'The scrap book was just lying there,' she babbled away as she continued to get lost in his eyes. 'On the bed. I would have felt awful if I had found it hidden under the mattress or at the bottom of a drawer somewhere, but it was just there, waiting to be found.'

'Not by me. Rachel knew that I would never go into her suite of rooms.'

Lesley shrugged. 'I wanted you to see that you're important to your daughter,' she murmured shakily, 'Even if you don't think you are because of the way she acts. Teenagers can be very awkward when it comes to showing their feelings.' He still wasn't saying anything. If he thought that she felt sorry for him, then how was it that he was staying put, not angrily stalking off? 'You remember being a teenager.' She tried a smile in an attempt to lighten the screaming tension between them.

'Vaguely. When I think back to my teenage years, I inevitably end up thinking back to being a daddy before I was out of them.'

'Of course,' Lesley murmured, her voice warm with understanding. At the age of fourteen, not even knowing it, he would have been a mere four years away from becoming a father. It was incredible.

'You're doing it again,' Alessio said under his breath.

'Doing what?'

'Smothering me with your sympathy. Don't worry. Maybe I like it.' His mouth curved into a wolfish smile but underneath that, he thought with passing confusion, her sympathy was actually very welcome.

He reached out and touched her face, then ran two fingers along her cheek, circling her mouth then along her slender neck, coming to rest at the base of her collarbone.

'Have you felt what I've been feeling for the past couple of days?' he asked.

Lesley wasn't sure she was physically capable of answering his question. Not with that hand on her collarbone and her brain reliving every inch of its caress as it had touched her cheek and moved sensuously over her mouth.

'Well?' Alessio prompted. He rested his other hand on her thigh and began massaging it, very gently but very thoroughly, just the one spot, but it was enough to make the breath catch in her throat.

'What do you mean? What are you talking about?' As if she didn't know. As if she wasn't constantly aware of the way he unsettled her. And was she conscious that the electricity flowed both ways? Maybe she was. Maybe that was why the situation had seemed so dangerous.

She had thought that she needed to get out because her attraction to him was getting too much, was threatening to become evident. Maybe a part of her had known that the real reason she needed to get out was because, on some level, she knew that he was attracted to her as well. That underneath the light-hearted flirting there was a very real undercurrent of mutual sexual chemistry.

And that was not good, not at all. She didn't do one-night stands, or two-day stands, or 'going nowhere so why not have a quick romp?' stands.

She did *relationships*. If there had been no guy in her life for literally years, then it was because she had never been the kind of girl who had sex just for the sake of it.

But with Alessio something told her that she could be that girl, and that scared her.

'You know exactly what I mean. You want me. I want you. I've wanted you for a while...'

'I should go up to bed.' Lesley breathed unevenly, nailed to the spot and not moving an inch despite her protestations. 'Leave you to your thoughts...'

'Maybe I'm not that keen on being alone with my thoughts,' Alessio said truthfully. 'Maybe my thoughts are a black hole into which I have no desire to fall.

Maybe I want your pity and your sympathy because they can save me from that fall.'

And what happens when you've been saved from that fall? What happens to me? You're in a weird place right now and, if I rescue you now, what happens when you leave that weird place and shut the door on it once again?

But those muddled thoughts barely had time to settle before they were blown away by the fiercely exciting thought of being with the man who was leaning towards her, staring at her with such intensity that she wanted to moan.

And, before she could retreat behind more weak protestations, he was cupping the back of her neck and drawing her towards him, very slowly, so slowly that she had time to appreciate the depth of his dark eyes; the fine lines that etched his features; the slow, sexy curve of his mouth; the length of his dark eyelashes.

Lesley fell into the kiss with a soft moan, part resignation, part despair; mostly intense, long-awaited excitement. She spread her hand behind his neck in a mirror gesture to how he was holding her and, as his tongue invaded the soft contours of her mouth, she returned the kiss and let that kiss do its work—spread moisture between her legs, pinch her nipples into tight, sensitive buds, raise the hairs on her arms.

'We shouldn't be doing this,' she muttered, breaking apart for a few seconds and immediately wanting to draw him back towards her again.

'Why not?'

'Because this isn't the right reason for going to bed with someone.'

'Don't know what you're talking about.' He leaned

to kiss her again but she stilled him with a hand on his chest and met his gaze with anxious eyes.

'I don't pity you, Alessio,' she said huskily. 'I'm sorry that you don't have the relationship with your daughter that you'd like, but I don't pity you. And when I showed you that scrap book it was because I felt the contents were something you needed to know about. What I feel is…understanding and compassion.'

'And what I feel is that we shouldn't get lost in words.'

'Because words are not your thing?' But she smiled and felt a rush of tenderness towards this strong, powerful man who was also capable of being so wonderfully *human*, hard though he might try to fight it.

'You know what they say about actions speaking louder…' He grinned at her. His body was on fire. She was right—words weren't his thing, at least not the words that made up long, involved conversations about feelings. He scooped her up and she gave a little cry of surprise, then wriggled and told him to put her down immediately; she might be slim but she was way too tall for him to start thinking he could play the caveman with her.

Alessio ignored her and carried her up the stairs to his bedroom.

'Every woman likes a caveman.' He gently kicked open his bedroom door and then deposited her on his king-sized bed.

Night had crept up without either of them realising it and, without the bedroom lights switched on, the darkness only allowed them to see one another in shadowy definition.

'I don't,' Lesley told him breathlessly as he stood in front of her and began unbuttoning his shirt.

She had already seen him barely clothed in the pool. She should know what to expect when it came to his body and yet, as he tossed his shirt carelessly on the ground, it was as if she was looking at him for the first time.

The impact he had on her was as new, as raw, as powerful.

But then, this was different, wasn't it? This wasn't a case of watching him covertly from the sidelines as he covered a few lengths in a swimming pool.

This was lying on his bed, in a darkened room, with the promise of possession flicking through her like a spreading fire.

Alessio didn't want to talk. He wanted to take her, fast and hard, until he heard her cry out with satisfaction. He wanted to pleasure her and feel her come with him inside her.

But how much sweeter to take his time, to taste every inch of her, to withstand the demands of his raging hormones and indulge in making love with her at a more leisurely pace.

'No?' he drawled, hand resting on the zipper of his trousers before he began taking those off as well, where they joined the shirt in a heap on the ground, leaving him in just his boxers. 'You think I'm a caveman because I carried you up the stairs?'

He slowly removed his boxers. He regretted not having turned some lights on because he would have liked to really appreciate the expression on her face as he watched her watching him. He strolled towards the side of the bed and stood there, then he touched himself lightly and heard her swift intake of breath.

'I just think you're a caveman in general,' Lesley feasted her eyes on his impressive erection. When he held it in his hand, she longed to do the same to herself, to touch herself down there. Her nerves were stretched to breaking point and she wished she was just a little more experienced, a little more knowing about what to do when it came to a man like him, a man who probably knew everything there was to know about the opposite sex.

She sat up, crossed her legs and reached out to touch him, replacing his hand with hers and gaining confidence as she felt him shudder with appreciation.

It was a strange turn-on to be fully clothed while he was completely naked.

'Is that right?'

As she took him into her mouth, Alessio grunted and flung his head back. He had died and gone to heaven. The wetness of her mouth on his hard erection, the way she licked, teased and tasted, his fingers curled into her short hair, made him breathe heavily, well aware that he had to come down from this peak or risk bringing this love-making session to an extremely premature conclusion, which was not something he intended to do.

With a sigh of pure regret, he eased her off him.

Then he joined her on the bed. 'Would I be a caveman if I stripped you? I wouldn't...' he slipped his fingers underneath the tee-shirt and began easing it over her head '...want to...' Then came the jeans, which she wriggled out of so that she remained in bra and pants, white, functional items of clothing that looked wonderfully wholesome on her. 'Offend your feminist sensibilities.'

For the life of her, Lesley couldn't find where she had misplaced those feminist sensibilities which he had mentioned. She reached behind to unhook her bra but he gently drew her hands away so that he could accomplish the task himself.

He half-closed his eyes and his nostrils flared with rampant appreciation of her small but perfectly formed breasts. Her nipples were big, brown, circular discs. She had propped herself up on both elbows and her breasts were small, pointed mounds offering themselves to him like sweet, delicate fruit.

In one easy movement, he straddled her, and she fell back against the pillow with a soft, excited moan.

She was wet for him. As he reached behind him to slip his hand under the panties, she groaned and covered her eyes with one hand.

'I want to see you, my darling.' Alessio lowered himself so that he was lightly on top of her. 'Move your hand.'

'I don't usually do this sort of thing,' Lesley mumbled. 'I'm not into one-night stands. I never have been. I don't see the point.'

'Shh.' He gazed down at her until she was burning all over. Then he gently began licking her breast, moving in a concentric circle until his tongue found her nipple. The sensitised tip had peaked into an erect nub, and as he took her whole nipple into his mouth so that he could suckle on it she quivered under him, moving with feverish urgency, arching back so that not a single atom of the pleasurable sensations zinging through her was lost.

She had to get rid of her panties, they were damp and uncomfortable, but with his big body over hers she couldn't reach them. Instead she clasped her hand to the back of his head and pressed him down harder on her breasts, giving little cries and whimpers as he carried on sucking and teasing, moving between her breasts and then, when she was going crazy from it, he trailed his tongue over her rib cage and down to the indentation of her belly button.

His breath on her body was warm and she was breathing fast, hardly believing that what was happening really was happening and yet desperate for it to continue, desperate to carry on shamelessly losing herself in the moment.

He felt her sharp intake of breath as he slipped her underwear down, and then she was holding her breath as he gently parted her legs and flicked his tongue over her core.

Lesley groaned. This was an intimacy she had not experienced before. She curled her fingers into his dark hair and tugged him but her body was responding with a shocking lack of inhibition as he continued to taste her, teasing her swollen bud until she lost the ability to think clearly.

Alessio felt her every response as if their bodies had tuned into the same wavelength. In a blinding, revelatory flash, he realised that everything else that had come before with women could not compete with what was happening right now, because this woman had just seen far more of him than anyone else ever had.

This had not been a simple game of pursuit and capture. She hadn't courted this situation, nor had he anticipated it. Certainly, there had come a point when he had looked at her and liked what he had seen; had wanted what he had seen; had even vaguely *planned* on having her because, when it came to him and women, wanting and having were always the same side of the coin.

But he knew that he hadn't banked on what was happening between them now. For the first time, he had the strangest feeling that this wasn't just about sex.

But the sex was great.

He swept aside all his unravelling thoughts and lost himself in her body, in her sweet little whimpers and her broken groans as she wriggled under him, until at last, when he could feel her wanting to reach her orgasm, he broke off to fumble in the bedside cabinet for a condom.

Lesley could hardly bear that brief pause. She was alive in a way she had never been before and that terrified her. Her relationships with the opposite sex had always been guarded and imbued with a certain amount of defensiveness that stemmed from her own private insecurities.

Having been raised in an all-male family, she had developed brilliant coping skills when it came to standing her ground with the opposite sex. Her brothers had toughened her up and taught her the value of healthy competition, the benefits of never being cowed by a guy, of knowing that she could hold her own.

But no one had been able to help her during those teenage years when the lines of distinction between boys and girls were drawn. She had watched from the sidelines and decided that lipstick and mascara were not for her, that sport was far more enjoyable. It wasn't about how you looked, it was about what was inside you and what was inside her—her intelligence, her sense of humour, her capacity for compassion—did not need to be camouflaged with make-up and sexy clothes.

The only guys she had ever been attracted to were the ones who'd seen her for the person she was, the ones whose heads hadn't swivelled round when a busty blonde in a short skirt had walked past.

So what, it flashed through her head, was she doing with Alessio Baldini?

She sighed and reached up to him as he settled back on her, nudging her legs apart, then she closed her eyes and was transported to another planet as he thrust into her, deep and hard, building a rhythm that drove everything out of her mind.

She flung her head back and succumbed to loud, responsive cries as he continued to fill her.

She came on a tidal wave of intense pleasure and felt her whole body shudder and arch up towards him in a wonderful fusing of bodies.

The moment seemed to last for ever and she was only brought back down to earth when he withdrew from her and cursed fluently under his breath.

'The condom has split.'

Lesley abruptly surfaced from the pleasant, dreamy cloud on which she had been happily drifting, and the uncomfortable thoughts which had been sidelined when he had begun touching her returned with double intensity.

What on earth had she done? How could she have allowed herself to end up in bed with this man? Had she lost her mind? This was a situation that was going nowhere and would never go anywhere. She was Lesley Fox, a practical, clever, not at all sexy woman who should have known better than to be sweet talked into sleeping with a man who wouldn't have looked twice at her under normal circumstances.

On every level, he was just the sort of man she usually wouldn't have gone near and, had he seen her passing on the street, she certainly would not have been the sort of woman he would have noticed. She would literally have been invisible to him because she just wasn't his type.

Fate had thrown them together and an attraction had built between them but she knew that she would be a complete fool not to recognise that that attraction was grounded in novelty.

'How the hell could that have happened?' Alessio said, his voice dark with barely contained anger. 'This is the last thing I need right now.'

Lesley got that. He had found himself tricked into marriage by a pregnancy he had not courted once upon a time and his entire adult life had been affected. Of course he would not want to repeat that situation.

Yet, she couldn't help but feel the sting of hurt at the simmering anger in his voice.

'It won't happen,' she said stiffly. She wriggled into a sitting position and watched as he vaulted upright and began searching around for his boxers, having disposed of the faulty condom.

'And you know that because?'

'It's the wrong time of month for that to happen.' She surreptitiously crossed her fingers and tried to calculate when she had last had her period. 'And, rest assured, the last thing I would want would be to end up pregnant, Alessio. As it stands, this was a very bad idea.'

In the process of locating a tee-shirt from a chest of drawers, he paused and strolled back to the bed. The condom had split and there was nothing he could do about that now. He could only hope that she was right, that they were safe.

But, that aside, how could she say that making love had been a very bad idea? He was oddly affronted.

'You know what. This. Us. Ending up in bed together. It shouldn't have happened.'

'Why not? We're attracted to one another. How could it have been a bad idea? I was under the impression that you had actually enjoyed the experience.' He looked down at her and felt his libido begin to rise once again.

'That's not the point.' She swung her legs over the side of the bed and stood up, conscious of her nudity, gritting her teeth against the temptation to drag the covers off the bed and shield herself from him.

'God, you're beautiful.'

Lesley flushed and looked away, stubbornly proud, and refusing to believe that he meant a word of that. Novelty was a beautiful thing but became boring very quickly.

'Well?' He caught her wrist and tilted her face so that she had no option but to look at him.

'Well what?' Lesley muttered, lowering her eyes.

'Well, let's go back to bed.'

'Didn't you hear a word I just said?'

'Every word.' He kissed her delicately on the corner of her mouth and then very gently on her lips.

In a heartbeat, and to her disgust, Lesley could feel her determination begin to melt away.

'You're not my type,' she mumbled, refusing to cave in, but his lips were so soft against her jaw that her disobedient body was responding in all sorts of stupidly predictable ways.

'Because I'm a caveman?'

'Yes!' Her hands crept up to his neck and she protested feebly as he lifted her off her feet and back towards the bed to which she had only minutes previously sworn not to return.

'So, what are you looking for in a man?' Alessio murmured.

This time, he drew the covers over them. It was very dark outside. Even with the curtains open, the night was black velvet with only a slither of moon penetrating the darkness and weakly illuminating the bedroom.

He could feel her reluctance, her mind fighting her body, and it felt imperative that her body win the battle because he wanted her, more than he had ever wanted any woman in his life before.

'Not someone like you, Alessio,' Lesley whispered, pressing her hands flat against his chest and feeling the steady beat of his heart.

'Why? Why not someone like me?'

'Because…' *Because safety was not with a man who looked like him, a man who could have anyone he wanted.* She knew her limits. She knew that she was just not the sort of girl who drew guys to her like a magnet. She never had been. She just didn't have the confidence; had never had the right preparation; had never had a mother's guiding hand to show her the way to all those little feminine wiles that went into the mix of attraction between the sexes.

But bigger than her fear of involvement with him was her fear of *not* getting involved, *not* taking the chance.

'You're just not the sort of person I ever imagined having any kind of relationship with, that's all.'

'We're not talking marriage here, Lesley, we're talking about enjoying each other.' He propped himself up on one elbow and traced his finger along her arm. 'I'm not looking for commitment any more than you probably are.'

And certainly not with someone like you; Lesley reluctantly filled in the remainder of that remark.

'And you still haven't told me the sort of man you would call "your type".' She was warm and yielding in his arms. She might make a lot of noises about this being a mistake, but she wanted him as much as he wanted her, and he knew that if he slipped his fingers into her he would feel the tell-tale proof of her arousal.

He could have her right here and right now, despite whatever she said about him not being her type. And who, in the end, cared whether he was her type or not? Hadn't he just told her that this wasn't about commitment and marriage? In other words, did it really matter if he wasn't her type?

But he was piqued at the remark. She was forthright and spoke her mind; he had become accustomed to that very quickly. But surely what she had said amounted to an unacceptable lack of tact! He thought that there was nothing wrong in asking her to explain exactly what she had meant.

His voice had dropped a few shades.

'You're offended, aren't you?' Lesley asked and Alessio was quick to deny any such thing.

Lesley could have kicked herself for asking him that question. Of course he wouldn't be offended! To be offended, he would actually have had to care about her and that was not the case here, as he had made patently clear.

'That's a relief!' she exclaimed lightly. 'My type? I guess thoughtful, caring, sensitive; someone who believes in the same things that I do, who has similar interests…maybe even someone working in the same field. You know—artistic, creative, not really bothered about the whole business of making money.'

Alessio bared his teeth in a smile. 'Sounds a lot of fun. Sure someone like that would be able to keep up with you? No, scrap that—too much talk. There are better things to do and, now that we've established that you can't resist me even though I'm the last kind of person you would want in your life, let's make love.'

'Alessio…'

He stifled any further protest with a long, lingering kiss that released in her a sigh of pure resignation. So this made no sense, so she was a complete idiot…

Where had the practical, level-headed girl with no illusions about herself gone? All she seemed capable of doing was giving in.

'And,' he murmured into her ear. 'In case you think that Italy is off the agenda because I'm not a touchy-feely art director for a design company, forget it. I still want you there by my side. Trust me, I will make it worth your while.'

CHAPTER SEVEN

EVERYTHING SEEMED TO happen at the speed of light after that. Of course, there was no inconvenient hanging around for affordable flights or having to surf the Internet for places to stay. None of the usual headaches dogged Alessio's spur-of-the-moment decision to take Lesley to Italy.

Two days after he had extended his invitation, they were boarding a plane to Italy.

It was going to be a surprise visit. Armed with information, they were going to get the full story from his daughter, lay all the cards on the table and then, when they were back in the UK, Alessio would sort the other half of the equation out. He would pay an informal visit to his emailing friend and he was sure that they would reach a happy conclusion where no money changed hands.

Lessons, he had assured her, would regrettably have to be learnt.

Lesley privately wondered what his approach to his daughter would be. Would similar lessons also 'regrettably have to be learnt'? How harsh would those lessons be? He barely had a relationship with Rachel and she privately wondered how he intended ever to build on it if he went in to 'sort things out' with the diplomacy of a bull in a china shop.

That was one of the reasons she had agreed to go to Italy with him.

Without saying it in so many words, she knew that he was looking to her for some sort of invisible moral back-up, even though he had stated quite clearly that he needed her there primarily to impart the technicalities of what she had discovered should the situation demand it.

'You haven't said anything for the past half an hour.' Alessio interrupted her train of thought as they were shown into the first class cabin of the plane. 'Why?'

Lesley bristled. 'I was just thinking how fast everything's moved,' she said as they were shown to seats as big as armchairs and invited to have a glass of champagne, which she refused.

She stole a glance at his sexy face, lazy and amused at the little show of rebellion.

'I came to do a job for you, thinking that I would be in and out of your house in a matter of a few hours and now here I am, days later, boarding a plane for Italy.'

'I know. Isn't life full of adventure and surprise?' He waved aside an awe-struck air hostess and settled into the seat next to her. 'I confess that I myself am surprised at the way things unfolded. Surprised but not displeased.'

'Because you've got what you wanted,' Lesley complained. She was so accustomed to her independence that she couldn't help feeling disgruntled at the way she had been railroaded into doing exactly what he had wanted her to do.

Even though, a little voice inside her pointed out, this rollercoaster ride was the most exciting thing she had ever done in her life—even though it was scary, even though it had yanked her out of her precious comfort zone, even though she knew that it would come to nothing and the fall back to Planet Earth would be painful.

'I didn't force your hand,' Alessio said comfortably.

'You went into the office and talked to my boss.'

'I just wanted to point out the world of opportunity lying at his feet if he could see his way to releasing you for one week to accompany me to Italy.'

'I dread to think what the office grapevine is going to make of this situation.'

'Do you care what anyone thinks?' He leant against the window so that he could direct one hundred per cent of his undivided attention on her.

'Of course I do!' Lesley blushed because she knew that, whilst she might give the impression of being strong, sassy and outspoken, she still had a basic need to be liked and accepted. She just wasn't always good at showing that side of herself. In fact, she was uncomfortably aware of the fact that, whilst Alessio might have shown her more of himself than he might have liked, she had likewise done the same.

He would not know it, but against all odds she had allowed herself to walk into unchartered territory, to have a completely new experience with a man knowing that he was not the right man for her.

'Relax and enjoy the ride,' he murmured.

'I'm not going to enjoy confronting your daughter with all the information we've managed to uncover. She's going to know that I went through her belongings.'

'If Rachel had wanted to keep her private life private, then she should have destroyed all the incriminating evidence. The fact is that she's still a child and she has no vote when it comes to us doing what was necessary to protect her.'

'She may not see it quite like that.'

'She will have to make a very big effort to, in that case.'

Lesley sighed and leaned back into the seat with her eyes shut. What Alessio did with his daughter was really none of her business. Yes, she'd been involved in bringing the situation to light, but its solutions and whatever repercussions followed would be a continuing saga she would leave behind. She would return to the blessed safety of what she knew and the family story of Alessio and his daughter would remain a mystery to her for ever.

So there was no need to feel any compunction about just switching off.

Yet she had to bite back the temptation to tell him what she thought, even though she knew that he would have every right to dismiss whatever advice she had to offer about the peculiarity of their relationship, if a 'relationship' was what it could be called. She was his lover, a woman who probably knew far too much about his life for his liking. She had been paid to investigate a personal problem, yet had no right to have any discussions about that problem, even though they were sleeping together.

In a normal relationship, she should have felt free to speak her mind, but this was not a normal relationship, was it? For either of them. She had sacrificed her feminist principles for sex and she still couldn't understand herself, nor could she understand how it was that she felt no regrets.

In fact, when he looked at her the way he was looking at her right now, all she felt was a dizzying need to have him take her.

If only he could see into her mind and unravel all her doubts and uncertainties. Thank goodness he couldn't. As far as he was concerned, she was a tough career woman with as little desire for a long-term relationship as him. They had both stepped out of the box, drawn to each other by a combination of proximity and the pull of novelty.

'You're thinking,' Alessio said drily. 'Why don't you spit it out and then we can get it out of the way?'

'Get what out of the way?'

'Whatever disagreements you have about the way I intend to handle this situation.'

'You hate it when I tell you what I think,' Lesley said with asperity. Alessio shrugged and continued looking at her in the way that made her toes curl and her mouth run dry.

'And I don't like it when I can see you thinking but you're saying nothing. "Between a rock and a hard place" comes to mind.' He was amazed at how easily he had adapted to her outspoken approach. His immediate instinct now was not to shove her back behind his boundary lines and remind her about overstepping the mark.

'I just don't think you should confront Rachel and demand to know what the hell is going on.' She shifted in the big seat and turned so that she was completely facing him.

The plane was beginning to taxi in preparation for taking off, and she fell silent for a short while as the usual canned talk was given about safety exits, but as soon as they were airborne she looked at him worriedly once again.

'It's hard to know how to get answers if you don't ask for them,' he pointed out.

'We know the situation.'

'And I want to know how it got to where it finally got. It's one thing knowing the outcome but I don't intend to let history repeat itself.'

'You might want to try a little sympathy.'

Alessio snorted.

'You said yourself that she's just a kid,' Lesley reminded him gently.

'You *could* always spare me the horror of making a mess of things by talking to Rachel yourself,' he said.

'She's not my daughter.'

'Then allow me to work this one out myself.' But he knew that she was right. There was no tactful way of asking the questions he would have to ask, and if his daughter disliked him now then she was about to dislike him a whole lot more when he was finished talking to her.

Of course, there were those photos, cuttings of him—some indication, as Lesley had said, that she wasn't completely indifferent to the fact that he was her father.

But would that be enough to take them past this little crisis? Unlikely. Especially when she discovered that the photos and cuttings had been salvaged in an undercover operation.

'Okay.'

Alessio had looked away, out through the window to the dense bank of cloud over which they were flying. Now, he turned to Lesley with a frown.

'Okay. I'll talk to Rachel if you like,' she said on a reluctant sigh.

'Why would you do that?'

Why would she? Because she couldn't bear to see him looking the way he was looking now, with the hopeless expression of someone staring defeat in the face.

And why did she care? she asked herself. But she shied away from trying to find an answer to that.

'Because I'm on the outside of this mess. If she directs all her teenage anger at me, then by the time she gets to you some of it may have diffused.'

'And the likelihood of that is…?' But he was touched at her generosity of spirit.

'Not good odds,' Lesley conceded. 'But worth a try, don't you think?' He was staring at her with an expression of intense curiosity and she continued quickly, before he could interrupt with the most obvious question: *why?* A question to which she had no answer. 'Besides, I'm good at mediating. I got a lot of practice at doing that when I was growing up. When there are six kids in a family, a dad worked off his feet, and five of those six are boys, there's always lots of opportunity to practise mediation skills.'

But just no opportunity to practise *being a girl*. And that was why she was the way she was now: hesitant in relationships; self-conscious about whether she had what it took to make any relationship last; willing not to get into the water at all rather than diving in and finding herself out of her depth and unable to cope.

Only since Alessio had appeared on the scene had she really seen the pattern in her behaviour, the way she kept guys, smiling, at arm's length.

He was so dramatically different from any man she had ever been remotely drawn to that it had been easy to pinpoint her own lack of self-confidence. She was a clever career woman with a bright life ahead of her and yet that sinfully beautiful face had reduced all those achievements to rubble.

She had looked at him and returned to her teenage years when she had simply not known how to approach a boy because she had had no idea what they were looking for.

For her, Alessio Baldini was not the obvious choice

when it came to picking a guy to sleep with, yet sleep with him she had, and she was glad that she had done so. She had broken through the glass barrier that had stood between her and the opposite sex. It was strange, but he had given her confidence she hadn't really even known she had needed.

'And mediation skills are so important when one is growing up,' Alessio murmured.

Basking in her new-found revelations, Lesley smiled. 'No, they're not,' she admitted with more candour than she'd ever done to anyone in her life before. 'In fact, I can't think of any skill a teenage girl has less use for than mediation skills,' she mused. 'But I had plenty of that.' She leaned back and half-closed her eyes. When she next spoke it was almost as though she was talking with no audience listening to what was being said.

'My mum died when I was so young, I barely remember her. I mean, Dad always told us about her, what she was like and such, and there were pictures of her everywhere. But the truth is, I don't have any memories of her—of doing anything with her, if you see what I mean.'

She glanced sideways at him and he nodded. He had always fancied himself as the sort of man who would be completely at sea when it came to listening to women pour their hearts out, hence it was a tendency that he had strenuously discouraged.

Now, though, he was drawn to what she was saying and by the faraway, pensive expression on her face.

'I never thought that I missed having a mother. I never knew what it was like to have one and my dad was always good enough for me. But I can see now that growing up in a male-only family might have given me confidence with the opposite sex but only when it came to things like work and study. I was encouraged to be as good as they were, and I think I succeeded, but I wasn't taught, well…'

'How to wear make-up and shop for dresses?'

'Sounds crazy but I do think girls need to be taught stuff like that.' She looked at him gravely. 'I can see that it's easy to have bags of confidence in one area and not much in another,' she said with a rueful shake of her head. 'When it came to the whole game-playing, sexual attraction thing, I don't think I've ever had loads of confidence.'

'And now?'

'I feel I have, so I guess I should say thank you.'

'*Thank you?* What are you thanking me for?'

'For encouraging me to step out of the box,' Lesley told him with that blend of frankness and disingenuousness which he found so appealing.

Alessio was momentarily distracted from the headache awaiting him in Italy. He had no idea where she was going with this but it had all the feel of a conversation heading down a road he would rather not explore.

'Always happy to oblige,' he said vaguely. 'I hope you've packed light clothes. The heat in Italy is quite different from the heat in England.'

'If I hadn't taken on this job, there's not a chance in the world that I would ever have met you.'

'That's true enough.'

'Not only do we not move in the same circles, we have no interests in common whatsoever.'

Alessio was vaguely indignant at what he thought might be an insult in disguise. Was she comparing him to the 'soul mate' guy she had yet to meet, the touchy-feely one with the artistic side and a love of all things natural?

'And if we *had* ever met, at a social do or something like that, I would never have had the confidence to approach you.'

'I'm not sure where you're going with this.'

'Here's what I'm saying, Alessio. I feel as though I've taken huge strides in gaining self-confidence in certain areas and it's thanks in some measure to you. I could say that I'm going to be a completely different person when I get back to the UK and start dating again.'

Alessio could not believe what he was hearing. He had no idea where this conversation had come from and he was enraged that she could sit there, his lover, and talk about going back on the dating scene!

'The dating scene.'

'Is this conversation becoming a little too deep for you?' Lesley asked with a grin. 'I know you don't do deep when it comes to women and conversations.'

'And how do you know that?'

'Well, you've already told me that you don't like encouraging them to get behind a stove and start cooking a meal for you, just in case they think, I don't know, they have somehow managed to get a foot through the door. So I'm guessing that meaningful conversations are probably on the banned list as well.'

They were. It was true. He had never enjoyed long, emotional conversations which, from experience, always ended up in the same place—invitations to meet the parents, questions about commitment and where the relationship was heading.

In fact, the second that type of conversation began rearing its head, he usually felt a pressing need to end the relationship. He had been coerced into one marriage and he had made a vow never to let himself be railroaded into another similar mistake, however tempting the woman in question might be.

He looked into her astute, brown eyes and scowled. 'I may not be looking for someone to walk down the aisle with, but that doesn't mean that I'm not prepared to have meaningful discussions with women. I'm also insulted,' he was driven to continue, 'That I've been used as some kind of trial run for the real thing.'

'What do you mean?' Lesley was feeling good. The vague unease that had been plaguing her ever since she had recognised how affected she was by Alessio had been boxed away with an explanation that made sense.

Sleeping with him had opened her eyes to fears and doubts she had been harbouring for years. She felt that she had buried a lack of self-confidence in her own sexuality under the guise of academic success and then, later on, success in her career. She had dressed in ways that didn't enhance her own femininity because she had always feared that she lacked what it took.

But then she had slept with him, slept with a man who was way out of her league, had been wanted and desired by him, and made to feel proud of the way she looked.

Was it any wonder that he had such a dramatic effect on her? It was a case of lust mixed up with a hundred other things.

But the bottom line was that he was no more than a learning curve for her. When she thought about it like that, it made perfect sense. It also released her from the disturbing suspicion that she was way too deep in a non-relationship that was going nowhere, a relationship that meant far more to her than it did to him.

Learning curves provided lessons and, once those lessons had been learnt, it was always easy to move on.

Learning curves didn't result in broken hearts.

She breathed in quickly and shakily. 'Well?' she flung at him, while her mind continued to chew over the notion that her involvement with him had been fast and hard. She had been catapulted into a world far removed from hers, thrown into the company of a man who was very, very different from the sort of men she was used to, and certainly worlds apart from the sort of man she would ever have expected herself to be attracted to.

But common sense had been no match for the power of his appeal and now here she was.

When she thought about never seeing him again, she felt faintly, sickeningly panicked.

What did that mean? Her thoughts became muddled when she tried to work her way through what suddenly seemed a dangerous, uncertain quagmire.

'I mean that you used me,' Alessio said bluntly. 'I don't like being used. And I don't appreciate you talking about jumping back into the dating scene, not when we're still lovers. I expect the women I sleep with to only have eyes for me.'

The unbridled arrogance of that statement, which was so fundamentally *Alessio,* brought a reluctant smile to her lips.

She had meant it when she had told him that under normal circumstances they would never have met. Their paths simply wouldn't have crossed. He didn't mix in the same circles as she did. And, even if by some freak chance they *had* met, they would have looked at one another and quickly looked away.

She would have seen a cold, wealthy, arrogant cardboard cut-out and he would have seen, well, a woman who was nothing like the sort of women he went out with and therefore she'd have been invisible. But the circumstances that had brought them together had uniquely provided them with a different insight into one another.

She had seen beneath the veneer to the three-dimensional man and he had seen through the sassy, liberal-minded, outspoken woman in charge of her life to the uncertain, insecure girl.

She was smart enough to realise, however, that that changed nothing. He was and always would be uninterested in any relationship that demanded longevity. He was shaped by his past and his main focus now was his daughter and trying to resolve the difficult situation that had arisen there. He might have slept with her because she was so different from what he was used to and because she was there, ready and willing but, whereas he had fundamentally reached deep and changed her, she hadn't done likewise with him.

'You're smiling.' Alessio was reluctant to abandon the conversation. When, he thought, was this dive back into the dating scene going to begin? Had she put time limits on what they had? Wasn't he usually the one to do that?

'I don't want to argue with you.' Lesley kept that smile pinned to her face. 'Who will you introduce me as when we get to Italy?'

'I haven't given it any thought. Where is all this hectic dating going to take place?'

'I beg your pardon?'

'You can't start conversations you don't intend to finish. So, where will you be going to meet Mr Right? I'm taking it you intend to start hunting when we return to England, or will you be looking around Italy for any suitable candidates?'

'Are you upset because I said what I said?'

'Why would I be upset?'

'I have no idea,' Lesley said as flippantly as she could. 'Because we both know that what we have isn't going to last.' She allowed just a fraction of a second in which he could have contradicted her, but of course he said nothing, and that hurt and reinforced for her the position she held in his life. 'And of course I'm not going to be looking around Italy for suitable candidates. I haven't forgotten why I'll be there in the first place.'

'Good,' Alessio said brusquely.

But the atmosphere between them had changed, and when he flipped open his lap-top and began working Lesley took the hint and excavated her own lap-top so that she too could begin working, even though she couldn't concentrate.

What she had said had put his nose out of joint, she decided. He wanted her to be his, to belong to him for however long he deemed it suitable, until the time came when he got bored of her and decided that it was time for her to go. For her to talk to him about dating other men would have been a blow to his masculine pride, hence his reaction. He wasn't upset, nor was he jealous of these imaginary men she would soon be seeking out. If they existed.

Her thoughts drifted and meandered until the plane began its descent. Then they were touching down at the airport in Liguria and everything vanished, except the reason why they were here in the first place.

Even the bright sunshine vanished as they stepped out and were ushered into a chauffeur-driven car to begin the journey to his house on the peninsula.

'I used to come here far more frequently in the past,'

he mused as he tried to work out the last time he had visited his coastal retreat.

'And then what happened?' It was her first time in Italy and she had to drag her eyes away from the lush green of the backdrop, the mountains that reared up to one side, the flora which was eye-wateringly exuberant.

'Life seemed to take over.' He shrugged. 'I woke up to the fact that Bianca had as little to do with this part of Italy as she possibly could and, of course, where she went, my daughter was dragged along. My interest died over a period of time and, anyway, work prohibited the sort of lengthy holidays that do this place justice.'

'Why didn't you just sell up?'

'I had no pressing reason to. Now I'm glad I hung onto the place. It may have been a bit uncomfortable had we been under the same roof as Rachel and Claudia, given the circumstances. I hadn't planned on saying anything to my mother-in-law about our arrival, but in all events I decided to spare her the shock of a surprise visit—although I've told her to say nothing to Rachel, for obvious reasons.'

'Those reasons being?'

'I can do without my teenage daughter scarpering.'

'You don't think she would, do you? Where would she go?'

'I should think she knows Italy a lot better than I do. She certainly would have friends in the area I know nothing about. I think it's fair to say that my knowledge of the people she hangs out with isn't exactly comprehensive.' But he smiled and then stared out of the window. 'I shudder to think of Claudia trying to keep control of my daughter on a permanent basis.'

The conversation lapsed. The sun was setting by the time they finally made it to his house, which they

approached from the rear and which was perched on
a hill top.

The front of the house overlooked a drop down to
the sea and the broad wooden-floored veranda, with
its deep rattan-framed sofas, was the perfect spot from
which you could just sit and watch the changing face
of the ocean.

Only when they had settled in, shown to their bedroom by a housekeeper—yet another employee keeping
a vacant house going—did Alessio inform her that he
intended visiting his mother-in-law later that evening.

'It won't be too late for her,' he said, prowling
through the bedroom and then finally moving to the
window to stare outside. He turned to look at her. In
loose-fitting trousers and a small, silky vest, she looked
spectacular. It unsettled him to think that, even with this
pressing business to conclude, she had still managed to
distract him to the point where all he could think of was
her returning to London and joining the singles scene.

He wouldn't have said that his ego was so immense
that it could be so easily bruised, but his teeth clamped
together in grim rejection of the thought of any man
touching her. Since when had he been the possessive
type, let alone jealous?

'It will also allow Rachel to sleep on everything, give
her time to put things into perspective and to come to
terms with returning with us on the next flight over.'

'You make it sound as though we'll be leaving tomorrow.' Lesley hovered by the bed, sensing his mood
and wondering whether it stemmed from parental concern at what was to come. She wanted to reach out and
comfort him but knew, with unerring instinct, that that
would be the last thing he wanted.

Yet hadn't he implied that they would be in the country for at least a week? She wondered why the rush was suddenly on to get out as quickly as possible. Did he really think that she had been using him? Had he decided that the sooner he was rid of her, the better, now that she had bucked the trend of all his other women and displayed a lack of suitable clinginess?

Pride stopped her from asking for any inconvenient explanations.

'Not that it matters when we leave,' she hastened to add. 'Would I have time to have a shower?'

'Of course. I have some work I need to get through anyway. I can use the time to do that and you can meet me downstairs in the sitting room. Unlike my country estate, you should be able to find your way around this villa without the use of a map.'

He smiled, and Lesley smiled back and muttered something suitable, but she was dismayed to feel a lump gathering at the back of her throat.

The sex between them was so hot that she would have expected him to have given her that wolfish grin of his, to have joined her in the shower, to have forgotten what they had come here for…just for a while.

Instead, he was vanishing through the door without a backward glance and she had to swallow back her bitter disappointment.

Once showered, and in a pair of faded jeans and a loose tee-shirt, she found him waiting for her in the sitting room, pacing while he jangled car keys in his pocket. The chauffeur had departed in the saloon car in which they had been ferried and she wondered how they were going to get to Claudia's villa, but there was a small four-wheel-drive jeep tucked away at the side of the house.

She had all the paperwork in a backpack which she

had slung over her shoulder. 'I hope I'm not under-dressed,' she said suddenly, looking up at him. 'I don't know how formal your mother-in-law is.'

'You're fine,' Alessio reassured her. A sudden image of her naked body flashed through his head with such sudden force that his heart seemed to skip a beat. He should have his mind one hundred per cent focused on the situation about to unravel, he told himself impatiently, instead of thinking about her and whatever life choices she decided to make. 'Your dress code isn't the issue here,' he said abruptly and Lesley nodded and turned away.

'I know that,' she returned coolly. 'I just wouldn't want to offend anyone.'

Alessio thought that that was rather shutting the door after the horse had bolted, considering she had had no trouble in offending *him*, but it was such a ridiculous thought that he swept it aside and offered a conciliatory smile.

'Don't think that I don't appreciate what you're doing,' he told her in a low voice. 'You didn't have to come here.'

'Even though you made sure I did by dangling that carrot of a fabulous new big job under my boss's nose?' She was still edgy at his dismissive attitude towards her but, when he looked at her like that, his dark eyes roving over her face, her body did its usual thing and leapt into heated response.

As if smelling that reaction, Alessio felt some of the tension leave his body and this time when he smiled it was with genuine, sexy warmth.

'I've always liked using all the tools in my box,' he murmured and Lesley shot him a fledgling grin.

His black mood had evaporated. She could sense it.

Perhaps now that they were about to leave some of his anxiety about what lay ahead was filtering away, replaced by a sense of the inevitable.

At any rate, she just wanted to enjoy this return to normality between them. For that little window when there had been tension between them, she had felt awful. She knew that she had to get a grip, had to put this little escapade into perspective.

She would give herself the remainder of what time was left in Italy and then, once they returned to the UK, whatever the outcome of what happened here, she would return to the life she had temporarily left behind. She had already laid the groundwork for a plausible excuse, one that would allow her to retreat with her dignity and pride intact.

It was time to leave this family saga behind her.

CHAPTER EIGHT

THE DRIVE TO Claudia's villa took under half an hour. He told her that he hadn't been back to Portofino for a year and a half, and then it had been a flying visit, but he still seemed to remember the narrow roads effortlessly.

They arrived at a house that was twice the size of Alessio's. 'Bianca always had a flair for the flamboyant,' he said drily as he killed the engine and they both stared at an imposing villa fronted by four Romanesque columns, the middle two standing on either side of a bank of shallow steps that led to the front door. 'When we were married and she discovered that money was no object, she made it her mission to spend. As I said, though, she ended up spending very little time here— too far from the action. A peaceful life by the sea was not her idea of fun.'

Lesley wondered what it must be like to nip out at lunchtime and buy a villa by the sea for no better reason than *you could.* 'Is your mother-in-law expecting me?'

'No,' Alessio admitted. 'As far as Claudia is concerned, I am here on a mission to take my wayward daughter in hand and bring her back with me to London. I thought it best to keep the unsavoury details of this little visit to myself.' He leaned across to flip open the passenger door. 'I didn't think,' he continued, 'That

Rachel would have appreciated her grandmother knowing the ins and outs of what has been going on. Right. Let's get this over and done with.'

Lesley felt for him. Underneath the cool, composed exterior she knew that he would be feeling a certain dread at the conversation he would need to have with his daughter. He would be the Big, Bad Wolf and, for a sixteen-year-old, there would be no extenuating circumstances.

The ringing of the doorbell reverberated from the bowels of the villa. Just when Lesley thought that no one was in despite the abundance of lights on, she heard the sound of footsteps, and then the door was opening and there in front of them was a diminutive, timid looking woman in her mid-sixties: dark hair, dark, anxious eyes and a face that looked braced for an unpleasant surprise until she registered who was at the door and the harried expression broke into a beaming smile.

Lesley faded back, allowing for a rapid exchange of Italian, and only when there was a lull in the conversation did Claudia register her presence.

Despite what Alessio had said, Lesley had expected someone harder, tougher and colder. Her daughter, after all, had not come out of Alessio's telling of the story as an exemplary character, but now she could see why he had dismissed Claudia's ability to cope with Rachel.

Their arrival had been unannounced; they certainly had not been expected for supper. Alessio had been vague, Claudia told her, gripping Lesley's arm as she led them towards one of myriad rooms that comprised the ground floor of the ornately decorated house.

'I was not even sure that he would be coming at all,' she confided. 'Far less that he would be bringing a lady friend with him...'

Caught uncomfortably on the outside of a conversation she couldn't understand, Lesley could only smile weakly as Alessio fired off something in Italian and then they were entering the dining room where, evidently, dinner had been interrupted.

Standing a little behind both Claudia and Alessio, Lesley nervously looked around the room, feeling like an intruder in this strange family unit.

For a house by the coast, it was oddly furnished with ornate, dark wooden furniture, heavy drapes and a patterned rug that obscured most of the marble floor. Dominating one of the walls was a huge portrait of a striking woman with voluptuous dark good looks, wild hair falling over one shoulder and a haughty expression. Lesley assumed that it was Bianca and she could see why a boy of eighteen would have been instantly drawn to her.

The tension in the room was palpable. Claudia had bustled forward, but her movements were jerky and her smile was forced, while Alessio remained where he was, eyes narrowed, looking at the girl who had remained seated and was returning his stare with open insolence.

Rachel looked older than sixteen but then Lesley knew by now that she was only a few weeks away from her seventeenth birthday.

The tableau seemed to remain static for ages, even though it could only have been a matter of seconds. Claudia had launched into Italian and Rachel was pointedly ignoring her, although her gaze had shifted from Alessio, and now she was staring at Lesley with the concentration of an explorer spotting a new sub-species for the first time.

'And who are *you*?' She tossed her hair back, a mane of long, dark hair similar to the woman's in the portrait, although the resemblance ended there. Rachel had her father's aristocratic good looks. This was the gangly teenager whose leather mini-skirt Lesley had stealthily tried on. She reminded Lesley of the cool kids who had ruled the school as teenagers, except now a much older and more mature Lesley could see her for what she really was: a confused kid with a lot of attitude and a need to be defensive. She was scared of being hurt.

'Claudia.' Alessio turned to the older woman. 'If you would excuse us, I need to have a quiet word with my daughter.'

Claudia looked relieved and scuttled off, shutting the door quietly behind her.

Immediately Rachel launched into Italian and Alessio held up one commanding hand.

'English!'

It was the voice of complete and utter authority and his daughter glared at him, sullenly defiant but not quite brave enough to defy him.

'I'm Lesley.' Lesley moved forward into the simmering silence, not bothering to extend a hand in greeting because she knew it wouldn't be taken, instead sitting at the dining room table where she saw that Rachel had been playing a game on her phone.

'I helped to create that.' She pointed to the game with genuine pleasure. 'Three years ago.' She dumped the backpack onto the ground. 'I was seconded out to help design a website for a starter computer company and I got involved with the gaming side of things. It made a nice change. If I had only known how big that game would have become, I would have insisted on putting my name to it and then I would be getting royalties.'

Rachel automatically switched off the phone and turned it upside down.

Alessio had strolled towards his daughter and adopted the chair next to her so that she was now sandwiched between her father and Lesley.

'I know why you've come.' Rachel addressed her father in perfect, fluent English. 'And I'm not going back to England. I'm not going back to that stupid boarding school. I hate it there and I hate living with you. I'm staying here. Grandma Claudia said she's happy to have me.'

'I'm sure,' Alessio said in a measured voice, 'That you would love nothing more than to stay with your grandmother, running wild and doing whatever you want, but it is not going to happen.'

'You can't make me!'

Alessio sighed and raked his fingers through his hair. 'You're still a minor. I think you will find that I can.'

Looking between them, Lesley wondered if either realised just how alike they were: the proud jut of their chins, their stubbornness, even their mannerisms. Two halves of the same coin waiting to be aligned.

'I don't intend to have a protracted argument with you about this, Rachel. Returning to England is inevitable. We are both here because there is something else that needs to be discussed.'

He was the voice of stern authority and Lesley sighed as she reached down to the backpack and began extracting her folder, which she laid on the shiny table.

'What's that?' But her voice was hesitant under the defiance.

'A few weeks ago,' Alessio said impassively, 'I started getting emails. Lesley came to help me unravel them.'

Rachel was staring at the folder. Her face had paled and Lesley saw that she was gripping the arms of the chair. Impulsively she reached out and covered the thin, brown hand with hers and surprisingly it was allowed to remain there.

'It's thanks to me,' she said quietly, 'That all this stuff was uncovered. I'm afraid I looked through your bedroom. Your father, of course, would have rather I didn't, but it was the only way to compile the full picture.'

'You looked *through my things*?' Dark eyes were now focused accusingly on her, turned from Alessio. Lesley had become the target for Rachel's anger and confusion and Lesley breathed a little sigh of relief because, the less hostility directed at Alessio, the greater the chance of him eventually repairing his relationship with his daughter. It was worth it.

It was worth it because she loved him.

That realisation, springing out at her from nowhere, should have knocked her for six, but hadn't she already arrived that conclusion somewhere deep inside her? Hadn't she known that, underneath the arguments about lust and learning curves, stepping out of comfort zones and finding her sexuality, the simple truth of the matter was that she had been ambushed by the one thing she had never expected? It had struck her like a lightning bolt, penetrating straight through logic and common sense and obliterating her defences.

'You had no right,' Rachel was hissing.

Lesley let it wash over her and eventually the vitriol fizzled out and there was silence.

'So, tell me,' Alessio said in a voice that brooked no argument, 'About a certain Jack Perkins.'

Lesley left them after the initial setting out of the information. It was a sorry story of a lonely teenager, unhappy at boarding school, who had fallen in with the wrong crowd—or, rather, fallen in with the wrong boy. Piecing together the slips of paper and the stray emails, Lesley could only surmise that she had smoked a joint or two and then, vulnerable, knowing that she would be expelled from yet another school, she had become captive to a sixteen-year-old lad with a serious drug habit.

The finer details, she would leave for Alessio to discover. In the meantime, not quite knowing what to do with herself, she went outside and tried to get her thoughts in order.

Where did she go from here? She had always been in control of her life; she had always been proud of the fact that she knew where she was heading. She hadn't stopped for a minute to think that something as crazy as falling in love could ever derail her plans because she had always assumed that she would fall in love with someone who slotted into her life without causing too much of a ripple. She hadn't been lying when she had told Alessio that the kind of guy she imagined for herself would be someone very much like her.

How could she ever have guessed that the wrong person would come along and throw everything into chaos?

And what did she do now?

Still thinking, she felt rather than saw Alessio behind her and she turned around. Even in the darkness he had the bearing of a man carrying the weight of the world on his shoulders, and she instinctively walked towards him and wrapped her arms around his waist.

Alessio felt like he could hold onto her for ever. Wrong-footed by the intensity of that feeling, he pulled her closer and covered her mouth with his. His hand crept up underneath the tee-shirt and Lesley stepped back.

'Is sex the *only* thing you ever think about?' she

asked sharply, and she answered the question herself, providing the affirmative she knew was the death knell to any relationship they had.

He wanted sex, she wanted more—it was as simple as that. Never had the gulf between them seemed so vast. It went far beyond the differences in their backgrounds, their life experiences or their expectations. It was the very basic difference between someone who wanted love and someone who only wanted sex.

'How is Rachel?' She folded her arms, making sure to keep some space between them.

'Shaken.'

'Is that all you have to say? That she's *shaken*?'

'Are you deliberately trying to goad me into an argument?' Alessio looked at her narrowly. 'I'm frankly not in the mood to soothe whatever feathers I've accidentally ruffled.' He shook his head, annoyed with himself for venting his stress on her, but he had picked something up—something stirring under the surface—even though, for the life of him, he couldn't understand what could possibly be bugging her. She certainly hadn't spent the past hour trying and failing to get through to a wayward teenager who had sat in semi-mute silence absorbing everything that was being said to her but responding to nothing.

He was frustrated beyond endurance and he wondered if his own frustration was making him see nuances in her behaviour that weren't there.

'And I'm frankly amazed that you could talk to your daughter, have this awkward conversation, and yet have so little to report back on the subject.'

'I didn't realise that it was my duty to *report back* to you,' Alessio grated and Lesley reddened.

'Wrong choice of words.' She sighed. Here were the

cracks, she thought with a hollow sense of utter dejection. Things would go swimmingly well just so long as she could disentangle sex from love, but she was finding that she couldn't now. She spiked her fingers through her short hair and looked away from him, out towards the same black sea which his villa down the road overlooked.

She could see the way this would play out: making love would become a bittersweet experience; she would be the temporary mistress, making do, wondering when her time would be up. She suspected that that time would come very quickly once they returned to England. The refreshing, quirky novelty of bedding a woman with brains, who spoke her mind, who could navigate a computer faster than he could, would soon pall and he would begin itching to return to the unchallenging women who had been his staple diet.

Nor would he want a woman around who reminded him of the sore topic of his daughter and her misbehaviour, which had almost cost him a great deal of money.

'Would it be okay if I went to talk to her?' Lesley asked, and Alessio looked at her in surprise.

'What would you hope to achieve?'

'It might help talking to someone who isn't you.'

'Even though she sees you as the perpetrator of the "searching the bedroom" crime? I should have stepped in there and told her that that was a joint decision.'

'Why?' Lesley asked with genuine honesty. 'I guess you had enough on your plate to deal with and, besides, I will walk away from this and never see either of you again. If she pins the blame on me, then I can take it.'

Alessio's jaw hardened but he made no comment. 'She's still in the dining room,' he said. 'At least, that's where I left her. Claudia has disappeared to bed, and frankly I don't blame her. In the morning, I shall tell her that my daughter has agreed that the best thing is to return to England with me.'

'And school?'

'As yet to be decided, but it's safe to say that she won't be returning to her old stamping ground.'

'That's good.' She fidgeted, feeling his distance and knowing that, while she had been responsible for creating it, she still didn't like it. 'I won't be long,' she promised, and backed away.

Like a magnet, his presence seemed to want to pull her back towards him but she forced herself through to the dining room, little knowing what she would find.

She half-expected Rachel to have disappeared into another part of the house, but the teenager was still sitting in the same chair, staring vacantly through the window.

'I thought we might have a chat,' Lesley said, approaching her warily and pulling a chair out to sit right next to her.

'What for? Have you decided that you want to apologise for going through my belongings when *you had no right*?'

'No.'

Rachel looked at her sullenly. She switched on her mobile phone, switched it off again and rested it on the table.

'Your dad's been worried sick.'

'I'm surprised he could take the time off to be worried,' Rachel muttered, fiddling with the phone and then eventually folding her arms and looking at Lesley with unmitigated antagonism. 'This is all your fault.'

'Actually, it's got nothing to do with me. I'm only

here because of you and you're in this position because of what you did.'

'I don't have to sit here and listen to some stupid employee preach to me.' But she remained on the chair, glaring.

'And I don't have to sit here, but I want to, because I grew up without a mum and I know it can't be easy for you.'

'Oh puh…lease….' She dragged that one word out into a lengthy, disdainful, childish snort of contempt.

'Especially,' Lesley persevered, 'As Alessio—your father—isn't the easiest person in the world when it comes to touchy-feely conversations.'

'*Alessio*? Since when are you on first-name terms with my father?'

'He wants nothing more than to have a relationship with you, you know,' Lesley said quietly. She wondered if this was what love did, made you want to do your utmost to help the object of your affections, to make sure they were all right, even if you knew that they didn't return your love and would happily exit your life without much of a backward glance.

'And that's why he never bothered to get in touch when I was growing up? *Ever*?'

Lesley's heart constricted. 'Is that what you really believe?'

'It's what I was told by my mum.'

'I think you'll find that your father did his best to keep in touch, to visit… Well, you'll have to talk to him about that.'

'I'm not going to be talking to him again.'

'Why didn't you come clean with your dad, or even one of the teachers, when that boy started threatening you?' She had found a couple of crumpled notes and had quickly got the measure of a lad who had been happy to extort as much of Rachel's considerable pocket money as he could by holding it over her head that he had proof of the one joint she had smoked with him and was willing to lie to everyone that it had been more than that. When the pocket money had started running out, he must have decided to go directly to the goose that was laying the golden eggs: pay up or else he would go to the press and disclose that one of the biggest movers and shakers in the business world had a druggie teenage daughter. 'You must have been scared stiff,' she mused, half to herself.

'That's none of your business.'

Some of the aggression had left her voice. When Lesley looked at her, she saw the teenage girl who had been bullied and threatened by someone willing to take advantage of her one small error of judgement.

'Well, you dad's going to sort all of that out. He'll make the whole thing go away.' She heard the admiring warmth in her voice and cleared her throat. 'You should give him a chance.'

'And what's it to you?'

Lesley blushed.

'Oh, right.' She gave a knowing little laugh and sniffed. 'Well, I'm not about to give anyone a chance, and I don't care if he sorts that thing out or not. So. He dumped me and I had to traipse around with my mum and all her boyfriends.'

'You *knew* your mum…err…? Well, none of my business.' She stood up. 'You should give your dad a chance and at least listen to what he has to say. He tried very hard to keep in touch with you but, well, you should let him explain how that went—and you should go get some sleep.'

She exited the room, closing the door quietly behind her. Had she got through to Rachel? Who knew? It would take more than one conversation to break down some of those teenage walls, but several things had emerged.

Aside from the fact that everything was now on the table—and, whether she admitted it or not, that would have come as a huge relief to Rachel—it was clear that the girl had had no idea just how hard her father had tried to keep in touch with her, how hard he had fought to maintain contact.

And Alessio had no idea that his daughter was aware of Bianca's wild, promiscuous temperament.

Join those two things together, throw into the mix the fact that Rachel had kept a scrapbook of photos and cuttings, and Lesley suspected that an honest conversation between father and daughter would go some distance to opening the door to a proper relationship.

And if Rachel was no longer at a boarding school, but at a day school in London, they would both have the opportunity to start building a future and leaving the past behind.

She went outside to find Alessio still there and she quietly told him what she had learned during the conversation with his daughter.

'She thinks you abandoned her,' she reinforced bluntly. 'And she would have been devastated at the thought of that. It might explain why she's been such a rebel, but she's young. You're going to have to take the lead and lower your defences if you want to get through to her.'

Alessio listened, head tilted to one side, and when she had finished talking he nodded slowly and then told her in return what he intended to do to sort the small matter of a certain Jack Perkins. He had already contacted someone he trusted to supply him with information about the boy and he had enough at his disposal to pay a visit to his parents and make sure the matter was resolved quickly and efficiently, never again to rear its ugly head.

'When I'm through,' Alessio promised in a voice of steel, 'That boy will think twice before he goes near an Internet café again, never mind threatening anyone.'

Lesley believed him and she didn't doubt that Jack Perkins' life of crime was about to come crashing down around his head. It had transpired that his family was well-connected. Not only would they be horrified at what their son had done, and the drug problems he was experiencing, but his father would know that Alessio's power stretched far; if he were to be crossed again by a delinquent boy, then who knew what the repercussions would be?

The problem, Alessio assured her, would wait until he returned to the UK. It wasn't going anywhere and, whilst he could hand over the business of wrapping it up to a trusted advisor and friend, he would much rather do it himself.

'When I'm attacked,' he said softly, 'Then I prefer to retaliate using my own fists rather than relying on my bodyguards.'

Everything, Lesley thought, had been neatly wrapped up and she was certain that father and daughter would eventually find their way and become the family unit they deserved to be.

Which left her...the spectator whose purpose had been served and whose time had come to depart.

They drove in silence back to Alessio's villa. He planned on returning to his mother-in-law's the following morning and he would talk to his daughter once again.

He didn't say what that conversation would be, but Lesley knew that he had taken on board what she had said, and he would try and grope his way to some sort of mutual ground on which they could both converse.

Alessio knew that, generally speaking, the outcome to what could have been a disaster had been good.

Jack Perkins had revealed problems with his daughter that would now be addressed, and Lesley's mediation had been pretty damn fantastic. How could his daughter not have known that he had tried his hardest? He would set her straight on that. He could see that Rachel had been lost and therefore far too vulnerable in a school that had clearly allowed too much freedom. He might or might not take them to task on that.

'Thanks,' he suddenly said gruffly as they pulled up into the carport at the side of the villa. He killed the engine and looked at Lesley. 'You didn't just sort out who was behind this but you went the extra mile, and we both know, gentle bribe or no gentle bribe, you didn't have to do that.' Right now, all he wanted to do was get inside the villa, carry her upstairs to the bedroom and make love to her. Take all night making love to her. He had never felt as close to any woman.

No, Lesley thought with a tinge of bitterness, she really had had no need to go the extra mile, but she had, and it had had nothing to do with bribes, gentle or otherwise.

'We should talk,' she said after a while.

Alessio stilled. 'I thought we just had.'

Lesley hopped out of the car, slammed the door behind her and waited for him. Just then, in the car, it had felt way too intimate. Give it just a few more seconds sitting there, breathing him in, hearing that lazy, sexy drawl, and all her good intentions would have gone down the drain.

'Want to tell me what this is all about?' was the first thing he asked the second they were inside his villa. He threw the car keys on the hand-carved sideboard by the front door and led the way into the kitchen where he helped himself to a long glass of water from a bottle in the fridge. Then he sat down and watched as she took the seat furthest away from him.

'How long,' she finally asked, 'Do you plan on staying here?'

'Where is that question leading?' For the first time, he could feel quicksand underneath his feet and he didn't like it. He wished he had had something stronger to drink; a whisky would have gone down far better than a glass of water. He didn't like the way she had sat a million miles across the room from him; he didn't like the mood she had been in for the past few hours; he didn't like the way she couldn't quite seem to meet his eyes. 'Oh, for God's sake,' he muttered when she didn't say anything. 'At least until the end of the week. Rachel and I have a few things to sort out, not to mention a frank discussion of where she will go to school. There are a lot of fences to be mended and they won't be mended overnight; it'll take a few days before we can even work out where the holes are. But what has that got to do with anything?'

'I won't be staying on here with you.' She cleared her throat and took a deep breath. 'I do realise that I promised I would stay the week, but I think my job here is done, and it's time for me to return to London.'

'Your job here *is done*?' Alessio could not believe what he was hearing.

'Yes, and I just want to say that there's every chance that you and your daughter will find a happy solution to the difficulties you've been experiencing in your relationship.'

'Your job here…*is done*? So you're *heading back*?'

'I don't see the point of staying on.'

'And I don't believe I'm hearing this. What do you mean you don't *see the point of staying on*?' He point-blank refused to ask *what about us?* That was not a question that would ever pass his lips. He remembered what she had said about wanting to head back out there, get into the thick of the dating scene—now that she had used him to reintroduce her to the world of sex; now that she had overcome her insecurities, thanks to him.

Pride slammed in and he looked at her coldly.

'What we have, Alessio, isn't going anywhere. We both agreed on that, didn't we?' She could have kicked herself for the plaintive request she heard in her voice, the request begging him to contradict her. 'And I'm not interested in having a fling until we both run out of steam. Actually, probably until we get back to London. I'm not in the market for a holiday romance.'

'And what are you in the market for?' Alessio asked softly.

Lesley tilted her chin and returned his cool stare. Was she about to reveal that she was in the market for a long-term, for ever, happy-ever-after, committed relationship? Would she say that so that he could naturally assume that she was talking about *him*? Wanting that relationship *with him*? It would be the first conclusion he would reach. Women, he had told her, always seemed to want more than he was prepared to give. He would assume that she had simply joined the queue.

There was no way that she would allow her dignity to be trampled into the ground.

'Right now…' her voice was steady and controlled, giving nothing away '…all I want is to further my career. The company is still growing. There are loads of opportunities to grow with it, even perhaps to be transferred to another part of the country. I want to be there to take advantage of those opportunities.' She thought she sounded like someone trying to sell themselves at an interview, but she held her ground and her eyes remained clear and focused.

'And the career opportunities are going to disappear unless you hurry back to London as fast as you can?'

'I realise you'll probably pull that big job out from under our feet.' That thought only now struck her, as did the conclusion that she wasn't going to win employee of the week if her boss found out that she had been instrumental in losing a job that would bring hundreds of thousands of pounds to the company and extend their reach far wider than they had anticipated.

Alessio wondered whether her thirst for a rewarding career would make her change her mind about not staying on, about not continuing what they had. It revolted him to think that it might. He had never had to use leverage to get any woman into his bed and he wasn't about to start now.

Nor had he ever had to beg any woman to stay in his bed once she was there, and he certainly wasn't about to start *that* now.

'You misjudge me,' he said coldly. 'I offered that job to your boss and I am not a man who would renege on a promise, least of all over an affair that goes belly up. Your company has the job and everything that goes with it.'

Lesley lowered her eyes. He was a man of honour. She had known that. He just wasn't a man in love.

'I also think that when I decide to embark on another relationship.'

'You mean after you've launched yourself back into the singles scene.'

She shrugged, allowing him to think something she knew to be way off mark. She could think of nothing less likely than painting the town red and clubbing.

'I just feel that, if I decide to get involved with anyone, then it should be with the person who is right for me. So, I think we should call it a day for us.'

'Good luck with your search,' Alessio gritted. 'And, now that you've said your piece, I shall go and do some work downstairs. Feel free to use the bedroom where your suitcase has been put; I shall sleep in one of the other bedrooms and you can book your return flight first thing in the morning. Naturally, I will cover the cost.' He stood up and walked towards the door. 'I intend to go to Claudia's by nine tomorrow. If I don't see you before I go, have a safe flight. The money I owe you will be in your bank account by the time you land.' He nodded curtly and shut the kitchen door behind him.

This is all for the best, Lesley thought, staring at the closed door and trying to come to terms with the thought that she would probably never see him again.

It was time for her to move on...

CHAPTER NINE

LESLEY PAUSED IN front of the towering glass house and stared up and up and up. Somewhere in there, occupying three floors in what was the most expensive office block in central London, Alessio would be hard at work. At least, she hoped so. She hoped he wasn't out of the country. She didn't think she could screw up her courage and make this trip to see him a second time.

A month ago, she had walked out on him and she hadn't heard from him since. Not a word. He had duly deposited a wad of money into her account, as he had promised—far too much, considering she had bailed on their trip a day in.

How had his talk with his daughter turned out? Had they made amends, begun the protracted process of repairing their relationship? Where was she at school now?

Had he found someone else? Had he found her replacement?

For the past few weeks, those questions had churned round and round in her head, buzzing like angry hornets, growing fat on her misery until… Well, until something else had come along that was so big and so overwhelming that there was no room left in her head for those questions.

She took a deep breath and propelled her reluctant feet forward until she was standing in the foyer of the building, surrounded by a constant river of people coming and going, some in snappy suits, walking with an air of purpose; others, clearly tourists, staring around them, wondering where they should go to get to the viewing gallery or to one of the many restaurants.

In front of her a long glass-and-metal counter separated a bank of receptionists from the public. They each had a snazzy, small computer screen in front of them and they were all impeccably groomed.

She had worked out what she was going to say, having decided beforehand that it wasn't going to be easy gaining access to the great Alessio Baldini—that, in fact, he might very well refuse to see her at all. She had formulated a borderline sob story, filled with innuendo and just enough of a suggestion that, should she not be allowed up to whatever floor he occupied, he would be a very angry man.

It worked. Ten minutes after she had arrived, a lift was carrying her up to one of the top floors, from which she knew he would be able to overlook all of London. She had no idea how much the rent was on a place like this and her head spun thinking about it. She had been told that she would be met at the lift, and she was, but it was only as they were approaching his office that nerves really truly kicked in and she had to fight to keep her breathing steady and even and not to hyperventilate.

She was aware of his personal assistant asking concerned questions and she knew that she was answering those questions in a reassuring enough voice, but she felt sick to the stomach.

By the time they reached his office suite, she was close to fainting.

She didn't even know if she was doing the right thing. The decision to come here had been taken and then rejected and then taken again so many times that she had lost count.

The outer office, occupied by his personal assistant, was luxurious. In one corner, a massive semi-circular desk housed several phones and a computer terminal. Against one of the walls was a long, grey bench-like sofa that looked very uncomfortable. Against the other wall was a smooth, walnut built-in cupboard with no handles, just a bank of smooth wood.

It was an intimidating office, but not as intimidating as the massive door behind which Alessio would be waiting for her.

And waiting for her he most certainly was. He had been in the middle of a conference call when he had been buzzed by his secretary and informed that a certain Lesley Fox was downstairs in reception and should she be sent away or brought up?

Alessio had cut short his conference call without any preamble. His better self had told him to refuse her entry. Why on earth would he want to have anything further to do with a woman who had slept with him, had not denied having slept with him as part of her preparations for entering the world of hectic dating and then walked out of his life without a backward glance? Why would he engage in any further conversation with someone who had made it perfectly clear that he was not the sort of man she was looking for, even though they had slept together? Even though there had been no complaints there!

He had made sure that the money owed to her was deposited into her bank account, and had had no word from her confirming whether she had received it or not, despite the fact that he had paid her over and above the agreed amount, including paying her for time she had not worked for him at all.

The time he had wasted waiting for a phone call or text from her had infuriated him.

Not to mention the time he had wasted just *thinking* about her. She was hardly worth thinking about and yet, in the past few weeks, she had been on his mind like a background refrain he just couldn't get out of his head.

And so, when he had been called on his internal line to be told that she was there in the building, that she wanted to see him, there had been no contest in his head.

He had no idea what she could possibly want, and underwriting his curiosity was the altogether pleasant day dream that she had returned to beg for him back. Perhaps the wild and wonderful world of chatting up random men in bars and clubs had not quite lived up to expectation. Maybe having fun with the wrong guy was not quite the horror story she had first thought. Maybe she missed the sex; she had certainly seemed to enjoy every second of being touched by him.

Or, more prosaically, maybe her boss had sent her along on something to do with the job he had put their way. It made sense. She knew him. Indeed, they had landed that lucrative contract without even having to tender for it because of her. If anything needed to be discussed, her boss would naturally assume that she should be the one to do it and there would be no way that she could refuse. At least, not unless she started pouring out the details of her private life, which he knew she would never do.

He frowned, not caring for that scenario, which he immediately jettisoned so that he could focus as he waited for her on more pleasurable ones.

By the time his secretary, Claire, announced her arrival, through the internal line to which she exclusively had access, Alessio had come to the conclusion that he was only mildly curious as to the nature of her surprise visit—that he didn't care a whit what she had to say to him and that the only reason he was even allowing her entry into his office was because he was gentlemanly enough not to have her chucked out from the foyer in full view of everyone.

Still, he made her wait a while, before sitting back in his leather chair and informing Claire that his visitor could be ushered in—cool, calm and screamingly forbidding.

Lesley felt the breath catch jaggedly in her throat as she heard the door close quietly behind her. Of course, she hadn't forgotten what he looked like. How could she when his image had been imprinted in her brain with the red-hot force of a branding iron?

But nothing had prepared her for the cold depths of those dark eyes or the intimidating silence that greeted her arrival in his office.

She didn't know whether to keep standing or to confidently head for one of the leather chairs in front of his desk so that she could sit down. She certainly felt as though her legs didn't have much strength left in them.

Eventually, she only scuttled towards one of the chairs when he told her to sit, simultaneously glancing at his watch as though to remind her that, whilst she might have been offered a seat, she should make sure that she didn't get too comfortable because he didn't have a lot of time for her.

This was the guy she had fallen in love with. She knew she would have dented his pride when she had walked out on him, but still she had half-hoped that he might contact her in some way, if only to ask whether she had received the money he had deposited into her account.

Or else to fill her in on what had happened in his family drama. Surely that would have been the polite thing to do?

But not a word, and she knew that had she not arrived on his doorstep, so to speak, then she would never have seen him again. Right now, those brooding dark eyes were surveying her with all the enthusiasm of someone contemplating something the cat had inadvertently brought in.

'So,' Alessio finally drawled, tapping his rarely used fountain pen on the surface of his desk. 'To what do I owe this unexpected pleasure?' To his disgust, he couldn't help but think that she looked amazing.

He had made one half-hearted attempt to replace her with one of the women he had dated several months ago, a hot blonde with big breasts and a face that could turn heads from a mile away, but he had barely been able to stick it out for an evening in her company.

How could he when he had been too busy thinking of the woman slumped in the chair in front of him? Not in her trademark jeans this time but a neat pair of dark trousers and a snug little jacket that accentuated the long, lean lines of her body.

On cue, he felt himself begin to respond, which irritated the hell out of him.

'I'm sorry if I'm disturbing you,' Lesley managed. Now that she was here, she realised that she couldn't just drop her bombshell on him without any kind of warning.

'I'm a busy man.' He gesticulated widely and shot her a curving smile that contained no warmth. 'But never let it be said that I'm rude. An ex-lover deserves at least a few minutes of my time.'

Lesley bit her tongue and refrained from telling him that that remark in itself was the height of rudeness.

'I won't be long. How is Rachel?'

'You made this journey to talk about my daughter?'

Lesley shrugged. 'Well, I became quite involved in what was going on. I'm curious to know how things turned out in the end.'

Alessio was pretty sure that she hadn't travelled to central London and confronted him at his office just to ask one or two questions about Rachel, but he was willing to play along with the game until she revealed the true reason for showing up.

'My daughter has been…subdued since this whole business came out in the open. She returned to London without much fuss and she seems relieved that the boarding school option is now no longer on the cards. Naturally, I have had to lay down some ground rules for her—the most important of which is that I don't want to hear from anyone in the school that she's been acting up.' Except he had been far less harsh in delivering that message than it sounded.

Rachel might have been a complete idiot, led astray for reasons that were fairly understandable, but he had to accept his fair share of the blame as well. He had taken his eye off the ball.

Now, there was dialogue between them, and he had high hopes that in time that dialogue would turn into fluent conversation. Would that be asking too much?

He had certainly taken the unfortunate affair by the horns and sorted it all out, personally paying a visit to the boy's parents and outlining for them in words of one syllable what would happen if he ever had another email from the lad.

He had shied away from taking the full hard line, however, confident that the boy's parents, who had seemed decent but bewildered, would take matters in hand. They both travelled extensively and only now had it dawned on them that in their absence they had left behind a lonely young man with a drug problem that had fortunately been caught in the bud.

Rachel had not commented on the outcome, but he had been shrewd enough to see the relief on her face. She had found herself caught up in something far bigger than she had anticipated and, in the end, he had come to her rescue, although that was something he had taken care not to ram home.

'That's good.' Lesley clasped her hands together.

'So is there anything else you want? Because if that's all…' He looked at the slender column of her neck, her down-bent head, the slump of her shoulders, and wanted to ask her if she missed him.

Where the hell had *that* notion come from?

'Just one other thing.' She cleared her throat and looked at him with visible discomfort.

And, all at once, Alessio knew where she was going with this visit of hers. She wanted back in with him. She had walked away with her head held high and a load of nonsense about needing to find the right guy, wherever the hell he might be. But, having begun her search, she had obviously fast reached the conclusion that the right guy wasn't going to be as easy to pin down as she had thought and, in the absence of Mr Right, Mr Fantastic Sex would do instead.

Over his dead body.

Although, it had to be said that the thought of her

begging for him was an appealing one. He turned that pleasant fantasy over in his head and very nearly smiled.

He was no longer looking at his watch. Instead, he pushed the chair away from the desk and relaxed back, his fingers lightly linked together on his flat, hard stomach.

Should he rescue her from the awkwardness of what she wanted to say? Or should he just wait in growing silence until her eventual discomfort propelled her into speech? Both options carried their own special appeal.

Eventually, with a rueful sigh that implied that far too much of his valuable time had already been wasted, he said, shaking his head, 'Sorry. It's a little too late for you.'

Lesley looked at him in sudden confusion. She knew that this was an awkward situation. She had appeared at his office and demanded to see him, and now here she was, body as stiff as a plank of wood, sitting in mute silence while she tried to work how best to say what she had come to say. No wonder he wanted to shuffle her out as fast as he could. He must be wondering what the hell she was doing, wasting his time.

'You're—you're busy,' she stammered, roused into speech as her brain sluggishly cranked back into gear just enough to understand that he wanted her out because he had more important things to do.

Once again, she wondered whether she had been replaced. Once again, she wondered whether he had reverted to type, back to the sexy blondes with the big breasts and the big hair.

'Have you been busy?' she blurted out impulsively, almost but not quite covering her mouth with her hand in an instinctive and futile attempt to retract her words.

Alessio got her drift immediately. No matter that the

question hadn't been completed. He could tell from the heightened colour in her cheeks and her startled, embarrassed eyes that she was asking him about his sex life, and he felt a groundswell of satisfaction.

'Busy? Explain.'

'Work. You know.' When she had thought about having this conversation, about seeing him again, she had underestimated the dramatic effect he would have on her senses. In her head, she had pictured herself cool, composed—a little nervous, understandably, but strong enough to say her piece and leave.

Instead, here she was, her thoughts all over the place and her body responding to him on that deep, subterranean level that was so disconcerting. The love which she had hoped might have found a more settled place— somewhere not to the forefront—pounded through her veins like a desperate virus, destroying everything in its path and making her stumble over her words.

Not to mention she'd hoped not to ask questions that should never have left her mouth, because she could tell from the knowing look in those deep, dark eyes that he knew perfectly well what she had wanted to know when she had asked him whether he had been 'busy'.

'Work's been…work. It's always busy. Outside of work…' Alessio thought of his non-date with a non-contender for a partner and felt his hackles rise that the woman staring at him with those big, almond-shaped brown eyes had driven him into seeking out someone for company simply to try and replace the images of her he had somehow ended up storing in his head. He shrugged, letting her assume that his private life was a delicate place to which she was not invited—hilarious, considering just how much she knew about him. 'What about you?' He smoothly changed the subject. 'Have you found your perfect soul-mate as yet?'

'What did you mean when you said that it was a little too late for me?' The remark had been playing at the back of her mind and she knew that she needed him to spell it out in words of one syllable.

'If you think that you can walk back into my life because you had a bit of trouble locating Mr Right, then it's not going to happen.'

Pride. But then, what the hell was wrong with pride? He certainly had no intention of telling her the truth, which was that he was finding it hard to rid his system of her, even though she should have been no more than a blurry memory by now.

He was a man who moved on when it came to women. Always had been—never mind when it came to moving on from a woman who had dumped him!

Just thinking about that made his teeth snap together in rage.

'I don't intend walking back into your life,' Lesley replied coolly. So, now she knew where she stood. Was she still happy that she had come here? Frankly, she could still turn around and walk right back through that door but, yes, she was happy she was here, whatever the outcome.

Alessio's eyes narrowed. He noticed what he had failed to notice before—the rigid way she was sitting, as though every nerve in her body was on red-hot alert; the way she was fiddling with her fingers; the determined tilt of her chin.

'Then why are you here?' His voice was brusque and dismissive. Having lingered on the pleasant scenario of her pleading to be a part of his life once again, he was irrationally annoyed that he had misread whatever signals she had been giving off.

'I'm here because I'm pregnant.'

There. She had said it. The enormous thing that had been absorbing every minute of every day of her life since she had done that home pregnancy test over three days ago was finally out in the open.

She had skipped a period. It hadn't even occurred to her that she could be pregnant; she had forgotten all about that torn condom. She had had far too much on her mind for that little detail to surface. It was only as she'd tallied the missed period with tender breasts that she remembered the very first time they had made love…and the outcome of that had been very clear to see in the bright blue line on that little plastic stick.

She hadn't bothered to buy more, to repeat the test. Why would she do that, when in her heart she knew that the result was accurate?

She had had a couple of days to get used to the idea, to move from feeling as though she was falling into a bottomless hole to gradually accepting that, whatever the landing, she would have to deal with it; that the hole wouldn't be bottomless.

She had had time to engage her brain in beginning trying to work out how her life would change, because there was no way that she would be getting rid of this baby. And, as her brain had engaged, her emotions had followed suit and a flutter of excitement and curiosity had begun to work their way into the equation.

She was going to be a mum. She hadn't banked on that happening, and she knew that it would bring a host of problems, but she couldn't snuff out that little flutter of excitement.

Boy or girl? What would it look like? A miniature

Alessio? Certainly, a permanent reminder of the only man she knew she would ever love.

And should she tell him? If she loved him, would she ruin his life by telling him that he was going to be a father—again? Another unplanned and unwanted pregnancy. Would he think that she was trapping him, just like Bianca had, into marriage for all the wrong reasons?

Wouldn't the kindest thing be to keep silent, to let him carry on with his life? It was hardly as though he had made any attempt at all to contact her after she had left Italy! She had been a bit of fun and he had been happy enough to watch her walk away. Wouldn't the best solution be to let him remember her as a bit of fun rather than detonate a bomb that would have far-reaching and permanent ramifications he would not want?

In the end, she just couldn't bring herself to deny him the opportunity of knowing that he was going to be a father. The baby was half his and he had his rights, whatever the outcome might be.

But it was still a bomb she'd detonated, and she could see that in the way his expression changed from total puzzlement to dawning comprehension and then to shock and horror.

'I'm sorry,' she said in a clear, high voice. 'I know this is probably the last thing you were expecting.'

Alessio was finding it almost impossible to join his thoughts up. Pregnant. She was pregnant. For once he couldn't find the right words to deal with what was going through his head, to express himself. In fact, he actually couldn't find any words at all.

'It was that first time,' Lesley continued into the lengthening silence. 'Do you remember?'

'The condom split.'

'It was a one in a thousand chance.'

'The condom split and now you're pregnant.' He leant forward and raked his fingers through his hair, keeping his head lowered.

'It was no one's fault,' Lesley said, chewing her lower lip and looking at his reaction, the way he couldn't even look at her. Right now he hated her; that was clear. He was listening to the sound of his life being derailed and, whether down to a burst condom or not, he was somehow blaming her.

'I wasn't going to come here...'

That brought his head up, snapping to attention, and he looked at her in utter disbelief. 'What, you were just going to disappear with my baby inside you and not tell me about it?'

'Can you blame me?' Lesley muttered defensively. 'I know the story about how you were trapped into a loveless marriage by your last wife; I know what the consequences of that were.'

'Those consequences being...?' When Bianca had smiled smugly and told him that he was going to be a father, he had been utterly devastated. Now, strangely, the thought that this woman might have spared him devastation second time round didn't sit right. In fact, he was furious that the thought might even have crossed her mind although, in some rational part of himself, he could fully understand why. He also knew the answer to his own stupid question, although he waited for her to speak while his thoughts continued to spin and spin, as though they were in a washing machine with the speed turned high.

'No commitment,' Lesley said without bothering to dress it up. 'No one ever allowed to get too close. No woman ever thinking that she could get her foot through the door, because you were always ready to bang that door firmly shut the minute you smelled any unwanted advances in that direction. And please don't look at me as though I'm talking rubbish, Alessio. We both know I'm not. So excuse me for thinking that it might have been an idea to spare you the nightmare of…of this…'

'So you would have just disappeared?' He held onto that tangible, unappealing thought and allowed his anger to build up. 'Walked away? And then what—in sixteen years' time I would have found out that I'd fathered a child when he or she came knocking on my door asking to meet me?'

'I hadn't thought that far into the future.' She shot him a mutinous look from under her lashes. 'I looked into a future a few months away and what I saw was a man who would resent finding himself trapped again.'

'You can't speculate on what my reactions might or might not have been.'

'Well, it doesn't matter. I'm here now. I've told you. And there's something else—I want you to know straight off that I'm not asking you for anything. You know the situation and that's my duty done.' She began standing up and found that she was trembling. Alessio stared at her with open-mouthed incredulity.

'Where do you think you're going?'

'I'm leaving.' She hesitated. This was the right time to leave. She had done what she had come to do. There was no way that she intended to put any pressure on him to do anything but carry on with his precious, loveless existence, free from the responsibility of a clinging woman and an unwanted baby.

Yet his presence continued to pull her towards him like a powerful magnet.

'You're kidding!' Alessio's voice cracked with the

harshness of a whip. 'You breeze in here, tell me that you're carrying my child, and then announce that you're on your way!'

'I told you, I don't want anything from you.'

'What you want is by the by.'

'I beg your pardon?'

'It's impossible having this sort of conversation here. We need to get out, go somewhere else. My place.'

Lesley stared at him in utter horror. Was he mad? The last thing she wanted was to be cooped up with him on his turf. It was bad enough that she was in his office. Besides, where else was the conversation going to go?

Financial contributions; of course. He was a wealthy man and in possession of a muddy conscience; he would salve it by flinging money at it.

'I realise you might want to help out on the money front,' she said stiltedly. 'But, believe it or not, that's not why I came here. I can manage perfectly well on my own. I can take maternity leave and anyway, with what I do, I should be able to work from home.'

'You don't seem to be hearing me.' He stood up and noticed how she fell back.

She might want him out of her life but it wasn't going to happen. Too bad if her joyful hunt for the right guy had crashed and burned; she was having his baby and he was going to be part of her life whether she liked it or not.

The thought was not as unwelcome as he might have expected. In fact, he was proud of how easily he was beginning to take the whole thing on board.

It made sense, of course. He was older and wiser. He had mellowed over time. Now that sick feeling of having an abyss yawn open at his feet was absent.

'If you want to discuss the financial side of things,

then we can do that at a later date. Right now, I'll give you time to digest everything.'

'I've digested it. Now, sit back down.' This was not where he wanted to be. An office couldn't contain him. He felt restless, in need of moving. He wanted the space of his apartment. But there was no way she would go there with him; he was astute enough to decipher that from her dismayed reaction to the suggestion. And he wasn't going to push it.

It crossed his mind that this might have come as a bolt from the blue for him, turning his life on its axis and sending it spiralling off in directions he could never have predicted, but it would likewise have been the same for her. Yet here she was, apparently in full control. But then, hadn't he always known that there was a thread of absolute bravery and determination running through her?

And when she said that she didn't want anything from him, he knew that she meant it. This situation could not have been more different from the one in which he had found himself all those years ago.

Not that that made any difference. He was still going to be a presence in her life now whether she liked it or not.

Lesley had reluctantly sat back down and was now looking at him with a sullen lack of enthusiasm. She had expected more of an explosion of rage, in the middle of which she could have sneaked off, leaving him to calm down. He seemed to be handling the whole thing a great deal more calmly than she had expected.

'This isn't just about me contributing to the mother and baby fund,' he said, in case she had got it into her head that it might be. 'You're having my baby and I intend to be involved in this every single step of the way.'

'What are you talking about?'

'Do you really take me for a man who walks away from responsibility?'

'I'm not your ex-wife!' Lesley said tightly, fists clenched on her lap. 'I haven't come here looking for anything and you certainly don't owe me or this baby anything!'

'I'm not going to be a part-time father,' Alessio gritted. 'I was a part-time father once, not of my own choosing, and it won't happen again.'

Not once had Lesley seen the situation from that angle. Not once had she considered that he would want actual, active involvement, yet it made perfect sense. 'What are you suggesting?' she asked, bewildered and on the back foot.

'What else is there to suggest but marriage?'

For a few frozen seconds, Lesley thought that she might have misheard him, but when she looked at him his face was set, composed and unyielding.

She released a hysterical laugh that fizzled out very quickly. 'I don't believe I'm hearing this. Are you mad? Get married?'

'Why so shocked?'

'Because…' *Because you don't love me. You probably don't even like me very much right now.* 'Because having a baby isn't the right reason for two people to get married,' she said in as controlled a voice as she could muster. 'You of all people should know that! Your marriage ended in tears because you went into it for all the wrong reasons.'

'Any marriage involving my ex-wife would have ended in tears.' Alessio was finding it hard to grapple with the notion that she had laughed at his suggestion of marriage. Was she *that* intent on finding Mr Right that she couldn't bear the thought of being hitched to him? It was downright offensive! 'You're not Bianca, and you need to look at the bigger picture.' Was that overly aggressive? He didn't think so but he saw the way she stiffened and he tempered what he was going to say with a milder, more conciliatory voice. 'By which I mean that this isn't about us as individuals but about a child that didn't ask to be brought into the world. To do the best for him or her is to provide a united family.'

'To do the best for him or her is to provide two loving parents who live separately instead of two resentful ones joined in a union where there's no love lost.' Just saying those words out loud made her feel ill because what she should really have said was that there was no worse union than one in which love was given but not returned. What she could have told him was that she could predict any future where they were married, and what she could see was him eventually loathing her for being the other half of a marriage he might have initiated but which had eventually become his prison cell.

There was a lot she could have told him but instead all she said was, 'There's no way I would ever marry you.'

CHAPTER TEN

THE PAIN STARTED just after midnight. Five months before her due date. Lesley awoke, at first disorientated, then terrified when, on inspection, she realised that she was bleeding.

What did that mean? She had read something about that in one of the many books Alessio had bought for her. Right now, however, her brain had ceased to function normally. All she could think of doing was getting on her mobile phone and calling him.

She had knocked him back, had told him repeatedly that she wasn't going to marry him, yet he had continued to defy her low expectations by stealthily becoming a rock she could lean on. He was with her most evenings, totally disregarding what she had said to him about pregnancy not being an illness. He had attended the antenatal appointments with her. He had cunningly incorporated Rachel into the picture, bringing his daughter along with him many of the times he'd visited her, talking as though the future held the prospect of them all being a family, even though Lesley had been careful to steer clear of agreeing to any such sweeping statements.

What was he hoping to achieve? She didn't know. He didn't love her and not once had he claimed to.

But, bit by bit, she knew that she was beginning to rely on him—and it was never so strongly proved as now, when the sound of his deep voice over the end of the phone had the immediate effect of calming her panicked nerves.

'I should have stayed the night,' was the first thing he told her, having made it over to her house in record time.

'It wasn't necessary.' Lesley leaned back and closed her eyes. The pain had diminished but she was still in a state of shock at thinking that something might be wrong. That she might lose the baby. Tears threatened close to the surface but she pushed them away, focusing on a good outcome, despite the fact that she knew she was still bleeding.

And then something else occurred to her, a wayward thought that needled its way into her brain and took root, refusing to budge. 'I shouldn't have called you,' she said more sharply than she had intended. 'I wouldn't have if I'd thought that you were going to fret and worry.' But she hadn't thought of doing anything *but* picking up that phone to him. To a man who had suddenly become indispensable despite the fact that she was not the love of his life; despite the fact that he wouldn't be in this car here with her now if she had never visited him in his office.

She had never foreseen the way he had managed to become so ingrained into the fabric of her daily life. He brought food for her. He stocked her up with pregnancy books. He insisted they eat in when he was around because it was less hassle than going out. He had taken care of that persistent leak in the bathroom which had suddenly decided to act up.

And not once had she sat back and thought of where all this was leading.

'Of course you should have called me,' Alessio said softly. 'Why wouldn't you? This baby is mine as well. I share all the responsibilities with you.'

And share them he had, backing away from trying to foist his marriage solution onto her, even though he had been baffled at her stubborn persistence that there was no way that she was going to marry him.

Why not? He just didn't get it. They were good together. They were having a baby. Hell, he had made sure not to lay a finger on her, but he still burned to have her in his bed, and the memory of the sex they had shared still made him lose concentration in meetings. And, yes, so maybe he had mentioned once or twice that he had learnt bitter lessons from being trapped into marriage by the wrong woman for the wrong reasons, but hadn't that made his proposal even more sincere—the fact that he was willing to sidestep those unfortunate lessons and re-tread the same ground?

Why couldn't she see that?

He had stopped thinking about the possibility that she was still saving herself for Mr Right. Just going down that road made him see red.

'I hate it when you talk about responsibilities,' she snapped, looking briefly at him and then just as quickly looking away. 'And you're driving way too fast. We're going to crash.'

'I'm sticking to the speed limit. Of course I'm going to talk about responsibilities. Why shouldn't I?' Would she rather he had turned his back on her and walked away? Was that the sort of modern guy she would have preferred him to be? He hung onto his patience with difficulty, recognising that the last thing she needed was to be stressed out.

'I just want you to know,' Lesley said fiercely, 'That if anything happens to this baby…'

'Nothing is going to happen to this baby.'

'You don't know that!'

Alessio could sense her desire to have an argument with him and he had no intention of allowing her to indulge that desire. A heated row was not appropriate but he shrewdly guessed that, if he mentioned that, it would generate an even bigger row.

What the hell was wrong? Of course she was worried. So was he, frankly. But he was here with her, driving her to the hospital, fully prepared to be right there by her side, so why the need to launch into an attack?

Frustration tore into him but, like his impatience, he kept it firmly in check.

Suddenly she felt that it was extremely important that she let him know this vital thing. 'And I just want you to know that, if something does, then your duties to me are finished. You can walk away with a clear conscience, knowing that you didn't dump me when I was pregnant with your child.'

Alessio sucked in his breath sharply. Ahead, he could see the big, impersonal hospital building. He had wanted her to have private medical care during the pregnancy and for the birth of the baby, but she had flatly refused, and he had reluctantly ceded ground. If, indeed, there was anything at all amiss, that small victory would be obliterated because he would damn well make sure that she got the best medical attention there was available.

'This is not the time for this sort of conversation.' He screeched to a halt in front of the Accident and Emergency entrance but, before he killed the engine, he looked at her intently, his eyes boring into her. 'Just try and relax, my darling. I know you're probably scared stiff but I'm here for you.' He brushed her cheek lightly and the tenderness of that touch brought a lump to her throat.

'You're here for the baby, not for me,' Lesley muttered under her breath. But then any further conversation was lost as they were hurried through, suddenly caught up in a very efficient process, channelled to the right place, speeding along the quiet hospital corridors with Lesley in a wheelchair and Alessio keeping pace next to her.

There seemed to be an awful lot of people around and she clasped his hand tightly, hardly even realising that she was doing that.

'If something happens to the baby...' he bent to whisper into her ear as they headed towards the ultrasound room '...then I'm still here for you.'

An exhausting hour later, during which Lesley had had no time to think about what those whispered words meant, she finally found herself in a private room decorated with a television on a bracket against the wall and a heavy door leading, she could see, to her own en-suite bathroom.

Part of her wondered whether those whispered words had actually been uttered or had they been a fiction of her fevered imagination?

She covertly watched as he drew the curtains together and then pulled a chair so that he was on eye-level with her as she lay on the bed.

'Thank you for bringing me here, Alessio,' she said with a weak smile that ended up in a yawn.

'You're tired. But everything's going to be all right with the baby. Didn't I say?'

Lesley smiled with her eyes half-closed. The relief

was overwhelming. They had pointed out the strongly beating heart on the scan and had reassured her that rest was all that was called for. She had been planning to work from home towards the beginning of the third trimester. That would now have to be brought forward.

'You said.'

'And—and I meant what I said when we were rushing you in.'

Lesley's eyes flew open and she felt as though her heart had skipped a beat. She had not intended to remind him of what he had said, just in case she had misheard, just in case he had said what he somehow thought she wanted to hear in the depths of her anxiety over her scare.

But now his eyes held hers and she just wanted to lose herself in possibilities.

'What did you say? I can't quite…um…remember.' She looked down at her hand which had somehow found its way between his much bigger hands.

'What I should say is that there was a moment back then when it flashed through my mind—what would I do if anything happened to *you*? It scared the living daylights out of me.'

'I know you feel very responsible…with me being pregnant.' She deliberately tried to kill the shoot of hope rising inside her and tenaciously refusing to go away.

'I'm not talking about the baby. I'm talking about you.' He felt as though he was looking over the side of a very sheer cliff, but he wanted to jump; he didn't care what sort of landing he might be heading for.

So far she hadn't tried to remind him that he wasn't her type and that they weren't suited for one another. That surely had to be a good sign?

'I don't know what I'd do if anything happened to

you because you're the love of my life. No, wait, don't say a thing. Just listen to what I have to say and then, if you want me to butt out of your life, I'll do as you say. We can go down the legal route and have the papers drawn up for custody rights, and an allowance to be made for you, and I'll stop pestering you with my attention.' He took a deep breath and his eyes shifted to her mouth, then to the unappealing hospital gown which she was still wearing, and then finally they settled on their linked fingers. It seemed safer.

'I'm listening.' *The love of his life*? She just wanted to repeat that phrase over and over in her head because she didn't think she could possibly get used to hearing it.

'When you first appeared at my front door, I knew you were different to every single woman I had ever met. I knew you were sharp, feisty, outspoken. I was drawn to you, and I guess the fact that you occupied a special place of intimate knowledge about certain aspects of my private life not usually open to public view fuelled my attraction. It was as though the whole package became irresistible. You were sexy as hell without knowing it. You had brains and you had insight into me.'

Lesley almost burst out laughing at the 'sexy as hell' bit but then she remembered the way he had looked at her when they had made love, the things he had said. *She* might have had insecurities about how she looked, but she didn't doubt that his attraction had been genuine and spontaneous. Hadn't he been the one to put those insecurities to bed, after all?

'It just felt so damned right between us,' he admitted, stealing a surreptitious look at her face, and encouraged that she didn't seem to be blocking him out. 'And the more we got to know one another the better it felt. I thought it was all about the sex, but it was much bigger than that, and I just didn't see it. Maybe after Bianca I simply assumed that women could only satisfy a certain part of me before they hit my metaphorical glass ceiling and disappeared from my life. I wasn't looking for any kind of involvement and I certainly didn't bank on finding any. But involvement found me without my even realising it.'

He laughed under his breath and, when he felt the touch of her hand on his cheek, he held it in place so that he could flip it over and kiss the palm of her hand. He relaxed, but not too much.

'Thanks to you, my relationship with Rachel is the healthiest it's ever been. Thanks to you, I've discovered that there's far more to life than trying to be a father to a hostile teenager and burying myself in my work. I never stopped to question how it was that I wasn't gutted when you told me about the pregnancy. I knew I felt different this time round from when Bianca had presented me with a future of fatherhood. If I had taken the time to analyse things, I might have begun to see what had already happened. I might have seen that I had fallen hopelessly in love with you.'

All his cards were on the table and he felt good. Whatever the outcome. He carried on before she could interrupt with a pity statement about him not really being the one for her.

'And I may not cry at girlie movies or bake bread but you can take me on. I'm a good bet. I'm here for you; you know that. I'll always be here for you because I'm nothing without you. If you still don't want to marry me, or if you want to put me on probation, then I'm willing to go along because I feel I can prove to you that I can be the sort of man you want me to be.'

'Probation?' The concept was barely comprehensible.

'A period of time during which you can try me out for size.' He had never thought he would ever in a million years utter such words to any woman. But he just had and he didn't regret any of them.

'I know what the word means.' The thoughts were rushing round in her head, a mad jumble that filled every space. She wanted to fling her arms around him, kiss him on the mouth, pull him right into her, jump up and down, shout from the rooftops—all of those things at the same time.

Instead, she said in a barely audible voice, 'Why didn't you say sooner? I wish you had. I've been so miserable, because I love you so much and I thought that the last thing you needed was to be trapped into marriage to someone you never wanted to see out your days with.' She lay back and smiled with such pure joy that it took her breath away. Then she looked at him and carried on smiling, and smiling, and smiling. 'I knew I was falling for you but I knew you weren't into committed relationships.'

'I never was.'

'That should have stopped me but I just didn't see it coming. You really weren't the sort of guy I ever thought I could have fallen in love with, but who said love obeys rules? By the time I realised that I loved you, I was in so deep that the only way out for me was to run as fast as I could in the opposite direction. It was the hardest thing I ever did in my entire life but I thought that, if I stayed, my heart would be so broken that I would never recover.'

'My darling... My beautiful, unique, special darling.' He kissed her gently on the lips and had the wonderful feeling of being exactly where he was meant to be.

'Then I found out that I was pregnant, and after the

shock had worn off a bit, I felt sick at the thought of telling you—sick at the thought of knowing that you would be horrified, your worst nightmare turned into reality.'

'And here we are. So I'm asking you again, my dearest—will you marry me?'

They were married in Ireland a month before their baby was born, with all her family in attendance. Her father, her brothers and her brothers' partners all filled the small local church. And, when they retired to the hotel which they had booked into, the party was still carrying on, as he was told, in typical Irish style. And just as soon as the baby was born, he was informed, they would throw a proper bash—the alcohol wouldn't stop flowing for at least two days. Alessio had grinned and told them that he couldn't wait but that, before the baby discovered the wonders of an Irish bash, she or he would first have to discover the wonders of going on honeymoon, because they had both agreed that wherever they went their baby would come as well.

And their baby, Rose Alexandra, a little girl with his dark hair and big, dark eyes, was born without fuss, a healthy eight pounds four ounces. Rachel, who was over the moon at the prospect of having a sibling she could thoroughly spoil, could barely contain her excitement when she paid her first visit to the hospital and peered into the little tilted cot at the side of Lesley's bed.

The perfect family unit, was the thought that ran through Alessio's mind as he looked at the snapshot picture in front of him. His beautiful wife, radiant but tired after giving birth, smiling down at the baby in her arms while Rachel, the daughter he had once thought lost to him but now found, stood over them both, her dark hair falling in a curtain as she gently touched her sister's small, plump, pink cheek.

If he could have bottled this moment in time, he would have. Instead, still on cloud nine, he leaned into the little group and knew that this, finally, was what life should be all about.

* * * * *

RETURN OF THE ITALIAN TYCOON

JENNIFER FAYE

To Michelle Styles, an amazing friend, who taught me so much, including that the important part of writing was what I decided to do after the dreaded 'R'. Thank you!

CHAPTER ONE

"CAN I SMELL YOU?"

Kayla Hill's fingers struck the wrong keys on her computer. Surely she hadn't heard her boss correctly—her very serious, very handsome boss. "Excuse me. What did you say?"

Angelo Amatucci's tanned face creased with lines as though he were deep in thought. "Are you wearing perfume?"

"Uh…yes, I am."

"Good. That will be helpful. May I have a smell?"

Helpful? With what? She gave up on answering an email and turned her full attention to her boss, who moved to stand next to her. What in the world had prompted him to ask such a question? Was her perfume bothering him? She sure hoped not. She wore it all the time. If he didn't like it or was allergic to it, she thought he'd have mentioned it before now.

Kayla craned her neck, allowing her gaze to travel up over his fit body, all six-foot-plus of muscle, until she met his inquisitive eyes. "I'm sorry but I… I don't understand."

"I just finished speaking with Victoria Van Holsen, owner of Moonshadows Cosmetics. She has decided that her latest fragrance campaign, even though she painstakingly approved it each step of the way, just won't do."

"She doesn't want it?" Kayla failed to keep the astonishment out of her voice.

A muscle in his jaw twitched. "She insists we present her with a totally new proposal."

"But this is a Christmas campaign. Everything should be finalized, considering it's already March." Then, realizing that she was speaking to a man with far more experience, she pressed her lips together, silencing her rambling thoughts.

"Now that information about her competitor's upcoming holiday campaign has been leaked, she wants something more noteworthy—something that will go viral."

"I thought the campaign was unique. I really like it." Kayla truly meant it. She wasn't trying to butter up her boss—that was just an unexpected bonus.

"The fact of the matter is, Victoria Van Holsen is a household name and one of our most important clients. Our duty is to keep her happy."

It was the company's motto—the client's needs come first. No matter what. And if Kayla was ever going to rise up the chain from her temporary detour as the personal assistant to the CEO of Amatucci & Associates Advertising to her dream job as an ad executive on Madison Avenue, she could never forget that the clients were always right. It didn't matter how unreasonable or outrageous their requests might be at times, keeping them happy was of the utmost importance.

"How can I help?"

"Stand up."

His face was devoid of emotion, giving no hint of his thoughts.

She did as he asked. Her heart fluttered as he circled her. When he stopped behind her and leaned in close, an army of goose bumps rose on her skin. Her eyes drifted closed as a gentle sigh slipped across her lips. Angelo Amatucci truly did want an up close and personal whiff of her perfume.

He didn't so much as touch a single hair on her, but she could sense him near her neck. Her pulse raced. If this most unusual request had come from anyone else, she'd swear they were hitting on her. But as Mr. Amatucci stepped to the front of her, his indifferent expression hadn't changed. Her frantic heart rate dipped back to normal.

There had never been any attempt on his part to flirt with her. Though his actions at times could be quite unpredictable, they were always ingenuous. She deduced that his sudden curiosity about her perfume had something to do with the Van Holsen account. But what could he be thinking? Because there was no way she was wearing a Moonshadows fragrance. One ounce of the stuff would set her back an entire paycheck.

"It seems to have faded away." A frown tugged at his lips.

"Perhaps this will be better." She pulled up the sleeve of her blue suit jacket and the pink blouse beneath it before holding out her wrist to him. "Try this."

His hand was warm and his fingers gentle as he lifted her hand to his face. Her heart resumed its frantic tap dancing in her chest. *Tip-tap. Tip-tap.* She wished it wouldn't do that. He was, after all, her boss—the man who held her career aspirations in the palm of his very powerful hand. A man who was much too serious for her.

Still, she couldn't dismiss that his short dark wavy hair with a few silver strands at the temples framed a very handsome, chiseled face. His dark brown eyes closed as he inhaled the fragrance, and she noticed his dark lashes as they swept down, hiding his mesmerizing eyes. It was a wonder some woman hadn't snatched him up—not that Kayla had any thoughts in that direction.

She had narrowly escaped the bondage of marriage to a really nice guy, who even came with her Mom's and Dad's stamp of approval. Though the breakup had been hard, it had been the right decision for both of them. Steven had wanted a traditional wife who was content to cook, clean and raise a large family. Not that there was anything wrong with that vision. It just wasn't what she envisioned for her future. She wanted to get out of Nowhereville, USA, and find her future in New York City.

When Mr. Amatucci released her arm, she could still

feel warmth where his fingers had once been. Her pulse continued to race. She didn't know why she was having this reaction. She wasn't about to jeopardize her rising career for some ridiculous crush on her boss, especially when it was perfectly obvious that he didn't feel a thing for her.

His gaze met hers. "Is that the only perfume you wear?"

She nodded. "It's my favorite."

"Could I convince you to wear another fragrance?"

He was using her as a test market? Interesting. She could tell him what he wanted to hear, but how would that help him develop a new marketing strategy? She decided to take her chances and give him honest answers.

"Why would I change when I've been using this same perfume for years?"

He rubbed his neck as she'd seen him do numerous times in the past when he was contemplating new ideas for big accounts. And the Van Holsen account was a very big account. The fact that the client had the money to toss aside a fully formulated ad campaign and start over from scratch was proof of their deep pockets.

Mr. Amatucci's gaze was still on her, but she couldn't tell if he was lost in thought. "How long have you worn that fragrance?"

"Since I was a teenager." She remembered picking out the flower-shaped bottle from a department store counter. It was right before her first ever school dance. She'd worn it for every special occasion since, including her first date with Steven. And then there was her high school graduation followed by her college commencement. She'd worn it for all the big moments in her life. Even the day she'd packed her bags and moved to New York City in search of her dreams.

"Talk to me." Mr. Amatucci's voice cut through her memories. "What were you thinking about just now?"

She glanced hesitantly at him. In all of the weeks she'd worked as his PA, they'd never ventured into a conversation that was the slightest bit personal. Their talks had always centered around business. Now, he'd probably think she was silly or sentimental or both.

"I was thinking about all the times in my life when I wore this perfume."

"And?"

"And I wore it for every major event. My first date. My first kiss. My—" A sharp look from him silenced her.

"So your attachment to the fragrance goes beyond the scent itself. It is a sentimental attachment, right?"

She shrugged. "I guess so."

She'd never thought of it that way. In fact, she'd never given her perfume this much thought. If the bottle got low, she put it on her shopping list, but that's as far as her thoughts ever went.

"So if our client doesn't want to go with a sparkly, feel-fabulous-when-you-wear-this campaign, we can try a more glamorous sentimental approach. Thanks to you, we now have a new strategy."

She loved watching creativity in action. And she loved being a part of the creative process. "Glad I could help."

He started to walk away, then he paused and turned back. "You were just promoted to a copywriter position before you took this temporary assignment as my PA, right?"

She nodded. What better way to get noticed than to work directly for one of the biggest names in the advertising industry.

"Good. You aren't done with this project. I want you to dig into those memories and write out some ideas—"

"But don't you have a creative team for this account?" She wanted to kick herself for blurting out her thoughts.

Mr. Amatucci sent her a narrowed look. His cool, professional tone remained unchanged. "Are you saying you aren't interested in working on the project?"

Before she could find the words to express her enthusiasm, his phone rang and he turned away. She struggled to contain her excitement. This was her big opening and she fully intended to make the most of it.

This was going to work out perfectly.

A smile tugged at Kayla lips. She'd finally made it. Though people thought she'd made a big mistake by taking a step backward to assume a temporary position as Mr. Amatucci's PA, it was actually working out just as she'd envisioned.

She'd gone after what she wanted and she'd gotten it. Well, not exactly, but she was well on her way to making her dreams a reality. With a little more patience and a lot of hard work, she'd become an account executive on New York's famous Madison Avenue in the exclusive advertising agency of Amatucci & Associates.

Her fingers glided over the keyboard of her computer as she completed the email to the creative department about another of their Christmas campaigns. Sure it was only March, but in the marketing world, they were working months into the future. And with a late-season snowstorm swirling about outside, it seemed sort of fitting to be working on a holiday project.

She glanced off to the side of her computer monitor, noticing her boss holding the phone to his ear as he faced a wall of windows overlooking downtown Manhattan. Being on the twenty-third floor, they normally had a great view of the city, but not today. What she wouldn't give to be someplace sunny—far, far away from the snow. After months of frigid temperatures and icy sidewalks, she was most definitely ready for springtime.

"Have you started that list?" Mr. Amatucci's piercing brown gaze met hers.

Um—she'd been lost in her thoughts and hadn't even realized he'd wrapped up his phone call. Her gaze moved from his tanned face to her monitor. "Not yet. I need to finish one more email. It shouldn't take me long. I think your ideas for the account are spot-on. Just wait until the client lays her eyes on the mock-ups."

Then, realizing she was rambling, she pressed her lips firmly together. There was just something about being around him that filled her with nervous energy. And his long stretches of silence had her rushing to fill in the silent gaps.

Mr. Amatucci looked as though he was about to say something, but his phone rang again. All eyes moved to his desk. The ringtone was different. It must be his private line. In all the time she'd been working for him, it had never rung.

It rang again and yet all he did was stare at the phone.

"Do you want me to get it?" Kayla offered, not sure what the problem was or why Mr. Amatucci was hesitant. "I really don't mind."

"I've got it." He reached over and snatched up the receiver. "Nico, what's the matter?"

Well, that was certainly a strange greeting. Who picked up the phone expecting something to be wrong? Then, realizing that she was staring—not to mention eavesdropping—she turned her attention back to the notes she'd been rewording into an email. She glanced up to see Mr. Amatucci had turned his back to her. He once again faced the windows and spoke softly. Though the words were no longer distinguishable, the steely edge of his voice was still obvious.

She looked at the paper on her desk, her gaze darting over it to find where she'd left off. She didn't want to sit here with her hands idle. No, that definitely wouldn't look good for her.

She was sending along some of Mr. Amatucci's thoughts about the mock-up of an ad campaign for a new client—a very demanding client. The account was huge. It would go global—like most of the other accounts her boss personally handled. Each of his clients expected Mr. Amatucci's world to revolve around them and their accounts. He took their calls, no matter the time—day or night. Through it all, he maintained his cool. To say Angelo was a workaholic was being modest.

As a result, he ran the most sought-after advertising agency in the country—if not the world. Stepping off the elevator, clients and staff were immediately greeted by local artists' work and fresh flowers. The receptionist was bright and cheerful without being annoying. Appointments were kept timely. The quality of the work was exemplary. All of it culminated in Amatucci & Associates being so popular that they had to turn away business.

"*Cosa!* Nico, no!" Mr. Amatucci's hand waved about as he talked.

Her boss's agitated voice rose with each word uttered. Kayla's fingers paused as her attention zeroed in on the man who never raised his voice—until now. He was practically yelling. But she could only make out bits and pieces. His words were a mix of English and Italian with a thick accent.

"Nico, are you sure?"

Had someone died? And who was Nico? She hadn't heard Mr. Amatucci mention anyone with that name, but then again, this call was on his private line. It was highly doubtful that it had anything to do with business. And she knew exactly nothing about his personal life—sometimes she wondered if he even had one.

"Marianna can't be pregnant!" The shouts spiraled off into Italian.

Pregnant? Was he the father? The questions came hard and fast. There was a little voice in the back of her mind that told her she should excuse herself and give him some privacy, but she was riveted to her chair. No one would ever believe that this smooth, icy-cool man was capable of such heated volatility. She blinked, making sure she hadn't fallen asleep and was having some bizarre dream. But when her eyes opened, her boss was standing across the room with his hand slicing through the air as he spoke Italian.

The paramount question was: Who was Marianna?

Angelo Amatucci tightened his grip on the phone until his fingers hurt. This had to be some sort of nightmare and soon he'd wake up. Could it be he'd been working a bit too much lately? Perhaps he should listen to the hints from his business associates to take a break from the frantic pace. That would explain why just moments ago when he'd been examining Ms. Hill's perfume—a scent he found quite inviting—that he'd been tempted to smooth his thumb along the silky skin of her wrist—

"Angelo, are you listening to me?" Tones of blatant concern laced Nico's voice, demanding Angelo's full attention. "What are we going to do?"

Nico was his younger brother by four years, and though their opinions differed on almost everything, the one area where they presented a unified front was their little sister, Marianna—who wasn't so little anymore.

"There has to be another answer to this. You must have misunderstood. Marianna can't be pregnant. She's not even in a serious relationship."

"I know what I heard."

"Tell me again."

"I wanted her to taste the wine from the vineyard. I think it's the best we've ever produced. Just wait until you try some—"

"Nico, tell me about Marianna."

"Yes, well, she has looked awfully pale and out of sorts since she returned home after her year of traveling. I thought she'd done too much partying—"

"*Accidenti!* She wasn't supposed to waste the year partying." Unable to stand still a moment longer, Angelo started to pace again. When his gaze met the wide-eyed stare of Ms. Hill, she glanced down at her desk. He made a point of turning his back to her and lowering his voice. "She was sent to Australia to work on the vineyards there and get more experience in order to help you. If I'd have known she planned for it to be a year of partying, I'd have sent for her. I could have put her to work at the office."

Nico sighed. "Not everyone is like you, big brother. We aren't all driven to spend every last moment of our lives working."

"And you didn't do anything about her being sick?"

"What was I supposed to do? I asked if she needed anything. She said no, that it was some sort of flu bug. What else was I supposed to do?"

Angelo's hand waved around as he flew off in a string of Italian rants. Taking a calming breath, he stopped in front of the windows and stared blindly at the snow. "And it took her confessing she was pregnant for you to figure it out?"

"Like you would have figured it out sooner? What do either of us know about pregnant women...unless there's something you haven't told me?"

"Don't be ridiculous!" Angelo had no intention of getting married and having a family. Not now. Not ever.

"She didn't have any choice but to come clean when I offered her some wine. She knew she couldn't drink it. Hard to believe that you and I will be uncles this time next year."

"Don't tell me you're happy about this development?"

"I'm not. But what do you want me to do?"

"Find out the father's name for starters."

"I tried. She's being closemouthed. All she said was that she couldn't drink the wine because she's eight weeks pregnant. Then she started to cry and took off for her room."

"Didn't you follow? How could you have just let her get away without saying more?"

"How could I? I sure don't see you here trying to deal with an emotional pregnant woman."

How had things spun so totally out of control? Angelo's

entire body tensed. And more importantly, how did he fix them? How did he help his sister from so far away?

Angelo raked his fingers through his hair. "She has to tell you more. How are we supposed to help if we don't even know which man is the father. She isn't exactly the sort to stay in a relationship for long."

"Trust me. I've tried repeatedly to get his name from her. Maybe she'll tell you."

That wasn't a conversation Angelo wanted to have over the phone. It had to be in person. But he was in the middle of overseeing a number of important projects. Now was not the time for him to leave New York. But what choice did he have? This was his baby sister—the little girl he remembered so clearly running around with a smile on her face and her hair in braids.

But a lot of time had passed since he'd left Italy. Would she open up to him? The fact his leaving hadn't been his idea didn't seem to carry much weight with his siblings, who were left behind to deal with their dysfunctional parents. Though he dearly missed his siblings, he didn't miss the constant barrage of high-strung emotions of his parent's arguments and then their inevitable reunions—a constant circle of epic turmoil.

Maybe the trouble Marianna had got herself into was some sort of rebellion. With their parents now living in Milan, there was only Nico at home to cope with their sister. And to Nico's credit, he never complained about the enormous responsibility leveled solely on his shoulders.

Now that their parents had moved on, Angelo didn't have any legitimate excuse to stay away. But every time the subject of his visiting Monte Calanetti surfaced, he pleaded he had too much work to do. It was the truth—mostly. Perhaps he should have tried harder to make more time for his siblings.

Stricken with guilt, anger and a bunch of emotions that Angelo couldn't even name, he couldn't think straight. As the oldest brother, he was supposed to look out for his brother and sister. Instead, he'd focused all of his time and energy on creating a thriving, wildly successful company.

In the process, he'd failed their wayward and headstrong sister.

And now her future would forever be altered.

He owed it to Marianna to do what he could to fix things. But how could he do that when he was so far away?

CHAPTER TWO

THIS ISN'T GOOD. Not good at all.

Kayla pressed Save on the computer. She needed to give Mr. Amatucci some space. She reached for her wallet to go buy a—a—a cocoa. Yes, that would suit the weather outside perfectly.

She got to her feet when her boss slammed down the phone. He raked his fingers through his short hair and glanced at her. "Sorry about that. Where were we?"

The weariness in his voice tugged at her sympathies. "Um…well, I thought that I'd go get some um…cocoa—"

"The Van Holsen account. We were talking about how we need to put a rush on it."

"Um…sure." She sat back down.

Kayla wasn't sure how to act. She'd never before witnessed her boss seriously lose it. And who exactly was Marianna? Was it possible Mr. Amatucci really did have a life outside this office—one nobody knew about? The thought had her fighting back a frown. Why should it bother her to think that her boss might have fathered a baby with this woman? It wasn't as if they were anything more than employee and employer.

Mr. Amatucci stepped up to her desk. "I'll need to go over this with you tomorrow afternoon."

"Tomorrow?"

She knew that he asked for the impossible at times and this happened to be one of those times. He'd caught her totally off guard. It'd take time to think out innovative ideas for the new campaign platform. And she had an important meeting that night, but there was no way she was telling her boss about that.

Mr. Amatucci arched a brow at her. "Is that going to be a problem?"

"Uh...no. No problem." She would not let this opportunity pass her by. "I'll just finish up what I was working on, and I'll get started."

He paused as though considering her answer. "On second thought, it'd be best to go over your ideas first thing in the morning."

"The morning?"

His gaze narrowed in on her, and she wished that her thoughts would quit slipping across her tongue and out her mouth. It certainly wasn't helping this situation. She was here to impress him with her capabilities, not to annoy him when he was obviously already in a bad mood.

"Ms. Hill, you seem to be repeating what I say. Is there some sort of problem I should be aware of?"

She hated that he always called her Ms. Hill. Couldn't he be like everyone else in the office and call her Kayla? But then again, she was talking about Angelo Amatucci—he was unlike anyone she'd ever known.

He was the first man to set her stomach aquiver without so much as touching her. She'd been so aware of his mouth being just a breath away from her neck as he'd sniffed her perfume. The memory was still fresh in her mind. Was it so wrong that she hadn't wanted that moment to end?

Of course it was. She swallowed hard. He was her boss, not just some guy she'd met at a friend's place. There could never be anything serious between them—not that he'd ever even noticed her as a desirable woman.

"Ms. Hill?"

"No, there won't be a...uh...problem." Who was she kidding? This was going to be a big problem, but she'd work it out—somehow—some way.

Her gaze moved to the windows and the darkening sky. With it only nearing the lunch hour, it shouldn't be so dark, which could only mean that they were going to get pounded with more snow. The thought of getting stuck at the office turned her nervous stomach nauseous.

Snow. Snow. Go away.

He gazed at her. "I didn't mean to snap at you—"

"I understand. You've got a lot on your mind."

"Thank you."

His gaze continued to hold hers. The dark depths of his eyes held a mystery—the story of the real man behind the designer suits and the Rolex watches. She had to admit that she was quite curious about him—more than any employee had a right to about her very handsome, very single boss. And that odd phone call only made her all the more curious. Maybe he wasn't as single as she'd presumed. The jagged thought lodged in her throat.

Mr. Amatucci's steady gaze met hers. "You're sure you're up for this project?"

She pressed her lips together, no longer trusting her mouth, and nodded. She'd have to reschedule tonight's meeting for the fund-raiser.

"Good. If you need help, feel free to ask one of the other PAs to take over some of your other work. The Van Holsen account is now your priority."

He gathered his tablet computer and headed for the door. "I've got a meeting. I'll be back later."

"Don't worry. I've got this."

Without a backward glance, he strode out of the room, looking like the calm, cool, collected Angelo Amatucci that everyone respected and admired for his creative foresight. But how he was able to shut down his emotions so quickly was totally beyond her.

What was she going to do about her meeting tonight? It didn't help that she'd been the one to set it up. Somehow she'd been put in charge of the Inner City League after-school program fund-raiser. The program was in a serious financial bind. ICL was a great organization that kept at-risk kids off the streets after school while their parents were still at work.

Kayla had been volunteering for the past year. Helping others was how her parents had raised her. They had always been generous with their spare time and money—not that they had much of either. Kayla may have hightailed it out of Paradise, Pennsylvania, as soon as she could, but there was still a lot of Paradise in her. And she'd swear that she got more back from the kids and the other volunteers than she ever gave to any of them. For a girl who was used to living in a small town of friends, it was a comfort to have such a friendly group to keep her from feeling isolated in such a large city of strangers.

There was no way she could reschedule tonight's meeting. They were running out of time until the charity concert and there was still so much to plan. Somehow she had to make this all work out. She couldn't let down the kids nor could she let down her boss. The thought of Angelo Amatucci counting on her felt good.

Not only was he easy on the eyes, but she really enjoyed working with him, even if he was a bit stiff and withdrawn most of the time. But now that she'd witnessed him emotionally charged, she couldn't help but wonder what it'd be like to get up close and personal with him.

Angelo shook his head.

Marianna pregnant! Impossible.

Okay, so it wasn't impossible, but why had she been acting so irresponsible? It wasn't as if she was married or even considering it. She changed romantic interests faster than he changed ties—never getting too serious—until now. Nico didn't even know the father's name. What was up with that?

"What do you think, Mr. Amatucci?"

He glanced up at his youngest and most promising account executive. This was a meeting to discuss the campaign for a new sports car that was going to be revealed later that year. The car was quite nice and was sure to create a buzz of attention.

But for the life of him, Angelo couldn't keep his mind wrapped around business—no matter how important the account. His head was in Italy at the village of Monte Calanetti—where he should be dealing with his sister's life-changing event.

Angelo glanced down at the presentation on his digital tablet and then back at the account executive. "I think you still have work to do. This presentation is flat. It isn't innovative enough. There's nothing here to sway a twentysomething consumer to take out a sizable loan on top of their college debt in order to have this car. I want the 'must have' factor. The part that says if I have this car all of my friends will be envious. This isn't just a car—this is a status symbol. Do you understand?"

Mike glanced down and then back at Angelo. "But this is what the client asked for."

"And it's your job to push the envelope and give the client something more to consider—to want." Maybe he'd been too quick in his determination that Mike was going to be an asset to Amatucci & Associates—unlike Kayla, who was constantly proving she was an independent thinker. "Try again."

Mike's mouth started to open but out of the corner of Angelo's eye he could see the copywriter give a quick shake of his head. Mike glanced back at Angelo. He nodded his agreement.

"Good. I expect to see something new in forty-eight hours."

Again the man's mouth opened but nothing came out. His lips pressed together, and he nodded. Now if only Angelo could handle his little sister in the same no-nonsense manner. He liked when things were easy and uncomplicated.

But now, with time to cool down, he realized that his only course of action was to return home—to return to Italy. His gut knotted as he thought of the expectations that he'd failed to fulfill. Back in Monte Calanetti he wasn't viewed as someone successful—someone influential. Back home he was Giovanni's son—the son who'd fled his family and their way of life, unlike his younger brother who took great pride in their heritage.

With the meeting concluded, Angelo made his way back to his office. With the decision made to leave first thing in the morning, he had to figure out how to handle his current workload. His clients would never accept having their accounts turned over to anyone else. They paid top dollar for one-on-one attention, and they would accept nothing less.

In order for him to stay on top of everything while traveling abroad, he needed someone who was good in a crisis, levelheaded and an independent worker. Kayla's beautiful face immediately sprang to mind. Could she be the answer?

He hesitated. She did have a habit of being a bit too chatty at times. But this was an emergency. Allowances would have to be made.

More importantly, he was impressed with her work ethic and her attention to details. She was hungry and eager—two elements that would serve her well. And best of all, she had an easy way with people—something that might come in handy on this trip.

He stopped next to her desk. "Ms. Hill." She glanced up. Her green eyes widened. How had he missed their striking shade of jade until now? He cleared his throat, focusing back on the business at hand. "How's the Van Holsen account coming?"

Color pinked her cheeks. "Mr. Amatucci, I… I haven't gotten to it yet. The phone has been ringing and I've been sending out information for some other accounts."

She looked worried as though she'd done something wrong. For the first time, Angelo wondered if everyone who worked for him was intimidated by him. He didn't like the thought of Ms. Hill being uncomfortable around him. He knew he wasn't an easy man to get to know, but he didn't like the thought of striking fear in the hearts of his employees.

"Relax. That's fine. Besides you'll have plenty of time to brainstorm on the flight."

"Excuse me. The flight?"

Since when did he speak without thinking it through first? It had to be this mess with Marianna. It had him off-kilter. "Something urgent has come up. I need to travel to Italy. And I need a competent person to accompany me."

"Me?" Excitement lit up her whole face. Before today, he'd never noticed that behind those black-rimmed reading glasses were not only mesmerizing green eyes but also a beautiful face—not that he was interested in her, or anyone. Ms. Hill clasped her hands together. "I've never been to Italy. I'd love it."

"Good. That's what I was hoping you'd say." But suddenly he wasn't sure spending so much time alone with her was such a good idea, especially now that he'd noticed the unique color of her mesmerizing eyes and her intoxicating scent. He swallowed hard. But it was too late to back out now. "You need to understand this trip will be business only, not a holiday."

"Understood."

"If you go, you'll need to be committed to your work 24/7. We can't afford to miss any deadlines. Is that acceptable?"

She hesitated and, for a moment, he worried that she would back out.

But then Ms. Hill's head bobbed. "I can do it."

"Make sure you are ready to go first thing in the morning."

"As in tomorrow morning?"

He nodded. "And expect to be gone for at least a week—

maybe two." Her mouth gaped and her eyes widened. It was obvious that he'd caught her off guard. But she wasn't the only one to be surprised today—by so many things.

When he'd approved her transfer to be his temporary PA, he'd made it perfectly clear that he demanded 100 percent focus and commitment from his employees. It was that extra push and attention to detail that put Amatucci & Associates head and shoulders above the competition.

If you wanted to be the best, you had to give it your all. And that is what he expected from all of his employees, even if it meant dropping family, hobbies and extracurricular activities in order to focus on the job. What he was asking of Kayla was no different than he'd ask of anyone.

When she didn't jump to accept his offer, he had no patience to wait for an answer. "That won't be a problem, will it?"

From the little he knew about his assistant, she didn't have a family. At least not in the city. And he hadn't seen or heard any hints of a man in her life. Maybe she was more like him than he'd originally thought.

Or was there something else bothering her? Was it the incident with the perfume? Perhaps that hadn't been one of his better moves. He was used to following his instincts when it came to his creative process, but there was something about his assistant that had him leaning a little closer to her slender neck and, for the briefest second, he'd forgotten the reason. His mind had spiraled in a totally inappropriate direction. That wouldn't happen again. He'd see to it.

After all, she wasn't his type. Her nondescript business suits, the way she pulled back her hair and the way she hid her luminous green eyes behind a pair of black-rimmed glasses gave off a very prim, old-fashioned persona. So why was he letting one unexplainable moment bother him?

"I could make arrangements to go, but I have so much work to do on the Van Holsen account—"

"If that's your only objection, then don't worry. The account can wait one day. In fact, take the rest of the day off. I expect to see you at the airport at 6:00 a.m.. Unless you'd like me to pick you up on the way."

"Uh, no." She shook her head vehemently. "I'll find my own way there."

He felt a bit obligated. He was, after all, asking her to drop everything on a moment's notice to help him out. He needed to make a concerted effort to be a little friendlier. "Are you sure? It's really no problem to swing by your place."

"You don't even know where I live."

"True. But since you're going out of your way to help me, I wouldn't mind going out of my way for you."

"Thank you. I appreciate it." She smiled, easing the stress lines from around her mouth.

Angelo found his attention straying to her kissable lips coated with a shimmery light pink gloss. Okay, so not every aspect of her was prim and proper. A fantasy of her pulling off her glasses and letting down her hair played in his mind. Realizing the direction of his wayward thoughts, he halted them.

With effort, his gaze rose over the light splattering of freckles on her pert nose to her intense green eyes. How had he failed to notice her beauty up until today? Had he been that absorbed in his work that he'd failed to see what was standing right in front of him?

He cleared his throat. "I'll pick you up at say five-thirty?"

"Mr. Amatucci—"

"If we're going to travel together, we should at least be on a first name basis. Please, call me Angelo." Now where in the world had that come from? He made a point of keeping his distance from his employees. But then again, he was taking her home with him, where she would meet his family, and that broke all of his professional rules. He reconciled himself with the fact that Kayla's time working for him was limited—soon his regular PA would be back. So maybe he could afford to bend the rules a bit.

"And please call me Kayla." She smiled again, and this time it reached her eyes, making them sparkle like fine jewels.

"We're going to my home in Italy. It's a small village in the Tuscany countryside—Monte Calanetti."

"I'm afraid I've never heard of it, but then again, I've never had the opportunity to travel abroad. Is it big? The village that is?"

He shook his head. "The last time I saw it— granted it has been quite a while—but it was as if time had passed it by. It is rather small and quaint. It is entirely a different world from New York City. Now, are you still interested in going?"

She hesitated and he worried that he'd have to come up with an alternate plan. As of right now, he didn't have one. He needed someone who was familiar with his accounts and wouldn't need a bunch of hand-holding. Kayla was his only viable option. He wasn't one to beg, but at this particular moment he was giving it serious consideration.

Her dimpled chin tilted up. "Yes, I am. It sounds like it'll be a great adventure."

"I don't know about that. The reason I'm going there isn't exactly pleasant, but then again, that isn't for you to worry about. You need to go home and pack."

"Okay. But what should I plan on wearing for the trip? Business attire?"

"Definitely something more casual. There won't be any business meetings, so use your best judgment." He had no doubt her casual attire was as dull and drab as her suits. Not that it mattered to him what she wore so long as she was ready to work.

Kayla gathered her things, and then paused. "Before I leave, should I make plane reservations?"

He shook his head. "No need. We'll take my private jet."

Her pink lips formed an O but nothing came out. And for a moment, he let himself wonder what it'd be like to kiss those full, tempting lips. Not that he would, but he could imagine that one kiss just wouldn't be enough. Something told him that lurking beneath that proper and congenial surface was a passionate woman—

Again, he drew his thoughts up short. The last thing he needed was to notice her feminine qualities. He wasn't about to mix business with pleasure. No way.

CHAPTER THREE

FLUFFY CLOUDS FLOATED past the jet's windows.

They'd soon be touching down in Italy.

A giddy excitement bubbled up in Kayla's chest as she glanced across the aisle at Mr. Amatucci—er—Angelo. She still had a problem remembering to call him by his given name after referring to him as Mr. Amatucci for so long. Being on a first-name basis left her feeling unsettled—not exactly sure how to act around him. If anything, Angelo was even more quiet and reserved than before. Had he sensed her attraction to him?

Impossible. She hadn't said or done anything to betray herself. She smoothed a hand over her gray skirt. She was worrying for nothing.

Just act normal.

She glanced at her boss. "Do you know how long until we arrive?"

Angelo turned in his leather seat to look at her. "What did you say?"

"I was wondering how long we have until we land in Italy."

"Not much longer." His dark gaze dipped to the pen and paper in her lap. "Are you working?"

"I am." Her body tensed as she read over her scribbled notes for the Van Holsen account. She didn't have anything innovative enough to measure up to the Amatucci standard. "I thought this would be a good time to flesh out some ideas."

"And you like doing it longhand?"

"I think better that way." She'd never really taken the time to consider her creative process, but yes, now that she thought about it, she did always start with pen and paper. She didn't move to the computer until she had a fully functioning idea.

"Is that for the Van Holsen account?"

"Yes, I've been doing what you suggested and going with a nostalgic appeal."

"Good. Can I see what you've come up with so far?"

She glanced down at all of her scribbles and half thoughts. And then her eyes caught sight of his name scrolled out in cursive. Her heart clenched. *What in the world?*

She must have done it while she'd been deep in thought. Immediately, her pen started crossing it out. The last thing she needed was for her boss to think she had a crush on him. That would be the end of her career.

"I… I don't exactly have anything solid yet." She was going to have to be careful in the future of what she wrote down just in case Mr. Curious decided to peer over her shoulder.

"I could help you. Let me see what you have." He held out his hand.

She really didn't want to hand over her notepad, but what choice did she have if she wanted to stay in his good graces? She glanced down at the scratched-out spot and squinted. She could still see his name—all fourteen letters. But that was because she knew it was there. She ran the pen over it a few more times.

With great hesitation, she handed over the legal pad. Angelo's acute gaze skimmed over the page. Her palms grew moist. He took his time reading, but he paused as he reached the bottom. That was where she'd vigorously scratched out his name, almost wearing a hole in the page.

"I'm guessing that you've ruled out this idea?" He gestured to the blob of ink.

"Most definitely. It wouldn't have worked."

"Are you sure? Maybe you should tell me what it was,

and then we can see if there's any value in pursuing it?" He sent her an expectant look.

"Honestly, it's not worth the effort. I was totally off the mark with it." A man like Angelo, who could have a gorgeous model or movie star on each arm, would never be interested in someone as plain and boring as herself.

He let the subject go and turned back to her notes while she sat there realizing just how "off the mark" her imagination had wandered. No way was she going down that romantic path again, even if it was paved with rose petals. All it'd do was lead her into making a commitment—having a family—everything she'd left behind in Paradise. She wanted to be different—she wanted to be professionally successful. She needed to show everyone back in her hometown that she'd made her dreams come true.

And then Angelo's gaze lifted to meet hers. She should glance away but the intensity of his gaze held her captive. Her heart raced. He didn't say anything, which was just as well, because she doubted she could have strung two words together. Had he figured out what she'd scribbled on the page? *Please, not that.* But then again, he didn't look upset. Instead, he looked like—like what? The breath hitched in her throat. Was he interested in her?

He glanced away and shook his head. "Sorry about that. Something you wrote down gave me an idea for the campaign, but then it slipped away."

Silly girl. What made her think he'd ever look at her that way? And why would she want him to? It'd be the beginning of the end of her rising career—her dream.

Get a grip, Kayla.

"No problem." She held out her hand, willing it not to shake. "If you let me have the pad back, I'll work on getting my thoughts more organized. Maybe we can discuss them as soon as we get situated in Italy." She wasn't quite sure where their accommodations would be since Angelo had personally handled the travel arrangements, but she was certain they would be nice.

"Sounds good. Just because we're out of town doesn't mean we should fall behind on our work. I don't plan to be here long—just long enough to take care of some personal business. If we're lucky, perhaps I can wrap it up in a day or two."

What had happened to a week—maybe two? Disappointment assailed her. But it would be for the best. After all, it'd get her home sooner to make sure the ICL fund-raiser was moving along without too many snags. But she still couldn't shake the disappointment.

He'd missed this.

Angelo maneuvered the low-slung sports car over the windy roads of the Tuscany hillside toward his home in Monte Calanetti. He was grateful to be behind the wheel. It helped to center his thoughts. On the plane, he'd noticed his assistant in the most unexpected way. With her peaches-and-cream complexion, he'd been tempted to reach out and caress her smooth skin. But it was her green, almost-jade eyes that sparkled and hinted at so much more depth to the woman than he already knew—or would expect to know. The last thing he needed to do was get distracted by his assistant.

Actually, now that he'd noticed her—really noticed her—it was getting harder and harder to keep his mind on business around her. Perhaps bringing her on this trip wasn't his best decision, after all, but it was a necessity. He needed her help. He assured himself that, in the end, it would all work out as long as he stayed focused on the business at hand.

Thankfully, Kayla was just temporary help until his assistant returned from maternity leave. Then life would get back to normal. As far as he was concerned, that wouldn't be soon enough.

"This is wonderful."

The sound of Kayla's excited voice drew him out of his thoughts. He took his eyes off the roadway for just a moment to investigate what she found so fascinating, but he only saw vegetation. "Sorry. I missed it."

"No, you didn't. It's this. The long grass and the trees lining the roadway. It's beautiful."

What? The woman had never been outside of the city? He supposed that was possible. He honestly didn't know much about her other than her excellent work ethic. That, in and of itself, would normally be enough for him, but since they were traveling together, what would it hurt to know a little more?

"Is this your first time outside New York City?"

"I'm not a native New Yorker."

They had something else in common. Still, after all of those years living in New York, it was home to him now. He thrived on the constant energy that flowed through the city. He couldn't imagine living anywhere else. "Where does your family live?"

He could feel her curious gaze on him, but he didn't turn to her. "They live in a small town in Pennsylvania."

"So you really didn't move all that far from home."

"That's not what my parents think."

He glanced at her and saw she'd pressed her lips together in a firm line. Something told him that she hadn't meant to share that bit of information. But why? What else was she holding back?

"Your parents aren't crazy about the big-city life?"

There was a moment of hesitation as though she were trying to figure out how to answer him. "It's not New York so much as the fact that I'm not in Paradise anymore. They had my whole life planned out for me, but I rejected it."

"You must have had one of those chopper mothers I've heard about."

Kayla laughed. The sound was melodious and endearing. In that moment, he realized that he'd never heard her laugh before. He really liked it and hoped she'd do it more often, but for the life of him, he had no idea what he'd said to cause such a reaction.

"Do you mean a helicopter mom?"

He shrugged. "I guess. I knew it was something like that."

"My mom wasn't too bad. I know friends that had mothers who were much more controlling. But my mom is pretty good."

Wait. Something wasn't adding up. He pulled to a stop at an intersection. If he went straight ahead, it'd lead them up the hill to the village. But if he veered to the right, it'd take them to Nico's boutique vineyard—their childhood home.

Checking the rearview mirror and finding no traffic behind them, he paused and turned to her. "So if your mother is so great, why did you flee to the big city?"

Kayla shifted in her seat as though she were uncomfortable—or was it that he was digging too deep into personal territory? He knew what that was like—wanting to keep a firm lid on the past. But he couldn't help himself. There was just something about Kayla that intrigued him—and it went much deeper than her beauty. He was genuinely interested in her as a person.

Her voice was soft when she spoke, and he strained to hear. "I didn't live up to my parents' expectations."

That was so hard to believe. He was a very particular employer, and Kayla lived up to and in some areas exceeded his expectations. "Do they know what a wonderful job you've done at Amatucci & Associates?"

Her gaze widened. "You really think so?"

Angelo didn't realize he'd kept his approval of her work under wraps. Then again, he wasn't the sort of man to go on about someone's performance. Yet, in this moment, something told him that Kayla really needed to hear his evaluation of her performance.

"I think you've done an excellent job—"

"You do?" She smiled brightly and practically bounced in her seat before clasping her hands together.

"I do—"

A horn beeped behind them.

The interruption was a welcome one. This conversation was getting a little too emotional for his comfort. He thought for a moment that in her glee she might throw her arms around him. He didn't do hugs—no way—and certainly not with an employee. He couldn't—wouldn't—let the lines between them blur.

Angelo eased the car forward, focusing once again on the road and his destination. He urged himself to ignore the funny feeling Kayla's obvious excitement had given him. He trained his thoughts on the scene he'd be walking into at the vineyard. His fingers tightened on the black leather steering wheel.

On second thought, maybe he should have dropped Kayla off at the hotel before venturing out here. But he hadn't exactly been thinking straight—not since Nico had dropped the bombshell that their little sister was about to have a baby. Angelo was about to become an uncle. He wasn't sure how he felt about that. He'd worked so hard to distance himself from his family—from his emotionally charged parents and their chaotic marriage. But now that they'd moved, what excuse did he have to stay away from his birthplace—the home of his brother and sister?

"Is this the way to the village?" Kayla sat up a little straighter.

"No, this is the way to my brother's vineyard."

"Oh, how exciting. I've never visited a vineyard. I can't wait to see it. I bet it's beautiful like those magazine photos. Will we be staying there?"

"No." Angelo's tone was brusquer than he'd intended, but her endless chatter combined with his pending reunion had him on edge.

He chanced a glance her way and found her eyes had widened in surprise. He couldn't blame her, but how did he explain his family dynamics to her? Then again, why did he feel a need to explain his family at all?

"It'll be best if we stay at a hotel in the village. I'm not sure if the internet at the vineyard has been updated." There, that sounded like a valid reason for them to have some space between him and his siblings.

"Oh, I hadn't thought about that. I know the Van Holsen account needs to be updated as soon as possible. I already contacted the art department and let them know that a whole new strategy will be coming their way."

"Good. I want everything to move ahead without delay."

Whether he liked it or not, he'd been right to bring Kayla along on this trip. She was efficient and quite good at her job. Now, if only he could be just as professional and keep his mind from meandering into dangerous territory. However, the more time he spent around her, the more he found himself being anything but professional.

CHAPTER FOUR

THE CAR TURNED to the right and lurched forward. Kayla grabbed for the door handle. She had no idea that the vineyard would be so far out in the country, but then again, this was her first trip to Italy. In fact, other than one business trip to Canada, this was her first expedition out of the country.

"Welcome to Calanetti Vineyard."

Kayla glanced around, taking in the neat lines of grapevines. "Does all of this belong to your brother?"

"No. His vineyard is just a small portion of this land, but he produces some of the highest quality wine in the country."

"And you grew up here?"

"I did." Angelo pulled the car to a stop in front of a two-story villa. The home featured earth tones that blended in well with the land. "My brother will be expecting us. I phoned him from the airport."

As if on cue, the front door of the villa swung open and a man stepped out. Kayla did a double take—it was like looking at a slightly younger version of Angelo. The man approached the car wearing an easy smile. His eyes were dark brown like his brother's, but there was an easiness in them. They were quite unlike Angelo's dark and mysterious eyes.

When Nico opened the car door for her and held out his hand, she accepted his offer. Then she noticed the biggest difference of all. Instead of her stomach quivering with nervous energy in response to Nico's touch, she had no reaction at all. What did that mean? How could two men who looked so much alike have her reacting in such opposite ways?

It had to be that Angelo was her boss. That must be it. There was simply no other reasonable explanation for the electric charge that Angelo gave her every time she felt his gaze on her or when their fingers brushed as they passed papers back and forth.

"Benvenuta." Nico's voice carried a thick, warm Italian accent. When she sent him a puzzled look, he smiled. *"Scusi.* Welcome."

She smiled back, immediately liking Angelo's brother. "I'm so glad to be here."

"My brother doesn't bring many visitors home. In fact, you are the first. You must be special—"

"Nico, this is my assistant." Angelo frowned at his sibling.

Nico's dark brows rose and then a knowing smile pulled at his lips. "I hope my brother doesn't work you too hard while you're in Italy. There's so much to see. I'd love to give you a tour of the vineyard—"

"She doesn't have time for that stuff. She's here to work." Any hint of the easiness Angelo had displayed in the car was gone—hidden behind an impenetrable wall. "Now where is Marianna?"

"I don't know."

"What? Didn't you tell her that I was on my way?"

"I did." Nico folded his arms over his broad chest and lifted his chin. "I think that's the reason she left so early this morning without even bothering to grab a bite to eat. I haven't seen her since, but then again, I haven't looked for her, either."

"You let her walk away—?"

"What did you want me to do? Lock her in her room?"

"Maybe if you'd have done that a while ago, we wouldn't be in this mess."

Nico's arms lowered and his shoulders straightened. "You're blaming me for this?"

Angelo's body visibly tensed. "Yes...no. If only I'd have known something was wrong, I could have..."

"Could have what?"

Kayla's gaze darted between the two men who glared at each other. It was time to do something and fast. "This certainly is a beautiful place you have here." She acted as though she were totally oblivious to the torrent of under-currents. "Angelo told me you produce some of the finest wine in Italy."

At last, the brothers quit glaring at each other. Nico turned to her. "My brother got that much right. I'd be happy if you'd sample some while you're here."

"I'd be honored."

This palpable tension certainly wasn't what she'd been expecting for a family reunion, but then again, after over-hearing the heated conversation when Nico had phoned the office, she shouldn't be too surprised. She turned her atten-tion to her always-in-control boss, who looked as though he was about to lose his cool edge and have a meltdown. *Intriguing.* There was definitely a lot more to him than what she'd witnessed so far.

"I should have come back before now." There was a weary, pained toned to Angelo's voice. "I let the past keep me away."

Nico turned back to his sibling. "What happened to you was a long time ago. It wasn't right, but a lot has changed since then. You no longer have an excuse to stay away."

"But I still have a company to run. I don't have time to drop everything and travel halfway around the globe to check up on things. As far as I knew, everything was all right."

"Maybe if you didn't work all the time and bothered to call occasionally, you'd know how things were going around here."

Questions crowded into Kayla's mind—questions that were absolutely none of her business. But that didn't stop her from wondering what had happened to drive Angelo away from his family. He obviously loved them or he wouldn't have let his cool composure slide. And what caused him to keep his emotions under lock and key in the first place?

Angelo raked his fingers through his hair. "Maybe I should have called more."

"Yes, you should have."

The thud of a door slamming shut punctuated Nico's words. Kayla hesitantly glanced off in the distance as a young woman marched toward them. Her brown hair was wild and curly as it fluttered in the breeze. Her lips pressed into a firm line and her eyes narrowed in on the two men. This must be Marianna.

"Enough!" The woman came to a stop between Angelo and Nico. "You two are being ridiculous. Anytime you both want to quit with the overprotective-brother routine, we can talk."

Though she was at least a foot shorter than her brothers, Marianna certainly didn't hesitate to step between them. Something told Kayla that little sister wasn't a shrinking violet with these two as her brothers. She'd definitely have to be strong-willed. Silently Kayla cheered her on.

Angelo's broad chest puffed up before he sighed. When he spoke, his voice was much gentler. "Marianna, if only I'd known—"

"Stop." The young woman pressed her hands to her hips and pulled back her slender shoulders. "Neither of you are to blame for my choices."

Angelo's brows drew together in a formidable line. "But—"

"I'm not done." Her shoulders remained ramrod straight. "I'm a grown woman, if you hadn't noticed. But then again, you've been off in the States and missed the fact that I've grown up. Maybe if you'd spent more time here, you'd have realized this."

Kayla's heart went out to Angelo. He'd obviously made mistakes where his family was concerned, and they weren't shy about calling him out on it. In his eyes, she could see pain and regret. Beneath his hard, protective shell lurked a vulnerable man.

Angelo's stance eased and his head lowered. "I know I should have been here for you—"

"No. This isn't what I want." Marianna shook her head, sending her hair flying. "I don't need you feeling guilty. I need you to understand that I can make my own decisions."

"See, I told you," Nico piped in. "Trying to deal with her isn't as easy as it sounds."

Angelo turned to his brother. "Maybe if you'd have told me sooner—"

Nico's dark brows drew together in a formidable line. "Told you—I tried calling you but I always got your voice mail. And you didn't call back."

"I... I was getting around to it."

Nico shook his head in disbelief. "I'm glad to know where I fit on your list of priorities."

"You don't understand." Angelo rubbed the back of his neck. "You don't know what it's like to have a lot of people relying on you to produce cutting-edge promotions and other people looking to you for a paycheck. It's not as easy as it sounds to run a successful company."

Nico expelled a disgusted sigh. "And you think turning this place into a renowned boutique vineyard has been easy? Yet I still found time to call you."

"Your message never said it was important."

"Stop!" Marianna pushed Angelo back. "You aren't helping anything by coming here and fighting with Nico."

Angelo took a deep breath and blew it out. "I know I wasn't here when you needed me, but I'm here now. Let me help."

Kayla watched all of this in utter amazement. She never would have guessed her boss was capable of such a wide range of emotions. So then why did he strive at the office for such an unflappable persona? What was she missing?

Kayla was about to introduce herself to Marianna, when the young woman stared up at Angelo and said, "And I wish you weren't here now. Not like this. Not with all of the fighting." When Angelo's brows rose and his mouth opened but nothing came out, Marianna added, "I don't want to play referee." Her hand moved protectively to her still-flat stomach. "It isn't good for the baby."

Angelo and Nico looked at each other as though neither had considered how their fighting would stress their sister—their pregnant sister.

Marianna moved to look at both of her brothers. "I'm fully capable of taking care of myself."

Nico rolled his eyes. Angelo crossed his arms but refrained from saying anything.

"I hope you'll both give me some space."

Angelo's brows rose. "But first, we want to know the name of the father."

"That's none of your business."

Nico stepped forward. "It is our business if he thinks he's going to get our sister pregnant and then just walk away."

Marianna's face filled with color.

Angelo pressed his hands to his sides. "We deserve the right to speak to this guy. He needs to know that we expect him to step up and do his part—"

"And I expect you both to mind your own business." Marianna started for the house.

Enough was enough. The time had come to make a hasty exit. It was obvious that Marianna was in over her head and that her brothers were only making the situation worse.

When Angelo turned to follow his sister, Kayla moved swiftly in front of him. "I'm not feeling so good." It wasn't totally a lie—her stomach was in knots watching the Amatucci siblings squabble. "Could you take me to the hotel?"

Angelo's worried gaze moved from her to his sister to her. "Sure." He turned to Nico. "We need to talk more."

"I figured as much."

"I'll be back after we get settled."

Nico shrugged. "I'll be here. I can't speak for Marianna."

"I don't think she needs anyone to speak for her. She certainly does have a mind of her own. Even if it gets her in trouble."

"She always was strong-willed. I think she's a lot like Mama."

"Agreed."

At last the two had something they agreed on—their little sister's character. And now that things were on a good note, it was definitely time to say goodbye.

Kayla cleared her throat, hoping to gain Angelo's attention. When he didn't turn her way, she proceeded to say, "Angelo, are you ready to go?"

She'd have rather had a tour of the vineyard and stretched her legs, but not under these strained circumstances. She couldn't help but wonder if it was the situation with their sister that had them at odds or if they had a history of not getting along.

Angelo glanced her way. "It was a long trip. I suppose you would like to lie down for a bit."

"That would be nice." She turned to Nico, who was still eyeing his brother with obvious agitation. "It was so nice to meet you. I hope that we'll see each other again."

"I suppose that'll depend on my brother and whether he trusts you with me—"

"Nico. Enough." Angelo's voice held an obvious note of warning. "We'll be staying at the Hotel Villa Bellezza. If Marianna cools down, phone me."

Angelo quietly followed her to the car and opened the door for her. "I'm sorry you had to witness that."

"Don't be." She searched for words of comfort. "Families are messy. It's what happens when people love each other. And I saw a lot of love back there."

"You did?"

"Most definitely." She stepped past him and got in the car.

She'd never met anyone who could get under her boss's skin like Nico. The man appeared to have needling his big brother down to a fine art. There was so much more to the polished, successful businessman standing next to her than she'd ever imagined. And she was anxious to know more.

CHAPTER FIVE

KAYLA GRIPPED THE armrest tightly.

The line of cypress trees was no more than a blur as Angelo accelerated away from the vineyard. He didn't say a word as they zigzagged through the valley before starting their ascent up a hillside. The vegetation was so green and lush that she couldn't imagine there was a village, much less a five-star hotel, within miles of here.

"I need to apologize." Angelo's voice broke the awkward silence. "I didn't mean to have you witness our family drama."

"It's okay. I know how families can be." She couldn't help but want to know more about him and his family. "Your parents, do they live around here?"

He shook his head, keeping his eyes on the road. "They left the vineyard to us kids and moved to Milan. It was best for everyone."

Kayla wasn't sure what to say to that. Obviously there wasn't a close relationship between him and his parents. Did she even want to know why? It'd just move them further from boss and employee and into a new relationship— one that she didn't want to examine too closely.

Angelo downshifted for a curve. "I know that you come from a close-knit family, so it'd be hard for you to understand a family that functions better apart than together."

Kayla was surprised that he kept talking about his private life when she hadn't even asked him anything. It was as if these thoughts were pent up inside him, and he needed to get them out if he was to have any peace.

She searched frantically for words of comfort. "Every family is different. Not better. Not worse. Just different."

"But this is my fault." His palm smacked the steering wheel. "I shouldn't have left for New York to go to college. I should have found a way to stay here. Marianna was so young when I left, and my parents—well, they were so consumed with each other that they didn't have time to worry about anyone else."

"I'm sure they did their best."

He shook his head. "You don't know my parents. They are the most passionate people I know. And not in a good way. One minute they love each other and the next they are getting divorced. That's the end. They never want to see each other again. To say our childhoods were unstable is putting it mildly."

Kayla struggled to keep her mouth from gaping open. Her parents were the most mild-mannered couple. Their voices were rarely raised to each other, and they still gazed lovingly at each other like a couple of starstruck teenagers. Kayla knew they wanted her to experience the same sort of love and happiness. That's why she didn't hold it against them for trying to guide her life. It's just that she was different. There was so much more to life than love, marriage and babies. And she wanted to experience all of it.

Angelo cleared his throat, but his voice still rumbled with emotion. "I just couldn't take any more of their fighting and making up. It was so unnerving to never know if my parents were passionately in love or on the verge of calling their divorce attorneys. And there was no way I could take Nico with me—not that he'd have gone. He has this unbreakable tie to the vineyard—to the village. He never would have done what I did. And maybe he's right. Maybe if I'd stayed then Marianna wouldn't be alone and having a baby."

"It's not your fault." Kayla resisted the urge to reach out to him. "Your sister is a grown woman. She has to be allowed to make her own choices. Right or wrong. You couldn't have prevented this."

"But maybe if I'd been here, she'd have felt like she still had a family that loves her. Then she wouldn't have taken off on this trip of hers only to let some smooth-talking guy take advantage of her." Angelo's body noticeably stiffened.

"I'm fairly certain that no one could take advantage of your sister. She seems quite strong, like her brothers. She just needs some time to sort things out."

He sighed. "I'm sure she's plenty confused. And I suppose Nico and I did nothing to help by arguing. It's just that every time my brother and I get together, we disagree. We are very different. That's why I reserved us a suite at the hotel. I knew staying at the vineyard would just lead to more drama, and that's the last thing any of us need."

"But you two didn't argue at the end."

"That's because we both agree that Marianna needs both of us—whether she likes it or not."

"Good. Maybe you can build on that."

"Perhaps."

She decided that enough had been said for now on that subject. Angelo needed time to calm down. "Is the hotel far from here?"

"No. It's just at the rise of the hill." His voice had returned to its normal reserved, unemotional tone.

"Really. I never would have guessed. I can't wait to see the village." But if Angelo was serious about this being a productive trip, she wasn't sure that she'd get to see much of Italy. The thought dampened her mood. "Do you think I'll have some time to look around the village?"

He glanced at her before turning back to the road. "There really isn't much to see."

She'd beg to differ with him. Everything about Italy was special for this American girl. This was the biggest adventure of her life. How could he think this place was anything but special?

"I… I've never been here before. I was just hoping to sneak in some sightseeing."

"As long as you get your work done, I don't care what you do with your free time."

Oh, good!

As the car climbed the hill, Angelo pulled to the side for an older truck that was barreling toward them. Once back on the road, the car's tire dropped into a rut and bounced Kayla. The seat belt restrained her, but her bare thigh brushed against his hand as it gripped the gearshift. Heat raced up her leg, under her skirt and set her whole body tingling.

"Sorry about that." He quickly moved his hand back to the steering wheel.

Had he noticed their touch? Had it affected him, too? Was that why he'd moved his hand? Or was she just being ridiculous? Definitely being ridiculous. She knew when men were interested in her, and Angelo certainly wasn't. A frown pulled at her lips.

So why then did it bother her? Sure, he was the most handsome man she'd ever laid eyes on. But, he was her boss—the key to her career. She wouldn't—she couldn't—let some ridiculous crush get in her way after everything she'd sacrificed to get here.

Time to think about something else.

"I didn't have time to do any research before we left New York. What should I see while I'm here?"

He shrugged. "Honestly, there's nothing special about Monte Calanetti. It's just small and old."

"I'm used to small towns. I grew up in one. And there's always something special about them."

He glanced her way and his dark brow rose. "What was special about your town?"

"A number of things." She wasn't sure that she wanted to delve into this subject with him. She'd finally got past her homesickness. The way she'd done that was by not thinking of her hometown and what made it special.

"Such as?"

She shook her head. "Never mind."

Before he could question her more, she spotted what she thought was the edge of Monte Calanetti. "Are we here?"

"We are."

She stared out the windshield, not exactly sure what to expect. There was a tall wall. As they eased past it she found rustic buildings of earth tones similar in color to Nico's villa. People stopped and glanced their way as though trying to figure out if they should know them.

As more and more people turned to stare, Kayla couldn't hold back her curiosity any longer. "Why are they staring?"

He shrugged. "It must be the car."

"The car?"

"Yeah, you know because it's a sports car. They probably don't see many around here."

"Oh." She glanced over at him. Was he sitting up a little straighter? And was his chin tilted just a little higher? *Interesting.* "The village looks quite intriguing. And small enough to explore on foot."

Angelo didn't say anything. He just kept driving. And sadly he didn't offer her a guided tour. She forced herself not to frown. Then again, why should he bend over backward for her? She was, after all, merely an employee. They weren't even friends. Though little by little, she was getting to know Angelo better and better. In fact, she'd learned more about him in the past forty-eight hours than she had in the past two months while working as his assistant.

The car slowed as they eased through a wrought iron gate and up the short paved drive to a two-story building. The outside was plain but there was an elegance in its simplicity. Beneath a black awning, a bronze plaque off to the side of the front door read: Hotel Villa Bellezza. The place looked old but well kept. It reminded her of maybe a duke's grand house. She couldn't wait to check out the inside.

A young man in a black uniform rushed outside and opened her door for her. He smiled at her before his gaze moved to Angelo. The smile dimmed. She had the feeling that the young man had jumped to the wrong conclusion—that she and Angelo were a couple, here for a romantic tryst. Nothing could be further from the truth. But for the first time, she imagined what it might be like if Angelo were to look at her as a woman—a woman he desired. The thought rolled around in her mind at a dizzying pace.

Angelo moved to her side and spoke softly in her ear. "Are you okay?"

His voice drew her from her thoughts. She swallowed and hoped she succeeded in composing herself. "Yes."

"Are you sure? You're a little pale."

She patted his arm, not a good move as her fingertips tingled where they made contact. "I'm fine. Honest."

Or she would be, once she quit fantasizing about her boss. He obviously wasn't attracted to her. He saw her as nothing more than his temporary assistant, and that's the way it'd have to remain if she hoped to convince him of her talents.

While Angelo took care of registering them, she took in her surroundings. The modest exterior had not prepared her for the beauty of the interior. The floor was gleaming marble while the walls and ceiling were masterpieces of art with ornate parquet. Kayla had to force her mouth to remain closed instead of gaping open. She'd never stayed anywhere so fancy.

She couldn't even imagine how much this visit would cost Angelo. And the fact that he could afford to stay in a place such as this without even batting an eye impressed her. They sure didn't have anything like this back in Paradise. Wait until she told her mother and father about this.

CHAPTER SIX

There was no time for fun and games.

Angelo didn't get to the top of his profession by taking time off. Now that they were settled into their suite and Kayla had rested for a bit, they needed to get back to work. As he waited for her to join him, he couldn't help but wonder what she made of his clash with his brother. He shouldn't have taken her to the vineyard. What had he been thinking?

Yet on the car ride here, she hadn't seemed to judge him. Instead, she'd acted as though she cared. It was as if she understood him. Her reaction surprised him. He wasn't used to letting people into his personal life. But from the moment he'd asked her to join him on this trip, the lines between personal and professional had become irrevocably blurred.

Kayla entered the common room between their bedrooms. Her auburn hair was loose and cascaded down past her shoulders. Her glasses were off and she was no longer wearing the drab gray business suit. Instead, she was wearing pink capris and a white cotton sleeveless top, which showed off her creamy shoulders and slender arms.

The breath hitched in his throat. Who was this gorgeous woman? And what had happened to his nondescript assistant?

"I hope you don't mind that I changed?"

Wow! All he could do was stare. It was as if she were some sort of butterfly who'd just emerged from a cocoon.

Kayla settled on the couch with her laptop. She gave him a strange look as though wondering why he had yet to say a word. The problem was he didn't know what to say. Ever since they'd left New York, the ground had been shifting under his feet. Now it was as though a fissure had opened up and he was teetering on the edge, scrambling not to get swallowed up.

She didn't appear to be too disturbed by his standoffishness, which was good. Before he took a seat anywhere near her, he had to get a hold on his rambling thoughts. Kayla wasn't just any woman. He couldn't indulge in a romantic romp with her, and then go about his life.

He was her boss and, more important, he couldn't afford to lose her because she was good—really good at her job. He'd already had ideas of promoting her, but he wasn't sure that she was ready to be advanced quite yet. He wanted to see how she handled the Van Holsen account, since he'd given her a lot of room to show him her stuff.

The tight muscles in his chest eased and he was able to breathe easier. Concentrating on work always relaxed him and put him back in his groove. Work was logical for the most part and it lacked emotions, again for the most part, depending on the client. But since he was the boss, he was able to hand off the more excitable clients to other account executives.

That was it. Focus on business and not on how appealing he found her. "How's the Van Holsen account coming?"

She glanced over the top of her laptop. "Thanks to your help, I think I've come up with some innovative ideas. Would you care to take a look?"

His gaze moved to the cushion next to her on the couch and his body tensed. He was being ridiculous. She wasn't the first beautiful woman that he'd been around. What in the world had got into him today? It had to be his return home. It had him feeling out of sorts.

Time to start acting like Angelo Amatucci, the man in charge. "Sure. I'll have a look."

He strode over to the couch and took a seat. Kayla handed over the laptop and their fingers brushed. Hers were soft, smooth and warm. A jolt of awareness zinged up his arm and the air hitched in his lungs. *Stay focused.* He didn't dare turn to look at her. Instead, he focused his gaze on the computer monitor.

He read over her ideas for the new fragrance campaign and was truly impressed. Not only had she taken his ideas and expanded upon them, but she'd also inserted some of her own. He loved her initiative. Kayla was exactly the kind of innovative person that he wanted at Amatucci & Associates. Talented people like Kayla were the assets that would keep his company one of the most sought-after advertising agencies in the world.

"This is really good." He turned to her. When her green gaze met his, the rest of his thoughts scattered.

"You really like it?"

He nodded. His line of vision momentarily dipped to her pink frosted lips before meeting her gaze again. He struggled for a nonchalant expression. "I think you've captured a touching nostalgic note with a forward-thinking view. This should capture both the new and old consumer."

Her tempting lips lifted into a broad smile that lit up her eyes. "Now we just have to hope the client will approve."

"I wouldn't worry about that. Send this along to the art department and have them start working on some mock-ups."

Her smile dimmed a bit. "You're sure about this?"

"Of course I am. Don't look so surprised. You don't think you got the position as my assistant just because you're beautiful, do you?"

Now why in the world had he gone and said that? But it was the truth. She was stunning. In fact, he was considering changing the dress code at the office. He really enjoyed this different look on her. Then again, if she looked this way in the office, he'd never get any work done.

Color bloomed on her creamy cheeks. "You think I'm beautiful?"

He stared back into her eyes longer than was necessary.

In that moment, his ability to speak intelligently was de-batable. He merely nodded.

"No man has ever called me that."

At last finding his voice, Angelo said, "I'm having a hard time believing that."

"Steven was more matter-of-fact and sparing on com-pliments. It wasn't that he was a bad man. In fact, it's quite the opposite. He was really good to me. He just wasn't good with flowery words."

"This Steven, he's from Paradise, too?"

She nodded. "High-school sweethearts."

"The man must need glasses badly to have missed your beauty. Both inside and out. Is he still your boyfriend?" Part of Angelo wanted her to say yes to put a swift end to this surreal moment, but a much stronger part wanted her to be free.

"We…we broke up before I moved to New York."

The field was wide-open. Exhilaration flooded through Angelo. His hand reached out, stroking the smooth, silky skin of her cheek. The backs of his fingers skimmed down over her jaw, and then his thumb ran over the plumpness of her bottom lip. Her sudden inhale drew air over his fingers.

In her eyes, he noted the flames of desire had been ig-nited. She wanted him as much as he wanted her. And in that moment, he didn't want to think—he just wanted to act. He wanted to forget everything and enjoy this moment with the girl with wavy red hair.

His heart pounded as he leaned forward. He needed her and her understanding ways more than he imagined possible. Their lips met. He was a man who knew what he wanted and he wanted Kayla. Yet he fought back the urge to let loose with his mounting need. Instead, his touch was tentative and gentle. He didn't want to do anything to scare her away—not now that he had her exactly where he wanted her.

Kayla's lips were rose-petal soft. And when she opened them up to him, a moan grew deep in his throat. She tasted sweet like chocolate. He'd never been a fan of candy until this moment. Now he couldn't get enough of her sugary sweetness.

His arms wrapped round her curvy form, pulling her close. The gentle scent of perfume wrapped around them— the teasing scent that he hadn't been able to forget since that day in the office. It was as though she'd cast some sort of magical spell over him.

In the next instant, his phone vibrated in his pocket, zapping him back to his senses. He pulled back and Kayla's confused gaze met his. He couldn't blame her. He was just as confused by what had happened.

He held up a finger to silence her inevitable questions— questions for which he had no answers. Because there was no way he was falling for her. Getting involved with her— with anyone—meant dealing with a bunch of messy emotions. The last thing in the world he wanted to do was end up like his parents. Just the memory of their turbulent life had Angelo immediately working to rebuild the wall between him and Kayla. He just couldn't—wouldn't—subject anyone to such miserable instability.

Angelo glanced down at the screen to see his brother's name pop up. Hopefully his sister had confessed all. Angelo couldn't wait to confront the man who'd walked away from his responsibilities.

Angelo lifted the phone to his ear. "Nico, do you have a name yet?"

There was a distinct sigh. "Is this how you answer your phone these days? Too important for a friendly greeting before diving into the heart of the matter?"

Angelo's back teeth ground together. He quickly counted to ten, okay maybe only to five, before addressing his sibling. "Hello, Nico. What did Marianna say?"

"Nothing."

He was losing his patience. "But why did you call?"

"You and Kayla need to return to the villa. Now. I'll explain everything when you both get here." The line went dead.

Angelo slipped the phone back into his pocket. He turned to Kayla, whose face was still filled with color. "We have to go."

"What happened?"

"I don't know. That was Nico and he summoned us back to the villa. It must be Marianna. I just pray there aren't complications with the baby." Before they left he needed to clear the air about their kiss that never should have happened. "Listen, about the kiss, I crossed a line. I... I don't know what I was thinking."

A myriad of expressions crossed over her face. "It's forgotten."

He didn't believe her. "Can we talk about it later?"

"I'd rather not. There's nothing to say. Besides, you have more important things to deal with." She jumped to her feet and moved away from him. "You should get going. I'll be fine here."

"Nico requested you, too." Angelo held back the startling fact that he'd feel better facing this crisis with her next to him.

Kayla pressed a hand to her chest. "But why me?"

"I don't know. But we have to go."

"Okay. Just let me grab my shoes and purse." She rushed back to her room.

Angelo got to his feet and paced back and forth. Of course he was worried about his sister, but there was something else fueling his inability to sit still—Kayla's off-the-cuff dismissal of his kiss.

The women he was used to spending time with never brushed off his advances, though each of them knew his rules in advance—nothing serious. So why did that rule not apply here? Probably because Kayla was off-limits. She was his assistant. He couldn't forget that going forward—no matter how much his personal life spun out of control while in Italy.

From this point forward, Kayla was off-limits.

CHAPTER SEVEN

HER THOUGHTS RACED so fast that it unsettled her stomach.

Kayla stared out of the passenger window as she clasped her hands tightly together. Angelo expertly guided the rented sports car along the narrow, tree-lined road. How in the world had she lost control of the situation?

She inwardly groaned. As fantastic as that kiss had been, it couldn't have come at a worse time. Angelo at last had noticed her work and complimented her professionally. And what did she turn around and do, stare at him like some lovesick teenager—encouraging him to kiss her.

Sure, she was wildly attracted to him. What woman with a pulse wasn't? He was gorgeous with that short, dark hair, olive skin and dark, sensual eyes. But he was her boss—the man in charge of her professional future—her dreams.

She couldn't afford any more blunders. She had to remain aloof but professional. Surely it wasn't too late to correct things between them. At least he hadn't mentioned anything about sending her back to New York on the next plane, but then again they'd rushed out of the hotel so quickly that he didn't have time to think of it. His thoughts were on his sister.

Kayla sure hoped there wasn't anything wrong with Marianna. This was the first time Kayla had ever witnessed Angelo visibly worried. He obviously cared a great deal for his family though he never let on at the office—when he was working he was 100 percent professional—

So then what happened back there at the hotel?

Angelo pulled the car to a skidding halt in front of the villa. Before she could summon an answer to that nagging question, Angelo had her car door opened. She would figure it out later. Right now, she would offer her support in whatever capacity to Angelo's family.

Nico rushed into the drive. "About time you got here."

"We came right away." Angelo frowned at his brother. "What's the matter with Marianna?"

"Marianna?" Nico's brows drew together in a questioning look. "This has nothing to do with our sister."

"Then why in the world did you have us rush over here?" Angelo's voice took on a sharp edge.

Kayla breathed a sigh of relief. She had no idea what Nico wanted, but she was fully relieved that mother and baby were okay. However, she did have to wonder why Nico wanted her here? Was he hoping that she'd play referee?

Nico's eyes opened wide and his face became animated. "You are never going to believe this—"

"I might if you'd get to the point."

Nico smiled in spite of his brother's obvious agitation. "What would you say if I told you that I was just approached by representatives of Halencia? Monte Calanetti has just made the short list of locations for the royal wedding of Prince Antonio and Christina Rose."

Angelo rolled his eyes. "Nico, this is no time for joking around—"

"I'm not. I'm perfectly serious."

Kayla's mouth gaped open. A royal wedding. Wow! She really was in Europe because nothing like this ever happened back in the States. Wait until she told her family. They would never believe it.

Her gaze moved to Angelo. He still wasn't smiling. In fact, he didn't look the least bit excited about this news. She had absolutely no ties to this village and she was over-the-moon happy for them. So why was he so reserved?

Angelo pressed his hands to his trim waist. "You called us back here to tell us this?"

"Brother, you're not understanding. The royal family of Halencia wants us to make a pitch as to why Monte Calanetti should be the location for the soon-to-be king and his intended bride's wedding."

"And?"

Nico shook his head. "What aren't you understanding? This is where you come in. You and Kayla. This is what you two do for a living—pitch ideas, convince people to go with the products you represent. That's what we need."

Nico wanted Angelo and her to help? Really? For a royal wedding?

The breath caught in her throat as she held back a squeal of excitement. If she'd ever wanted a chance to stand out and gain a promotion, this was a prime opportunity. Plus, it'd mean continuing to work with Angelo. But once they got back to New York, away from this romantic countryside, things would go back to normal. Wouldn't they?

Surely they would. This project was huge. It was amazing. An honest-to-goodness royal wedding. She didn't even know where they'd begin, but she couldn't contain her excitement. She'd show Angelo how good an ad executive she could be. Just wait and see.

Pitch a wedding to royalty?

Angelo had never done such a thing. Weddings weren't his thing. He knew nothing about love and romance. He was highly unqualified for this project. But he wasn't about to admit any of this to Nico. No way. So how was he supposed to get out of this?

Nico smiled as he led them straight through the modestly decorated villa that still looked much the same as it did when he'd been a child. Once everyone was situated on the veranda with cold drinks, Nico turned to him. "So what do you think?"

"About what?"

"You know, coming up with a pitch for the village?"

Angelo wanted to tell his brother that he was too busy and that he couldn't possibly fit it into his schedule. He highly doubted his brother would hear him. Nico had selective hearing when he wanted something bad enough—like Angelo being a silent investor in the vineyard.

Angelo turned to Kayla to see what she thought about the idea, hoping she'd make some excuse to get them out of this situation. But her green eyes sparkled with excitement. How wrong could he have been to look to her for support? Was there a woman alive who didn't get excited about weddings? Or was it the part about pitching it to a real-life prince that had caught her full attention?

Angelo's gut tightened when he thought of Kayla being starstruck over the royal prince. He shrugged off the uneasy sensation. It was none of his concern. Besides, it wasn't as if she was attracted to him. She couldn't dismiss their kiss fast enough.

His jaw tensed as he recalled how easily she'd brushed off their moment. He could have sworn she'd been as into him as he was into her. It just showed how little he understood women.

He drew up his thoughts, refusing to dwell on the subject. In the meantime, Kayla had engaged his brother in light conversation about the vineyard and how it'd been their childhood home. Angelo looked around the place and was truly impressed by what his brother had done to bring this place back to life. It looked so different than when they were kids, when the place was dying off.

Angelo had actually thought that his brother was crazy for wanting to devote his time and money into reviving the vineyard, but with Nico's determination, he'd made a go of the place. In fact, this boutique vineyard might not produce a large quantity of wine, but what it did produce was of the finest quality. Angelo kept his private wine collection stocked with it. Calanetti wines impressed a great number of influential guests that he'd entertained.

The chime of Kayla's laughter drew his thoughts back to the moment. Nico was entertaining her with a tale from when they were kids. As the oldest, Angelo had always been put in charge of his siblings while his parents went out. But this one time, Angelo hadn't been paying attention and they'd sneaked off. What Nico failed to add, and what he probably didn't know, was that had been one of Angelo's scariest moments—not knowing what had happened to his brother and sister.

"Are you telling them about the royal wedding?" Marianna joined them. Her face was a bit on the pale side and there were shadows beneath her eyes.

Nico leaned back in his chair. "I just told Angelo about it. He's thinking it over."

Marianna turned to Angelo. "You have to think it over? But why? This will be the biggest thing you've ever done."

"You really want me to do the pitch?"

She nodded. "Please. It would be so wonderful for everyone. Couldn't you just this once help your family?"

Guilt landed squarely on his shoulders with the force of a full wine barrel. He owed his brother and sister this. It'd put Monte Calanetti on the map. And the benefits the village would reap from the royal wedding taking place here were countless.

But he was already fully obligated. And he couldn't do it all on his own. He'd need help. A good copywriter. His gaze strayed to Kayla. He'd already witnessed just how talented she was with words and images. He could easily imagine her taking on some more of his workload, allowing him time to work on the wedding proposal.

They'd have to work closely together—closer than ever. There was no way he'd let her loose with the company's most important clients. But would they be able to manage it after the kiss?

"So what do you say, Angelo?" Nico looked at him. "The village is all abuzz with the news, and you know that pitching a wedding isn't my area of specialty."

"Please Angelo, will you do it?" Marianna looked at him, openly pleading with him with her eyes.

He'd never been good at telling her no. And now that she was standing there carrying some stranger's baby—some man that his sister wouldn't even introduce to their family—his resistance to her plea was nonexistent. If playing host to a royal wedding made her happy, how could he deny it to her? The decision for once was quite simple.

"Okay. I'll do it."

"You will?" The words echoed around the patio.

"Why does everyone sound so shocked? It'll be good publicity for the firm." But that wasn't his reason for agreeing—it was to see the smiles on the two women in his life... and his brother.

Marianna launched herself into his arms. Warmth swelled in his chest. He may not have been here to protect her and watch over her as he should have been, but at least he could give her something to look forward to while she sorted out the rest of her life.

Marianna pulled back and sent him a watery smile. "Thanks."

He turned to Kayla. She looked like an excited kid on Christmas Eve. "How about you? Are you up for taking on some more responsibility?"

Kayla didn't waste a moment before uttering, "Definitely. Just tell me what needs done."

"Good." He turned to his brother. "It looks like you've hired yourself a team. I'll get started on the pitch as soon as we get back to New York."

"New York?" Nico's brows gathered together.

"Yes, that's where we work. I'll send through what I come up with, but it's going to take me a little time. I have a rush project that I—we—have to wrap up—"

"This can't wait. You have to get started on it right away."

Angelo didn't like the worried tone of his brother's voice. "Why? What haven't you told us?"

Nico got to his feet. "Does anyone need anything else to drink?"

Angelo knew a stalling tactic when he saw one. "Nico, spit it out. What is the catch?"

After Nico finished refilling Kayla's iced tea, he turned to his brother. "The catch is the pitch has to be completed in no more than three weeks' time."

"Three weeks." Angelo leaned back in his chair. "You sure don't give a person much time."

"And—"

"There's more?"

Nico nodded. "The presentation has to be given to the royal family at the palace in Halencia."

Nico sank down into his chair while Angelo charged to his feet. "This changes everything. I wasn't planning to stay in Italy for three weeks. Nico, don't you understand? I have a business to run."

"You're the boss. Can't you put someone else in charge while you're here?"

Angelo never sloughed off his work on other people. He stayed on top of things. Some people called him a control freak. He considered it the only way to keep the company on track. "That's not the point. There are certain things only I can do."

"The point is that when we need you, you're never here." Nico got to his feet and faced him. "Why should I have thought this would be any different?"

His brother's words were pointed and needled at his guilt. "That's not fair. I've lent you money for the vineyard—"

"This isn't about you writing out a check. I'm talking about you personally investing yourself—your time—in something that's important to your family."

Angelo turned to Marianna, looking for support, but she moved to Nico's side. When he sought out Kayla, she was busy studying her iced tea glass with such intensity that it was as if she'd never seen glassware before. He was alone in this. He knew what he should do, but it was so hard to just hand over the reins of the company he'd built from the ground up.

Three weeks was a long time to be away. And yet it wasn't much time to create a compelling campaign for a wedding—a royal wedding. It had just started to sink in what a big deal this really was for his brother and sister, and the village, plus it would be amazing for his company— that is if they won the pitch.

Angelo raked his fingers through his hair. Letting go of the reins at Amatucci & Associates went against every business instinct. Yet, he couldn't turn his back on his siblings again. "Okay. I'll stay."

Marianna turned to Kayla. "Will you stay, too?"

"Yes, Kayla," Nico chimed in. "Will you help my brother? I get the feeling that he won't be able to do it without you."

Kayla's eyes flashed with surprise. "I don't know that I need to stay in Italy to do it."

"It'd be most convenient," Marianna pointed out. "I'm sure Angelo will need your input. After all, we're talking about a wedding. And my brothers, well, they aren't ex-actly romantic."

"Hey!" Nico and Angelo protested in unison.

Both women burst out in laughter. Angelo supposed the dig was worth it as his sister's face broke into a smile. And when he turned to Kayla, the happiness reflected in her eyes warmed a spot in his chest. She was a very beautiful woman. Why, oh, why did it have to be now when they were practically attached at the hip that he truly realized his attraction to her?

When she caught him staring, the breath hitched in his throat. He should glance away, but he couldn't. He was in awe of her. Was it being away from the office that had him more relaxed about the proper conduct between employer and employee? Nonsense. He knew what he was doing. He could keep this together.

He gazed directly at the woman who took up more and more of his thoughts. "Well, don't keep us in suspense. Will you remain in Italy and lend a hand?"

CHAPTER EIGHT

THIS WAS A very bad idea.

But it was so tempting. How could she let such a rare opportunity pass her by?

Kayla worried her bottom lip. Though she wouldn't be working directly on the royal wedding, she'd be close at hand. Perhaps she could add an idea here and there. Oh, what she wouldn't give to actually work on the project itself. Yet, she understood with the magnitude of a royal wedding that only the best of the best would work on the project, and that meant Angelo.

But she was needed back in New York. The ICL fundraiser was quickly approaching, and seeing as it was her idea—it was her responsibility to make sure it went off without a hitch. However, she had put Pam, an associate at the after-school program, in charge while she was gone. And how much could possibly go wrong in three weeks?

"Please say you'll stay." Marianna looked so hopeful. "I could use someone on my side against my brothers, who think they know everything."

That sold her. Marianna could definitely use some help keeping her brothers in line while she figured out her next move. "Okay, I'll stay."

Everyone smiled except Angelo.

Aside from the fund-raiser, there was nothing waiting for her back in New York, not even a goldfish. When she wasn't at the office, she was at the after-school program helping kids with their homework followed by a game of dodgeball or basketball or volleyball. She wasn't very good at any of the games, but she gave it her best effort.

For the moment, she was giving herself permission to

enjoy Italy before she set to work. And this was the perfect place to start. She'd love to see more of the vineyard, and it'd give Angelo some private time with his siblings.

"Would you mind if I had a look around the vineyard?" Kayla's gaze met Nico's.

"My apologies. I should have offered to give you a tour earlier. I've had other thoughts on my mind—" his gaze strayed to his sister and then back to her "—with uh…the royal wedding."

"That's okay. I totally understand." Kayla got to her feet. "I've never been to a vineyard before. I'll just show myself around."

"Nonsense. Angelo can give you the grand tour while I make some phone calls and spread the good news. And make sure he shows you the chapel." Nico turned a smile to Angelo. "You can handle that, can't you, brother?"

Angelo's jaw tightened, but he didn't argue. Kayla took that as progress between the brothers. Not wanting to give Angelo time to change his mind, she set off for the vines, hoping Angelo would follow.

He did, and he proved to be quite an insightful guide. He explained to her the difference between a larger vineyard and this boutique vineyard. While Nico produced fewer barrels of wine—less than five thousand cases a year—it was carefully processed to the highest quality with the least amount of oxidation.

As much as the history and current production of wine interested her, it was the bell tower in the distance that drew her attention. She headed for the weathered building that sat on the other side of the wall that lined the edge of the vineyard. "Is this the chapel your brother mentioned?"

"Yes. Nico and I explored it as kids. We considered it our castle. I was the king and Nico was the daring knight fighting off dragons." Angelo smiled at the long-forgotten memory.

"You and your brother must have had a lot of fun."

"Now that I think about it, we did have some good times."

She smiled. "This looks like a great place for an adventure. Can we go inside the chapel?"

"It's nothing you'd be interested in."

"Sure I would." Her steps grew quicker as she headed for the opening in the wall that led to the little chapel. Maybe this was her chance to let Angelo know that she'd be more than willing to help with the wedding pitch—in fact, this was the opportunity of a lifetime. Now, how did she broach the subject with Angelo?

She stopped next to the four steps that led to two tall, narrow wooden doors. It looked as though time had passed it by. Okay so it needed a little TLC, but it had a charm about it that transcended time. "Your brother is so lucky to have this piece of history on his land. Imagine all of the weddings and christenings that must have taken place here."

"Technically it's not on Nico's land." Angelo pointed over his shoulder to the wall. That divides the vineyard. The other side is Nico's."

"So who owns this land, then?"

"This is Palazzo di Comparino. Its owner, Signor Carlos Bartolini, recently passed away. From what I understand, there's a young woman staying there now."

"You know this chapel gives me an idea—it'd be perfect for the royal wedding."

"I don't know." Angelo rubbed his chin. "It needs work."

She pulled open one of the doors and peered inside at the rows of pews. The place was filled with dust and cobwebs. "It's nothing that can't be done rather easily." This was her chance to put herself out there. "You know I could help you with the pitch."

Angelo didn't immediately respond. The breath hitched in her throat as she waited—hoping that he'd latch on to her offer. The experience from working on such a prestigious project had immeasurable potential, from a promotion at Amatucci & Associates to making her résumé stand out—head and shoulders above the rest.

"I don't think so. You'll have enough to do with the other accounts that need looking after." The disappointment must have filtered across her face because his stance eased and his voice softened. "I appreciate the offer, but I don't want you getting overwhelmed."

It teetered on the tip of her tongue to ask him if this had anything to do with the kiss, but she hesitated. She couldn't bring herself to tarnish that moment. The memory of how his eyes had devoured her before his lips had claimed hers still made her heart race.

If it wasn't the kiss, why was he turning away her offer of help? Was it just as he said, not wanting to give her too much work? Or did he feel she wasn't up to the task of working on something so important?

With the wind temporarily knocked out of her sails, she turned back to the villa. She wasn't giving up. She would show Angelo that she was invaluable.

What was the problem?

Two days later, Angelo paced around the hotel suite. He needed a fresh approach to the wedding. It had to be something amazing—something unique to Monte Calanetti that would appeal to a prince and his intended bride. But what?

He was stuck. This had never happened to him before. He inwardly groaned as his mind drew a total blank. This was ridiculous. He clenched his hands into tight balls. He had absolutely nothing. And that was so not like him.

He liked to think outside the box. He liked to push boundaries and experiment, but all he could think of was why would anyone would want to get married in Monte Calanetti? What special qualities did they see in the village for it to make the royals' short list?

He poured himself a cup of the now-lukewarm coffee.

The silence of the suite was getting to him. Kayla had cleared out early that morning, claiming she wanted some fresh air while she worked on the mock-ups for the Van Holsen account and answered emails. She'd been great about taking on additional responsibilities, allowing him time to brainstorm. Not that it was helping him much.

In fact, she'd done such an exceptional job that maybe he should see what she could do with this wedding stuff. After all, she was a girl, and didn't they all dream about their weddings?

Suddenly the image of Kayla in a white dress formed in his mind. His body tensed. As quickly as the image came to him, he vanquished it. She'd be a beautiful bride, but for someone else. He wasn't getting married—ever.

Determined to stay on point and to get her input on the wedding, he headed downstairs to the pool area. He opened the door and stepped outside, momentarily blinded by the bright sunlight. Once his vision adjusted, he glanced around, quickly locating his assistant. She was at a shaded poolside table. She lifted her head and smiled, but it wasn't aimed at him.

She wasn't alone. A young man stood next to her table. Angelo's gut knotted. He told himself that it was because she was supposed to be working, not flirting. His only interest was in her getting her work done in a timely fashion. But as the chime of her laughter carried through the gentle breeze, Angelo's mouth pulled into a frown.

He strode toward the table. Kayla didn't even notice him approach as she was captivated by the young man.

Angelo cleared his throat. "Hello, Kayla."

Both heads turned his way. Kayla's eyes opened wide with surprise. The young man drew himself up to his full height as though he was about to defend his right to be flirting with Kayla. The guy had no idea that Angelo had no intention of challenging his right to gain Kayla's attention. After all, it would be for the best if she was interested in someone—as long as it wasn't him. But that would all have to wait, because right now she was on the clock. And he needed her help.

Angelo used his practiced professional voice, the one that let people know that he meant business. "How's the Van Holsen account coming?"

"Uh, good. Dino was just asking about the royal wedding."

"He was?" Angelo stepped between Kayla and the young man. "What do you want to know?"

The young man glanced down, not meeting Angelo's direct gaze. "I… I was just curious if the rumor was true that they might pick Monte Calanetti for the wedding."

"It is. Is there anything else?"

Dino shrugged his shoulders. "I guess not."

"Good. Kayla has work to do now. If you'll excuse us."

"Uh, sure." Dino leaned to the side to look at Kayla. "I'll see you around."

"Bye."

Angelo took a seat next to Kayla. "It seems you've found yourself an admirer."

"Who? Dino?" She shook her head. "He was just interested in what I knew about the royal wedding, which wasn't anything more than he's heard through the grapevine. How's the pitch for the wedding coming?"

"Good." *Liar.*

He wasn't about to admit that he, Angelo Amatucci, couldn't come up with a dynamic pitch that would turn the prince's and his bride's heads. No way. What would Kayla think of him? No. Scratch that. He didn't want to know what she'd think. She'd probably laugh at him.

"I'm glad to hear it's going well. I know that I'm not the only one who's anxious for the pitch. Imagine a royal wedding. The whole world will be watching it and you'll have played a big part in it."

"Not a big part."

"You're too modest. You're like the village hero now."

Just what he needed was more pressure. He swallowed down his uneasiness. "You're assuming that the prince will choose this village, and that's a big leap."

"But why wouldn't they pick Monte Calanetti? From the little I've seen, I think it's a lovely village."

"That's just because you didn't grow up here."

Her green eyes widened. "You really didn't like living here?"

He shook his head, but he wasn't going to get into the details of his childhood or his strained relationship with his parents. Kayla had already been privy to more about his private life than anyone else ever. But something told him that his family secrets were safe with her.

Not in the mood to talk anymore about this village or dwell on the fact that he'd wasted two days without coming up with anything striking or fascinating, he decided to turn the conversation around. "How is the work going?"

CHAPTER NINE

COULD SHE PRETEND she hadn't heard Angelo?

Kayla had spent a large chunk of time at this poolside table. With most of the guests either off sightseeing or attending other engagements, it was a peaceful place for her to jot out more ideas for the Van Holsen account. But after going back and forth between the art department and the very demanding client, they were still missing the mark.

It didn't help that her ideas for the Van Holsen account had stalled. For the past half hour or so, she'd been jotting out ideas for the fund-raiser back in New York. The event was their last hope to keep the after-school program going for so many at-risk kids and it was weighing heavy on her mind. There were still so many details to iron out.

And as exciting as it was to be working with Angelo Amatucci on what could be the project to catapult her career, she couldn't forget the children. They were relying on her to make their lives a little better by raising money to keep their facility open.

"Kayla, did you hear me?"

The sound of Angelo's voice startled her back to the here and now. "Sorry. I just had a thought."

"About the account?"

She nodded. "It's coming along."

"Why don't you tell me what you have so far and we can work on it together?"

She glanced down at her closed notebook. "That's okay. I know you have more important things to concentrate on. I've got this."

Angelo's dark brows drew together. "Listen, I know that

things haven't exactly been right between us since, well, you know…the kiss. If that's still bothering you—?"

"It's not." Yes, it was. But not the way he was thinking. The kiss had been better than she'd ever imagined. And she knew that it could never happen again. She had too much on the line to risk it all by fooling around with her boss.

The truth of the matter was the pad of paper also contained her thoughts for the benefit concert. Angelo had a strict policy about not taking on charity accounts—he believed there were too many good causes and not enough time to help them all. Kayla couldn't understand his stance, but then again she'd never been in charge of a large company. Maybe there was more to it than what she knew.

The one thing she did know was that she couldn't let Angelo find out that she was organizing a fund-raiser while on this trip. She didn't want him to have a reason not to consider her for a promotion or worse yet to have her replaced as his assistant. She wasn't sure how he would handle the situation. In all of her time at Amatucci & Associates, she'd never witnessed anyone going against company policy. Angelo was a man no one wanted to cross.

"I'm just jotting out some ideas. Nothing specific yet." She caught herself worrying her bottom lip, hoping he wouldn't take exception to her not coming up with something more concrete. After all, they were on a timetable and the clock was ticking. "I spent the morning on the phone with the art department and Mrs. Van Holsen—"

His brows drew together into a formidable line. "Why didn't you get me?"

"I… I didn't want to disturb you. I'm supposed to be here to lighten your load."

He shook his head. "I can't spend all of my time on one campaign. That isn't fair to the other clients. I have to stay on top of everything. Next time you speak with a client, I expect to be in on the call. Understood?"

"Yes."

He let the subject go as he continued on with some other business items. "By the way, while I was on the phone with the office I mentioned that we'd been unavoidably detained in Italy, but I didn't go into specifics. I don't want any rumors starting up that we put off longtime clients in favor of this royal wedding pitch. I won't risk my company's reputation for something that is never going to happen."

Kayla's mouth gaped before she caught it and forced her lips together. "Is that really what you think?"

He nodded. "Pretty much."

"But why?"

"Well, I can't see what a royal couple would find so endearing about Monte Calanetti. I think everyone, including my brother and sister, are getting worked up over something that will never happen."

"I don't understand. If that's truly what you think then why go to all of the bother to delay your return to New York and work on a campaign that you're certain will fail?"

He shrugged. "It's an obligation that I owe them." He raked his fingers through his hair. "I owe it to Nico and Marianna—you know, for skipping out on them. For letting them fend for themselves with parents who were more wrapped up in their marital drama than worrying about their children."

"I'm sorry—"

"Don't be. I didn't tell you any of that so you'd feel sorry for me. In fact, I don't know why I mentioned it at all."

"I'm glad you did. I'd like to think that we've become more than coworkers." When she met his drawn brows, she realized that she'd said more than she should have. "I… I don't mean about the kiss. I just thought we might be friends, too."

A wave of relief washed over his face easing the stress lines. "I would like that."

"You would?"

Slowly he nodded, and then a smile tugged at his lips. "Yes, I would."

She couldn't help but smile back. She noticed how the worry lines bracketing his eyes and mouth smoothed. She'd never seen him look so worried before. Why would that be? He was amazing at creating winning pitches. He was amazing in a lot of ways.

Realizing that she was staring, she turned away, but by then, her heart was beating faster than normal. Images of the kiss they'd shared clouded her mind. She'd tried to put it out of her head, but the memory kept her awake late into the night. What had it meant? Had it meant anything? Because there was no way that a wealthy, successful businessman who could have his choice of women would fall for his assistant.

Kayla reached for a tall, cool glass of iced tea. "Would you like something to drink? I could go and get you something."

"Thanks. But I'm all right." He looked at her as though studying her. "Can I ask what direction you think the wedding pitch should take?"

"Really?" She sat up straighter. "You want my input?"

He nodded. "I thought you might have some ideas that I hadn't thought of."

"I do…have ideas, that is." She struggled to gather her thoughts.

"I'm listening."

She'd done a lot of thinking about this—probably too much, considering she hadn't even been invited to help with the royal pitch until now. "I'm thinking that regardless of whether they go big or small, they're going to want elements that play into an elegant yet traditional event."

"That's true. If they wanted a contemporary feel, they certainly wouldn't come to Monte Calanetti." He rubbed the back of his neck.

"What's bothering you?"

"I'm just trying to figure out why this village made the short list for the royal wedding. I mean, there's nothing special here. I've gone round and round with this, but I still have no answer. It's not like it has amazing history like Rome or the heartbeat of the nation like Milan or the stunning architecture of Venice. This is a little, old village."

"And it's tripping you up when you're trying to come up with a unique pitch."

Angelo hesitated as though he wasn't sure whether or not to confide in her. Then he sighed. "Yes, it's giving me a bit of a problem. No matter which way I go at it, I just can't find that special quality that will put Monte Calanetti head and shoulders above the other locations."

Kayla smiled and shook her head. "You just don't see it because you take this place for granted. It's your home, but to outsiders, it's something special."

His gaze met hers. "You think it's special?"

She decided a neutral stance was best. "I haven't made up my mind yet."

"Then how can you tell me that I'm blind to what's in front of me when you haven't even made up your mind?" His voice held a disgruntled tone.

She smiled, liking the fact that she could get past his polished persona and make him feel real genuine emotions. "I mean that I need to see the village." When he opened his mouth to protest, she held up her hand, stopping him. "And driving straight through it to get to the hotel does not count. It was more of a blur than anything."

"What are you saying?"

"I'm saying that tomorrow you and I will start exploring Monte Calanetti. You can tell me all about it. You know, the little things that a tourist wouldn't know—the parts that make the village special."

"Don't be too disappointed when it doesn't live up to your expectations."

"I think you'll actually end up surprising yourself."

His gaze narrowed in on her. "You really want to walk all through the village?"

She nodded. "If you want to come up with a winning pitch to make all of the citizens, not to mention your brother and sister very happy, you're going to have to see it differently."

"I'm not sure that's possible. But if you insist on it, I will give you the grand tour."

"I would like that."

"Now, if you'll excuse me, I promised to swing by my brother's villa. He wants to show me the latest improvements at the winery." He got to his feet. "Of course, if you'd like to accompany me, you're welcome."

Kayla glanced down at her rather sparse list of notes. "I think my time would be better spent here doing some research."

"You're sure?"

She nodded. "I am. But thank you for the invite."

The truth was, she and Angelo were getting along a lot better than they had in the office. She'd been working for him for weeks now and they'd only ever addressed each other with mister and miss, but now they were on a first-name basis. And then there was that kiss...er...no she wasn't going to think about it. No matter how good it was or how much she wished that he'd kiss her again—

Her thoughts screeched to a halt. Did she want him to kiss her again? She turned to watch his retreating form. His broad shoulders were evident in the linen suit jacket. His long, powerful legs moved at a swift pace, covering the patio area quickly.

Yes, she did want to be kissed again. Only this time she wanted him to kiss her because he wanted her and not because he was exhausted and stressed after a run-in with his siblings. But that couldn't happen. She needed this job.

A quick fling with her boss in the warm sunshine of

Tuscany wasn't worth throwing away her dreams—the rest of her life. No matter how tempting Angelo might be, she just couldn't ruin this opportunity.

And she couldn't return to Paradise as a failure.

CHAPTER TEN

WHY EXACTLY HAD he agreed to this?

The last thing Angelo wanted to do was take a stroll through Monte Calanetti. It was like taking a walk back through history—a history that he preferred not to dwell on. Still, he had to admit that having Kayla along would make the journey back in time a little more tolerable, but he still didn't see how it was going to help him create a winning pitch.

He paced back and forth in the hotel lobby, waiting for Kayla to finish getting ready for their outing. He'd also wanted to check with the front desk to make sure that extending their stay wouldn't be an issue.

"Mr. Amatucci, you're in luck." The concierge strode up to him. "We've just had a cancellation. And with a bit of juggling we've been able to keep you and your assistant in your suite of rooms." The young man, who was polished from the top of his short cut hair down to his spiffed-up dress shoes, looked quite pleased with himself. "Is there anything else I can do for you?"

"Actually there is." Angelo wasn't sure it was a good idea, but he decided that Kayla deserved a night out for being such a good sport. "I've heard that Mancini's is quite a popular restaurant."

"Yes, it is. We're so lucky to have had Raffaele Mancini return to the village. Mancini's is so popular that they only take reservations."

That's what Angelo suspected. "Would you mind making a reservation for myself and my assistant for tomorrow evening?"

The concierge's face creased with worry lines.

"Is there a problem?"

"Well, sir. They're usually booked well in advance."

Angelo wasn't used to being put off. Even in New York he didn't have a problem getting into the most popular restaurants. How in the world was it that he was being turned down in little old Monte Calanetti? Impossible.

"Do you know who I am?"

The young man's eyes opened wide, and then he nodded.

Angelo got the distinct impression that the young man didn't have a clue who he was or what power he wielded outside of the Tuscany countryside. He felt as though he'd stepped back in time, becoming a nobody who faded into the crowd. With his pride pricked, he gave the young man a pointed look. But he knew that he was letting his past get the best of him. He swallowed down the unwarranted agitation. Of course the young man didn't know him. The concierge wasn't much more than a kid.

Angelo decided upon a new approach. "Forgive me. My tone was uncalled-for just now. When you call for the reservations, tell them that the owner of Amatucci & Associates is requesting a table as we are considering including them in the pitch for the royal wedding."

Maybe he had put it on a little thick just now, but he wanted—no, he needed to prove to everyone including himself that he had far surpassed everyone's expectations of him—especially his father's. Angelo's gut churned at the memory of his father turning to him in anger and saying, *You'll never amount to anything.*

"Yes, sir." The concierge attempted a nervous smile. "I'll do that right away. I had no idea, sir—"

"It's okay." Angelo tipped the young man handsomely to make up for his brusqueness. "I just need you to know that this dinner is very important." But suddenly Angelo was no longer talking about business or proving himself to the villagers or even the royal wedding. His mind was on Kayla. He liked making her happy, and he was hoping this dinner would earn him another smile or two.

"I'll get right on it, sir."

"Thank you. I appreciate it."

Angelo moved over to the small sitting area in the lobby to wait for Kayla. Just about to reach for the newspaper to find out what was going on around the world, Angelo caught a movement out of the corner of his eye. Curious to see if it was Kayla, he turned.

His gaze settled on her slender form. He stood transfixed as he took in her beauty. Kayla's auburn wavy hair hung loose and flowed down over her shoulders. A pair of sunglasses sat atop her head like a hair band. Her face was lightly made up and her reading glasses were nowhere in sight. A sheer tan cardigan covered her arms while beneath was a lacy white tank top. She looked so stunning that all of the villagers would be too busy trying to figure out if she was a movie star to take any notice of him.

"Is everything all right with the suite?" She stopped next to him.

He swallowed hard and glanced away, telling himself to relax. This was still the same Kayla that he'd been working closely with for weeks. He gazed at her again, trying to see her as the levelheaded assistant that he'd come to rely on. Spending the day with her, leisurely strolling about was going to be a struggle. He just had to keep in mind that they had a mission to accomplish—a royal wedding to brainstorm.

"Angelo?" She sent him a concerned look.

"Um…sorry. Yes, the suite is ours for the duration."

She pressed a hand to her chest. "That's good. You had me worried for a moment there."

"Nothing at all to worry about. Are you ready for your grand tour?"

She smiled and nodded. "Yes, I am. I'm really looking forward to it."

Without thinking, he extended his arm to her. Surprise lit up her eyes but in a blink it was gone. She slipped her arm in his. He didn't know why he'd made the gesture. It just felt right. So much for the promise he'd made himself to remain professional around her. They hadn't even left the hotel and he was already treating her like...like... Oh, whatever.

Angelo led her out of the hotel into the sunshiny afternoon. He had to admit that it was nice to get away from the stress of the wedding pitch. The whole project had ground to a complete halt. He sure hoped this outing would refill his creative well. If nothing else, maybe it would help him relax so he could start brainstorming again.

He glanced over to find Kayla taking in their surroundings. "I thought we would walk since the village isn't far from here."

"Sounds fine by me. I've been cooped up in the hotel long enough. Back in New York, I'm used to doing a lot of walking."

"Really. Where do you walk?" He didn't know why but he was truly interested.

"I walk to the subway and then to the office. Sometimes, if the weather is right, I will duck out at lunch and stretch my legs."

"So you truly like to walk."

She nodded. "It sure beats eating like a bird. If you hadn't noticed, I do enjoy food." She rubbed her flat abs. "Especially pasta."

"Would you like to try some of the best Italian food in the region?"

"Definitely."

"Good. From what I've heard, you should be impressed with the restaurant I've chosen."

"Is it far from here?"

"Not at all. In fact, it's right here in Monte Calanetti. We have reservations for tomorrow night."

"I can't wait."

"Good. Consider it a date."

When her fine brows rose and her eyes glittered with unspoken questions, he realized he'd blundered. But he didn't take back the words. He liked the thought of having a friendly date with her.

They walked a bit before Kayla spoke. "What's it called?"

"Mancini's. It's an exclusive IGF-starred restaurant on the outskirts of the village. The chef is a friend of my brother's."

"This friend of your brother's, is he from around here?"

"Yes, he grew up here. After Raffaele achieved international success with his cooking, he returned to open his own restaurant. I suspect he was anxious to try running his own place, but I'm surprised he didn't start his business in one of the cities like Rome or Milan."

"Perhaps he just wanted to be home again. Have you really never considered moving back here?"

Angelo gave a firm shake of head. "Not even once."

"Don't you like it here?"

"It…it has a lot of memories. Not all of them good ones."

Angelo remembered how he'd been turned away from his home and told not to return. The buried memories came flooding back to him. The loud arguments between his parents. His brother and sister upset. And then there was the last time he came to his mother's defense. He'd experienced many a row with his father before that life-altering one—the one where his father threw him out of the house, telling him that he was old enough to make it on his own.

When Angelo had turned a pleading stare to his mother, she'd told him that he was a smart, strong young man and that it was time to make his way in life. That was when he'd had no choice but to follow his dreams. With the aid of his inheritance from his grandfather combined with his meager savings, he'd set out for New York.

Though he hated to leave his brother and sister, he didn't have a choice. His father was a stubborn man who wouldn't back down from an argument. And Angelo wasn't about to live any longer with his parents and their dysfunctional relationship. In fact, he hadn't even come back to Monte Calanetti to visit until his mother and father had moved to Milan. He had no intention of seeing his father again.

"I'm sorry. I didn't mean to upset you."

Kayla's voice drew him out of his thoughts. "What? Um…oh, you didn't."

She sent him an I-don't-believe-you look but said nothing more. They continued toward the village in silence. It felt so strange to be back here—when he'd left all of those years ago, he'd sworn that he'd never return. And he hadn't for a long time.

The truth was he missed his brother and sister. But he rarely made the journey home. It was too hard. There were too many unsettling memories lurking about, and he just didn't have the same draw to this place that his brother and sister did. He didn't understand Nico's need to cling to their heritage, not when there were so many adventures outside of Monte Calanetti to experience.

"This is beautiful." Kayla stood at the crumbling rock wall that surrounded the village, which was perched high upon a hill. "What an amazing view. What's with the wall?"

"The village is centuries old and used to be a strong-hold against attacks."

"I couldn't imagine there being unrest here. I mean, did you ever see anything so peaceful?" There was a distinct note of awe in Kayla's voice. "There's something almost magical about it."

"I used to think that, too."

"You did?"

He nodded, recalling days of long ago. "I used to come to this spot when I was a kid." What he failed to mention is that he came here to get away from his parents' arguing.

"I'd pretend that I was the defender of the kingdom. Many sword battles took place where you're standing."

"Really? So you were Sir Lancelot?" She eyed him up as though imagining him in a coat of armor.

He was no knight—not even close to it. He'd just been a kid trying to escape the battlefield between his parents, but he didn't want to get into any of that. A gentle breeze rushed past them and he willed it to sweep away the unsettling memories. He didn't want the past to ruin this day.

"Look." She pointed to a flock of little birds as they took flight. They soared up into the sky, circled and swooped low before rising again. "Aren't they beautiful?"

He was never a bird-watcher, but he had to admire the symmetry of their movements. He couldn't help but wonder what else he'd been missing. His gaze strayed back to Kayla. How had he missed noticing how amazing she was both inside and out?

"And listen."

He did as she asked. "I don't hear anything."

"Exactly! There's nothing but the rustle of the leaves. It's so freeing."

Now that he could agree on. He'd been searching for quietness like this ever since he'd moved to New York, but he'd never been able to find it—until now. "It clears the mind."

"Good. We want clear heads when we tour Monte Calanetti." She turned and pointed off in the distance. "I just love the rows of grapevines. I wonder how they get the lines so straight."

"I'm betting if you were to ask Nico that he'd tell you anything you want to know about running a vineyard. He's very proud of his work."

"You mean all of that is Nico's land?"

Angelo nodded. "It has been passed down through the family. When my father couldn't make a go of it, they passed the land down to us kids. I was already working in New York and Marianna was too young, so Nico stepped up. He's worked really hard to rebuild the vineyard and make a name for the wine."

"Hardworking must be a trait of the Amatucci men."

"Some of them anyhow." His father wasn't big on work, which was evident by the poor condition of the vineyard when he'd handed it over to his children. "Come on. I thought you wanted to see Monte Calanetti."

"I do."

With Kayla's hand still tucked in the crook of his arm, Angelo took comfort in having her next to him. This was his first stroll through the village since that dreadful day when his father cast him out of their family home. These days when he returned to Italy, he either stayed in the city or at the villa. He just wasn't up for the curious stares or worse the questions about why he left.

As they strolled through the village, Angelo warned himself not to get too comfortable with Kayla. Soon this vacation illusion would end, and they'd be back in New York, where he'd transform back into Mr. Amatucci and she'd once again be Ms. Hill. Everything would once again be as it should.

CHAPTER ELEVEN

NEVER ONE TO lurk in the shadows, Angelo led Kayla into the center of Monte Calanetti. Their first stop was at the *caffè* shop. He'd never met a woman who loved coffee as much as Kayla. She savored each sip before swallowing. He loved to watch her facial features when she'd take her first sip—it was somewhere between total delight and ecstasy. He longed to be able to put that look on her face…and not with coffee…but with a long, slow, deep, soul-stirring kiss.

He'd given up the futile effort of fighting his lustful thoughts for Kayla. He couldn't lie to himself. He found her utterly enchanting. And as long as he stuck with his daydreams of holding her—of kissing her passionately—they'd be fine. It wasn't as if she could read his mind.

They stepped out of the shop and onto the busy sidewalk. As they started to walk again, he reminded himself not to get too caught up in having Kayla by his side. She was the absolute wrong person for him to have a dalliance with beneath the Tuscany sun. He was her escort—her friend—nothing more. He forced his thoughts to the quaint shops that offered such things as locally grown flowers and to-die-for baked goods. There was a little bit of everything. And he could tell by the rapt stare on Kayla's face that she was enthralled by all of it.

"Angelo, is that you?"

They both stopped at the sound of a woman's excited voice. Angelo glanced over his shoulder to see an older woman rushing toward them. She looked vaguely familiar.

"It is you." The woman couldn't be much more than five feet tall, if that. She beamed up at him. "I knew you'd come back."

It took him a moment, but then the woman's gentle smile and warm eyes clicked a spot in his memory—Mrs. Caruso. He hadn't seen her since he was a teenager. Back then, she'd had long dark hair that she kept braided over one shoulder. Now, her dark hair had given way to shades of gray, and instead of the braid, her hair was pinned up.

Kayla elbowed him, and at last, he found his voice. "Mrs. Caruso, it's good to see you."

"What kind of greeting is that?" She grabbed him by the arms and pulled him toward her. When he'd stooped over far enough, she placed a hand on either side of his head, and then kissed each cheek. "You've been gone much too long. You've been missed."

She pulled him back down to her and gave him a tight hug. He hugged her back. Heat warmed his face. He wasn't used to public displays of affection...no matter how innocent they might be. This would never happen back in the States. But then again, Monte Calanetti was a lifetime away from New York City, and the same rules didn't seem to apply here.

They chatted for a bit as she asked one question after the other about what he'd been doing with himself. The years rolled away as she put him at ease with her friendly chatter. The best part was that she really listened to him—as she'd done all of those years ago when he was a kid. Mrs. Caruso and her husband ran the local bakery. They'd never had any children of their own. Angelo always suspected that it wasn't from the lack of wanting or trying. Without little ones of her own, she'd doted on the kids in the village.

"You are going to do the royal wedding pitch, aren't you?" She smiled and clapped her hands together as though she'd just solved the world's problems.

"Nico asked me to work on it. My assistant and I just extended our stay here in order to work up a presentation for the royal family."

"Wonderful!" Mrs. Caruso beamed. "Now I'm more

certain than ever that the village will host the wedding. Everyone will be so grateful to both of you."

"I don't know about that—"

"You're just being modest. You always were." Mrs. Caruso's gaze moved to Kayla. "Now where are my manners? Angelo, introduce me to your girlfriend."

His girlfriend? Hadn't she heard him say Kayla was his assistant? His gaze moved from her to Kayla, who was smiling. Why wasn't she correcting the woman? Was she just being polite? Or should he be concerned that she was taking this friendly outing far too seriously?

"Hi, I'm Kayla." She held out a hand while Angelo struggled to settle his thoughts. "I'm actually Mr. Amatucci's assistant."

Mrs. Caruso's brows rose as her gaze moved back and forth between them. "I could have sworn that you two were— Oh, never mind me. I'm just so glad that you're both here to help with the wedding."

They promised to stop by the bakery soon and moved on down the walkway. He still didn't know why Mrs. Caruso would think they were a couple. Then he glanced down to where Kayla's hand was resting on his arm. Okay, so maybe from the outside the lines in their relationship appeared a bit blurred, but they knew where they stood. Didn't they?

He swallowed hard. "I'm sorry about back there with Mrs. Caruso jumping to conclusions about us."

"It's okay. It was a natural mistake."

A natural mistake? Wait. What exactly did that mean?

He glanced over at Kayla. "But you know that you and I...that we're, um...that nothing has changed. Right?"

She smiled up at him. "Relax. We're just two business associates enjoying a stroll through the village. It's a mission. We have to learn as much about this place as possible so that you can do some brainstorming about the pitch when we return to our suite."

She said all of the right things, but why did they sound

so wrong to his ears? Maybe he was just being hypersensitive. He took a deep breath and blew it out. "Exactly." Now he needed to change the subject to something a little less stressful. "Mrs. Caruso certainly seemed hopeful about the royal wedding."

"She did. It seems as if the whole village is buzzing with excitement about it."

"I just hope they don't end up disappointed."

She lightly elbowed him. "They won't be. You'll see to that."

At this particular moment, she had a lot more faith in his abilities than he did. "I don't know if I'm that good. This is just a small village and we're talking about a royal wedding—the sort of thing they write about in history books."

"And who better to sell the royal couple on the merits of Monte Calanetti?" She gazed up at him with hope in her eyes. "You just need to loosen up a bit and enjoy yourself."

"I am relaxed." As relaxed as he got these days.

She sighed and shook her head. "No, you aren't. Let down your guard and enjoy the sun on your face."

"Why is this so important to you?"

"Because I want you to really see Monte Calanetti and get excited about it." Her gaze met his and then dipped to his mouth. "I think if you're passionate about something it will show."

The temperature started to rise. He knew what she was thinking because he was thinking the same thing. He zeroed in on her inviting lips. He was definitely feeling passionate. Would it be wrong to kiss her again?

Someone bumped his shoulder as they passed by, reminding him that they were in the middle of the village. Not exactly the place for a passionate moment or even a quick peck. Besides, he couldn't give her the wrong impression. He didn't do relationships.

Before he could decide if he should say something,

Kayla slipped her arm in his and they started to walk again. They made their way around the piazza, taking in the various shops from a shoe boutique to a candy shop. Monte Calanetti offered so much more than he recalled.

Maybe it wasn't quite the small backward village he'd conjured up in his memory—the same village where he'd once got into a bit of mischief with harmless pranks. Those were the carefree days that he hadn't known to appreciate as they flew by.

"What are you smiling about?" Kayla sent him a curious look.

He was smiling? He hadn't realized his thoughts had crossed his face. "I was just recalling some antics I'd gotten into as a kid."

"Oh, tell me. I'd love to hear."

"You would?" He wouldn't think something like that would interest her. When she nodded, he continued. "There was this one time when I glued a coin to the sidewalk outside the market. You wouldn't believe how many people tried to pry it free."

Her eyes twinkled. "So you didn't always play by the rules."

He shrugged. "What kind of trouble did you get into?"

"Me? Nothing."

"Oh, come on, confess. There has to be something."

She paused as though giving it some serious consideration. "Well, there was this one time the neighborhood boys attached some fishing line to a dollar. It was similar to what you did. They'd lay it out in front of my parents' market, and when someone went to pick up it up, they'd tug on the line."

"See, I knew you weren't as innocent as you appeared."

"Hey, it wasn't me. It was them. I… I was just watching."

"Uh-huh." He enjoyed the way her cheeks filled with color. "It's good to know you have some spunk in you. That will come in handy in this business."

* * *

Kayla was in love—with the village, of course.

Brilliant sunshine lit up the heart of Monte Calanetti. The piazza was surrounded by a wide range of small shops to satisfy even the most discerning tastes. But it was the large fountain in the center of the village square that drew Kayla's attention. She tugged on Angelo's arm, leading them toward it.

The focal point of the fountain was a nymph draped in a cloak. She held a huge clamshell overhead. The sunshine sparkled and danced over the fine billowing mist from the continuous jets of water. Kayla stopped at the fountain's edge. She smiled, loving the details of the sculpture that included a ring of fish leaping out of the water.

"I take it you like the fountain." Angelo's deep voice came from just behind her. "You know there's a tradition that if you toss a coin and it lands in the shell, you get your wish."

Her gaze rose to the clamshell—suddenly it didn't look quite so big. "You'd have to be awfully lucky to get it all the way up there."

"Why don't you give it a try?"

"I… I don't think so. I was never good at those types of things."

Angelo held a coin out to her. "Here you go." His fingers pressed the money into her palm. "I made a wish once and it came true."

"Really?" She turned to him. "What was it?"

He shook his head. "You aren't supposed to tell your wish."

"But that doesn't apply if your wish has already come true. So, out with it."

The corner of his very inviting lips lifted. "Okay. I wished that someday I'd get to travel the world."

"Wow. It really did come true." She thought really hard, but was torn by what she should wish for. She could wish for the fund-raiser to be a huge success. Or she could wish for her promotion to ad executive. But fountains should be for fanciful dreams.

"Don't look so worried. Turn around."

She did as he said. The next thing she knew, his body pressed to her back—his hard planes to her soft curves. His breath tickled her neck. Her heart thumped and her knees grew weak. Thankfully he was there holding her up.

His voice was soft as he spoke. "You make the wish and I'll help you get the coin in the shell. Ready?"

She nodded. Together with their hands touching, they swung. The coin flipped end over end through the air.

Let Angelo kiss me.

Plunk! The coin landed in the clamshell.

"We did it!"

At that moment, Angelo backed away. "Did you ever doubt it?"

"I couldn't have done it without you." She turned around, hoping her wish would come true.

"Did you make your wish?"

Disappointment washed over her. Of course he wasn't going to kiss her. She'd let herself get caught up in the moment. That wouldn't happen again.

"We should keep moving." She turned to start walking. "We don't want to miss anything."

"Wait." He reached out for her hand. "Aren't you going to tell me what you wished for?"

"Um…no. I can't." When he sent her a puzzled look, she added, "If I tell you, it won't come true."

"Well, we wouldn't want that to happen."

Her hand remained in his warm grasp as they continued their stroll. Was it her imagination or was Angelo's icy professional persona melting beneath the Tuscany sun? She smiled. He was definitely warming up.

CHAPTER TWELVE

SIMPLY *CHARMING*.

At this particular moment, Kayla had no better word for it. And she wasn't just talking about the village. She gave Angelo a sideways gaze. Handsome, thoughtful and entertaining. "Quite a combo."

"What?"

Oops! She hadn't meant to vocalize her thoughts. "I... I was just thinking Monte Calanetti has quite an amazing combination of old-world charm and modern day functionality."

They meandered away from the fountain. On the edge of the piazza, they passed by a well that she was certain had seen its days of women gathering to fill their buckets. While waiting for their turn, she imagined they'd shared the happenings of the village—the historic form of gossiping around the water cooler. It was so easy to envision how things used to be. Something told Kayla that this village hadn't changed a whole lot over the years.

The sunshine warmed the back of her neck, but it was Angelo's arm beneath her fingertips that warmed her insides. She resisted the urge to smooth her fingers over his tanned skin. She was in serious danger of forgetting that he was her boss—the key to her future promotion.

As the bell towers rang out, Kayla stared at the cobblestone path that wound its way between the brick buildings. A number of the homes had flower boxes with red, yellow and purple blooms. There were also flowerpots by the various shaped doors painted in every imaginable color. In other places, ivy snaked its way along the bricks. This area was quite picturesque and made Kayla forget that she was in the center of the village.

A rustling sound had her glancing upward. She craned her neck, finding fresh laundry fluttering in the breeze. She couldn't help but smile. It was a lovely, inviting sight. But as much as she liked it, it was the man at her side that she found utterly captivating.

Angelo Amatucci might be icy cool in the office, but she'd found that once he thawed out, he was a warm, thoughtful man. Not that she was falling for his amazing good looks or his dark, mysterious eyes. Her priority was her career—the reason she'd left her home in Paradise. And she wasn't about to ruin her future by throwing herself at her boss.

She chanced a quick glance his way. But then again—

No. She pulled her thoughts up short. This wasn't getting her anywhere.

She was supposed to be touring Monte Calanetti to get ideas for the wedding pitch. If they were going to sell the royal couple on this location for the wedding, she needed to know as much about it as possible. And of what she'd seen so far, she loved it. This village and its occupants would give the wedding an old-world feel with lots of heart.

The villagers sent puzzled glances their way as though they should know who Angelo was but couldn't quite place his face. And then there were a few people that ventured to ask if he was indeed Angelo. When he confirmed their suspicions, he wasn't greeted with a simple hello or a mere handshake; instead, he was yanked into warm hugs. She could see the frown lines etched on his face, but to his credit he didn't complain. There were even a few tears of happiness from the older women who remembered him when he was just a young boy.

Angelo took her hand in his as though it were natural for them. Kayla liked feeling connected to him—feeling his long fingers wrapped around hers.

"I'm sorry about that." Angelo started walking again. "I didn't expect anyone to remember me."

"You must have spent a lot of time in the village as a kid."

"I did. It was my escape from the monotony of working around the vineyard." His jaw tensed and a muscle twitched.

"I take it that's why you let your brother have the run of Calanetti Vineyards?"

He nodded. "Nico is as passionate about the winery as I am with advertising. How about you? Do you have any brothers or sisters?"

Kayla shook her head. "My parents wanted more children, but that didn't work out. So with me being an only child, they heaped all of their hopes and dreams onto me."

"Hmm…sounds a bit daunting for one person."

"It is. That's why I had to leave Paradise."

"Somehow I just can't imagine life in Paradise could be such a hardship."

She shrugged. "It's great. The people are wonderful. It's the perfect place to raise kids."

"But you weren't ready for kids?"

The thought of taking on that sort of responsibility still overwhelmed her. "I have to figure out me first and accomplish some things on my own before I can be there 24/7 for others. And my parents, as much as I love them, didn't understand this."

"They wanted you to graduate high school and settle down."

She nodded. "They had it all planned out. I'd get married, have lots of kids and when the time came my husband and I would take over the family store."

"Doesn't sound so bad."

"No. It isn't. But I always had a dream of going to college and making a name for myself. I wanted to move to the city. I wanted to climb the corporate ladder. I wanted to—"

She bit off her last words. Heat rushed up her neck and warmed her face. She couldn't believe that she'd gotten so comfortable around Angelo that she'd just rambled on about her dreams. For a moment, she'd forgotten that she was talking to her boss.

Not good, Kayla. Not good at all.

She freed her hand from his. It was time she started acting like his employee, not his girlfriend. The time had come to get back to reality.

Angelo stopped walking and turned to her. "What aren't you saying? What do you want to do?"

"Um…nothing. It's no big deal. Let's keep going. I want to see the whole village." She turned to start walking again.

Angelo reached out, catching her arm in his firm grip. "Not so fast." She turned back, glancing up at his serious gaze. "Kayla, talk to me." His hand fell away from her arm. "I've told you all sorts of things that I don't normally share with people. I'd like to know what you were about to say and why you stopped. Surely by now you know that you can trust me."

Could she trust him? She supposed it depended on the subject. With her safety—most definitely. With her dreams—perhaps. With her heart— Wait, where had that come from?

"Kayla, what is it?"

She wasn't good at lying so that left her with the truth, but she didn't know how Angelo would take it. "I came to New York because I wanted…er… I want to be an ad executive."

His brows scrunched together. "And?"

She shrugged. "And that's it."

"That's what you didn't want to tell me?"

Her gaze moved to the cobblestone walkway. "It's just that I got comfortable around you and forgot to watch what I was saying."

"Oh, I see. Since I'm the boss, you feel like you have to screen what you say to me?"

She nodded.

"How about this? For the duration of this trip, I'm not

your boss. We're just business associates or how about friends? Would you like that?"

Her gaze met his and she found that he was being perfectly serious. "But what about when we return to New York?"

"Obviously things will have to change then, but for right now, I'd like to just be Angelo, not Mr. Amatucci. I'd forgotten what it's like just to be me again."

"And I like you calling me Kayla." Her gaze met his. Within his eyes she found a comforting warmth. "Consider yourself a friend."

He held out his hand to her. She accepted it. A shiver of excitement raced up her arm. They continued to stare deep into each other's eyes, even though it was totally unnecessary. She knew she should turn away. She knew that it was the proper thing to do with her boss. But as he'd just pointed out they were friends—for now.

His voice grew deeper. "I couldn't think of a better friend to have."

Her heart fluttered in her chest. What had just happened?

Angelo turned and tucked her hand back in the crook of his arm. Why did it suddenly feel as though their relationship had just taken a detour? How would they ever find their way back to just being boss and employee now?

Monte Calanetti is a diamond in the rough.

Had that thought really just crossed his mind?

Before he'd left the hotel a few hours ago, he'd envisioned Monte Calanetti as he had when he was a child— suffocating with its traditional ways and its resistance to growth and to modernization. But somehow, with Kayla by his side, he'd seen the village from a different perspective —he'd seen it through her very beautiful, very observant eyes. With her passion and romantic tendencies, she might just be the key he needed to pull this wedding pitch together. But did he dare ask for her help?

Sure, she had talent. He'd witnessed it firsthand with the Van Holsen account. But did he trust her with a project that was so important to his family? After all, his brother and sister, not to mention the entire village, were counting on him to represent them properly to the royal couple. But how was he supposed to do that when he kept hitting one brick wall after the other?

They walked some more before Kayla turned to him. "Thank you for showing me your hometown. I love it."

"Really?" He failed to keep the surprise from his voice.

"Of course I do. How could you not? Not only that but it has the most delicious aromas and it's so peaceful." Just then two scooters whizzed by them. "Okay, so it isn't totally peaceful."

"You'll get used to them. Scooters are very popular around here."

A couple more scooters zoomed down the road causing Kayla to step into the grass. She took a moment, taking in her surroundings. "Is this where you went to school?"

Angelo glanced at the back of the building off in the distance. The years started to slip away. "Yes, it is."

"I bet you were a handful back then."

As a young kid, he'd been the complete opposite of the way he is now. "I believe the word they used was *incorrigible*."

Now why had he gone and admitted that? Letting down his defenses and opening up about his past would only lead to confusion and misunderstandings, because sharing was what people did when they were getting serious. And that wasn't going to happen. He refused to let it happen. No matter how ripe her lips were for a kiss. Or how her smile sent his pulse racing.

"You probably picked on all of the girls and pulled on their ponytails."

He shook his head. "Not me. I didn't have time for girls, not until I was a bit older."

"And then I bet you broke a lot of hearts."

He wasn't sure about that, but there was one girl, Vera Carducci, and he'd had the biggest crush on her. He hadn't thought of her in years.

"See. I was right." Kayla smiled triumphantly.

"Actually, I was the one who got dumped."

"That's so hard to believe—"

"It's the truth." Why did he feel the need to make Kayla believe that his life was far from idyllic? What was it about her that had him letting down his guard? He had to do better. He couldn't let her get too close. It'd only cause them pain in the end.

Kayla walked over to a tree in the school yard. Her fingers traced over the numerous carvings from initials to hearts. "Was this the kissing tree?"

He nodded, suddenly wishing they were anywhere but here.

"I bet your initials are here…somewhere." Kayla's voice drew him back to the present. "Want to point me in the right direction?"

"Actually, they aren't here."

Her eyes opened wide. "Really? I thought for sure that you would have been popular with the girls."

He shrugged, recalling his fair share of girlfriends over the years. But he'd never kissed them here. Not a chance.

"Surely you stole a kiss or two." Her gaze needled him for answers.

"Not here."

"Why not?"

Oh, what did it matter if he told her? It wasn't as if there was any truth to the legend. It was all a bunch of wishful thinking.

"There's some silly legend attached to the tree that says whoever you kiss here will be your soul mate for life."

Kayla's green eyes widened with interest. "Really? And you don't believe it?"

He shook his head. "It's just an old wives' tale. There's nothing to it."

"And yet you've made a point not to kiss anyone here." She stepped closer to him. "If you don't believe in such superstitions, prove it."

His pulse kicked up a notch. Why was there a gleam in her eyes? Was she challenging him? Did she really expect him to kiss her here?

Instead of the idea scaring him off, it actually appealed to him. His gaze dipped to her lips. Kayla was the only woman he had ever contemplated kissing here—wait, when did that happen? He gave himself a mental jerk, but it didn't chase away the tempting thought.

What was it about Miss Kayla Hill that had him wishing there were such things as happily-ever-afters instead of roller-coaster relationships? He'd had so much turbulence in his life that he couldn't stand anymore. But Kayla was different. She had a calming presence.

This wasn't right. He should make it perfectly clear that he was no Romeo, but the way she kept staring at him, challenging him with her eyes, filled him with a warm sensation. He didn't want it to end. What would it hurt to let her remain caught up in her romantic imaginings?

Without thinking about the pros and cons of what he was about to do, he dipped his head and caught her lips with his own. Her lips were soft and pliant. He wrapped his arms around her slender waist and pulled her to him. She willingly followed his lead. Her soft curves pressed to him and a moan swelled deep in his throat. How in the world was he ever going to let her go? He'd never felt anything this intense for anyone—ever.

He wanted to convince himself that it was because she was forbidden fruit—his assistant. But he couldn't buy that. There was something so special about her that he couldn't diminish the connection with such a flimsy excuse. He knew as sure as he was standing there in a liplock with her that if their situation were different and he wasn't her boss that he'd still desire her with every fiber of his body.

His mouth moved over hers, slow at first. Yet when she met him move for move, the desire burning in him flared. Her mouth opened to him and she tasted sweet like the sun-ripened berries she'd sampled back in the village. He'd never tasted anything so delectable in his life. He doubted he'd ever experience a moment like this again.

There was something so special about Kayla. It was as though no matter what he did, she could see the real him. But could she see his scars, the ones that kept him from letting people get too close?

Her hands slid up over his shoulders and wrapped around the back of his neck. Her touch sent waves of excitement down his spine. He wanted her. He needed her. But his heart and mind were still guarded.

If he let her get any closer, she'd learn of his shame— of his ultimate pain—and then she'd pity him. Pity was not something that he could tolerate. He was Angelo Amatucci. A self-made man. He needed no one's sympathy. He needed no one.

Anxious to rebuild that wall between them, he braced his hands on her hips and pushed her back. Her eyes fluttered open and confusion showed in them.

"We should head back to the hotel. I... I have work to do."

Disappointment flashed in her eyes. "Oh. Okay."

He retraced their steps. "I have a conference call this afternoon."

Kayla fell in step beside him. He should say something. Explain somehow. But he didn't know what to say because that kiss left him utterly confused by the rush of emotions she'd evoked in him. Somehow, some way, she'd sneaked past his well-placed barriers and with each smile, each touch, she was getting to him. That wasn't part of his plan.

Unable to decide what to do about his undeniable attraction to his assistant, he turned his attention to something much less stressful—the village. For the first time, he saw its charms. Kayla had opened his eyes to everything he'd blocked out, from the amazing artisans, to the detailed architecture, to the warm and friendly people. He had so much to work with now. The pitch would be amazing if he could pull it all together, even though he was still unsure about the wedding aspect.

Still, Monte Calanetti had some of the best food in the world. It was sure to impress even the royal couple. And to be truthful, he was quite anxious to try Raffaele's restaurant—if the rumors were anything to go by, it was out of this world.

Although his desire to go to dinner had more to do with Kayla than the food. He hungered for more of her melodious laugh and her contagious smiles. Though he shouldn't, he'd come to really enjoy her company.

As productive as they were, working as a team, he was enjoying getting to know her on a personal level. After all, it wasn't as if this thing, whatever you wanted to call it, would carry over to New York. He'd make sure of it. But what would it hurt to enjoy the moment?

CHAPTER THIRTEEN

ANGELO SWIPED HIS key card and opened the suite door for Kayla. When she brushed past him, he noticed the softest scent of wildflowers. He inhaled deeply, enjoying the light fragrance as he followed her into the room, wishing he could hold on to her delicate scent just a little longer.

When she stopped short, he bumped into her. He grabbed her shoulders to steady her. She turned in his arms and gazed up at him with those big luminous green eyes. His heart pounded in his chest.

"Wasn't the afternoon wonderful?"

Was it his imagination or was her voice soft and sultry? And was she looking at him differently? Or was it that he wanted her so much that he was projecting his lusty thoughts upon her?

He swallowed down the lump in his throat. "Yes, it was a really nice day."

"Thank you so much for spending the day with me. I promise to pay you back." She stood up on her tiptoes and leaned forward.

She was going to repeat their kiss. His heart pounded. His brain told him that it shouldn't happen, but his body had other thoughts. He started to lean forward—

Buzz. Buzz. His phone vibrated in his pocket, breaking the spell.

He pulled back. After retrieving the phone from his pocket, he checked the screen. "It's the conference call. I have to take it. Can we talk later?"

He moved to his room to take the call in private. He actually welcomed the interruption. It gave him time to figure out how to handle this change of dynamics with Kayla.

The phone call dragged on much longer than he'd anticipated. When he finally disconnected the call, he found Kayla was still in the suite working on her laptop.

He cleared his throat and she glanced up, but her gaze didn't quite reach his. "Sorry about the interruption."

"No problem." Her voice didn't hold its normal lilt. She lifted her reading glasses and rested them on her head.

As much as he'd like to pretend that the kiss hadn't happened, he couldn't. It was already affecting their working relationship and that was not acceptable. "I need to apologize. That kiss…back at the tree, it shouldn't have happened. You must understand that it can't happen again."

"Is that what you really want?"

"Yes. No. I don't know." He raked his fingers through his hair. "Maybe I was wrong about this. Maybe it'd be better if you flew back to New York."

"What?" She jumped to her feet. Her heated gaze was most definitely meeting his now.

"This isn't going to work between us." He glanced away, knowing he'd created this problem. "We can't keep our hands off each other. How are we supposed to concentrate on all of the work we have to get done?"

She stepped up to him and poked him in the chest. "You're not firing me. I won't let you—"

"Wait. Who said anything about firing you?" He wrapped his hand around her finger, fighting off the urge to wrap his lips around it. "Certainly not me. You are very talented. Do you honestly think that I'd sack you over a kiss or two—kisses that I initiated?"

"Then what?" She pulled her finger from his hold as though she'd read his errant thought. "You don't think you can keep your hands to yourself around me?"

"Yes… I mean, no." He absolutely hated this feeling of being out of control—of his emotions or whatever you called it ruling over his common sense. "You confuse me."

"How so?" Her gaze narrowed in on him. When he didn't answer her, she persisted. "Tell me. I want to know."

He sighed. "It's nothing. Just forget I said anything."

"What is this really about? It has to be about more than just a kiss."

His gaze lifted and met hers head-on. How could she understand him so well? No other woman had ever seen the real him—they'd always been more interested in having a good time. But then again, he'd gone out of his way to hook up with women who didn't have serious, long-term plans where he was concerned.

His strong reaction to Kayla was due to a lot more than just the kiss. She made him feel things—want things—that he had no business feeling or wanting. And the way she'd moved him with that passionate kiss hadn't done anything to settle him. It had only made him want her all the more. What was up with that? He'd never desired a woman with every single fiber of his being. Until now.

Kayla stepped closer and lowered her voice. "Angelo, I think we've grown close enough on this trip that you can talk to me and know that it won't go any further. Tell me what's eating you up inside."

He knew what she was after—the secrets of his past. But was he ready for that? Did he have the courage to peel back those old wounds? Was he ready to deal with her reaction? Could he stand having her think less of him?

The answer was a resounding no.

Angelo inhaled a deep breath and blew it out. He wasn't prepared to open that door. It wasn't as if they were involved romantically. They didn't have a future, just the here and the now.

But there was something else…

He needed her—well…er…her help. He couldn't do this wedding pitch alone. The admission twisted his gut in a knot. He was not a man accustomed to reaching out to others.

He made a point of being the man handing out assignments, making suggestions and overseeing operations. He was never at a loss for how to accomplish things—especially an advertising pitch. This was supposed to be his area of expertise—his specialty.

What was wrong with him? Why couldn't he come up with a solid pitch? And what was Kayla going to think of him when he made this request? Would she think less of him?

Wanting to get it over with, he uttered, "I need your assistance."

"What?" Her brow creased. "Of course I'll help you. That's what I'm here for." She took a seat on the couch. "What do you need?"

His gaze met hers briefly, and then he glanced away. "I... I'm having issues with this pitch. Weddings and romance aren't my thing." That much was the truth. He avoided weddings like the plague—he always had a prior business engagement. "I thought maybe you'd have some experience with them."

"Well, um... I have a bit of experience." Her cheeks took on a pasty shade of white.

"You don't look so good. I'll get you something to drink."

"You don't have to wait on me. I can get it."

She started to get up when he pressed a hand to her shoulder. "I've got this."

He retrieved a bottle of water from the fridge and poured it in a glass for her. This was his fault. He'd had her gallivanting all around Monte Calanetti in the sun. She must have worn herself out.

He moved to her side and handed over the water. "Can I get you anything else?"

She shook her head. "Thanks. This is fine."

He sat down beside her as she sipped at the water. "I'm sorry if I pushed you too hard in the village. I should have brought you back here sooner—"

"No, that's not it. The visit was perfect. I wouldn't have changed anything about it." She sent him a smile, but it didn't quite reach her eyes.

"I don't believe you. There's something bothering you." He stopped and thought about it. "And it started when I mentioned the wedding pitch. Do you feel that I'm expecting too much of you?"

"That's not it." She placed a hand on his knee. The warmth of her touch could be felt through his jeans. "I'm just a bit tired."

"Are you sure that's all it is? It doesn't have anything to do with your broken engagement?"

Her eyes widened. "That's been over for a long time. I've moved on."

Moved on? Surely she wasn't thinking those kisses—that they'd somehow lead to something. He swallowed hard and decided it was best to change topics. "Have you made many friends since you moved to New York?"

"I haven't had much time. But I made a few at the after-school program." She pressed her lips together and turned away.

He was missing something, but he had no idea what that might be. "What do you do at this after-school program?"

She shrugged. "It's no big deal. So what can I do to help you with the wedding pitch?"

"Wait. I'd like to hear more about this program. What do you do? And how do you have time?" It seemed as if she was always in the office working long hours without a complaint.

"I do what is necessary. It all depends on the day and how many volunteers show up. Sometimes I help with homework and do a bit of tutoring. Other times I play kickball or a board game."

"You do all of that on top of the overtime you put in at the office?"

"It's not that big of a deal." She toyed with the hem of her top. "I don't have anything waiting for me at home, so why not put my spare time to good use?"

"You shouldn't dismiss what you do. There are very few people in this world who are willing to go out of their way for others. It's impressive."

Her eyes widened. "You really think so?"

"I do. Why do you seem so surprised?"

"It's just that at the office you've banned employees from taking on charitable accounts."

"It has to be that way." He raked his fingers through his hair. "There are only so many hours in the workday. I write out enough checks each year to various organizations to make up for it."

Kayla nodded, but she certainly didn't seem impressed. Uneasiness churned in his gut. Maybe she would be more understanding if she knew the amount of those checks.

"I'm sure those organizations appreciate the donations."

Guilt settled over him. What was up with that? It wasn't as if he didn't do anything. He just couldn't afford the time to take on more accounts—especially for free. He was still working on growing Amatucci & Associates into the biggest and the best advertising firm. Speaking of which, he needed to get moving on this pitch. Time was running out before his trip to Halencia.

"I need to ask you something."

She reached for the glass of water. "Ask away. Then I need to go check my email. I'm waiting on some responses about the Van Holsen account."

He shook his head, thinking this was a bad idea. "Never mind. You have enough to deal with."

She arched a thin brow at him. "You can't back out now. You have me curious."

He just couldn't admit to her that he had absolutely no direction for the pitch. Three wasted days of jotting down ideas and then realizing that they were clichéd or just plain stupid—certainly nothing that he would present to the royal family.

"If it doesn't bother you—you know, because of your broken engagement—I wanted to ask you some wedding questions."

She reached out and squeezed his hand. "I appreciate you watching out for my feelings but talking about weddings won't reduce me to tears. I promise. Let's get started."

His gaze met hers and his breath caught in his throat. He was going to have to be really careful around her or he just might be tempted to start something that neither of them was ready for. And once he got something started with her, he wasn't sure he'd ever be able to end it when reality crashed in around them.

CHAPTER FOURTEEN

THIS IS IT!

At last, it was her big break.

Kayla grinned as she sat by the pool the next day. She could hardly believe that at last her plans were all coming together. If only she could keep her attraction to Angelo under wraps. Was that even possible at this point?

Who'd have thought that the wish she'd made at the fountain would actually come true?

Angelo had kissed her—again.

Her eyelids drifted closed as her thoughts spiraled back to their amazing day beneath the Tuscany sun. The day couldn't have gone any better. She'd always treasure it. And then there had been that mind-blowing, toe-curling kiss—

"And what has you staring off into space with a smile on your face?"

Kayla glanced up to find Angelo gazing at her. "Um… nothing. I… I mean I was thinking about the wedding."

"How about the Van Holsen account? We don't want to forget about it."

"Of course not. I've sent out the new concepts to the art department."

"Good." He took a seat next to her. "You know if you're having problems you can talk to me?"

Was he referring to personal problems? Or business ones? Since they'd arrived in Italy the lines had blurred so much that she wasn't sure. But she decided that it was best for her career to take his comment as a purely professional one.

"I understand." She smoothed her hands down over her white capris. "And so far the accounts are all moving along.

I should have some drafts back from the art department this afternoon to run by you."

"Sounds good. Can I see what you've come up with so far for the royal wedding?"

She pushed her notebook over to him. "Go ahead."

The seconds slowly passed as his gaze moved down over the first page. "But this is all about Monte Calanetti." He shoved aside the pages. "There's nothing here about the wedding itself. Nothing sentimental or romantic."

Oh, boy.

This was not the start she'd imagined. She swallowed a lump in her throat. To be honest, she wasn't ready to present her ideas to him. They were only partial thoughts—snippets of this and that.

She'd have to think fast on her feet if she wanted him to keep her on this account, because she wasn't about to let this opportunity slip through her fingers. She leveled her shoulders and tilted her chin up, meeting his frown. "I think the main focus should be all about the location."

"You do?"

She nodded. "The royal couple have already been taken by the village's charm." Kayla lowered her voice and added, "I was taken by it, too. It'd be the perfect backdrop for a wedding. And that's the part I think we should exploit."

Angelo's eyes widened and he was quiet for a moment as though considering her words. "What issues do you have with basing the pitch on the wedding itself? You know with all of the pomp and circumstance. We could even throw in a horse-drawn carriage for good measure."

Kayla smiled, loving the idea of six white horses leading a shiny white carriage with gold trim. And then her imagination took a wild turn and there was Angelo next to her in the carriage. Her insides quivered at the thought. Then, realizing that she was getting off point, she gave herself a mental jerk.

"We don't know anything about what the bride wants for the actual ceremony. But we need to show them that no matter whether it is a big, splashy affair, which seems most reasonable considering it's a royal wedding, or whether they want something smaller and more intimate, that Monte Calanetti can be quite accommodating."

Angelo leaned back and crossed his arms as he quietly stared at her. He was taking her suggestions seriously. She inwardly cheered. Not about to lose her momentum, she continued. "No matter what the size of the ceremony, we need to show them that we are willing to work with the bride. We need to show them that the whole community will come together to make it a day that neither of them will ever forget."

"So you think our approach should be two-pronged, showing the village both as intimate and accommodating."

Kayla nodded. "The tour you gave me was a great start. But if we are going to sell the royals on the virtues of this village, I think we need to dig deeper."

Angelo nodded. "Sounds reasonable. What do you have in mind?"

Before she could continue, her phone vibrated on the table. She'd turned off the ringer, not wanting to bother anyone else who was around the pool.

"Do you need to get that?" Angelo's gaze moved from her to the phone.

"Um…no."

Angelo cocked a brow. "It could be the office."

"I already checked my voice mail and sorted everything that needs attention." She wanted to get back to their conversation, but he kept glancing at her phone. Knowing he wasn't going to let up on this subject until he found out why she was so hesitant to answer, she grabbed her phone and checked the ID. Just as she'd suspected, the call was from the States but it wasn't the office—it was Pam, the woman handling the fund-raiser while Kayla was in Italy.

"It's nothing urgent." Kayla would deal with it later.

"Are you sure?"

"I am." This wasn't Pam's first call of the day nor would it likely be her last.

Why was Angelo looking at her that way? It was as though he could see that she was holding something back. And the last thing Kayla needed was for him not to trust her. Because this royal wedding was the opportunity of a lifetime. She planned to grasp it with both hands and hold on tight. Having Angelo make her an official part of this pitch would be the validation she needed to show her parents that she'd made the right decision with her life. At last, they'd be proud of her and her choices.

"Okay." He waved away the phone and grabbed for her notebook again. "You need to add more detail to these notes."

"I will, but I was thinking we need to visit each of the establishments in the village again. I could write up very specific notes about their specialties—things that will be hard to find elsewhere—items that the village is especially proud of."

His eyes lit up. "And I know exactly where we'll start."

"You do?" She smiled, knowing he liked her ideas. "Where?"

"Mancini's. You did bring something pretty, formal— Oh, you know what I mean."

"A little black dress?"

"Yes, that will do nicely. We have reservations at seven. Consider it a research expedition during which I want to hear more of your thoughts."

Her mounting excitement skidded to a halt upon his assurance that this evening would be all about business. She didn't know why she should let it bother her. This is what she wanted—for things to return to a business relationship. Wasn't it?

* * *

Time flew by far too fast.

A week had passed since their dinner at Mancini's. Angelo had been quite impressed with the service and most especially the food. What Raffaele was doing spending his time here in the countryside was beyond Angelo. The man was a magician in the kitchen. He could head up any restaurant that he set his sights on from Rome to New York. Although, it was lucky for Angelo, because Mancini's award-winning menu was going to be the centerpiece of the pitch.

Angelo stood in the middle of the hotel suite. He really liked what he saw. His gaze zeroed in on Kayla. They'd had a couple of tables brought in. The room had been rearranged so that the area loosely resembled an office more than a relaxing, posh hotel room. And it seemed to be helping them to stay on track.

Feeling the pressure to get this right, Angelo had relented and had Kayla pass along some of their other accounts to his top ad executive. Their attention needed to be centered on the wedding, especially since he'd already lost time spinning his wheels. One of the accounts they had retained was Victoria Van Holsen's account. The woman simply wouldn't deal with anyone but himself or Kayla. Victoria, who was quite particular about who she dealt with, had surprisingly taken to Kayla's sunny disposition. It seemed no one was immune to Kayla's charms—him included.

There was so much more to Kayla than he'd given her credit for when he'd hired her as his temporary assistant. Sure, her résumé had been excellent and her supervisors had nothing but glowing reports about her. Still, he was so busy rushing from meeting to meeting, cutting a new deal and approving the latest cutting-edge promotion that he never had time to notice the girl behind the black-rimmed glasses and the nondescript business suits.

While in Italy, he'd witnessed firsthand her passion for her work. She invigorated him to work harder and dig deeper for fresh ideas to top her own, which was nearly impossible as she came up with ideas for the wedding that never would have crossed his mind. To say she was a hard worker was an understatement. She was amazing and it wasn't just her work ethic that fascinated him.

Her smile lit up his world like the golden rays of the morning sun. And when he would lean over her shoulder, he'd get a whiff of her sweet, intoxicating scent. It conjured up the image of a field of wildflowers in his mind and always tempted him to lean in closer for a deeper whiff.

Then there were times like now, when she was concentrating so hard that her green eyes grew darker. She lifted her hand and twirled a long red curl around her finger. He noticed that she did this when she was unsure of something. He wondered what was troubling her now.

He moved closer. "Need some help?"

She glanced up with a wide-eyed stare as though she'd been totally lost in her thoughts. "Um…what?"

This wasn't the first time she'd been so lost in her thoughts that she hadn't heard him. "I said, would you like some help?"

"Sure. I was contemplating the piazza. I'm thinking it should play a prominent part in the wedding processional."

Her words sparked his own imagination. They made a great couple…um, team. He couldn't remember the last time he'd felt this invigorated. "How about having a horse-drawn carriage circle the fountain, giving the villagers a chance to cheer on the future queen?"

"I don't know. The bride will be a bundle of nerves. I don't know if she'll want to spend the time waving at people—"

"Sure she will."

Kayla sent him a doubtful look. "What would you know about weddings?"

"Nothing." His jaw tightened. And he planned to keep it that way. "You're forgetting one important thing."

"And what's that?"

"The villagers are the part that makes the village special."

A smile eased the worry lines on her face. "I'm glad you were paying attention while on our tour. And if the bride is willing, I think the villagers should play a prominent role in the festivities."

"And along the route there could be large royal flags waving in the breeze—"

"No. That's too impersonal." Her eyes sparkled. "What if we hand out small complimentary flags to the onlookers to welcome the newest member of the royal family?"

Angelo paused as he considered the idea. "I like it. It'll be a sea of color."

"I also think the chapel should be included in the pitch." Before he could utter a word, she rushed on. "The place is so beautiful. Sure it needs some work, but it has such a romantic feel to it. Just imagine it filled with roses— No, make that lilies. And the glow of the candles would add to the magic. Can't you just imagine it all?"

"No." He didn't believe in magic or romance. They were just fanciful thoughts. "I can't imagine anyone wanting to get married in such a dump—"

"It's not a dump!"

He ignored her outburst. "Besides, you're forgetting that I talked to the new owner and she wants nothing to do with the wedding."

"And that's it...you're just giving up? She could change her mind."

What was Kayla getting so worked up for? He wasn't making up these problems. "The chapel is crumbling. We are not putting it in the pitch. The royal couple would laugh us out of the room if we presented it—"

"They would not." Her words were rushed and loud. "They'd love its charm."

His muscles tensed. He hated conflict. "We're not using it!"

Her fine brows drew together as she crossed her arms. "You're making a mistake!"

He wasn't used to people challenging his decisions and they certainly didn't raise their voice to him. This argument was ending now. "This is my company—my decision! We're not including the chapel." When she went to speak, he added, "End of story."

She huffed but said nothing more.

For a while, they worked in an uncomfortable silence. He kept waiting for Kayla to rehash their disagreement, but she surprised him and let it go. He didn't know how much time had passed when they started to communicate like normal again.

Angelo rubbed his jaw. "Perhaps our best option is to take all of these photos and do a workup of each setting. We can have sketches made up of how each wedding scenario would work. Nothing sells better than letting the client see it with their own eyes. I'll have the art department start on it right away. They'll be on solid overtime until our meeting with the happy couple."

"You never said— Where is the meeting? At Nico's villa?"

"No. The meeting is in Halencia. It's an island not far from here."

"Oh, how exciting. You must be nervous to be meeting a real prince and his bride."

"Me? What about you?"

"What about me?"

"You're part of this team. You'll be going, too. I hope you have something in your suitcase suitable for a royal meeting. If not, perhaps you can find an outfit or two in the village."

Kayla's mouth gaped open and he couldn't help but chuckle. She looked absolutely stunned. Surely she didn't think that he'd put her to all of this work and then leave her behind. He was never one to take credit for another person's work, and he wasn't about to start now. Kayla deserved this honor.

But he sensed something else was on her mind. He could see the subtle worry lines marring her beautiful complexion when she didn't think he was looking. He had no doubt she was still smarting over his unilateral decision to scrap the chapel proposal. She had to accept that he knew what he was doing.

Just then a cell phone vibrated, rattling against the tabletop. Not sure whose phone it was, Angelo headed for the table in time to witness Kayla grabbing her phone and turning it off without bothering to take the call. She'd been doing it a lot lately.

He cleared his throat. "You know, just because I'm here doesn't mean you can't take a phone call from home now and then."

She shook her head. "It...it was nothing."

"Are you sure about that? I get the distinct feeling that the call was definitely something."

"I told you it's nothing important." Her voice rose with each syllable. "Why are you making such a big deal of it?"

"I just thought it might be important."

Her gaze didn't meet his. Her voice was heated and her words were rushed. "It's nothing for you to worry about. Besides, we have work to do."

He'd never witnessed Kayla losing her composure— ever. What was wrong with her? And why wouldn't she open up to him?

"Kayla, if you need a break—"

"I don't." She ran her fingers through her long red curls before twisting the strands around her fingertip. "Can we get back to work?"

His jaw tightened. These heated exchanges reminded him of his parents, and not in a good way. Kayla had just reinforced his determination to remain single. He wanted absolutely nothing to do with a turbulent relationship.

"Work sounds like a good idea." He turned to his laptop. Before he could even type in his password, Kayla softly called out his name. In fact, her voice was so soft that he was sure he'd imagined it. He glanced over his shoulder to find her standing next to him.

Her gaze was downcast and her fingers were laced together. "I'm sorry for snapping. I didn't mean to grouch at you. I... I—"

Before she could go any further, he uttered, "It's okay. We're both under a lot of pressure, working night and day to get this pitch perfected."

Her eyes widened in surprise. "Thanks for understanding. It won't happen again."

He didn't doubt that she meant it, but he was a realist and knew that blowups happened even in the best of relationships. So where did they go from here?

When he didn't immediately say anything, she added, "The phone call was a friend. I'll deal with it later."

Not about to repeat their earlier argument, he let her comment slide. "Then let's get back to work. We have the menu to work into the layout."

He didn't miss the way she played with her hair—the telltale sign she was nervous. Oh, that call was definitely something important. All of his suspicions were now confirmed. So what could be so important that it had her jumping for the phone, and yet she refused to take the call in front of him? A boyfriend? But she'd already stated categorically that she didn't have one, and he believed her.

So what had her nervous and fidgeting with her hair? What didn't she want him to know? And why was he more concerned about her blasted phone calls and mysterious ways than he was about this presentation that was quickly approaching?

He really needed to get his head in this game or Monte Calanetti would lose the pitch before they even gave their presentation in Halencia. But with Kayla so close by it was difficult at times to remember that she was here to work and not to fulfill his growing fantasies.

Moonbeams danced upon the window sheers as Kayla leaned back in her chair. They'd been working on this pitch night and day, trying to make it beyond amazing. A yawn passed her lips. Not even coffee was helping her at this point.

"You should call it a night." Angelo stared at her over the top of his laptop. "I've got this."

Not about to let him think she wasn't as dedicated to this project as he was, she said, "If you're staying up, so am I."

He sent her an I-don't-believe-you're-so-stubborn look. "If you insist—"

"I do." She crossed her arms. Even that movement took a lot of effort.

He arched a brow, but he didn't argue. "How about we take a break? I'm starved."

"Sounds good to me, but I don't think there's any room service at this hour."

"Who needs room service? There's still half of a pizza in the fridge."

"Oh. I forgot."

In no time, Angelo warmed them each a couple of slices in the microwave in their kitchenette. After handing her a plate, he moved to the couch. "Sorry, I can't provide you anything else."

"This is plenty. It reminds me of my college days. Leftover pizza for breakfast was a common staple in the dorms."

Angelo leaned back, kicked off his loafers and propped his feet up on the coffee table. There was no longer any boss/employee awkwardness between them. Being closed up in a hotel suite, no matter how fancy, left no room for cool distances. In fact, they'd shared some passionate disagreements over the pitch, which only led them to better, outside-the-box ideas. But it was far too late for any passionate conversations—at least the professional ones.

"I'm surprised your parents let you go to college." Angelo's voice roused her from her exhaustion-induced fantasy.

"Why?"

"Because they had your life planned out to be a wife, to be a mom and to take over the family business. Why spend the money and time on an advanced degree if you weren't going to use it?"

The fact that Angelo Amatucci, star of Madison Avenue, was truly interested in her life sent her heart fluttering. "It was hard for them to object when I won an academic scholarship. Plus, they knew I had my heart set on earning a degree. My guess is they thought I'd go, have fun with my friends for a few years and eventually realize my place was with them in Paradise." Her gaze met his. "Didn't your parents expect you to return to Italy after you graduated college?"

He glanced away as he tossed his plate of half-eaten pizza onto the table. "My family is quite different from yours. Their expectations weren't the same."

"I have a hard time believing that, after seeing how much your brother and sister miss you. Maybe you can slow down and fly here more often."

"I don't know." He rubbed the back of his neck. "I'd have to find someone to help with the special accounts—someone the clients would trust."

"Do you have anyone in mind?"

His steady gaze met hers, making her stomach quiver.

"I have an idea or two. And how about you? Is Amatucci & Associates just a stepping-stone for you? Do you have other plans for your future?"

"I'm exactly where I want to be."

His gaze dipped to her lips and then back to her eyes. "That's good to know. I want you here, too." He glanced away. "I mean at the company. You've become really important to me." He cleared his throat. "To the company. You know, it's really late. Let's call it a night and pick up where we left off tomorrow. You know, with the pitch."

Kayla sat there quietly as her normally calm, composed boss tripped and fell over his words. She wanted to tell him to relax because she liked him, too—a lot. The words teetered on the tip of her tongue when he jumped to his feet and moved across the room to shut down his computer.

Disappointment settled in her chest. Shouting her feelings across the room just didn't seem right, nor did she have the guts to do it. And by the rigid line of his shoulders, he wasn't ready to hear the words. She had to accept that the fleeting moment had passed—if it had truly been there at all.

She tried to tell herself that it was for the best. Taking a risk on revealing her feelings to Angelo was putting all of her hopes and dreams on the line, but she wasn't much of a gambler. She liked sure bets. At the moment, the odds were really good that she'd gain a promotion if they pulled off this royal pitch. And that's what she needed to focus on—not on the way Angelo's intense gaze could make her stomach do a series of somersaults.

CHAPTER FIFTEEN

THIS COULDN'T BE HAPPENING.

Two days before Angelo's private jet was scheduled to sweep them off to the Mediterranean island of Halencia, Kayla received yet another phone call from Pam. However with Angelo hovering so close by and forever checking over her shoulder to see the progress she was making with their pitch, she couldn't answer the call. No way. No how.

Kayla sent the call to voice mail before returning to the email she was composing. But a thought had been nagging at her that perhaps after their talk Angelo might have changed his stance on the company doing some charity work. There were so many worthy causes out there that really could use the power of Amatucci & Associates to make a difference. And she wasn't just thinking of her beloved after-school program.

There were countless other organizations that were worthy of a helping hand. Perhaps it was worth a shot. What was the worst that could happen? He would tell her to drop the subject and get back to work? Because surely at this point he wouldn't fire her, would he?

"You've done a really good job with this pitch." And she meant it. Angelo was very talented and creative. If he weren't, he wouldn't be at the top of his game. "It might be a nice idea if you'd considered implementing a charity program at the office. I know a lot of people would be willing to help—"

"No."

Just a one-word answer? Really? Kayla tried to accept it as his final word, but she was having problems swallowing such a quick dismissal. Why did he have to be so close-minded? Was he that worried about his bottom line?

She stared at him. How was it possible that the same man who had escorted her around the village and had shared some of his childhood memories with her could be opposed to helping charities? There had to be something more to his decision.

Maybe if she understood, she could change his mind—make him see that charities needed his special kind of help. Not everyone was gifted in getting the word out in so many different capacities from tweeting to commercials and radio spots. Not to mention that Angelo had an army of contacts in Hollywood willing to help him when needed.

"Why are you so opposed to the idea of helping out charity organizations?"

"You just aren't going to let this go, are you?"

She shook her head. How could she be honest with him about what had her distracted when she knew that it would put her job in jeopardy? Maybe if she understood his reasons, it would bridge the divide. "Explain it to me."

He raked his fingers through his hair and pulled out a chair next to her. "When I came to the States, I was alone. I didn't know anyone. And I'll admit that it wasn't easy and there were a few scary moments."

This certainly wasn't the explanation that she was expecting, but she liked that he was opening up to her, little by little. "I can't even imagine what that must have been like for you. I mean, I moved to New York City and I didn't know a soul here, but I was only a car ride away from my family. You practically moved halfway around the world."

"I didn't have a choice." His lips pressed together into a firm line as though stopping what was about to come out of his mouth.

"What do you mean?"

"Nothing. It's just that when I was in school, I got caught up in the football team and my dream of graduating college started to fade into the rearview mirror. Now granted, that isn't the same as working for a charitable organization, but

I learned a valuable lesson—if I wanted to be the best at whatever I decided to do, I had to commit myself 100 percent. I couldn't let myself get distracted."

Was that happening to her with the fund-raiser? Was she spreading herself too thin? Was she trying to cover too many bases?

She didn't want to accept that she was setting herself up to fail. He had to be wrong. "Couldn't you have done both in moderation?"

"You're not understanding me—I had to succeed—I had to be the best to get anywhere in New York City. Competition is fierce and if I failed, I couldn't go home."

"Sure you could have—"

"You don't know what you're talking about." His intense stare met hers, warning her not to delve further into that subject. "The point is that I know what happens when people become distracted for any reason—no matter how good the cause. They lose their focus. Their ambition dwindles. And that can't happen to Amatucci & Associates. I hate to say it, but it's a cutthroat business. If we lose our edge, the competitors will swoop in and steal away our clients."

Between the lines she read, if she lost her edge—if she didn't give 100 percent—she'd lose her dream. She'd fail and return to Paradise with her tail between her legs. Her stomach twisted into a queasy knot.

She clasped her hands together. Knowing all of this, there was no way she was about to confess to Angelo that she was spending every free moment handling a fund-raiser that seemed to hit one snag after the next. He'd think she wasn't dedicated to her career—that couldn't be further from the truth.

She cleared the lump from the back of her throat. "And that's why you compromise and write generous checks each year to the various organizations?"

He nodded. "I didn't say I wasn't sympathetic. But the office policy stands. End of discussion."

She was more than happy to change subjects, and he'd touched upon one that she was most curious about. "And your parents—"

"Are not part of this discussion."

They might not be, but that didn't mean that she didn't understand a whole lot more about them now. At last, the pieces of his family life started to fall into place. She had wondered why they weren't at the villa to greet Angelo. Nor were they around to help their daughter cope with her unplanned pregnancy. There was definitely discord, and it must run quite deep if Angelo still wasn't ready to broach the subject.

Something told her that he'd closed himself off from that part of his life and focused on his business not so much because he was worried about losing focus, but rather because he found his business safe. It lacked the ability to wound him the way family could do with just a word or a look. That was why he was so cold and professional most of the time. It was his shield.

That was no way to live. There was so much more in life to experience. And she desperately wanted to show him that…and so much more.

But how was she to help him if he wasn't willing to open up?

"Help! I don't know what to do. Everything is ruined."

Kayla's heart lurched at the sound of Pam's panicked voice. She gripped the phone tightly and reminded herself that Pam tended to overreact. Things with the ICL fundraiser had been going pretty well. Ticket sales were still lagging but the radio spots were helping. What could be wrong now?

"Pam, slow down."

"But we don't have time."

"Take a deep breath. It can't be as bad as you're thinking."

"No, it could be worse." Pam sniffled.

Okay. What had happened this time? Did Pam lose another file on her computer? Or misplace the phone number for the manager of the headline band? Pam did blow things out of proportion.

"Pam, pull yourself together and tell me what happened." While Kayla hoped for the best, she steeled herself for a catastrophe.

"They canceled."

Kayla sat up straight, knocking her empty water glass over. Surely she hadn't heard correctly. "Who canceled?"

"The band." Pam started to cry again.

Impossible. "The band quit?"

"Yes! What are you going to do?" She hiccupped.

"But they can't just quit. We have an agreement—a contract."

"That…that's what I said. They said there was a clause or some sort of thing in there that let them back out."

Kayla rubbed her forehead. This couldn't be happening. What was she supposed to do about it all the way in Italy?

"I… I just can't do this anymore. Everyone is yelling at me." The sniffles echoed across the Atlantic. "I can't."

Oh, no. She couldn't have Pam backing out on her, too. "Calm down." Kayla's hands grew clammy as she tightened her hold on the phone. "You can't quit. The kids are counting on us. We can't let them down."

"But what are you going to do? You have to fix this. I can't."

Kayla wanted to yell that she didn't know but that the whining wasn't helping anyone. "I don't know yet. What did the band say was the problem?"

"They got a contract with some big band to be the opening act on a cross-country tour. They leave before the concert."

It'd certainly be hard to compete with a national tour.

Most likely this was the band's big break and Kayla's heart sank, knowing that wild horses couldn't hold them back. And to be honest, she couldn't blame them. This was what they'd been working toward for so long now. But none of that helped her or the fund-raiser.

Kayla struggled to speak calmly. "Just sit tight. I'll think of something."

"You know of another band that can fill in at the last minute?"

She didn't have a clue where to find a replacement. In fact, she'd totally lucked into that first band. A friend of a friend knew the band manager, who liked the idea of free publicity. Where in the world would she locate another band?

"I need time to think." Kayla said, feeling as though the world was crumbling around her.

"But what do I tell people?"

"Tell them that we'll have an announcement soon."

Kayla ended the call. Her mind was spinning. She didn't know how she was going to save the event. The enormity of the situation was only beginning to settle in. With no headline act, there was no point. The tickets would have to be refunded. The Inner City League after-school program would cease to exist.

All of those at-risk kids would be turned away.

No! She refused to fail them. Visions of Gina's smiling face, Patrick's pout when she didn't have time to throw the ball with him and Lilly's anxious look as she'd handed Kayla a new drawing filled her mind. And there were so many more faces—all counting on her to come through for them.

Something splashed her hand. Kayla glanced down to see a tear streak down the back of her hand. She lifted her fingers and touched her cheek, finding it damp. At that moment, she heard the door to the suite open. She took a deep calming breath and dashed the back of her hands across her cheeks.

"I'm back." Angelo's deep voice echoed through the large room. "Did I miss anything?"

Talk about a loaded question. "Um…no." She struggled to sound normal as she kept her back to him. She blinked repeatedly and resisted the urge to fan her overheated face. "Nothing much happened around here."

"You were right about approaching my brother." He paused. "Kayla?"

"Yes."

"Is there a reason I'm talking to the back of your head?"

She shook her head. "I'm just finishing up an email."

"Do you want to hear this?"

"Um…yes. Of course. I can do two things at once."

There was an extended pause as though he was deciding if she were truly interested or not. "Well, I asked Nico for permission to offer up his vineyard as one of the sites for the wedding. The photographer from the village is stopping by tomorrow to take some professional photos."

"I'm glad the meeting went smoothly between you and your brother. What about the new owner of the neighboring vineyard? What did you say her name was?"

"Louisa something or other." He rubbed the back of his neck. "I talked to her about using her vineyard, since it's larger than Nico's place, but she was adamant that she wants absolutely nothing to do with the wedding."

"Really? How odd."

"Not as odd as this."

"What do you mean?" Kayla hated putting on this pretense, but she knew that he would never abide her splitting her work hours between the royal wedding and a charity event. He'd already made that abundantly clear.

"You won't face me and there's something off with your voice." His approaching footsteps had her body tensing. He knelt down next to her. He placed a finger beneath her chin and turned her face to his. "Now tell me, what's got you upset?"

His voice was so soft and comforting. All she wanted to do in that moment was lean into his arms and rest her face in the crook of his neck. She wanted to feel the comfort and security of his strong arms holding her close. She wanted him to tell her that everything would be all right—that they would work together to find a solution.

But none of that could or would happen. Angelo would never understand how she'd knowingly gone behind his back to work on this fund-raiser instead of focusing solely on the royal wedding. She'd never be able to justify her actions to his satisfaction.

"I'm fine." Her gaze didn't meet his.

"You're not fine. Not by a long shot." As though he'd been privy to her thoughts, he reached out and pulled her to him.

She shouldn't do this. It wasn't right. But her body had other thoughts and willingly followed his lead. Her cheek pressed against the firmness of his shoulder and she inhaled the spicy scent of his cologne mingled with his male scent. It was quite intoxicating.

Her eyes drifted closed and for a moment she let go of everything. The silent tears streamed down her cheeks. She took comfort in the way Angelo's hands rubbed her back. It wove a spell over her and relaxed muscles that she hadn't realized were stiff.

"I'm sorry for working you too hard."

She dashed her fingers over her cheeks and pulled back. "You aren't making me work this hard—I want to do it. I want to do everything to make our pitch stand out."

He ran his hands up her arms, sending goose bumps racing down her skin. "But not to the point where you've worn yourself to a frazzle. Look at you. You've gotten yourself all worked up."

She shook her head. No matter how much she wanted

to open up to him, she couldn't. They only had two days until they had to catch a plane to Halencia, and they still didn't have a completed pitch. And what they had didn't sparkle. And it didn't scream "pick me." There was something missing, but she just couldn't put her finger on it. And now, add to it the problem with the fund-raiser and she was at a total loss.

"Kayla, if you won't talk to me, how can I help?"

Her gaze met his, and she saw the worry reflected in his eyes. "You can't."

"Why don't you give me a chance?"

He just wasn't going to let this go. His eyes begged her to open up to him—to trust him. But she couldn't give up her dream of being the sort of person that Angelo Amatucci would want as an ad executive—she'd given up everything to follow this dream. She couldn't return to Paradise and face her parents as a failure.

"The truth is I... I have a headache." And that wasn't a lie. The stress of everything had her temples pounding.

He studied her for a moment as though weighing her words. "Did you take anything for it?"

"I was about to, but I hadn't made it there yet."

Angelo nodded as though he knew what needed to be done. "Go lie down on the couch and rest—"

"But I have stuff that needs done—"

"Later. Right now, you're going to rest. I'll get some medication for you."

His thoughtfulness only made her feel worse—about everything—most especially that she couldn't open up to him. She was certain that he would have some amazing suggestion that would save the fund-raiser, but she just couldn't risk everything she'd worked for. Instead, she'd have to pray for a miracle.

CHAPTER SIXTEEN

He was as ready as he would ever be.

Angelo kept telling himself that, hoping it would sink in.

As the royal limo ushered them through the streets of Halencia toward the palace, Angelo stared out the window. Mounting tension over this meeting had his body stiff. This sort of reaction was unfamiliar to him. Usually he was calm, cool and collected. He was the expert when it came to marketing. But ever since he'd let his guard down around Kayla, he'd lost that cool aloofness that he counted on when doing business.

She'd gotten past his defenses and had him connecting with his emotions. He just hoped he hadn't lost his edge— the confidence needed to execute a pitch and sell the buyer on his—er—their ideas.

The flight had been a short one as Halencia was just a small island nation not far off the coast of Italy. Angelo had noticed how Kayla kept to herself, working on her computer. He had no idea what she'd been working on because at that point the pitch had been locked in. They had the talking points nailed down and the graphics were in order. He'd made sure to include what he considered the key element—a sample menu from Raffaelle's restaurant. All combined, he hoped this pitch would clinch the royal couple's interest.

Kayla had even insisted on bringing along some of the baked goods for the royal couple to sample. They were fresh baked that morning and delivered to their hotel suite. He'd tried to taste them, but Kayla had smacked his hand away with a warning glance. Everyone in Monte Calanetti was excited and more than willing to do their part to help.

But Kayla had him worried. She'd been so quiet on the flight here. And now as she leaned against the door of the limo with her face to the window, the bubbly woman who toured Monte Calanetti was gone. He didn't recognize this new person.

He cleared his throat. "Are you feeling all right?"

Kayla turned to him, the dark circles under her eyes were pronounced. His gut tightened.

She smiled, but her lips barely lifted at the corners. "Sure. I'm fine."

He wasn't going to argue the point when it was obvious that she was anything but fine. "You did an excellent job preparing the pitch."

She shrugged. "I don't know. I guess it all depends on what the royal couple says."

He shook his head. "It doesn't matter whether they chose Monte Calanetti or not for the wedding, I know for a fact that you went above and beyond for this project." He hated how his praise seemed to barely faze her. She'd worn herself out and he'd been so busy trying to tie up all of the loose ends for this pitch that he'd failed to notice.

On the flight to Halencia, he'd been mulling over how to recognize Kayla's tremendous effort. He decided to share part of it with her now. "And when we get back to New York, you'll be rewarded for your accomplishments not only with the royal pitch but also with the success of the Van Holsen account."

Her eyes widened. "Really? I... I mean thank you."

Before she could say more, her phone buzzed. She swiped her finger over the screen and frowned. Her fingers moved rapidly over the touch screen as her frown deepened.

Even Angelo had his limits. Work could wait. They were almost at the palace and having her upset was not going to be a good way to start their meeting with the royal couple. He reached out and snagged her phone from her.

She glanced up and her mouth gaped open. Then her lips pressed together into a firm line and her gaze narrowed.

She held out her hand. "It's important."

"It can wait."

"No, it can't."

The car slowed as they eased through the gates leading up the drive to the palace. "We're here. Forget the rest of the world and enjoy this adventure. It isn't every day you get a royal invitation to a palace."

Kayla turned to the window as they wound their way up the paved drive lined with statues and greenery. It was very prestigious and yet it wasn't overly pretentious. In fact, he found it quite a fitting reflection of their nobility. He just hoped that they'd find the prince and his bride to have the same unassuming demeanor.

When the palace came into view, Angelo was taken by surprise at the enormity of it. The palace stood three stories high and appeared to be a large square with towers at each corner. The outside was painted a sunny yellow while the numerous windows were outlined in white. Grand, sweeping stairs led the way to a large patio area with two enormous doors in the background that granted access to the palace.

There weren't that many things in life that still took Angelo's breath away, but he had to admit that this palace was an amazing piece of architecture. And with the abundance of greenery and bright flowers, it was definitely like stepping into paradise. He couldn't even imagine what it must be like calling this place home.

The car swung up the drive and stopped right in front of the palace. To one side was a garden with a fountain in the center. It was quite inviting. He could easily imagine taking Kayla for a stroll through it after dinner as the setting sun cast a watermelon hue over the sky. They'd stop to admire a flower and she'd turn to him. The breeze would rush through her hair as her gaze would meet his. Then his attention would move to her lips. No words would be necessary as they'd lean into each other's arms.

"Angelo, this is amazing."

Kayla's voice jerked him from his daydream, which was in fact amazing. "Um…yes. This is quite beautiful."

"Is this your first visit?"

"It is. I've never done business in this part of the world before." Though he had done business in a great many other countries.

As beautiful as the grounds were, Angelo's attention was drawn back to Kayla. He had plans for her. A surprise after their big presentation. At first, he'd been hesitant, but now, seeing how weary she was, he was certain that he'd made the right decision. He just hoped she would relax long enough to enjoy it.

He still had the feeling that she was keeping something from him—something that was eating at her. But what was it? Was she worried that he'd make another move on her?

The thought left him feeling unsettled. Granted, he wasn't that good at reading women. They were forever a mystery to him, but he'd swear that she was into him and his kisses. She'd come alive in his arms. He was certain that he hadn't imagined that. So then, what had her putting an unusually big gap between them in the limo?

He was impressive.

Kayla sat in one of the plush chairs in the palace's state room. Instead of taking a closer view of the ornate ceiling with large crystal chandeliers, the red walls with white trim, the huge paintings of historical figures or the priceless statues on pedestals, her entire attention was focused on Angelo as he stood in the front of the room in his freshly pressed navy suit and maroon tie. Every inch of him looked as if he'd just stepped off the cover of a men's magazine. He was definitely the most handsome man she'd ever laid her eyes on.

And his presentation was truly impressive. If this didn't sell the royal couple on the benefits of holding the royal wedding in Monte Calanetti, then nothing would. Angelo's talk was informative while containing bits of entertainment. Sure, he'd gone over it with her back in Italy, but somehow here in front of the royal prince and his bride, it seemed so much more special—more dynamic.

"Monte Calanetti offers a variety of services from a world-renowned chef to the most delicious bakery." Angelo moved off to the side while Kayla started the slideshow presentation on a large high-definition screen. "You can see here an overview of the village—"

With the slideshow up and running, Kayla's thoughts spiraled away from the presentation she knew verbatim. Instead, she was amazed by the man making the presentation. Though he didn't have the best one-on-one people skills, he was truly amazing when he was selling an idea. His voice was strong, sure and unwavering. His tone was cajoling. And his posture was confident but not cocky. No wonder he was the best in the business.

So then how in the world was he so inept when it came to dealing with people—people like his family? People like her? Why did he have to make it so tough to get close to him?

Why couldn't he let his guard down and take a chance on love like the crown prince and his Cinderella bride? Kayla's gaze moved to the soon-to-be couple, envious that they seemed to have it all—success, stability and most of all love.

But as they sat there surrounded by their staff, Kayla didn't see any telltale signs of love. There were no clasped hands. No loving gazes when they thought no one was looking. No nothing.

Kayla gave herself a mental jerk. She was overthinking things. Of course they were being all businesslike. This was their wedding—a wedding that would have all of the world watching. That had to be their focus right now.

Still, there was something that nagged at her about the couple, but she brushed it off. Whatever it was—bridal nerves or such—it was absolutely none of her business. She had enough of her own problems.

He'd nailed it.

Angelo wore an easy smile. The presentation had gone without a hitch. Everything had fallen into place just as he'd practiced it over and over again with Kayla in their hotel suite. He had a good feeling that Monte Calanetti would be in serious contention for the site of the royal wedding.

After the slideshow presentation was over, Angelo asked, "Are there any questions?"

"Yes." The bride, Christina Rose, sat up straight. "I didn't see anything in your presentation about the chapel. I'm particularly interested in it."

Angelo's gut knotted. He'd been wrong. His gaze sought out Kayla. He was certain that she'd be wearing an I-told-you-so look. But her chair was empty? Where had she gone? The next thing he knew Kayla was standing next to him. What in the world?

"Hi. I'm Kayla." She sent him an I've-got-this smile. "The chapel is my part of the presentation."

He moved away and went to take a seat. What in the world did Kayla have up her sleeve? He thought they'd settled this back in Monte Calanetti—no chapel presentation. His back teeth ground together as he remembered that call had been his.

Angelo leaned back in his chair while Kayla put photos of the chapel up on the screen with a pitch that he'd never heard before, but it sounded like music to his ears. So the little minx had gone behind his back and done exactly what he'd told her not to do.

And he couldn't be happier.

After Kayla finished her short presentation, the bride

spoke up again. "The chapel—you mentioned that it had just switched ownership—the new owner—have they approved the use of it for the wedding?"

Seriously? That had to be the first question. Kayla's gaze momentarily strayed to him. He had no help to offer her, but he was anxious to see how she handled the question.

Kayla laced her fingers together. "At this moment, we have not obtained a release for the use of the chapel." The bride's face creased with frown lines. That was definitely not a good sign. "Knowing the chapel is of particular interest to you, we will make it a priority to secure its use for the wedding."

The young woman's eyes lit up, but she didn't say anything as she glanced over at the crown prince. He didn't speak to Kayla, either, but rather conversed softly with his advisors, who had a list of questions.

Kayla handled the inquiries with calm and grace. Angelo couldn't have done any better. She certainly was full of surprises, and he couldn't be happier having her by his side.

It wasn't until much later that Angelo walked with her toward their rooms. This was their first chance to talk privately since the presentation. As they strolled along the elegant hallways, Kayla waited anxiously to hear Angelo's thoughts on how she'd handled her part of the meeting. She hoped he wasn't too upset about her ignoring his dictate about the chapel.

Angelo stopped and turned to face her. "Stop looking so worried. You did an excellent job today."

"I did?"

He nodded. "I owe you an apology for not listening to you and a thank-you for being so prepared."

"Really? Even though I didn't do what you said?"

He gazed deep into her eyes. "I think you have excellent instincts and the courage to follow them. You've got what it takes to have a very bright future."

In her excitement, she threw her arms around him. He had no idea how much she needed this one perfect moment.

Coming back to earth, she grudgingly let go of him and stepped back. "Thank you for the opportunity."

"You earned it. And you did well by knowing all of the answers to their questions. And you took notes of things that particularly interested them. I couldn't have done any better."

"You really mean that? You're not just saying these things to make me feel better."

He chuckled. "Did anyone ever tell you that you don't take compliments well?"

She shrugged. "I guess I'm still wound up."

"We make a great team."

It was the first time he'd ever referred to them in that manner and she liked it. She really liked it. More than that, she liked him a lot—more than was wise. But that didn't stop her heart from pounding in her chest when he gazed deeply into her eyes.

He was going to kiss her—again. She should turn away. She should pretend she didn't know that he was interested in her. But her body had a will of its own, holding her in place. She knew that nothing good would come of it, but she wanted him to kiss her more than she wanted anything in that moment.

Angelo turned and continued down the hallway. The air that had been caught in her lungs rushed out. What had happened? It took her a second to gather her wits about her, and then she rushed to catch up to him.

They continued on in silence until they stopped outside her bedroom door. He turned to her again. "Thank you for everything. If I had done this alone, I wouldn't have stood a chance of winning their favor. You were my ace in the hole."

His gaze caught and held hers.

"I… I was?"

He nodded and stepped closer. "How could anyone turn you down?"

Her heart pitter-pattered harder and faster. She didn't want this moment to end—not yet. It was her very own fairy tale. "Do you want to come inside?"

He tucked a loose curl behind her ear. Then the back of his fingers grazed down her cheek. "I don't think that would be a good idea. We're expected at dinner with the royal couple. It wouldn't look right if we were late."

The hammering of her heart drowned out her common sense. Because when he was looking at her that way and touching her so sweetly, all she could think about was kissing him—

She lifted up on her tiptoes and pressed her lips to his. He didn't move at first and she wondered if there was some way that she had misread the situation. But then his arms wrapped around her and pulled her hard against him. She'd been here before, but it never failed to excite her. He was thoughtful, sweet and kind. Nothing like her boss at the office. This was a different side of him, and she found him utterly irresistible.

Angelo braced his hands on her hips, moving an arm's length away. "We need to stop now or we are never going to make it to that dinner."

"Who needs dinner?" There was only one thing she was hungry for at that moment and she was staring at him.

"Don't tempt me." He smiled at her. "I don't think that would help our pitch." He pressed a kiss to her forehead and proceeded down the hallway to his room.

In that moment, Kayla felt lighter than she had in days. Suddenly anything seemed possible. Maybe she'd given up on the fund-raiser too soon. She pressed a hand to her lips. Perhaps everything would work out in the end, after all.

She sure hoped so.

CHAPTER SEVENTEEN

"I DON'T UNDERSTAND."

Kayla's gaze narrowed in on Angelo as they stood beneath the crystal chandelier in the marble foyer. He'd been acting mysterious ever since they'd given their pitch to the royal couple the day before. Was it the kiss? It couldn't be. He hadn't been distant at the royal dinner. In fact, he'd been quite attentive—even if the evening hadn't ended with any more kisses.

"Trust me." His dark eyes twinkled with mischief. "You will understand soon enough."

"It'd be easier if you'd just tell me where we're going. If this has something to do with the pitch, you should tell me. I would have brought my laptop. Or at least I could have grabbed my tablet."

"You don't need it." He took her hand and guided her out the door, down the palace steps and into an awaiting limo. "Trust me."

"But how do I know if I'm dressed appropriately. The only formal clothes I have with me I wore yesterday for the pitch and then the dinner with the royal couple. I thought that we'd be leaving today."

"I've delayed our departure."

He had? She didn't recall him mentioning anything to her. Then again, she'd been so caught up in her thoughts lately that she might have missed it.

"Don't worry. I ran it past your boss." He winked at her. "He's fine with it."

"He is, huh?" She wondered what Angelo was up to and why he was in such a good mood. "But why aren't we flying back to Italy? I thought you'd be anxious to wrap things up there before we return to New York."

"It can wait."

She had absolutely no idea where they were headed. The curiosity was eating at her. But the driver knew. She turned to the front to ask him.

"Don't even think of it," Angelo warned as though he knew exactly what she intended. "He's been sworn to secrecy."

Her mouth gaped open. Angelo really did know what she was thinking. Thankfully he didn't know everything that crossed her mind or else he'd know that she'd gone against his express wishes and worked on the fund-raiser during work hours.

And worst of all, her efforts were for naught. She'd reached out to everyone she could think of, but she had yet to come up with another big-name band on such short notice. But ever the optimist, she wasn't canceling the event until the very last minute. There just had to be a way to help the kids.

"Hey, no frowning is allowed."

She hadn't realized that her thoughts had transferred to her face. "Sorry. I was just thinking of all the work I should be doing instead of riding around with you."

"You'll have plenty of time for work later. In fact, when we return to New York I imagine that you'll have more work than you'll ever want."

She sent him a quizzical look. Was he trying to tell her something?

"Quit trying to guess. You aren't going to figure out our destination."

The car zipped along the scenic roadway. Angelo was totally relaxed, enjoying the terrific view of the tranquil sea. But she couldn't relax. Not yet. Not like this. Not with the fate of the fund-raiser hanging over her head.

Kayla desperately wanted to ask Angelo for help, but she just couldn't bring herself to trust him, knowing his adamant stance on such matters. But if she didn't ask Angelo for help, what did that say about their relationship? Did it mean what they'd shared meant nothing?

The thought left a sour taste in her mouth. The Angelo she'd got to know so well here in Italy put his family above his own needs even at the risk of one of his most important accounts. But that was his family? And she was what?

She had absolutely no answer.

Realizing that he was still holding her hand, her heart thumped. She was certainly more than his assistant—but how much more?

He turned to her. Their gazes caught and held. Her heart started to go *tap-tap-tap*. Oh, yes, she was definitely falling for her boss.

But what would happen when this trip was over? What would their relationship be like when they returned to the reality of their Madison Avenue office? Or worse yet, what if he found out that she'd been working on the fund-raiser instead of devoting all of her attention to her work?

"Relax. Everything will be okay." Angelo raised her hand to his lips and pressed a gentle kiss to the back of her hand.

Her stomach shivered with excitement. Throwing caution to the wind, she uttered, "When you do that, relaxing is the last thing on my mind."

"In that case…" He pulled her close and with her hand held securely in his, he rested his arm on his leg. His voice lowered. "You can get as worked up as you like now."

His heated gaze said a hundred things at once. And all of them made her pulse race and her insides melt. He wanted her. Angelo Amatucci, the king of Madison Avenue, was staring at her with desire evident in his eyes.

If she were wise, she would pull away and pretend that none of this had happened. But her heart was pounding and her willpower was fading away. She'd been resisting this for so long that she was tired of fighting it—tired of denying the mounting attraction between them.

Maybe this thing between them wouldn't survive the harsh glare of the office, but that was days away. They were to remain in Italy until the royal couple had all of the inquiries answered and their decision made. In the meantime, what was so wrong with indulging in a most delightful fantasy?

Once again, Angelo seemingly read her mind—realizing that she'd come to a decision. He turned to her and leaned forward. His lips were warm as they pressed to hers. Her eyes drifted closed as her fingers moved to his face, running over his freshly shaved jaw. His spicy aftershave tormented and teased. It should be illegal for anyone to smell so good. A moan bubbled up in the back of her throat.

The car stopped, jostling them back to the here and now. Angelo was the first to pull away. Disappointment coursed through her. Her eyes fluttered open and met his heated gaze.

"Don't look so disappointed. There will be time for more of this later." He smiled and her discontentment faded away. "Remember, I have a surprise for you."

"Did I forget to tell you that I love surprises?"

He laughed. "I was hoping you would."

She glanced out her window, finding nothing but lush greenery, flowers and trees. She struggled to see around Angelo, but with his arm draped loosely around her, she couldn't see much.

"I can't see." She wiggled but his strong arm kept her next to him—not a bad place to be, but she was curious about their location. "Where are we?"

"My, aren't you impatient? You'll soon see."

She couldn't wait. Though she still had problems to resolve, for just this moment she let them shift to the back of her mind. She might never have this kind of experience again, and she didn't want to miss a moment of it. And it had nothing to do with the surprise that Angelo had planned for her.

It had everything to do with the man who could make her heart swoon with those dark, mysterious eyes.

Mud. Seriously.

Angelo frowned as he sat submerged in a mud bath. He felt utterly ridiculous. This was his first trip to a spa, and though he'd set up the appointment for Kayla, he'd thought he might find out what he was missing. After all, Halencia was known for its world-renowned spa. It ought to be renowned for the exorbitant prices and, worse yet, the cajoling he had to do to get an appointment at the last moment. He'd finally relented and name-dropped—the prince's name certainly opened up their schedule quickly. But it had been worth it when Kayla's face lit up.

He glanced sideways at her as she leaned back against the tub's ledge with her eyes closed. Her long red wavy hair was twisted up in a white towel, safe from this muck. She definitely wasn't the prim-and-proper girl that he'd originally thought her to be when he'd hired her as his temporary assistant. No, Kayla definitely had a bit of a naughty, devil-may-care attitude. And that just intrigued him all the more.

"I'm sorry." Angelo didn't know what else to say. "I guess I should have done more research before making the reservations, but we were so pushed for time with the royal pitch that it just slipped my mind."

Kayla lifted her head. "It's really no problem. I'm enjoying myself."

"But how was I to know that they would set us up for a couple's spa day?"

Her eyes lit up. Her smile stretched into a grin and her eyes sparkled with utter amusement.

"Hey, you aren't inwardly laughing at me, are you?"

"Who? Me? No way." She clutched her bottom lip between her teeth as her shoulders shook.

He wasn't used to being the source of entertainment, but she certainly seemed to be enjoying herself. He supposed that made it worth it. Although, when he'd found out what was involved in the deluxe package, he did think that she was going to balk and walk away. But he'd been worried for no reason.

Kayla wasn't shy. In fact, she could be quite bold. The memory of her in hot pink lacy underwear before she'd stepped into the mud had totally fogged up his mind. Although, when he'd had to strip down to his navy boxers, he'd been none too happy. How could he have overlooked the need to bring swimsuits? Talk about taking down each other's defenses and getting down to the basics.

"What are you thinking about?"

He turned to Kayla, finding her studying him. "Nothing important. So, are you enjoying your trip?"

"Definitely. But…"

"But what?"

"I get the feeling that you aren't enjoying it. Why is that? Is it because of your sister's situation?"

He shrugged. "I suppose that has something to do with it."

"What else is bothering you? I'd think after being gone for so long that you'd be happy to be back in Italy."

"And you would be wrong. Returning to Monte Calanetti and interacting with my siblings and villagers is one of the hardest things I've ever had to do."

She arched an eyebrow and looked at him expectantly.

Why had he opened his mouth? He didn't want to get into this subject. It would lead to nothing but painful memories. And he couldn't even fathom what Kayla would think of him after he told her the truth about his past—about how he ended up in New York.

She reached out her hand and gripped his arm. "You know that you can talk to me. Openness and honesty are important to a relationship—even a friendship or whatever this is between us. Besides, I'm a really good listener."

Even though they were submerged in this mineral mud

stuff, her touch still sent a jolt up his arm and awakened his whole body. After telling himself repeatedly that she was off-limits, he wanted her more with each passing day. He turned and his gaze met hers.

She was the most beautiful woman he'd ever laid his eyes on and it wasn't just skin-deep. Her beauty came from the inside out. She was kind, thoughtful and caring. She was everything he would ever want in a woman—if he were interested in getting involved in a serious relationship.

But he wasn't. He jerked his gaze back to the large window that gave an amazing view of the Mediterranean Sea, but it wasn't the landscape that filled his mind—it was Kayla. She consumed far too many of his thoughts.

"Angelo, talk to me." Her voice was soft and encouraging.

For the first time in his life, he actually wanted to open up. And though his instinct was to keep it all bottled up inside, he wondered if that was the right thing to do. Maybe if Kayla, with her near-perfect home life, were to see him clearly she wouldn't look at him with desire in her eyes.

But could he do it? Could he reveal the most horrific episode in his life? More than that, could he relive the pain and shame?

He gazed into Kayla's eyes, finding compassion and understanding there. He swallowed hard and realized that perhaps he had more strength than he gave himself credit for. Though taking down his ingrained defenses to expose the most vulnerable part of himself would be extremely hard, he firmly believed it would be for the best. If it would put an end to this thing between him and Kayla, how could he hold back?

He cleared his throat. "Remember when I told you that I left Italy to go to school in the States?"

She nodded. "It's the bravest thing I've ever heard. I couldn't have done it—"

"But the thing is… I didn't do it because I wanted to."

Her brows drew together. "What are you saying?"

"My father and I didn't get along and that's putting it mildly." Angelo's body tensed as his mind rolled back in time. "My parents have always had a rocky relationship. On and off. Divorcing and remarrying." He shook his head, chasing away the unwelcome memories. "It was awful to listen to them."

He stopped and glanced at Kayla, whose expression was one of compassion. And then she did something he didn't expect. She reached over, grabbed his arm again and slid her hand down into the mud until she reached his hand. She laced her fingers tightly around his and gave him a big squeeze.

He exhaled a deep breath and continued. "My father is not a small man and he can be quite intimidating. When I'd had enough and my mother needed help with his temper, I… I'd step between them. My father did not like that at all."

"You don't have to tell me this."

"Yes, I do." He'd started this and he was going to see it through to the end. "It didn't matter what I did, it was never up to my father's expectations. I don't think there was anything I could have done to please him. And by the time I graduated school, I was done trying. And he was done trying."

"One day he blew up at me for not doing something in the vineyard. His bad mood spilled over to my mother— this was one of their good periods, so she didn't want to ruin things with him. When I tried to intervene between him and her by trying to soothe him, my father…he…he threw me out."

Kayla's fine brows rose. "But surely he calmed down and let you back in."

Angelo shook his head as he stared blindly out the window. Suddenly he was back there on that sunny day. His father had pressed a meaty hand to Angelo's chest, sending him stumbling out the front door. His mother's expression was one of horror, but she didn't say a word—not one thing—to contradict her husband. Instead, she'd agreed with him. Angelo's hurt had come out as anger. He'd balled up his hands and lifted them, taunting his father into a fight. But his father had told him that he wasn't worth the effort. How did a father do that to his son? How did he turn his back on him?

Angelo blinked repeatedly. "He told me that I was worthless and that I would never amount to anything. And then he told me to never darken his doorway again. He closed the door in my face."

"But your mother—"

"Wanted to make her husband happy. Don't you get it? Neither of them...they...didn't want me." His gut tightened into a knot and the air caught in his lungs as he fought back the pain of rejection.

This is where Kayla would turn away—just like his parents. She would know he was damaged goods. Not even his own parents could love him. He couldn't face Kayla. He couldn't see the rejection in her eyes.

"So you just left?" Her voice was soft.

He nodded. "I wasn't about to go back."

"But you were just a kid."

"I was man enough to make it on my own. I didn't have a choice. I couldn't live with him after that. And he didn't want me there. Nico brought my clothes to me, and with the money I'd saved from odd jobs over the years and my inheritance from my grandfather, I left. If it wasn't for Nico and Marianna, I'd have never looked back."

"And this is why you avoid serious relationships?"

He shrugged. "There isn't any point in them. The relationship will fail and somebody will get hurt. It's best this way."

"Best for who? You? You know that not everyone will treat you like your parents."

Suddenly he turned to her. His gaze searched her eyes. What was she saying?

Her warm gaze caressed him. "You can't keep yourself locked away from love because you're afraid. Some things are worth the risk."

She is worth the risk.

He leaned over and dipped his head, seeking out her lips. Every time he thought he'd learned everything there was to know about Kayla, she surprised him again. What did he ever do to deserve her?

He deepened the kiss. She responded to his every move. Her heated touch was melting the wall of ice inside him that he used to keep everyone out. Every second with their lips pressed together and their fingers intertwined was like a soothing balm on his scarred heart.

He needed her. He wanted her. He…he cared oh, so much about her.

A person cleared their throat in the background. "Do you need anything?"

Yeah, for you to leave.

Fighting back a frustrated groan, Angelo pulled back. If it wasn't for their attendant, he might have continued that kiss to its natural conclusion. Yes, he'd have definitely followed her into the shower and finished it.

In what seemed like no time, they were ushered from the mud bath into a shower and then into a private Jacuzzi. Angelo didn't know what to do with his hands. Well, he knew what he wanted to do with them, but with their attendant floating in and out, those plans would have to wait for later. For now, he stretched his arms along the rim of the tub and pulled her close to him. He just needed to feel that physical connection.

"Are you enjoying yourself?" He just had to be sure.

"This is perfect. Thank you."

"Well, not quite perfect. I did overlook the need for swimsuits." The heat of embarrassment crept up his neck.

"And miss seeing you in your boxers?" She waggled her brows at him. "I think it worked out perfectly."

"But you had to ruin your…um, clothes. They're all stained now."

"Oh, well. It was worth the sacrifice."

"Don't worry. I'll make sure to replace your…things." Why did he get so tripped up around her? It wasn't like him. But then again, everything was different when he was around Kayla.

"Will you be picking them out yourself?" Her eyes taunted him.

"Sure. Why not?"

"Do you have much experience with women's lingerie? And exactly how will you know what sizes to get?"

Boy, this water was starting to get hot—really hot. "Fine." His voice came out rough, and he had to stop to clear his dry throat. "I'll give you the money and you can get what you need."

She grinned at him. "I never thought of you as the kind to take the easy way out."

He had the distinct feeling there was no winning this conversation. No matter which way he went, he was doomed. "I'll make you a deal."

"Oh, I like the sound of this. Tell me more."

"We'll go together. I'll pick them out, but you have to promise not to wear them for anyone else."

Her eyes widened and then narrowed in on him. "Why, Mr. Amatucci, are you hitting on me?"

"I must be losing my touch if it took you this long to figure it out." He didn't even wait for her response before his head dipped and he caught her lips with his own.

Their relationship was unlike anything he had known previously—he never tired of Kayla. In fact, he missed her when she wasn't next to him. And her kisses, they were sweet and addicting.

What was wrong with him? He never acted like this.

And he never took part in flirting. He never had to. Normally women gravitated to him and things were casual at best. But with Kayla it was different—he was different. He barely recognized himself. It was as if he'd let down his shield of Mr. Angelo Amatucci, Madison Avenue CEO, and could at last be himself.

However, Kayla had taught him that a relationship didn't have to be turbulent like his parent's relationship. She'd opened his eyes to other possibilities. She'd shown him through her patience and understanding that, with openness and honesty, things didn't have to be kept bottled up inside until they exploded.

She hadn't been afraid to voice her disagreement over ideas for the wedding pitch. Nor had she been shy about vocalizing her objection to his no-charity-projects rule at the office. And though he hadn't agreed with her on some of the things, he'd been able to communicate it without losing his temper. Was it possible that he wasn't like his parents? Or was Kayla the key to this calm, trusting relationship?

He wasn't sure what it was, but the one thing he was certain about was that he wanted to explore this more—this thing that was growing between them.

When their attendant entered the room, they pulled apart. Disappointment settled in his chest. But the thought of picking up where they'd left off filled him with renewed vigor. This wasn't the end—it was just the beginning.

"I just have one question." Kayla gave him a puzzled look. "What exactly are we supposed to wear when we leave here? Please don't tell me that we're going commando."

He burst out laughing at the horrified look on her face.

"Hey, this isn't funny."

"Relax. I have another surprise waiting for you."

The worry lines on her face eased. "You do? Aren't you a man of mystery today?"

"I try."

"So tell me what it is."

He shook his head. "Just relax and let the water do its magic. You'll learn about your next surprise soon enough."

CHAPTER EIGHTEEN

CINDERELLA.

Yep, that's exactly how Kayla felt as she stepped out of the limo. Her nails were freshly manicured, her face was done up by a makeup artist and her hair was swept up with crystal-studded bobby pins. And that was just the beginning.

Angelo had surprised her with a gorgeous navy blue chiffon dress. Wide satin straps looped over her shoulders while a pleated bodice hugged her midsection. The tea-length skirt was drawn up slightly in the front while the back of the skirt flirted with her ankles. The thought that Angelo had picked it out for her and that it fit perfectly amazed her.

And there was lingerie—she wasn't even going to ask how he got all of her sizes right. Heat tinged her cheeks. Some things were best left unknown. Her silver sandals, though a bit tight, looked spectacular. And he'd even thought to present her with a sparkly necklace and ear-rings. The man was truly Prince Charming in disguise.

She looped her hand through the crook of his arm as he escorted her into a very posh restaurant. Tall columns, a marble floor and white table linens greeted them. Palms grew in large urns. The soft lighting and instrumental music made the ambience quite romantic. When the maître d' led them to the back of the restaurant and out a door, she wondered where they were going.

She soon found them standing on the terrace overlooking the Mediterranean Sea. A sweet floral scent filled the air. Kayla glanced up to find a wisteria vine woven through an overhead trellis. The beautiful bunches of delicate purple flowers were in full bloom. Lanterns hung from chains and gave off a soft glow. The whole setup was just perfect for a first date—this was a date, wasn't it?

Her gaze strayed to Angelo. What exactly had been his intention in giving her this magical day? Suddenly she decided she didn't want to analyze it—she just wanted to enjoy it.

The maître d' stopped next to a table by the railing. The view was spectacular, but even that word didn't cover the magnificence of the sight before her. The sea gently rolled inland, lapping against the rocks below the balcony. The glow of the sinking sun danced and played with the water, sweeping away her breath. She didn't know such a beautiful place existed on earth.

"If this is a dream, I don't want to wake up."

Angelo smiled at her. "Trust me. I'm having the same dream and I have no intention of waking up anytime soon."

"You have made this a day I'll never forget."

"Nor will I."

She continued to stare across the candlelit table at Angelo, who was decked out in a black tux that spanned his broad shoulders—the place where'd she'd been resting her head not so long ago. Even his dark hair was styled to perfection. Her fingers itched to mess up the thick strands while losing herself in another of his kisses. But that would have to wait until later. It would be the sweetest dessert ever.

The maître d' presented the menus and explained the wine list to Angelo before walking away. Everything sounded delightful.

Angelo peered over the menu at her. "I hope you brought your appetite."

She nodded, eating him up with her eyes. This was going to be a very long dinner.

However much Kayla wanted to throw caution to the wind, there was still a small hesitant voice in the back of her mind. And try as she might, it was impossible to ignore. She'd worked so hard to get to where she was at Amatucci & Associates—did she really want to jeopardize her dreams? And worse yet, if she did continue to thrive there, would she always wonder if her flourishing was due to the fact that she'd had a fling with her boss?

"Did I tell you how beautiful you look?" The flickering candlelight reflected in his dark eyes as he stared across the table at her.

"You don't look so bad yourself."

"You mean this old thing?" He tugged on his lapel. "I just grabbed it out of the back of my closet."

His teasing made her laugh. Maybe she'd worry about all of the ramifications tomorrow. "Is it possible that we never have to go back to New York? Couldn't we just live here in this little piece of heaven and never let the moment end?"

"Mmm... I wish. I've never enjoyed myself this much. But we can make the most of our time here." His eyes hinted at unspoken pleasures that were yet to come. "You know if we weren't in public and there wasn't a table separating us, I'd finish that kiss we started back at the spa."

Her stomach shivered with the anticipation. "Then I guess I have something more to look forward to."

"We both do."

Like Cinderella swept away in her carriage...

The limo moved swiftly over the darkened roadway back to the palace. All Kayla could remember of the dinner was staring across the table at her date. Angelo had presented one surprise after the other, and somewhere along the way, she'd lost her heart to him.

She didn't know when her love for him had started. It was a while back. Maybe it was when she first witnessed how much Angelo cared about his family. Or maybe it was when he'd given her a tour of his village and told her about pieces of his past—finally letting down that wall he kept between them. Then somewhere, somehow, Angelo Amatucci had sneaked into her heart.

Kayla loved him wholly and completely.

The revelation shook her to her core. Part of her wanted to run from him—from these feelings. They had the power to destroy everything she'd built for herself back in New York. But how did she turn off the powerful emotions that Angelo evoked in her? And did she want to?

Just a look and he had her heart racing. Her body willingly became submissive to his touch. And she reveled in the way he'd looked at her back at the spa. He had no idea that her insides had been nothing more than quivering jelly when she stripped down to her undies. But when his eyes had lit up with definite approval and then desire, her nervousness was quickly forgotten.

In his eyes, she saw her present and her future. She saw a baby with Angelo's dark eyes and her smile. Startlingly enough, the thought didn't scare her off. In fact, she liked it. Maybe it was never the idea of a family that frightened her, but rather she'd had her sights set on the wrong man.

"Hey, what has you so quiet?" Angelo reached out and pulled her to his side.

"Nothing." *Everything.*

"I hope you had a good day."

"It was the best." She turned her head and reached up, placing a kiss on the heated skin of his neck. There was a distinct uneven breath on his part.

His fingers lifted from her shoulder and fanned across her cheek. "No, you're the best."

They both turned at once and their lips met. There was no timidity. No hesitation. Instead, there was a raw hunger—a fiery passion. And it stemmed from both of them. Their movements were rushed and needy. Their breath mingled as their arms wrapped around each other. Reality reeled away as though it was lost out there in the sea.

Right now, the only thing Kayla needed or wanted was

Angelo. If they were to have only this one moment together, she wanted it to be everything. She wanted memories that would keep her warm on those long lonely winter nights back in New York.

Angelo moved his mouth from hers. His hands held her face as his forehead rested against hers. His breathing was ragged. "I don't want to leave you tonight."

She knew her response without any debate. "I don't want you to go."

For once, she was going to risk it all to have this moment with the man she loved—even if he didn't love her back.

The limo pulled to a stop at the foot of the palace's sweeping white stairs that were lit with lanterns trailing up each side. Angelo didn't follow protocol. He opened the door before the driver could make it around the car. Angelo turned back and held out his hand to help her to her feet.

With both of them smiling like starstruck lovers, they rushed up the steps and inside the palace. Brushing off offers of assistance from the staff, hand in hand they swiftly moved to the second floor. They stopped outside her bedroom door and Angelo pulled her close. His mouth pressed to hers. He didn't have to say a word; all of his pent-up desire was expressed in that kiss.

When he pulled back, he gazed into her eyes. "Are you sure about this?"

She nodded and opened the door. She'd never been so sure about anything in her life. She led the way into the room. This would be a night neither of them would ever forget.

CHAPTER NINETEEN

WHAT IN THE world had he let happen?

Angelo raked his fingers through his hair, not caring if he messed it up or not. He'd already messed things up big-time with Kayla. In the bright light of the morning sun, he stood on the balcony of his suite in the royal palace. He'd woken up in the middle of the night after a nightmare—a nightmare he'd thought he'd done away with long ago.

After leaving Italy, he'd had nightmares about his father turning him out—of his father throwing his clothes out in the drive and telling him that he was not welcome there ever again. In his dream, and in real life, his mother had cried, but she didn't dare go against her husband's wishes even if it meant sacrificing one of her own children.

But last night his nightmare had been different. It was Kayla who'd turned him away. She'd told him that she never wanted to see him again. He'd begged and pleaded, but she'd hear none of it. Her face had been devoid of emotion as she slammed the door in his face. With nowhere to go, he'd walked the dark streets of New York. When a mugger attacked him, Angelo had sat up straight in bed. His heart had been racing and he'd broken out in a cold sweat.

Angelo gave his head a firm shake, trying to erase the haunting images. Of course, he knew that he wasn't going to end up homeless, but he also knew that the dream was a warning of looming trouble. If his own parents could turn him out, why couldn't Kayla? How could he risk getting close to her, knowing how unreliable relationships could be? After all, his own parents were quite familiar with the divorce courts as they broke up and got back together on a regular basis. Angelo's chest tightened.

The only thing he could do was end things with Kayla—quickly and swiftly. There was no way to put the genie back in the bottle, but that didn't mean that they had to continue down this road—no matter how tempted he was to do just that. He couldn't put his tattered heart on the line only to have it shunned again. The price was just too high.

A knock at his door alerted him to the fact that their car was waiting to take them to the airstrip. It was time to return to Italy. More than that, it was time to face Kayla. He didn't know what to say to her—how to explain that everything they'd shared was a big mistake.

By the time he made it downstairs, Kayla was already in the car. Not even the clear blue sky and the sight of the beautiful gardens could lighten his mood. He was in the wrong here. Things had spiraled totally out of control yesterday, and it had been all his doing.

"Good morning." He settled in the seat next to her, making sure to leave plenty of room between them.

Her face was turned away. "Morning."

That was it. The only conversation they had as his luggage was loaded in the rear. Time seemed suspended as he waited for the car to roll down the driveway. This was going to be a very long trip back to Italy. And a very quiet one.

It wasn't until they were on his private jet and airborne that he realized ignoring the situation wasn't going to make it go away. They still had to work together.

"We need to talk."

Kayla turned to him. "Funny you should pick now to talk."

"What's that supposed to mean?"

"It means that you didn't have time to talk last night. You had one thing on your mind and now that you've gotten it, you want to give me the big kiss-off."

"Hey, that's not fair. I didn't set out to hurt you. You were as willing for last night as I was."

"You didn't even have the decency to face me this morning. You slunk away in the middle of the night."

"That's not true." Not exactly. "I couldn't sleep and I didn't want to wake you up." The truth was that he'd never gone back to sleep after that nightmare. He just couldn't shake the feeling of inevitable doom.

She eyed him up. "So then I jumped to the wrong conclusion? You weren't trying to get away from me?"

The hurt look in her eyes tore at him. This was all about him, not her. She was wonderful—amazing—perfect. He just wasn't the guy for her. But how did he make that clear to her?

He got up from his seat and moved across the aisle and sat beside her, still not sure what to say. Somehow, someway he had to say the right words to make her realize that she was amazing, but they just weren't going to have more than they'd shared yesterday.

He resisted the urge to pull her into his arms and kiss away the unhappiness written all over her face. Instead, he took her hand in his. "Kayla, you are the most wonderful woman I have ever known. And yesterday was very special. I will never ever forget it—"

"But you don't want to see me again." She jerked her hand away.

"No—I mean yes." He blew out a breath. "I'm not the man to settle down into a serious relationship."

"Is that what you tell all of your women?"

"No. It's not." She eyed him with obvious disbelief reflected in her eyes. "I'm telling you the truth. I never let anyone get this close to me."

She crossed her arms. "Then why me? Why did I have to be the one that you let get close only to reject me after one night?"

Frustration balled up in his gut—not at her, at himself for being unable to explain this properly. He'd been a scared young man with no one to turn to for help. Thank goodness for his inheritance or else he never would have been able to make it in the States. But did either of his parents care? No. Did they ever write or phone? No. Not until he'd made it on his own did he hear from his mother—she was marrying his father again and she wanted him to be there. Angelo didn't bother to respond. The only family he acknowledged these days was his brother and sister.

He didn't need a romantic relationship. Love was overrated. His business gave him happiness and a sense of accomplishment—that was all he'd ever need.

And somewhere along the way, he'd stumbled upon his explanation to Kayla. "You have to understand that for years now the only thing I've had to count on in my life was my career, and then it was my business. I've put everything I am into it—"

"But what does that have to do with me—with us?"

He reached out as though to squeeze her arm, but when her eyes widened, he realized that he was making yet another mistake and pulled back. "One of the reasons that Amatucci & Associates was able to grow so rapidly into a top advertising firm is that I gave it 110 percent of my attention—to the point of spending many nights on the couch in my office."

Her eyes grew shiny and she blinked repeatedly. "So what you're saying is that your company is now and will always be more important to you than me."

Is that what he was saying? It sure sounded much harsher when she said it. His gut twisted in a painful knot, knowing that he couldn't be the man worthy of her heart.

"You have to understand. I'm losing my edge. I fumbled this wedding pitch. If it wasn't for you, it would have been a disaster. The thing is I don't fumble accounts. I always maintain my cool. I keep my distance so that I am able to view projects objectively. But since we've been in Italy—since that first kiss—I haven't been able to maintain a professional distance. I've been all over the place, and that can't happen—I can't lose focus. It's what keeps me ahead of my competitors."

He did his best work when he relied on his head and not his heart. It was all of the talk about romance and weddings that had him thinking there was something between him and Kayla. That was all. Exhaustion and too much talk of love.

"I really need to work now." Kayla's voice was icy cold and dismissive.

"Do me a favor." He wanted to say something to lighten her mood.

"Depends."

"Remind me to stay far, far away from any other accounts where there's a wedding involved."

She didn't smile. She didn't react at all. Her head turned back to her computer.

He felt compelled to try again to smooth things over. Was that even possible at this point? "Is there anything I can help you with?"

Her narrowed gaze met his straight on. "You've helped me quite enough. I can handle this on my own. I'm sure you have something requiring your objective view and professional distance."

He moved back to his seat on the other side of the aisle. The fact that she was throwing his own words back in his face hurt. But he deserved it and so much more. He'd lost his head while in Halencia and now Kayla was paying the price.

For the rest of the flight, Kayla didn't say a word, and though he longed for her understanding—he had to accept that it was too much for her to take in. There was a part of him that wasn't buying it, either. It was the same part of him that couldn't imagine what his life was going to be like without her in it.

He leaned back in his seat, hearing the wheels of the plane screech as they made contact with the tarmac. Instead of returning to Italy, he longed to be in New York—a return to a structured, disciplined work atmosphere.

Back at the office there'd be no cucumber waters with sprigs of mint and the most adorable woman dressed in nothing more than a white fluffy robe that hid a lacy hot pink set of lingerie. His mouth grew dry as he recalled how Kayla had stared at him over the rim of her glass with those alluring green eyes.

He drew his thoughts to a sharp halt. He reminded himself that his regular PA should be returning from her maternity leave soon—real soon. If he could just keep it together a little longer, his life would return to normal. But why didn't that sound so appealing any longer?

It doesn't matter.

Kayla kept repeating that mantra to herself, wishing her heart would believe it. Three days had passed since she'd woken up alone after a night of lovemaking. How could Angelo just slip away into the night without a word? Did he know how much it would hurt her? Did he even give her feelings any consideration?

It doesn't matter.

Today was the day they learned whether their royal wedding pitch had been accepted or not. Kayla replayed the presentation in her head. She couldn't help wondering—if she hadn't been so distracted by the problems with the fundraiser and with her growing feelings for Angelo could she have done more? She worried her bottom lip. For months and months, she'd done everything to be the best employee, and now that it counted, she'd lost her focus. She'd let herself fall for her boss's mesmerizing eyes, devilish good looks and charms.

It doesn't matter.

Dismissing their time together was his choice. Why should she let it bother her? She didn't need him. She squeezed her eyes shut, blocking out the memories of being held in his arms—of the tender touch of his lips. How could such a special night go so terribly wrong? Had she totally misread what Angelo had been telling her?

None of it matters!

She had important work to do. Angelo had just departed for his brother's villa to speak to him about their sister. Kayla had declined his stilted offer to take her with him. She may have made a mess of things with Angelo, but there was still time to pull together the after-school program fund-raiser.

Kayla focused on the email she was composing to the manager of another New York City band. She could only hope they had a cancellation because the most popular bands were booked well into the future. With her name typed at the bottom, she reread it, making sure it contained plenty of appeals to the man's generous side. After all, who could possibly turn down a group of needy kids? She sure couldn't. Once she was certain there weren't any typos, she pressed Send, hoping and praying that this appeal to the Spiraling Kaleidoscopes would turn things around.

Her thoughts immediately turned to her faltering career at Amatucci & Associates. She grabbed frantically for some glimmer of hope that there was a way to get back to their prior boss-employee relationship. But every time Angelo looked at her, her heart ached and her mind went back in time to those precious moments they'd spent together, wondering if any of it was real.

Ending things now was for the best. It was all of this talk about a wedding that had filled her head with these ridiculous romantic notions. And after working so closely with Angelo these past few weeks, it was only natural that she would project them onto him. The truth was that she wasn't ready to fall in love with him—or anyone. She didn't want to settle down yet. She still had her dreams to accomplish and her career to achieve.

A message flashed on the computer screen. She had a

new email. Her body tensed and she said a silent prayer that it would be good news.

She positioned the cursor on the email and clicked, opening the message on to the screen:

To: Kayla Hill
From: Howard Simpson
RE: Spiraling Kaleidoscope Booking
Thanks so much for thinking of us for your fund-raiser. I am sorry but we are already booked solid for that weekend, in fact, we're booked for the month. Next time consider booking well in advance.

The backs of Kayla's eyes stung. She continued to stare at the email, wishing the letters would rearrange themselves into an acceptance letter, but they refused to budge. This was it. She was out of ideas and out of time. No other band at this late date was going to be available.

Another email popped into her inbox.

To: Ms. Kayla Hill
From: Ms. Stephanie Dyer, Public Relations, Paper Magic Inc.
RE: ICL after-school program fund-raiser
It has recently come to our attention that the fund-raiser no longer has a headline performer. And it is therefore with great regret that we will have to pull our sponsorship...

Her vision blurred. She'd made a mess of everything. And she had no idea how she was ever going to face the children of the after-school program and tell them that she'd let them down—that the doors of the center were going to close.

Just then the door of the suite swung open. It must be the maid. Kayla swiped a hand across her cheeks and sniffled.

She was a mess. Hopefully the cleaning lady wouldn't notice. And if she did, hopefully she wouldn't say anything.

"I'll just move out of your way." Kayla closed her laptop, preparing to move down to the pool area to work.

"Why would you have to get out of my way?"

That wasn't the maid's voice. It was Angelo's. He was back. But why?

When she didn't say a word, he moved to her side. "Kayla, what's the matter?"

She didn't face him. "I… I thought you were the maid."

"Obviously, I'm not. I forgot my phone so I came back. I didn't want to miss a call from the royal family about the pitch."

"Oh, okay." She kept her head down and fidgeted with the pens on the table.

"Kayla, look at me."

She shook her head.

"Kayla." He knelt down next to her.

Oh, what did it matter? She lifted her face to him. "What do you need?"

"I need you to explain to me what's wrong." The concern was evident in the gentleness of his voice. "I thought we had everything worked out between us."

"Is that what you call it?" He really wanted to know? Then fine. She'd tell him. "I call it ignoring the big pink elephant in the middle of the room."

But that wasn't the only reason she'd been crying. It seemed in the past few days that everything she cared about was disintegrating.

"Kayla, talk to me."

His phone chimed. Saved by the bell so to speak. He checked the caller ID and then held up a finger for her to wait. He straightened and moved to the window, where he took the call.

This was her chance to escape his inevitable interrogation. She didn't know where she would go. Suddenly gelato sounded divine. So what if she was wallowing in her own misery? She deserved some sugary comfort—until she figured out what to do next.

She moved to her room to splash some water on her face, repair her makeup and grab her purse. When she was ready to go, there was a knock at her door. She knew it was Angelo. She sighed. Why couldn't he just leave well enough alone?

"Kayla, we need to talk."

CHAPTER TWENTY

"NO, WE DON'T." Kayla moved to the door and swung it open. "Not unless it's about work. Other than that we have nothing to say."

Frown lines bracketed Angelo's face. "Did I hurt you that much?"

She glared at him. He really didn't expect an answer, did he? "Please move. I'm on my way out."

He moved aside and she passed by. She'd reached the exterior doorknob when he said, "Kayla, that was the prince's representative on the phone."

That stopped her in her tracks. Her heart pounded in her chest. *Please don't let the wedding fall through, too.* She turned and scanned Angelo's face. There were no hints of what had transpired on the phone.

"And…"

"The royal couple is steadfast in their decision that the chapel must be a part of the wedding. The bride was totally taken with the place. From what I understand that's the reason Monte Calanetti was placed on the short list."

"Did you try again to talk Louisa into letting them use it?"

His face creased with worry lines. "I did. And no matter what I said, she wanted no part of the wedding."

Kayla worried her bottom lip. This wasn't good. Not good at all. "This is all my fault. I shouldn't have let the royal couple believe we could deliver something that we obviously can't."

"It's not your fault. I thought that Louisa would change her mind. What I don't understand is why she's so adamant to avoid the royal wedding. Aren't all women romantics at heart?"

"Obviously not. And it's my fault. Everything is falling apart because of me."

Kayla's chin lowered. How could this be happening? Instead of helping everyone, she was about to let them all down. Most of all, she was about to let down the man she loved—correction, the man she worked for.

Angelo stepped up to her and grabbed her by the shoulders. "I've had enough of the riddles. There's more going on here than the royal wedding. I want to know what it is. Let me help you."

Her heart wanted to trust him. It wanted to spill out the problems so that they could work together to solve them. Perhaps it was time she let go of her dream of being an ad executive at Amatucci & Associates.

The price for her career advancement was far too steep. In her haste to escape her home and make a name for herself, she feared that she'd lost a part of herself. Now she realized that deep down where it counted, she still had the same principles that she'd been raised with. Her caring hometown and loving family had shown her what was truly important in life.

And the fact was she could never be happy as an ad executive, knowing she'd stepped over other people's hopes and dreams to get there. It was time to put her faith in Angelo's kindness and generosity.

She needed his help.

Why wouldn't she let him in?

Why did she insist on refusing his help?

Then Angelo remembered how their night of lovemaking had ended. His jaw tightened as he recalled how badly he'd handled that whole situation. No wonder she didn't trust him. If the roles were reversed, he'd feel the same way. But he couldn't give up. He couldn't just walk away and leave her upset.

"I know you don't have any reason to trust me, but if

you'll give me a chance, I'd like to help." His tone was gentle and coaxing. "I did my best for Nico and Marianna when they asked me—"

"But they are family. And…and I'm, well, just an employee."

His thumb moved below her chin and tilted her face upward until their gazes met. "I think you know that you're much more than that."

It was in that moment the air became trapped in his lungs. In her worried gaze he saw something else—something he hadn't expected to find. And it shook him to his core.

He saw his future.

It was in that moment that he realized just how much she meant to him.

He, the man who was intent on remaining a bachelor, had fallen head over heels, madly, passionately in love with his assistant. She was everything he'd been trying to avoid. Excitable, emotional and compassionate. The exact opposite of the cool, collected businessman image he'd created for himself.

The how and the when of these emotions totally eluded him. The startling revelation left him totally off-kilter and not sure what to say or do next. All that kept rolling through his mind was…

He, Angelo Amatucci, loved Kayla Hill.

"Angelo, what is it?"

"Um…nothing. And don't try changing the subject. We were talking about you and what has you so upset."

She breathed out an unsteady breath. "It's the emails."

"What emails? From the office?"

She shook her head. "Emails from the band's manager and the sponsors. Everyone's pulling out and…and it's in shambles—"

"Whoa. Slow down. I think we better take a seat and you need to start at the beginning."

Once seated on the couch, everything came bubbling to the surface. She told him about how she was involved with the after-school program. It came out about how the program was about to lose their lease unless they could come up with money to cover a hefty increase in the lease. And then she told him that she was heading up a fund-raiser—a big fund-raiser.

In fact, he'd heard about the fund-raiser. It was all over the radio and the papers. At the time, he'd been surprised his company hadn't been approached for a donation, but now he knew why.

"And this fund-raiser, you've been organizing it while you were here in Italy?"

She nodded. "I didn't have a choice."

So this is what she'd been hiding from him. "And you didn't think to mention it?"

"I thought about it." His mouth opened to respond but she cut him off. "And don't you dare blame this on me. I tried." Her voice rose and her face filled with color. "Every time I mentioned helping a charitable organization, you didn't want any part of it. Me not telling you before now is as much your fault as mine. I couldn't risk my job."

His voice rose. "You thought I'd fire you?"

She shouted back. "Wouldn't you have? Correction, aren't you going to now that you know?"

What he wanted to do was leave. Kayla was loud, emotional and making him extremely uncomfortable. She had him raising his voice—something he avoided at all costs. In that moment, he had flashbacks of his parents' endless arguments. He refused to end up like them.

He started for the door. The walls started to close in on him.

"Where are you going?"

"Out." His head pounded.

"And my job?"

"I don't know." He honestly didn't. He was torn between

his newfound feelings for her and the fear that they'd end up miserable like his parents. The pain in his temples intensified.

He stormed out the door, covering as much ground as he could cover with no destination in mind. He just had to get away from the arguing.

Over the years he'd worked so hard to control as much of his life as possible—keeping it the exact opposite of his emotional, turbulent parents. And then in one afternoon, he found himself back exactly where he'd started—in the middle of a heated relationship. That was unacceptable. His home and his office were kept orderly and on an even keel. Everything was how he wanted it—so then why couldn't he control his own traitorous heart?

CHAPTER TWENTY-ONE

HAD SHE BEEN FIRED?

Impossible.

But she was resigning from Amatucci & Associates effective as soon as she completed this one final task. Kayla sat across from Louisa Harrison on her patio. The Tuscany sun beamed bright overhead, but Louisa had the white table shaded by a large yellow umbrella. The woman was quiet, reserved and poised. Not exactly the easiest person to get to know.

"Thank you so much for taking the time to see me." Kayla fidgeted with the cup of coffee that Louisa had served just moments ago.

"I'm new here so I don't get much company."

Kayla gazed up at the huge palazzo. "Do you live here alone?"

Louisa nodded.

"You must get lonely in this big place all by yourself." Kayla pressed her lips together, realizing she'd once again said too much. "Sorry. I shouldn't have said that. Sometimes I don't think before I speak."

"It's okay. Most people probably would get lonely." Louisa played with the spoon resting on the saucer. "I moved here to get away from the crowd in Boston."

So Louisa wanted to be alone—perhaps that was the reason for her refusing to host a royal wedding that would bring a huge crowd of onlookers, not to mention the press. So was Louisa an introvert? Or was there another reason she preferred a quiet atmosphere?

First, Kayla had to build some friendly bridges. Hopefully she'd do a better job of that going forward. She genuinely liked Louisa. And she felt sorry for the woman, being so secluded from life.

And then a thought struck Kayla—if she wasn't careful and didn't stop pushing people away, she might end up alone just like Louisa. First, she'd shoved away her ex because she just didn't share his vision of the future. And now, there was Angelo, who had given her one amazing opportunity after the next. And how did she repay him but by having an utter meltdown.

She hadn't spoken to him since he'd stormed out of their suite that morning. He'd never returned. And she'd been so busy losing her cool that she never did get to ask him for help with the fund-raiser.

At the moment, though, she had to focus on Louisa. "You know, we have something in common. I'm new here, too. Except I'm not staying. I'm only here on a business trip with my boss, Angelo Amatucci."

Louisa's cup rattled as she placed it on the saucer. "I met Mr. Amatucci. I suppose he sent you here to convince me to change my mind about the royal wedding?"

Kayla could hear the obvious resistance in Louisa's voice. She'd have to tread lightly if she were to learn anything. "Actually, he didn't send me. He doesn't even know I'm here."

Louisa's eyes widened. "Then why have you come?"

"I need to be honest with you. I am here about the use of the chapel."

Louisa's mouth pressed together in a firm line and she shook her head. "I haven't changed my mind. I told Mr. Amatucci numerous times that I wouldn't agree to it."

"But I was wondering if there was something we could do to make the idea acceptable to you. The fact of the matter is this event could really help the village's economy. And the royal couple is adamant about using the chapel. If it's not available, they'll move on to the next village on their list."

Surprise reflected in the woman's eyes. "It's really that important?"

Kayla nodded. "I haven't lied to you so far. I need you to believe me now."

Louisa's light blue gaze met hers. "I do believe you. As much as I'd like to help, I just can't do it."

Kayla leaned forward. "If you tell me the problem, maybe I can find a way around it."

"I… I just can't have all of those people and reporters poking around here."

Something told Kayla that Louisa had spent more time in front of the paparazzi's cameras than she preferred. Her sympathy went out to the woman, but there had to be a compromise. "What if I make it my personal mission to ensure that you aren't photographed or even mentioned in the press coverage?"

Louisa's eyes opened wide. "You can do that?"

"Remember, we are dealing with royalty here. They have far-reaching hands. I'll let them know about your stipulation, and I'm sure they'll be able to handle the press."

There was a moment of silence. "If you're sure. I suppose it'd be all right."

Kayla resisted the urge to reach out and hug the woman, not wanting to scare her off. Instead, she leaned forward and squeezed Louisa's arm.

"Thank you." Kayla sent her a smile. "Now, if you don't mind, I'd love to hear more about your plans for this place. It's absolutely beautiful here."

Kayla sat back and sipped her coffee. She was happy that she could provide Angelo with this parting gift. With her resignation already typed up on her laptop, it was time for her to print it out.

That evening, Angelo had plans to dine with his brother and sister. While he was off having some family time, she would catch a plane home. Her moment beneath the Tuscany sun was over, and it was time to face the harsh reality of being jobless and heartbroken.

CHAPTER TWENTY-TWO

THIS HAS TO WORK.

Angelo sat in the back of a limousine outside Kayla's apartment. He'd been trying to call her ever since he'd found her resignation letter and the hotel suite empty, but she wasn't taking his calls. He'd just arrived in New York earlier that day after wrapping things up in Italy. Thanks to Kayla, Monte Calanetti was hosting the royal wedding.

He'd have left earlier but he couldn't. Nico and Marianna had been counting on him to stay until the royal decree was announced. Now that he and his siblings had achieved a peaceful relationship, it was as if they were truly a family again—something Angelo hadn't known how much he'd missed. And though Marianna still refused to divulge the name of the father of her baby, she knew without a doubt that both he and Nico were there for her—to support her no matter what decision she made about her future.

He'd returned to New York with orders from his brother and sister to track down Kayla and sweep her off her feet.

Since she'd been gone, he'd had time to realize how black-and-white his life was without her in it. He'd overreacted when he realized that he loved her. But now that he'd come to terms with the depth of his emotions, he hoped what he had planned was enough for her to give him—give them—a second chance.

Thanks to Kayla's very helpful assistant, who was a romantic at heart, he and Pam had secretly been able to piece the fund-raiser back together. And Kayla had been notified that a very special sponsor would be sending a car to escort her to the event.

He hated waiting. It seemed like forever since he'd last

laid his eyes on her. He wanted to march up to her apartment and beg her forgiveness, but he couldn't take the chance that she'd slam the door in his face. Worst of all, she'd end up missing her big night at the fund-raiser. He couldn't let that happen.

Instead, he'd stayed behind in the limo and sent up his driver with instructions not to mention that he was waiting. He needed a chance to talk to Kayla face-to-face. There was so much that he wanted to say—to apologize for—but he still hadn't found the right words.

The car door swung open and Kayla slid in the car next to him. She wore the navy dress he'd given her for their date in the Mediterranean. It hugged all of her curves and dipped in just the right places. It left him speechless that any woman could look so good.

When her gaze landed on him, her eyes opened wide. "What are you doing here?"

"What does it look like?"

Her gaze scanned his dark suit. "It looks like…like you're set for a night on the town."

"And so I am."

"Well, it can't be with me. I'm quite certain that it goes against your rules to date an employee."

"Ah, but what you're forgetting is that you're no longer an employee of Amatucci & Associates." He sighed. "We need to talk."

"Now's not the time. I have a fund-raiser to attend. Alone." She reached for the door handle, but before she could open it, the car started moving.

"And it looks like I'm your ride."

Her gaze narrowed in on him. "Angelo, there's nothing left to say. You said it all back in Tuscany."

"Not everything. Why did you quit without even talking to me?"

"First, I have a question for you. I thought it was strange when an internationally acclaimed rock band wanted to play for our fund-raiser on short notice. No one would tell me how Slammin' Apples heard about our need for help. Now I know. It was you, wasn't it?"

He wasn't so sure by the tone of her voice if this was going to go his way or not. "I was the one who called in a favor or two to have the band show up tonight."

"That isn't just any band. They are amazing. They've won national awards."

Angelo was going to take this all as a good sign. "I'm glad that you are pleased."

Her brows gathered together. "I didn't ask for your help."

"Kind of like how I didn't ask for your help with gaining permission from Louisa to use the chapel."

She shrugged. "I don't quit in the middle of projects."

He hoped this news would thaw her demeanor. "And thanks to you, Monte Calanetti is the official host of the royal wedding."

"Really?" A big smile bowed her lips and eased her frown lines. "I mean, I'm really happy for them."

"I knew you would be. Nico and Marianna send along their sincerest thank-yous." This was his chance to fix things. "I'm sorry about what was said in Tuscany. I never ever meant for you to quit. I need to make things right. You're far too talented to let go."

The light in her eyes dimmed. He'd obviously not said the right thing. For a man who made his fortune coming up with just the right words to turn people's heads and convince them to buy certain products or ideas, why was he messing this up so badly? Why couldn't he find the words to tell Kayla what she truly meant to him?

And then he knew what it was—what was holding him back. He was afraid that she wouldn't feel the same. He didn't want her to close the door on him as his parents had done so many years ago.

But still, he had to do it. He had to put himself out there if he ever wanted to win Kayla back. And that was something he most definitely wanted. After their month in Tuscany —he couldn't imagine another day without Kayla's sunny smile or her beautiful laugh.

Yet before he could sort his thoughts into words, the car pulled to a stop. Without waiting for the driver, Kayla swung the door open.

"Kayla, wait."

Without a backward glance, she faded into the sea of people waiting to get into the convention center. Though he rushed to get out of the car, by the time he did so she'd vanished—lost in the excited crowd.

He'd lost his chance to speak his piece. Maybe showing her how he felt would be better. He just hoped that his other surprise worked, because he just couldn't lose her now, not after she'd shown him that there was a different way to live—one with love in it.

CHAPTER TWENTY-THREE

KAYLA'S HEART ACHED.

She bit down on the inside of her lower lip, holding in the pain. Her legs were on automatic pilot as they kept moving one after the other, weaving her way through the throng of people. She didn't have a particular destination in mind. She just needed to put distance between her and Angelo before she crumbled in front of him.

After all they'd shared, how could Angelo look at her and see nothing more than an Amatucci & Associates asset? Was that truly all she was to him? The thought slugged her in the chest, knocking the breath from her.

And the sad thing was, for the longest time that's what she thought she'd wanted—Angelo to look at her and see her for all of her creative talent. But now things had changed—they'd changed considerably. Now she wanted him to see oh so much more—to see the woman that loved him with all of her heart.

After passing through security, she made her way to the front of the hall where the stage was set up. The kids of the ICL after-school program rushed up to her.

"Ms. Hill." Her name was repeated in chorus.

"Hi." With so many happy, smiling faces looking at her, it was like a temporary bandage on her broken heart. She forced a smile to her lips. "Is everyone here?"

"Yeah!"

The parents made their way up to her, shaking her hand and thanking her. She wanted to tell them that she hadn't done this, that it had been Angelo, but every time she opened her mouth to explain someone else thanked her.

And then her parents stepped in front of her. Her mother's eyes were misty as she smiled at her and her father looked at her. "You've done us proud."

They drew together into a group hug—something she'd grown up doing. No matter how old she got, some things didn't change.

Kayla pulled back. "But what are you two doing here?"

"Honey—" her mother dabbed at her eyes "—you don't think that we'd miss this after the invitation you sent."

Invitation? That she had sent? Something told her that Angelo had orchestrated this, too. Suddenly she wasn't so upset with him. For him to listen to her and give her this chance to show her parents what she'd accomplished while in New York touched her deeply. She wished he was around so that she could apologize for overreacting in the limo. More than that, she wanted to thank him.

The lights dimmed and one of the security guards approached her. They guided her through the barrier, around the stage and up a set of steps. When she stepped on the stage, she was awed by the number of people in the audience. She wondered if Angelo was out there somewhere or if he'd given up and gone home. The thought of him giving up on her left her deeply saddened.

Oh, boy. This wasn't good. She couldn't think about Angelo. Not here. Not now. She had to keep it together for all of the excited faces in the audience who were counting on her to pull this off. She'd made it this far—just a little longer.

And then as if perfectly timed, pink-and-silver balloons fell from the ceiling, scattering across the stage. *What in the world?*

The head of the outreach program stood at the microphone. Mr. Wilson was an older gentleman who'd already raised his family. Now he and his wife spent their time helping the children enrolled in the program.

"Kayla, join me." He turned to the audience. "Everyone,

please give the mastermind behind this amazing event a round of applause."

The clapping and cheers were unbelievable. And it would have been so much better if Angelo was standing next to her—after all, he'd been the one to save the fund-raiser. Not her.

As she peered at the countless smiling faces, her gaze connected with Angelo's. Her heart picked up its pace. What was he still doing here?

When quiet settled over the crowd, Mr. Wilson continued. "Kayla, would you like to say something?"

Though her insides quivered with nerves, she moved up to the microphone. Back at her apartment, she'd planned out what to say, but now standing here in front of thousands of people, including Angelo, the words totally escaped her.

She swallowed hard and relied on her gut. "I want to say a huge thank-you to everyone who helped with this event. Those people who helped with the planning and the organizing, please stand." Afraid to start naming names and forgetting someone, she stuck with generalities. "This was most definitely a group effort, and what a fabulous group. So please give them a round of applause."

She handed the microphone back to Mr. Wilson before she herself started clapping. Her gaze moved back to the last place she'd seen Angelo, but he was no longer there. She searched the immediate area but saw no sign of him. Her heart sank.

And then a familiar voice came across the speaker system. "Kayla, I know I say everything wrong when it comes to you. But I want you to know that I think you are the most amazing woman I've ever met."

Just then Angelo stepped on the stage and approached her. Her heart pounded in her chest. He stopped in front of her.

"What are you doing?" Heat flamed in her cheeks.

"Kayla, you've opened my eyes and my heart to the way

life can be if I let down my guard." He took her hand in his and gave it a squeeze. "I couldn't imagine doing that with anyone but you."

Kayla's eyes grew misty. It was a good thing that Angelo was holding her hand or she might have fallen over, because everything from her neck down felt like gelatin.

He handed the microphone back to Mr. Wilson as the band started to play. "Can I have this dance?"

He wanted to dance right here? Right now? In front of everyone?

Surely this all had to be a dream. If so, what did it matter if she accepted? She nodded and he pulled her into his arms as the band played a romantic ballad.

Angelo stared deeply into her eyes. "I never thought it was possible for me to feel this way, but I love you."

A tear of joy splashed on her cheek, a trait she inherited from her mother. "I love you, too."

"Does that mean I can rip up your resignation?"

"You still want me?"

"Always and forever."

EPILOGUE

Three months later...

"Do YOU HAVE time for a new account?"

Kayla turned from her computer monitor to face Angelo. Was he serious? It was hard to tell as he was smiling at her. Ever since the charity concert, Angelo had been a different man in the office. He'd let his guard down and put on a friendly face, but one thing that hadn't changed was that he still expected perfection—or as close to it as anyone could get with their work.

"I don't know. Since we succeeded with the royal pitch, we've been flooded with new accounts. It really put Amatucci & Associates heads and shoulders above the competition."

"Yes, it did. And I couldn't have done it without you."

She knew that praise from Angelo didn't come willy-nilly. He truly had to mean it or he wouldn't say anything. "Thank you. But you were the driving force behind it."

"How about we just settle for 'you and I make a great team'?" He approached her and held out his hand to her.

She placed her hand in his, all the while wondering what he was up to. He pulled her gently to her feet, and then his hands wrapped around her waist. What in the world was up with him? He never acted this way at the office —ever.

"About this account—" he stared deep into her eyes, making her heart flutter "—if you decide to take it, it'll be all yours."

The breath hitched in her throat. Was he saying what she thought he was saying? "It'll be my first solo account?"

He smiled and nodded. "I thought that might get your attention."

As much as she wanted to spread her wings, she also didn't want to mess up. "Are you really sure that you want to give me so much responsibility?"

"I'm quite confident that you'll handle it perfectly. You are amazingly talented in so many ways." His eyes lit up, letting her know that his thoughts had momentarily strayed to more intimate territory.

She lightly swiped at his arm. "We aren't supposed to talk about those things at the office. What if someone overheard?"

"Then they'd know that I'm crazy about you."

She couldn't hold back a smile as she shook her head in disbelief at this side of Angelo, which had been lurking just beneath the surface for so long. "Now tell me more about this account. I'm dying to hear all about it before I make up my mind."

"It's a wedding."

"Are you serious?" He nodded and she rushed on. "I don't know. Don't you remember all of the headaches we had with the royal wedding? I couldn't imagine having a nervous bride lurking over my shoulder. I don't think I'd be good at mollifying a bridezilla."

"I don't think you give yourself enough credit. Look at how you handled me and opened my eyes to a thing or two."

"I know. Talk about a lot of hard work to get past your stiff, cold shell—"

"Hey!" His mouth formed a frown, but his eyes twinkled, letting her know that he was playing with her. "There's no need to throw insults."

"I wasn't. I was just stating the obvious." She grinned at him, letting him know that she was playing, too. "We could take an office poll and see which boss they like best—pre-Italy Mr. Amatucci or post-Italy?"

"I think we'll pass on that idea. Besides, you're going

to be too busy for such things now that you have this very special account."

"Special, huh? How special are we talking?"

Angelo reached into his pocket and pulled out a box. He dropped down to one knee. "Kayla, I love you. Will you be my bride?"

With tears of joy in her eyes, she nodded vigorously. "Yes. Yes, I will. I love you, too."

* * * * *

A BRIDE WORTH MILLIONS

CHANTELLE SHAW

For Rosie and Lucy, best sisters and best friends!

CHAPTER ONE

'I'VE BEEN THINKING.'

'Really?' Luca De Rossi could not disguise the scepticism in his voice as he glanced at the blonde in bed beside him. Giselle Mercier was exquisite, and she was an inventive lover, but Luca doubted that the French model with baby-blue eyes and a penchant for expensive jewellery was about to announce that she had discovered a solution for world peace, or a cure for cancer.

His suspicions were confirmed when she held up her left hand so that the enormous diamond on her third finger was set ablaze by the early-morning sunbeams streaming into the penthouse.

'Yes. I've been thinking that I don't want to get married at a registry office. I want our wedding to be in a church, or even a cathedral.'

Giselle glanced towards the window and the view of the elegant spires of the Duomo—Milan's magnificent cathedral.

'And I want to wear a wedding dress. Think what a fantastic publicity opportunity it would be for De Rossi Designs,' Giselle purred when Luca frowned. 'The press would go mad for pictures of a wedding gown designed by the creative director of DRD for his bride.'

'There will be no press coverage of our wedding,' Luca said tersely. 'You seem to be forgetting that our marriage will be a temporary arrangement. I only require you to be my wife for one year. After that we will divorce and you will receive one million pounds—as we agreed.'

Giselle threw back the sheet to reveal her naked, golden-tanned body, and hooked one lissom thigh across Luca's hip. 'Perhaps you'll decide that you don't want a temporary marriage,' she murmured. 'Last night was amazing, *chéri*. I think we could have something special…'

Luca muttered something ugly beneath his breath as he swung his legs over the side of the bed. It was true that the sex last night had been good—albeit in the vaguely uninspiring way that sex always was with any of his mistresses. But it meant nothing to him. Just as it always meant nothing.

He didn't know why Giselle had suggested that their relationship could be in any way 'special'. They had made an arrangement that suited both of them and he could not conceal his impatience at her attempt to try and change the rules.

He strode across the room and stared moodily out of the window, while his mistress ran her eyes hungrily over his bare buttocks and muscular thighs. In the sunlight, Luca's thick black hair, which had a tendency to curl at his nape, gleamed like polished jet. His broad shoulders were tanned a dark bronze, the same as the rest of his body, even his buttocks, which made Giselle wonder if he sunbathed in the nude.

She had never had a lover as skilful and tireless as Luca De Rossi. No wonder the tabloids dubbed him the 'Italian Stallion'! He was as famous for his affairs with the countless female celebrities who wore his designs to red-carpet events as he was for his undeniable artistic talent and his flair for designing clothes that flattered women whatever their shape.

Luca was sinfully sexy and filthy rich. He was also in urgent need of a wife, so that he could keep his ancestral home: Villa De Rossi—a palatial house on the shores of Lake Como. It was something to do with the terms of his grandmother's will. Luca had to be married by his thirty-fifth birthday or the villa, which had been owned by the De Rossi family for three hundred years, would be sold.

Giselle did not understand all the details and did not particularly care. The important thing was that Luca had asked *her* to be his bride. The deal included an amazing pay-off, as well as lots of other perks—such as the diamond solitaire ring that Luca had promised she could keep when they went their separate ways.

But Giselle had no intention of going anywhere. It had occurred to her that, even though a million pounds was more than she was ever likely to earn from modelling, it made sense to hang on to her soon-to-be husband for as long as possible. After all, if he was willing to pay her one million pounds for one year of marriage then even Giselle's poor grasp of mathematics could work out the amount she should receive after two or three years of being Luca's wife. And of course if they had a child then Luca would have to pay maintenance and school fees.

Really, the future looked very promising, Giselle decided.

'Luca...' she said huskily. 'Why don't you come back to bed?'

Luca ignored the invitation. A familiar sense of frustration at the situation he found himself in made his blood boil, and he felt a strong urge to smash his fist through the window. He rested his brow against the glass and looked down on Corso Vittorio Emanuelle II, Milan's famous shopping precinct.

Despite the early hour, people were already milling

in the glass-domed walkways where all the top fashion brands, including De Rossi Designs, had boutiques. The fashion label that Luca had created fifteen years ago had become a global success, and the iconic DRD logo was a byword for haute couture and high-end ready-to-wear clothes that complemented the exclusive leather shoes, handbags and accessories that De Rossi Enterprises—founded eighty years ago by Luca's great-grandfather Raimondo—was famous for.

It was thanks to Luca that the family business had been saved from the brink of bankruptcy and now enjoyed an annual sales revenue of over a billion pounds. But he had never received praise or thanks from his grandparents when they had been alive, Luca reflected bitterly.

He walked back over to the bed, frowning when he saw the soft expression in Giselle's eyes. The last thing he wanted was for her think that she was in any way special to him, or that their relationship could become permanent. He had met her days after he had learned of his grandmother's will, when he had been reeling from shock and consumed with rage.

Giselle had been just another blonde at a party, but when she had tearfully confided that she had been dropped from her modelling contract, and was worried about how she would be able to afford the rent on her flat, Luca had seen a way to resolve both their problems. He had money, but he needed a wife. Giselle needed money and she had agreed to his marriage deal.

It was as simple as that, and he did not need her to complicate things with messy emotions that he was incapable of reciprocating.

'The jewellers who sold you my diamond ring have a matching necklace on display in the window.' Giselle arranged herself on the pillows so that her breasts tilted forward provocatively. 'It would be nice to have the set.' She pouted when Luca ignored her attempt to pull him down onto the bed. 'Why are you getting dressed? It's the week-end and you don't have to go to work today, do you?'

Luca forbore from pointing out that he hadn't built up his successful fashion label at the same time as running De Rossi Enterprises by working weekdays, from nine till five. Twenty-four/seven was nearer the mark. For the past fifteen years he had slogged his guts out to restore the De Rossi brand, but he faced losing everything he had achieved if he did not give in to his grandmother's outra-geous attempt to blackmail him from beyond the grave.

Nonna Violetta had wanted him to marry, and marry he would, Luca thought with a grim smile as he stared down at his bride-to-be. But it would be a sham marriage, a busi-ness deal, and the only reason he intended to go through with it was because it would allow him to give Rosalie the special care she needed.

'I have to go to England,' he told Giselle as he pulled on his trousers, followed by a shirt and jacket.

The superb tailoring of the suit he had designed him-self emphasised his lean, six-feet-plus frame, and the shirt moulded his powerful abdominal muscles.

'I've been invited to a society wedding,' he said drily.

Giselle's pout switched from sexy to sulky. 'You could take *me*. Who is getting married?'

'Charles Fairfax is someone I know from school. He's marrying the sister-in-law of my good friend Sultan Kadir of Zenhab.'

'You're friends with a *sultan*?' Giselle's eyes widened. 'I bet he's mega-rich. Will I meet him when I'm your wife?'

Not if he could help it, Luca thought to himself. Kadir Al Sulaimar was his closest friend, and would understand his reasons for marrying Giselle. But the truth was that

Luca felt uncomfortable about his fake marriage. He was a world-weary cynic, but when he had acted as best man to Kadir at his wedding to his beautiful English wife, Lexi, nine months ago, Luca had witnessed the intense love between the couple and had briefly felt envious of something that he could never have.

'Who is this sister-in-law of the Sultan that your friend Charles is marrying?' Giselle flicked through the pages of a gossip magazine that she had brought with her because Luca only kept boring books at the penthouse. 'Is she a celebrity?'

'Unlikely.' Luca had a vivid recollection of Athena Howard's sapphire-blue eyes, her oval-shaped face, and the determined chin that hinted at a stubborn streak in her nature. In Zenhab he had felt curious because Athena shared no physical resemblance with her sister. Lexi, with her silvery-blond hair and slender figure, had been a breathtakingly beautiful bride, but her sister and chief bridesmaid had faded into the background.

Luca had simply been carrying out his duties as best man when he had stood beside Athena for the wedding photographs and later led her onto the dance floor. She was petite in stature, and the top of her head had only reached his mid-chest. Following Zenhabian tradition she had worn a headscarf during the wedding ceremony, but at the private reception Luca had been surprised to see her long braid of dark brown hair—until she had explained that Lexi was her adoptive sister and they were not related by blood.

A memory slipped into Luca's mind of the perfume that Athena had worn at the wedding—an evocative fragrance of old-fashioned roses that had stirred his senses as they had walked together in the palace gardens. Stirred rather more than his senses, in actual fact, he recalled ruefully.

He could not explain to himself why he had kissed Athena Howard, or why the memory of that brief kiss still lingered in his subconscious.

Giselle's petulant voice pulled him from his thoughts. '*Why* can't I come to the wedding with you? Anyone would think you were trying to avoid being seen with me.'

'That's not true, *cara*. But I can't turn up at a wedding with an uninvited companion.'

The hard gleam in Giselle's eyes warned Luca that damage limitation was needed. His fiancée had been blessed with beauty at the expense of brains, but she was well aware that his thirty-fifth birthday was two weeks away. He felt a surge of impotent fury that everything that mattered to him lay in the hands of a brainless bimbo. It wasn't Giselle's fault, he reminded himself. She was the solution—not the cause of his problems.

'While I'm away, why don't you visit the jewellers and buy that diamond necklace?'

He dropped a credit card onto the bed and Giselle snatched it up.

'I might as well get the matching earrings, too.'

'Why not?' Luca murmured drily.

So what if his bride-to-be had an avaricious streak a mile wide? he thought five minutes later, as he walked out of the building and climbed into the chauffeur-driven car waiting to take him to the airport. What were a few diamonds when he would soon have everything he wanted?

Inexplicably, the memory of a pair of sapphire-blue eyes slid into his mind. He gave an indifferent shrug. Later today Athena Howard would become Mrs Charles Fairfax. He had only agreed to attend the wedding as a favour to Kadir.

Luca frowned, thinking of the phone call he'd received from the Sultan of Zenhab.

'Lexi is upset that we can't fly to England for her sister's wedding because the baby is due any day. We'd both be grateful if you would attend the wedding in our place and try and talk to Athena. Lexi is worried that her sister is making a mistake by marring Charles. You and I both know from our schooldays that Charlie Fairfax is a charmless oaf,' Kadir had reminded Luca. 'But if Athena seems happy then you won't need to hang around. However, if you detect that she's having doubts about the marriage...'

'What do you expect me to do?' Luca had demanded.

'Stop the wedding from going ahead,' Kadir had replied succinctly. 'I don't know how, exactly, but I'm sure you'll think of something.'

She did not look so much like a meringue as a cream puff, Athena decided as she studied her reflection in the mirror in her bedroom at Woodley Lodge, the country house of Lord and Lady Fairfax. But it was too late now to wonder why she had allowed herself to be persuaded to choose this crinoline-inspired wedding dress with a skirt so wide that she could be mistaken for the White Cliffs of Dover. The puffed sleeves broadened her top half, while the enormous skirt with its layers of white satin ruffles accentuated her lack of height and made her look dumpy.

'You'll be marrying into the aristocracy in front of five hundred guests,' her mother had reminded Athena when she had tentatively remarked that a simpler style of dress might suit her better. 'You need a dress that will make you the centre of attention.'

Butterflies performed a clog dance in Athena's stomach at the prospect of five hundred people looking at her as she walked down the aisle. Please God, she prayed she didn't do something embarrassing like trip on her long skirt and annoy Charlie.

She hoped he was in a better mood than he had been the previous evening. She had felt awful when she'd spilt red wine on the cream velvet carpet in the sitting room. Lady Fairfax had said that it didn't matter, although she'd compressed her lips into a thin line, but Charlie had made a fuss and had said she was like a bull in a china shop.

Athena bit her lip. Sometimes Charlie said quite hurtful things—almost as if he didn't care about her feelings. During the past year that they had been engaged, she had tried her best to be a gracious and elegant hostess at the dinner parties he had asked her to organise. But she would be the first to admit that she was clumsy—especially when she was nervous—and she always seemed to do something wrong that earned Charlie's criticism.

Heaven knew what he would say when he heard of her latest catastrophe. While inserting the contact lenses she wore because she was short-sighted she had dropped a lens—the last of her disposable lenses as it turned out—down the plughole of the sink, which meant that she would have to wear her glasses to the wedding.

Athena glanced longingly out of the window at the cloudless September sky. It was a beautiful day, and she would love to be outside, but she'd had to spend hours having her hair styled in an elaborate 'up-do', which required dozens of hairpins and so much hairspray that her hair felt as rigid as a helmet. And a make-up artist had applied a heavy foundation to her face which made her feel as though she was wearing a mask. Dramatic eye make-up and a cherry-red shade of lipstick certainly made her noticeable.

The person in the mirror did not look like her. Somewhere in all the wedding preparations Athena Howard had turned into someone she didn't recognise, she thought ruefully.

She tried to reassure herself that the sick feeling in the

pit of her stomach was just pre-wedding nerves. But her sense of panic would not go away. Her legs felt as if they had turned to jelly and she sank down onto the edge of the bed.

Why was she about to get married in a four-thousand-pound dress that did not suit her? That amount of money would keep the orphanage she supported in India running for months. She thought of the House of Happy Smiles in Jaipur, which was in desperate need of funds, and wished that instead of paying for an expensive wedding the money could have been donated to the fundraising campaign she had set up for the orphanage. She didn't want an extravagant wedding—she would have been happier with a small event—but what she wanted didn't matter.

It was typical of her that she had tried so hard to please everyone—her parents, Lady Fairfax and Charlie—that she had ignored the voice inside her head warning her that she was making a mistake. It had taken a phone call from her sister last night to make her confront her doubts.

'Do you love Charles Fairfax with all your heart? And does he love you?' Lexi had asked her. 'If you can't say yes to both those questions you should cancel the wedding.'

'I can't cancel it!'

The tension Athena had felt during her conversation with her sister gripped her again now. Through the window she could see the huge marquee on the lawn. Dozens of waiters in white jackets were scurrying to and fro, carrying trays of glasses for the champagne reception which was to take place after the four o'clock wedding ceremony at the village church. Later in the evening there would be a banquet for five hundred guests, followed by a firework display.

Charlie had said that three members of the House of Lords who were friends of his father's were on the guest list, as well as a minor member of the royal family. Calling off the wedding at this late stage was not an option. It was all her parents had talked about for months, and her father, for the first time in Athena's life, had told her that he was proud of her.

Lexi's words played in Athena's head. *'Do you love Charles Fairfax with all your heart?'*

A picture flashed into her mind of Lexi and Kadir on their wedding day. A huge state celebration befitting the Sultan of Zenhab and his bride had been followed by a private ceremony at the palace for close family and friends. The couple's happiness had been tangible, and the adoration in Kadir's eyes as he had looked at his wife had been deeply moving.

Charlie had never looked at *her* like that, Athena thought, unconsciously gnawing on her lip until she tasted blood. His eyes had never blazed with fierce possession, as if she was the most precious person in the world and the absolute love of his life.

She and Charlie had a different relationship from Lexi and Kadir, she told herself. Charlie worked long hours in the City, and it wasn't his fault he was often tired and tetchy.

Because he stayed at his London flat during the week, and she lived at her parents' house in Reading, they had only seen each other at weekends since they had got engaged. Either she had stayed at Woodley Lodge when Charlie had visited his parents, or she had gone to his flat in London. But even there they were rarely alone, because his friend Dominic always seemed to be around.

Sometimes Athena gained the impression that she was in the way, and that Charlie would rather go to his club with Dominic than spend time with her.

And then there was the subject of sex—or rather the lack

of it. She had never been able to bring herself to tell Charlie what had happened to her when she was eighteen—it was too personal, too shameful, and she never wanted to speak about it. And she had felt relieved when Charlie had said he was happy to wait until they were married before they slept together because he wanted to do things 'properly'. But lately she had been concerned about the lack of sexual spark between them.

Lexi and Kadir had barely been able to keep their hands off one another at their wedding, she remembered. Lexi had confided that she was sure that her baby, which was due any day now, had been conceived on her wedding night.

Charlie's kiss lacked a vital ingredient—but Athena would never have known it if Kadir's best man had not kissed her. She closed her eyes and tried to try to block Luca De Rossi's handsome face from her mind. But his sculpted features—the slashing cheekbones, aquiline nose and the faintly cynical curve of his mouth—had haunted her subconscious since she had met him in Zenhab.

She had heard of his reputation as a playboy and assumed she would not find any man who thought that women had been put on earth solely for his pleasure appealing. So it had been a shock when one smouldering glance from Luca's amber-gold eyes had turned her insides to molten liquid. She had never met a man as devastatingly sexy. He had stirred feelings in her that she had not known existed—or perhaps she had simply done a good job of suppressing her sensuality since she was eighteen, she thought ruefully.

She hadn't expected Luca to kiss her when they had walked together in the palace gardens in the moonlight, and she certainly had not expected that she would respond to the sensual magic of his lips and kiss him back. She had pulled out of his arms after a few seconds, assailed with guilt as she had frantically reminded herself that she was engaged to Charlie. Back in England she had tried to forget about the kiss, but sometimes in her dreams she relived the incandescent pleasure of Luca De Rossi's lips on hers...

What was she doing? *Why* was she thinking about a kiss she had shared with a notorious playboy she was never likely to meet again when all her thoughts should be on the man she was set to marry in two hours' time?

Athena jumped up from the bed and paced up and down the bedroom. Of course one kiss with a notorious playboy nine months ago had meant nothing. But deep down hadn't it made her realise that there was something missing from her relationship with Charlie? She had ignored her misgivings because the wedding preparations had already been well under way, and by marrying the future Lord Fairfax she had felt she was making up for her parents' disappointment that she was not the brilliantly academic daughter they had hoped for.

She had convinced herself that she was doing the right thing, but now she felt as though iron bands were crushing her ribs, and she couldn't breathe properly as her feeling of panic intensified and solidified into a stark truth.

She did not love Charlie with all her heart.

She had been flattered when he had shown an interest in her, and frankly astounded when he had proposed. Her parents had been over the moon that she was going to marry a member of the landed gentry. She remembered that at her engagement party Lexi had warned her that she shouldn't marry to earn their parents' approval. She had assured her sister that she loved Charlie, but she had been fooling herself—and probably Lexi, too, Athena thought bleakly.

She took a shuddering breath and ordered herself to

calm down. Perhaps if she spoke to Charlie he would be able to reassure her that he loved her and that everything would be all right. It was supposed to be bad luck for the bride to see the groom before the wedding on the day, but she *had* to see him and be reassured that she was simply suffering from a bad case of nerves.

Charlie's bedroom was in a private wing of the house. As Athena hurried along the corridor she almost collided with the Fairfaxes' dour butler, Baines.

'Master Charles gave strict instructions that he does not want to be disturbed while he is changing into his wedding attire,' Baines told her in a disapproving tone.

Usually Athena felt intimidated by the butler, but she resisted the urge to slink away back to her room and said coolly, 'Thank you, Baines, but I must see my future husband.'

The butler looked as though he wanted to argue, but then he nodded his head stiffly and walked away.

She paused outside Charlie's room and took a deep breath. Just as she was about to knock she heard voices from the other side of the door.

'This is the last time we can be together for a while. I'm going to have to play the role of devoted husband for the next few months.'

'I guess so,' a second voice drawled. 'It will be unbearable for both of us. You say that Athena wants to try for a child straight away?'

'Oh, she's mad keen to have a baby.' Charlie laughed. 'She'll be an ideal brood mare, because to be honest she's not overly bright or ambitious for a career. I'll need a few drinks before I bed her, but with any luck she'll get pregnant quickly and I won't have to touch her again because all she'll be concerned about is the sprog—leaving you and I free to carry on where we left off.'

Athena's hand was shaking so much that she could barely grip the door handle. Had Charlie been joking? Why had he said such horrible things about her to the other person in his bedroom? She recognised the second voice—but it *couldn't* be who she thought…

She turned the handle and flung open the door with such force that the heavy oak creaked on its hinges.

'Athena!'

Charlie's startled shout reverberated around the room, before fading to leave a deafening silence that was broken by his best man's amused drawl. 'Well, that's let the cat out of the bag.'

'I don't understand—' Athena choked.

But of course she *did* understand—even though she was 'not overly bright'. Charlie's top hat and cravat were scattered across the floor, together with the grey morning suit that he was to wear to the wedding, and he was in bed with his friend Dominic. The best man was also naked—apart from his top hat, which was perched at a jaunty angle on his head.

'For God's sake, Athena, what are you doing here?' Charlie sprang out of bed and hastily thrust his arms into a silk dressing gown.

How ironic that this was the first time she had seen her fiancé's naked body, Athena thought, swallowing down her hysteria.

'I needed to talk to you.' Her earlier doubts about marrying Charlie were nothing compared to the shock she felt now, at seeing him with his best man. 'Charlie…I…I've realised that I can't marry you. And this…' her gaze flew to Dominic '…this confirms that I was right to have second thoughts.'

'Don't be stupid—of course you have to marry me,' Charlie said sharply as he walked over to her and caught hold of her arm. 'You can't back out of the wedding now. My mother would have a fit. And think about how upset *your* parents would be,' he added cleverly, going directly for her weak spot. 'It will be all right, Athena,' he said, in a more conciliatory tone. 'Dom and I…' He shrugged. 'It means nothing…it's just a fling.'

'No, it isn't. I heard the two of you when I was outside the bedroom. What I don't understand is why you asked me to marry you when you know you're—' she broke off helplessly.

'Gay,' Charlie finished for her. He gave a mocking laugh. 'That's why I need a wife—to give me an air of respectability. There's still discrimination against gay men working in the City, and if I came out it would wreck my career. It would also devastate my father if he found out. The shock, so soon after his heart surgery, could finish him off. But if I marry and provide an heir I'll keep the parents happy and my inheritance safe—coincidentally.'

'But you can't live a lie for the rest of your life—and nor can you expect me to,' Athena said shakily. 'I realise it will be hard, but you need to be honest about who you are.'

Despite her shock, she felt some sympathy for Charlie's situation—especially as she knew his father was frail after undergoing a heart bypass operation. But she felt hurt that Charlie had expected her to provide a cover for his true sexual preference.

'I'm sorry, but I won't marry you.'

'You *have* to.' Charlie gripped her arm harder to prevent her from leaving the room.

She shook her head. 'I realised this morning that I don't love you, and I see now that you have never loved me. Let me go, Charlie.'

'You *need* to marry me.' Desperation crept into his voice. 'You want children. Who else do you think will want to marry a twenty-five-year-old virgin with a hang-up about sex?' Charlie said viciously.

Athena paled. 'Please don't be nasty, Charlie. Can't we at least end this as friends?'

His face was mottled red with anger. 'You silly bitch. If you refuse to marry me you'll ruin *everything*.'

She had to get away. From somewhere, Athena found a burst of strength to tear herself out of Charlie's grasp. As she fled from the room his voice followed her down the corridor.

'I didn't mean it. Come back, Athena, and let's talk. We can work something out.'

She ran into her bedroom and closed the door, leaning back against the wood while her chest heaved as if she had just completed a marathon.

Charlie and Dominic! Why hadn't she guessed? There had been signs, she realised, but she had simply thought the two men were good friends. No wonder Charlie had said he was happy to wait until they were married before they slept together. He had sensed that she had inhibitions about sex and he had used her—only asked her to marry him so that she would be a smokescreen to hide his relationship with Dominic.

Her stomach churned. What was she going to do? What reason could she give for calling the wedding off, even supposing she found the courage to walk downstairs and face Lord and Lady Fairfax? She would not expose Charlie's secret relationship with Dominic. He had done an unforgivable thing by trying to trick her into marriage, but it was against her nature to betray him. It was up to Charlie to be honest with his parents about his private life.

Oh, God, what a mess!

She stared at the phone, feeling tempted to call her sister. Lexi would know what to do. But it wouldn't be fair to worry her when she was so close to giving birth, and Athena knew that her sister *would* worry about her. Although Lexi now lived far away, in the desert kingdom of Zenhab, the bond between the sisters had grown stronger since Lexi had married Kadir and become utterly confident of his love.

Voices sounded from out in the corridor, and when Athena opened her door a crack she saw her parents emerging from the guest bedroom across the hall. Her father looked elegant, in top hat and tails, and her mother was wearing a spectacular wide-brimmed hat covered in lilac silk roses.

'Who would have guessed that our daughter will be related by marriage to *royalty*?' Veronica Howard said excitedly.

'*Distantly* related,' her husband pointed out. 'According to the *Encyclopedia of Genealogy* Lord Fairfax is a seventh cousin twice removed of the royal family. But, yes, Athena has certainly done well.'

Athena quickly closed the door. Tears filled her eyes. She couldn't bear to disappoint her parents again, as she had done on many occasions—such as when she had failed to get into university. She was the only Howard not to study at Oxford, as her father had said so sadly.

But the alternative was to continue with the wedding and marry Charlie even though she had discovered the truth about him.

There was another option. *You could disappear*, whispered a voice in her head. It would be cowardly, her conscience argued. But she felt trapped in a truly appalling situation and in her despair all she wanted to do was run away.

She could still hear her parents' voices out on the landing. Her only escape route was via the window, but her bedroom was on the second floor, overlooking a gravel path at the side of the house. Although the walls of the house were covered in ivy, and the thick, gnarled stems looked strong enough to support her weight...

Without giving herself time to think, she did at least remember to grab her bag, containing her phone and other essentials that she had packed for when she and Charlie flew to their honeymoon in the Seychelles. She wouldn't need the daring black lace negligee she had bought for her wedding night now, she thought bleakly.

From the window the ground did not look too far away, but when she climbed out onto the windowsill and grabbed hold of the ivy, the drop down to the gravel path seemed terrifyingly distant. It had been a stupid idea, she acknowledged. She froze with fear, unable to haul herself back through the window, but too afraid to climb down the ivy.

Oh, dear God! She looked down and instantly felt dizzy and sick with terror.

'Let go and I'll catch you.'

The voice from below was vaguely familiar, but Athena couldn't place it. She couldn't do anything but cling to the twisting vines that were beginning to tear under her weight. Suddenly the ivy was ripped away from the wall—and she screamed as she plummeted towards the ground.

CHAPTER TWO

WOLF'S EYES—amber irises flecked with gold and ringed with black—were watching her intently, Athena discovered as her eyelashes fluttered open. She saw heavy brows draw together in a frown above an aquiline nose.

'Athena.' The voice was as rich and dark as molasses, and the sexy accent sent a tingle down her spine. 'You must have fainted. Is that how you came to fall out of the window?'

The concern in the voice penetrated Athena's hazy thoughts. She blinked, and focused on the darkly masculine face centimetres from hers.

'Luca?'

She was suddenly aware that his strong arms were holding her. Her mind flashed back to those terrifying minutes when she had clung to the ivy growing on the wall. She remembered the sensation of falling, but nothing more.

'I caught you when you fell,' Luca told her—which explained why she wasn't lying on the gravel path with multiple fractures to her limbs.

The fact that her rescuer was Luca De Rossi was yet another shock to add to a day from which she fully expected to wake up and find had been a nightmare.

He certainly felt real. She became aware that her cheek was resting against his broad chest, and she could make out the shadow of dark hair beneath his white shirt. The spicy sent of his aftershave stirred her senses and reminded her of that moonlit night in the Zenhab palace gardens, his dark head descending as he brushed his lips across hers.

Heat unfurled deep inside her and her face flooded with colour. 'What are *you* doing here?' she mumbled.

'I'm a wedding guest. I knew Charles Fairfax at Eton and he sent me an invitation.' Luca frowned. 'My name must be on the guest list.'

'I've never seen the guest list.' Tears, partly from the shock of falling, filled Athena's eyes. 'Can you believe that? I don't even know who has been invited to my own wedding.'

Luca had caught Athena before she'd hit the ground, so he knew that she could not be concussed, but she still wasn't making any sense. He controlled his impatience and set her down on her feet. She swayed unsteadily. Her face was as white as her dress.

The designer in him shuddered as he studied the abomination of a wedding dress. A skirt that wide should theoretically have worked well as a parachute when she'd fallen out of the window, he thought sardonically.

He glanced up at the window ledge and his mouth compressed as he imagined the serious injuries she might have sustained if he hadn't caught her.

'It was stupid to stand beside an open window if you were feeling faint.'

'Stupid' summed her up, Athena thought bitterly. She remembered how Charlie had described her as 'not overly bright' and her insides squirmed with humiliation.

'I didn't faint. I climbed out of the window because I need to get away.' Her voice rose a notch. 'I *can't* marry Charles!'

Over Athena's shoulder Luca watched a group of waiters struggling to carry a huge ice sculpture of a swan into the marquee. In another part of the garden cages containing white doves were being unloaded from a van, so that they could be released during the reception. The wedding promised to be a circus and the woman in front of him looked like a clown, with a ton of make-up plastered over her face and that ridiculous dress. He barely recognised her as the unassuming, understated Athena Howard he had met in Zenhab.

'Here.' He handed her the pair of spectacles that had sailed through the air just before she had landed in his arms.

'Thank you.' She put them on and blinked at him owlishly.

'I don't remember that you wore glasses in Zenhab.'

'I usually wear contact lenses, but I've been so busy for the last few weeks with the wedding preparations I forgot to order a new supply.'

Athena felt swamped by a familiar sense of failure and inadequacy. It was true that she was forgetful. 'If only you were not such a daydreamer, Athena,' had been her parents' constant complaint when she was growing up. 'If you stopped writing silly stories and concentrated on your homework your maths results might improve.'

Thinking about her parents made Athena feel worse than ever. She had never been able to live up to their expectations. And then she pictured Charlie and Dominic in bed together and shame cramped in the pit of her stomach that she wasn't even capable of attracting a man—certainly not a man like Luca De Rossi. The thought slid into her head as she studied his sculpted facial features and exotic olive colouring. He was watching her through heavy-lidded eyes and his lips were curled in a faintly cynical expression that made him seem remote but at the same time devastatingly sexy.

A van with the name of a fireworks company on its sides drove up to the house. She remembered Charlie had said that Lord and Lady Fairfax had spent thousands of pounds on a lavish firework display as a finale for the wedding reception. The sight of the van escalated her feeling of panic.

'I have to get away,' she told Luca desperately.

Luca recalled Kadir's instruction to stop the wedding if Athena had had second thoughts. The fact that she had risked her neck to escape marrying Charlie Fairfax was pretty conclusive evidence that she had changed her mind.

'I parked my car next to the gamekeeper's lodge. If we leave now we might get away without anyone noticing.'

Athena hesitated, and glanced up at Charlie's bedroom window in the far corner of the house. She thought she saw a movement by the window, but it must have been a trick of the light because when she peered through her glasses again there was no one there. She was gripped with indecision. Should she go with Luca, a man she had only met once before but who was a good friend of her brother-in-law? Or should she stay and face the emotional fireworks that were bound to explode when she announced to Lord and Lady Fairfax and her parents that the wedding was off?

'What are you waiting for?'

Luca's impatient voice urged her to turn and follow him along the path. Moments later he halted by a futuristic-looking sports car which, despite its long, sleek body, had a tiny, cramped interior.

'I won't fit in there,' Athena said, looking from the car to her voluminous wedding dress.

'Turn around.' There was no time for niceties, Luca decided as he lifted the hem of her skirt up to her waist and untied the drawstring waistband of the hooped petticoat beneath her dress.

'What are you *doing*?' Athena gasped when Luca tugged the petticoat down and she felt his hands skim over her thighs.

She blushed at the thought of him seeing the sheer stockings held up by wide bands of lace. He held her hand to help her balance while she stepped out of the petticoat. Without the rigid frame her dress was less cumbersome and she managed to squeeze into the passenger seat. Luca bundled her long skirt around her and slammed the door shut.

Thank heavens she wasn't wearing her veil, Athena thought, stifling a hysterical laugh that turned to a sob. It was bad enough that the elaborate bun on top of her head was being squashed by the low roof.

Her thoughts scattered when Luca slid behind the wheel and fired the engine. He gave her no time to question her actions as he accelerated down the driveway.

Heaven knew how fast they were travelling. Trees and hedges flashed past as they raced along the narrow country lanes and Athena closed her eyes as she imagined Luca overshooting a bend and catapulting the car into a field.

'Where do you want to go?'

She did not reply because she had no idea what she was going to do next. Her priority had been to escape from the wedding and she had not planned any further ahead.

'Do you want me to take you home? Where do you live?'

Luca groped for his patience *and* the gearstick. Although the skirt of Athena's wedding dress had deflated without the hooped petticoat, the car was still filled with yards of white satin. *Dio*, he could do without being landed with a runaway bride when he had enough problems of his own.

The text message he had received from Giselle announcing that she wanted to get married in Venice had left him feeling rattled. He had arranged a civil wedding ceremony at the town hall in Milan. As soon as the legal formalities were done he would get Villa De Rossi and the security he so desperately wanted for his daughter, and Giselle would get a million pounds.

Why did women always have to complicate things? Luca thought irritably. More worryingly, why was Giselle trying to make something of their sham wedding, which as far as he was concerned could never be anything but a business arrangement?

'I can't go home. I live with my parents, and I don't think they will want to see me once they find out what I've done,' Athena said in low voice.

'Do you have a friend you could stay with for a while? Maybe someone you work with who will help you out?'

She had grown apart from her old friends since she had moved into Charlie's social circle, Athena realised. And although she had tried to get to know his friends she had never felt accepted by the City bankers and their sophisticated wives.

'I don't have a job,' she admitted.

And without an income she had no means of supporting herself, she thought worriedly. The few hundred pounds in her savings account was not enough for her to be able to rent somewhere to live while she looked for a position as a nursery assistant.

'If you don't work, what do you do all day?' Luca drawled.

He thought of Giselle, whose sole occupation seemed to be shopping. It was funny, but when he had met Athena at Kadir and Lexi's wedding she hadn't struck him as one of the vacuous 'ladies who lunch' brigade. Actually, she had seemed rather sweet, although she was not his type. He went for blondes with endless legs and a surfeit of sexual confidence—not petite brunettes with eyes big enough to drown in.

He hadn't planned to kiss her when he had walked with her in the palace gardens during the evening reception at Kadir and Lexi's wedding. It must have been the effect of the bewitching Zenhabian moon, Luca thought derisively. Athena had given him a shy smile, and for some inexplicable reason he had brushed his mouth across hers.

He had felt her lips tremble and for a crazy moment he had been tempted to deepen the caress, to slide his hand to her nape and crush her rosebud mouth beneath his lips. His arousal had been unexpectedly fierce, and her soft, curvaceous body had sent out an unmistakable siren call. But the sparkle of an engagement ring on her finger had caught his eye and he'd abruptly bade her goodnight before returning to the palace.

Imagination was a funny thing, he brooded. He could almost taste Athena on his lips, and he recognised her perfume—that delicate fragrance of old-fashioned roses that filled the car and teased his senses.

'Over the past few months I've attended courses on French cookery and flower arranging and learning how to be a perfect hostess, so that I could arrange dinner parties for Charlie's business clients,' Athena said stiffly. At least she would never have to stuff another mushroom now she was not going to be Charlie's wife.

She caught her breath when Luca slammed on the brakes as they approached a sharp bend in the road. Coming towards them was a fleet of silver saloon cars decorated with white ribbons—obviously heading for Woodley Lodge to drive the bride and groom and other members of the wedding party to the church.

Her heart juddered. *Oh, God! What had she done?* Had Charlie broken the news to his parents that the wedding was off and the reason why? What would her parents think when they heard that she had run away?

She remembered her mother's hat, covered in lilac silk roses, the pride in her father's voice, and suddenly the dam holding back her emotions burst. Tears poured in an unstoppable stream down her cheeks and she sniffed inelegantly, feeling more wretched than she had ever felt in her life.

'Here,' Luca said gruffly, pushing a tissue into her hands.

He had never seen a woman cry so hard before. He was used to crocodile tears when one of his mistresses wanted something. Women seemed to have an amazing ability to turn on the waterworks when it suited them, he thought sardonically. But this was different. Athena was clearly distraught and he felt uncomfortable with her raw emotions.

He reached into the glove box and took out a hip flask. 'Have a few sips of brandy and you'll feel better.'

'I never drink spirits,' she choked between sobs.

'Then today seems a good day to start,' he said drily.

Athena did not like to argue—especially when she glanced at Luca's hard profile. She took a cautious sip of brandy and felt warmth seep through her veins.

'You're probably wondering why I've decided not to marry Charlie.'

'Not particularly. Kadir asked me to make sure you were happy, and if not to stop the wedding. I'm not interested in the reason why you've changed your mind.'

'Kadir asked you to stop the wedding?'

Luca glanced at her, and was relieved to see that the brandy had brought colour back to her cheeks. 'Lexi was sure you were making a mistake, and Kadir would do anything to prevent his wife from worrying—especially when she's about to go into labour.'

He had done what he had been asked to do, Luca

brooded. But neither Kadir nor Athena seemed to have planned further than halting the wedding. He could not abandon her, but the only place he could think of taking her was back to his hotel. Perhaps she would get a grip on her emotions there and then take herself out of his life so that he could concentrate on his own pre-wedding problems with Giselle.

Athena took another sip of brandy and felt herself relax a little. She had a headache from crying and she closed her eyes, lulled by the motion of the car…

The strident blare of a horn woke her, and she was confused when she saw that they were in a traffic jam. A glance at her watch revealed that she had slept for forty minutes.

Her memory returned with a jolt. She had run away from her wedding—dubbed by society commentators as 'the wedding of the year'. Luca De Rossi had helped her to escape in his sports car. For some reason the sight of his tanned hands on the steering wheel evoked a quiver in her belly. A picture flashed into her mind of those hands caressing her, his dark olive skin a stark contrast to her pale flesh.

She swallowed. 'Where are we?'

'London. Mayfair, to be exact. I've brought you to my hotel to give you time to decide what your plans are.' Luca handed her another tissue. 'You might want to clean yourself up before we go inside.'

Athena had recognised the name of the exclusive five-star hotel that overlooked Marble Arch and Hyde Park. Her heart sank when she pulled down the car's sun visor to look in the vanity mirror and saw her face streaked with black mascara and red lipstick smudged across her chin like a garish Halloween mask.

She did her best with the tissue, and when Luca had

parked in the underground car park and they'd taken the lift up to the hotel's opulent reception area, she shot into the ladies' cloakroom to avoid the curious stares of the other guests, who were clearly intrigued to see a tearful bride.

In one of the private cubicles she ran a sink of hot water and scrubbed the make-up off her face. Her elaborate bun had slipped to one side of her head, and she began the task of removing the dozens of hairpins before brushing her hair to get rid of the coating of hairspray. She gave a start when her phone rang from the depths of her bag, and the sight of her mother's name on the caller display caused her stomach to knot with tension.

Out in the hotel lobby, Luca tapped his foot on the marble-tiled floor and tried to contain his impatience as he waited for Athena to emerge from the cloakroom. Long experience of women warned him that she might be in there for hours while she reapplied her make-up. While he was waiting he reread the latest text message he had received from Giselle.

I have decided to ask my four young nieces to be brides-maids at our wedding and I've seen the most adorable dresses for them to wear.

The message included a photo of a sickly-sweet child dressed in a shepherdess costume. Luca ground his teeth. *Bridesmaids!* Giselle was pushing his patience to its limit. And another text revealed that she knew she had the upper hand.

I hope you will be amenable, chéri, because I'm sure I don't need to remind you that you will be thirty-five in two short weeks.

The warning in Giselle's second text was clear. *Do what I want, or...* Or what? Luca thought grimly. It was unlikely that his bimbo bride would give up a million pounds over an argument about bridesmaids, but he dared not risk upsetting her when he was so close to his goal.

His phone rang and he frowned when he saw that the caller was the other thorn in his side: his grandmother's brother, Executive Vice President of De Rossi Enterprises, Emilio Nervetti.

'This continued uncertainty about who will head the company is affecting profits.' Emilio went straight for the jugular. 'I intend to ask the board to support a vote of no confidence in your leadership. Under the terms of my dear sister Violetta's will, two weeks from now you stand to lose your position as chairman unless you marry before your birthday—which you show no signs of doing.'

'On the contrary,' Luca said curtly. 'My wedding is arranged for next week—*before* I turn thirty-five. My marriage will allow me to continue in my role as chairman of De Rossi Enterprises, and after I have been married for one year I will not only secure the chairmanship permanently, but also the deeds to Villa De Rossi, and the right to use the De Rossi name for the fashion label I created.'

For a few seconds an angry silence hummed down the line, before Emilio said coldly, 'I am sure the board members will be relieved to know that you intend to give up your playboy lifestyle for a life of decency and sobriety. But I'm afraid I cannot be so confident. You inherited your mother's alley-cat morals, Luca. And God knows what genes you inherited from your father—whoever he was.'

Luca cut the call and swore savagely beneath his breath. His great-uncle's dig about his parentage was expected, but it still made him seethe. Emilio had only been given a position on the board of De Rossi Enterprises because his sister—Luca's grandmother—had married Luca's grand-father. *He* was the rightful De Rossi heir, Luca thought grimly, even though his grandparents had disapproved of him.

Luca's grandfather, Aberto De Rossi, had lacked the vision of his father, founder of De Rossi Enterprises, Raimondo De Rossi. But at least Aberto had been a steady figure at the head of the company. With no son to succeed him Aberto had given his daughter Beatriz a prominent position on the board—with disastrous results.

Beatriz had been too busy with her party lifestyle to take an interest in running the company, and her scandalous private life had brought disrepute to the De Rossi brand name and resulted in falling profits.

Eventually Aberto had run out of patience with his daughter and had named his illegitimate grandson as his heir—with the stipulation that Luca could only inherit with his grandmother's agreement, and only after her death. Aberto had also voiced his reservations about Luca's decision to study fashion design alongside a business degree.

However, at the age of twenty Luca had presented his first collection at New York Fashion Week and received critical acclaim. The launch of his fashion label, DRD, had restored the De Rossi brand to the prestige it had known under the legendary Raimondo. But, according to the terms of Luca's grandmother's will, he faced losing everything. All his hard work and achievements had meant nothing to Nonna Violetta—and he knew why.

He was a *bastardo*—the product of a brief union between his mother and a croupier she had met in a casino—and in his grandparents' eyes not a true De Rossi. He had inherited his talent for innovative design from his great-grandfather, but Luca had been a shameful reminder to his grandparents that their only daughter had made the family a laughing stock.

Luca's jaw clenched. He had done everything he could to win his grandparents' approval, but it had never been enough to earn their love. And after Aberto had died, Violetta had become increasingly demanding, saying that Luca must marry and provide an heir. Presumably she had believed that an heir from the *bastardo* De Rossi was better than no heir at all, he thought bitterly.

His grandmother had threatened to use her casting vote with the board to have him replaced as head of the company. And even after her death she still sought to control her grandson by stipulating in her will that he must be married by his thirty-fifth birthday or the Villa De Rossi would be sold to a consortium that was eager to turn the house into a hotel. Luca would also be removed from his role as chairman of De Rossi Enterprises and barred from holding any other position within the company. And, although he owned DRD, he would lose the right to use the De Rossi name for his fashion label.

Luca's lip curled. Nonna Violetta's ultimate betrayal had been that threat to ban him from using the name he had been given at birth for his design business. It was a vindictive reminder that he had only been called De Rossi because his mother hadn't known his father's surname. Despite everything he had done to restore the fortunes of the company, to his grandparents when they had been alive, and to some of the board members of De Rossi Enterprises, he would always be a *bastardo*.

Anger burned in his gut, and with it another emotion he did not want to recognise. He had once assumed he had been hurt too often by his grandmother and no longer cared what she thought of him. But when he had heard the details of her will he had felt sick to his stomach.

He did not care so much if he lost control of De Rossi Enterprises, and he could always rename his fashion label—he might even enjoy the challenge of starting again and rebranding his designs, and he only wished he could stand at his grandmother's grave and laugh at her attempt to manipulate him. But there was one very good reason why he couldn't. Two reasons, he amended. The first was the Villa De Rossi and the second was his daughter Rosalie, whom he loved and was determined to protect at all costs—even if that cost was his pride.

His phone pinged, heralding another text from Giselle. *Dio*, he needed to return to Italy so that he could keep his future bride satisfied with sex until she had signed her name on the marriage certificate, Luca thought sardonically.

He glanced across the lobby and saw Athena walk out of the cloakroom. She looked younger without the heavy make-up, and now that her hair was loose he saw that it still fell almost to her waist and was not, in fact, a dull brown, but a warm chestnut shade that shone like raw silk.

As she came towards him he could see that she had been crying again. Behind her glasses her eyes were red-rimmed. He wondered if she was regretting her decision not to marry Charles Fairfax but reminded himself that he did not care.

Her wedding dress was drawing attention from the other hotel guests. He supposed he could take her up to his suite and ply her with the cups of tea that the British seemed to consume in great quantities in times of crisis, but he did not have the time or the patience to listen to her problems when he had enough of his own.

Another text arrived from Giselle. He would have to phone her—but while he did what could he do with Athena?

Luca spotted a waiter who worked in the hotel's cocktail bar. 'Miguel, this is Miss Athena Howard. Will you take her into the bar and make her a cocktail?' He smiled briefly at Athena. 'I have to make a phone call. I'll join you in a few minutes.'

To Athena's relief there were only a few people in the bar, and she was able to hide behind a large potted fern to avoid attracting more curious looks. She knew that one of her first priorities must be to buy some different clothes, but she did not relish the idea of walking along Oxford Street in her wedding dress.

'Have you decided what you would like to drink?'

'Um…' She stared at the cocktail menu. She certainly wasn't going to ask the waiter for a Sex on the Beach! 'Can you recommend something fruity and refreshing?'

'How about an Apple Blossom?'

It sounded innocuous enough. 'That would be lovely.'

The waiter returned minutes later with a pretty golden-coloured drink decorated with slices of lemon. Athena sipped the cocktail. It tasted of apples and something else that she could not place, and it was warming as it seeped into her bloodstream.

Her mind replayed the phone call from her mother.

Veronica Howard, typically, had not given her daughter an opportunity to speak, but instead had launched into a tirade about how Athena had once again let her parents down.

'How *could* you jilt poor Charles, almost at the altar, and run off with an Italian playboy who, I am reliably informed, changes his mistresses as often as other men change his socks? What were you *thinking*, Athena? Did you even stop to consider how mortified your father and I would feel when Lady Fairfax explained what you had done? Poor Charles is heartbroken.'

'Wait a minute… Luca isn't…' Athena had tried to interrupt her mother. 'How do you know about Luca?'

What she had meant was how did her mother know that Luca had helped her to run away from the wedding—but, as so often happened with Athena, her words had come out wrong.

'Charles watched you drive off with this Luca in his flash sports car,' Veronica had said shrilly. 'Apparently he'd had suspicions that you were seeing another man behind his back, but he hoped that once you were married you would be happy with *him*. You can imagine how shattered poor Charles was when he discovered *today* that you are having an affair with his old school friend.'

'I'm not having an affair with anyone. It's Charlie who—'

Athena had been tempted to tell her mother the true reason why she had refused to marry Charlie, but despite the callous way he had used her she had been unable to bring herself to betray his deeply personal secret.

'You need to persuade Charles to tell his parents the true situation,' she had told her mother.

'Actually, I *need* to go and talk to the photographer from *High Society* magazine and explain why they can no longer feature a five-page spread of your wedding in their next issue,' Veronica had said coldly. 'Your father and I will *never* live this down,' she'd snapped as a final rejoinder, before ending the call.

Athena finished her drink and the waiter immediately reappeared with another. She blinked away her tears as she sipped the second cocktail. Her parents—particularly her mother—had never listened to her, she thought miserably.

When she was a child they had ignored her requests to give up the tennis lessons and violin lessons, the ballet classes in which she had been the least graceful dancer—

more like an elephant than a swan, as the other girls had taunted her. It hadn't been until she'd left school, having scraped her exams, with the words *'Athena is an average student'* written on every school report and emblazoned on her psyche, that her parents had given up their hope that she would show late signs of academic brilliance.

Even when she had qualified as a nursery assistant—a job that she loved—they had kept on at her to reapply for university so that she could at least train to be a teacher. She believed she had been a disappointment to her parents all her life. It was partly for that reason that she had never told them she had been sexually assaulted by her Latin tutor when she was a teenager. She had always wondered if the assault had somehow been her fault, she brooded, as she drained her glass and took a sip of the second cocktail that the waiter had brought over to her—or was it the third?

If she had betrayed Charlie she would have had to admit to her parents the humiliating fact that her ex-fiancé preferred his best man to her. Was she *really* so unattractive that no man would want her, as Charlie had said? He had accused her of having a hang-up about sex, and the truth was that he was right, Athena acknowledged, swallowing a sob and gulping down the rest of her cocktail.

The waiter must have noticed her empty glass, because he arrived at her table with another drink. She had lost track of how many cocktails she'd had—and actually she didn't care.

Through the door of the bar she could see Luca De Rossi in the lobby, talking into his phone. He was drop-dead gorgeous, and she noticed every woman who walked past him paused to give him a lingering look. He seemed unaware that he was the centre of attention, but it was more likely that he was used to women staring at him, Athena thought ruefully. A man like Luca would not have to try very hard. One smile from his sensual mouth and most women would melt—like she had in Zenhab.

A memory slipped into her mind of him kissing her when they had been in the palace gardens. She had been watching the water droplets from the fountain sparkle like diamonds in the moonlight, but at the same time had been intensely aware of Luca standing beside her. When he had bent his head and brushed his lips over hers she had responded unthinkingly, beguiled by his simmering sensuality.

Why had he kissed her?

She watched him walk into the bar and stride over to where she was sitting. His charcoal-grey suit was expertly cut to show off his superb physique and his silky black hair was just a fraction too long, curling over his collar. He was dark, devastating, and undoubtedly dangerous—and it suddenly seemed imperative to Athena to find out the reason he had kissed her at her sister's wedding.

The room spun when she stood up, and the floor seemed strangely lopsided as she walked towards him. She felt oddly brimming with self-assurance—as if all her inhibitions had disappeared. Even Charlie's cruel taunt that no man would want a twenty-five-year-old virgin no longer hurt. Luca De Rossi, sex god and notorious womaniser, had kissed her once before, and it was possible—likely, even, she decided with a whoosh of confidence—that he wanted to kiss her again.

Perhaps inevitably, she tripped on the hem of her wedding dress, but Luca caught her in his strong arms as she had known he would. He was her hero and her handsome knight, she thought, giving him a beaming smile.

'I think I might be a bit tipsy,' she announced, trying to focus on him. 'Although I don't know why. All I've had to drink are a few lovely cocktails called Apple Bosoms.' She giggled. 'Oops, I didn't mean to say bosom.'

The word had come into her mind because while she had been admiring Luca she'd felt a tingling sensation in her breasts and her nipples had felt hot and hard beneath the stiff bodice of her wedding dress. 'I meant Apple *Blossoms*,' she said carefully, wondering why her tongue felt too big for her mouth. 'Anyway, the cocktails are made with apple juice.'

'And calvados and vodka,' Luca murmured as he attempted to unwind Athena's arms from around his neck.

At least she had stopped crying, but she had clearly had too much to drink, and her wedding dress was still attracting attention from the hotel guests who had come into the bar.

'I think I had better take you up to my room and order you some strong coffee,' he told her, keeping his tone light and hoping he could whisk her out of the bar without her causing a scene.

She swayed, and would have fallen if he had not caught her. *'Santa Madonna!'* he growled beneath his breath, his patience ebbing away fast. It was obvious that she could not walk, so he did the only thing he could and swept her up into his arms.

'I think that's a *very* good idea,' Athena said over loudly. 'Take me upstairs, Luca, and kiss me like you did in Zenhab.'

CHAPTER THREE

IT FELT AS though someone was using a pneumatic drill to bore into her skull. Wincing with pain, Athena forced her eyes open. Without her glasses her vision was blurred, but she was certain she did not recognise the elegant decor of eau-de-Nil walls and dusky blue furnishings.

Her mouth was parched. She carefully turned her head and made out a glass of water on the bedside table.

So she was in a bed. *But whose bed?*

Random memories came into her mind. Charlie and his best man Dominic in bed together... Her crazy idea to climb out of the window at Woodley Lodge and her terror when the ivy had given away and she had fallen...

Her brother-in-law Kadir's friend Luca De Rossi had caught her before she'd hit the ground. And Luca had helped her to run away from her wedding—at least he had driven her away in his sports car and brought her to his hotel. She had a vague recollection of being in a hotel bar and Luca saying that he would take her up to his suite and make her coffee.

Which meant that this must be Luca's room—and she must be...*in Luca's bed*!

Another piece of the jigsaw slotted into place. She remembered that Luca had undone the lacing at the back of her dress before lifting the wedding gown over her head. *Oh, God!* Her face burned as she recalled with excruciating clarity how she had stood in front of him in her under-wear and said, 'Take me, Luca, I'm all yours.'

She thought he'd murmured, 'Lucky me,' in a dry tone. But she couldn't be sure, and after that her memory was blank.

Carefully she turned her head the other way on the pil-low and was relieved to find that she was alone in the bed. But the tangled silk sheets seemed to suggest that a lot of activity had taken place between them.

Athena's heart juddered to a standstill.

Had she? Could she have had sex with Luca and not remember anything about it? He was a notorious woman-iser, and she had literally thrown herself at him. Perhaps he had accepted her offer.

In a strange way it would be a relief if she'd lost her virginity without being aware of it, she thought, nibbling her lower lip with her teeth. She had allowed the incident that had happened years ago, with a university professor friend of her parents who had been giving her extra Latin tuition, to affect her for far too long. If she *had* had sex with Luca it couldn't have been too traumatic if she had no recollection of it.

She sat up and instantly felt very sick. The sheet slipped down and she saw she was wearing the white push-up bra that was part of the pretty bridal underwear set she had hoped would excite Charlie on their wedding night. Gri-macing, she peeped beneath the sheet and discovered that the matching lacy thong was still in place, which suggested that her virginity was also intact.

'Good morning,' a gravelly voice said, followed curtly by, 'Although it beats me if there is anything *good* about it.'

Athena whipped her head round and instantly regretted moving so quickly as the room and her stomach lurched in unison. Luca was sitting in an armchair close to the bed. He was dressed entirely in black, and his tight-fitting sweater moulded his torso so that she could see the delineation of his powerful abdominal muscles beneath the fine wool.

Lifting her gaze higher, she noted that the night's growth of dark stubble on his jaw accentuated his raw sexual magnetism. His mouth was curled in an even more cynical expression than usual, and she felt unnerved by the assessing expression in his amber eyes. The fact that he was dressed seemed to indicate that he had *not* accepted her drunken invitation the previous night, but Athena was desperate for confirmation.

'If I spent last night in your bed, where did you sleep?'

His black brows snapped together, but his voice was deceptively soft as he drawled, 'Where do you *think* I might have spent the night?'

Her jerky glance at the rumpled sheets betrayed her. Luca's eyes narrowed and he swore. 'Are you suggesting that I took advantage of you while you were paralytic? Could you be *any* more insulting?'

She swallowed and rested her aching head against the pillows. 'I'm sorry…but I don't remember anything that happened after you brought me to your suite last night… and I need to know if you…if we…'

He moved with the speed of an attacking cobra as he sprang up from the chair and leaned over the bed, placing his hands on either side of her head.

'You are not in my bed. This hotel suite has two bedrooms. Let's get a few facts straight,' he said grimly. 'Number one—if we'd had sex I guarantee you would remember. Number two—I only make love to women who are conscious and capable of participating. Number three…'

Luca's wolf's eyes gleamed with a hard brilliance '...I dislike being manipulated, Miss Howard.'

'What do you mean?' she asked shakily.

His face was so close to hers that even without her glasses she could almost count his thick black eyelashes. The rigid line of his jaw warned her that his hold on his temper was tenuous. But despite his anger Athena did not feel the wariness that she usually felt with men. Far from it. She hardly dared to breathe as her senses reacted to the warmth emanating from Luca's body and the intangible scent of his maleness.

Molten heat washed over her entire body and pooled between her thighs. She was painfully aware of the ache in her breasts and her pebble-hard nipples chafing against her lacy bra cups. The intensity of her desire shocked her, yet deep down she felt relieved at this proof that she had normal sexual needs just like any other woman, and that the assault when she was a teenager had not destroyed her sensuality.

She pictured Luca lowering his body onto hers and pinning her to the mattress with his hard thighs. She imagined how it would feel to have her breasts crushed against his chest and her lips crushed beneath his mouth as he kissed her with fierce passion.

The urge to moisten her dry lips with the tip of her tongue was overwhelming. She saw his eyes narrow as he watched the betraying gesture, and she sensed from his sudden stillness that he knew she wanted him to kiss her.

He jerked upright, leaving her confused by her reaction to him and pink cheeked with embarrassment.

'*This* is what I mean,' he said harshly, dropping a pile of newspapers onto the bed.

Athena tried to ignore her pounding headache as she sat upright and peered at the headline on one of the papers. 'What does it say? I can't read it without my glasses. Thank you...' she murmured when Luca shoved her spectacles into her hand.

She put them on and drew a sharp breath as she saw clearly the newspaper headline and the photograph below it of Luca holding her in his arms in the hotel bar. She had her arms wrapped tightly around his neck and a silly grin on her face that in the cold light of day made her want to die of mortification.

'Bride Jilts Toff for Italian Playboy!' screamed the headline, followed by a paragraph explaining how The Honourable Charles Fairfax had been left heartbroken after his fiancée Athena Howard had run off with his old school friend from Eton College, famous fashion designer Luca De Rossi, an hour before their lavish wedding was due to take place.

'Oh, my God,' Athena said faintly. There were a hundred questions in her mind and she voiced the top one. 'How did the journalists know you had brought me to your hotel?'

'Drop the innocent act,' Luca growled. 'Obviously you tipped off the press about our location and told them this lie about us having an affair.'

'No... No, I *didn't*!' she stammered, suddenly realising that behind Luca's unreadable expression his anger was simmering like a volcano about to erupt. 'Why would I have done that?'

He shrugged. 'I don't know. Maybe you had a row with Charlie and wanted to hurt him. You used me as your stooge. I helped you to escape from Woodley Lodge because I believed your helpless *"I can't marry Charlie because I don't love him"* routine, and this is the thanks I get,' he said savagely as he picked up another newspaper with a similar sensational headline and screwed it up in his fist. 'I don't know why you did it. Who understands what goes on in women's minds?' Luca muttered.

His jaw clenched as he recalled his phone conversation with Giselle half an hour ago. The story about him stealing Athena from under his old school friend's nose had made the headlines in Italy as well as England, and Giselle had refused to be placated or to listen to him when he'd tried to explain that none of it was true.

'*Is* this Athena woman with you at your hotel in London?' Giselle had demanded.

He had been unable to deny it . 'Yes, but...'

The rest of his words had been drowned out by Giselle's shrill tones.

'You've made me look a fool to my family and friends. *Everyone* knew that you and I were supposed to be getting married, but a week before our wedding you've been caught with your pants down with your best friend's bride.'

'I have *not* been caught with my pants down,' Luca had said grittily, 'and neither is Charles Fairfax my best friend.'

At Eton, Charlie had been an irritating boy from a lower year who had hung around him and Kadir because Kadir was a sultan. Privately Luca had suspected that Charlie wasn't interested in women, and he'd been surprised to hear that he was getting married.

'And your family only know about our wedding,' he'd continued, 'because against my advice *you* told them. I said we should keep the news of our marriage of convenience a secret. I'm sure I don't need to remind you that you will be well paid for being my temporary wife.'

'You're damned right, I'll be well paid,' Giselle had said in a hard voice. 'I'm upping my price, *chéri*. I want two million, or the marriage deal is off.'

He had underestimated Giselle, Luca acknowledged. He had dismissed her as an airhead. But she understood that the closer it got to his birthday the more valuable she was. He was unlikely to find another woman prepared to marry him within the next two weeks and be his wife in name only.

Giselle had believed she was calling the shots, but Luca had had enough of being manipulated—first by his grand-mother and now by a gold-digger. He had not lost his temper —that wasn't how Luca operated. But anyone who had crossed swords with him in the boardroom would vouch that behind Luca De Rossi's charming smile lay a heart made of ice and an implacable will that was second to none.

'I swear I didn't tell the newspapers that you and I are… involved.'

Athena's soft voice dragged Luca from the memory of his row with Giselle and the grim realisation that, although calling her bluff and telling her to get lost had been infi-nitely satisfying, he had blown everything.

'But I think I can guess who did.' Athena bit her lip. 'I suspect it was Charlie.'

'Why would Charlie tell the press that you'd jilted him and run off with one of the wedding guests?' Luca said impatiently. 'The story makes him look foolish in public. I remember at school he was a pompous oaf—he'll hate people believing that you dumped him for another man.'

'He has to put the blame on me to hide the fact that *he* is having an affair with…' Athena hesitated. She believed Charlie really had tipped off the press that she was at the hotel with Luca, but her innate sense of loyalty stopped her from revealing his secret relationship with Dominic. 'With someone else,' she finished flatly.

'Charlie is having an affair?' Luca's brows lifted in surprise.

Athena could be lying, he reminded himself. But he found he believed her. This morning she looked young and curiously innocent, with her face scrubbed of make-up and her long chestnut-brown hair rippling down her back. She had tugged the sheet right up to her chin, but not before he had glimpsed firm, round breasts that reminded him of plump peaches framed by a wispy white lace bra.

She kept darting shy glances at him from beneath the sweep of her lashes. But the sexy underwear that he'd seen last night when he had removed her wedding dress and put her into bed indicated that she was as sexually confident as he would expect of a woman in her mid-twenties who had been about to get married.

'When did you discover that Charlie was being unfaithful?'

'Just before I climbed out of the window.' Athena pushed a heavy swathe of hair back from her face. 'I knew I couldn't go ahead with the wedding. I panicked, and all I could think of was to get away. I thought Charlie would explain the truth about why the wedding was cancelled. I was horrified when my mother told me on the phone that Charlie had accused me of running off with you, but I never thought that he would lie to the *press*.'

She looked down at the lurid newspaper headlines and missed the flash of anger in Luca's eyes.

'Are you saying you already *knew* Charlie had accused you of having an affair with me?' Luca asked in a dangerous voice.

'Mum said that Charlie saw us drive off in your car. I assumed he had told his parents and mine that he'd suspected me of seeing another man in the weeks before the wedding. Of course you and I know he was lying…'

Her voice tailed off as Luca swore savagely.

'But now the story is in the newspapers and the whole damn world believes that you and I are lovers,' he grated. 'If you knew last night that Charlie had lied to the press, why the hell didn't you *say* so? I might have been able to stop the story from being printed.'

'I…I didn't think.' Her mother would say that was nothing new, Athena thought bleakly. And she did not actually remember much about the previous evening after she'd drunk several cocktails.

'I don't suppose there's any point telling the newspapers the truth about why I ran away. Charlie will deny it was him who was unfaithful and everyone will think I'm accusing him unfairly out of spite. We can only hope that the story will quickly be forgotten.' She gave Luca a hopeful look. 'I'm sure no one will pay much attention to gossip in the tabloids.'

Dio! Her chirpy optimism caused Luca to grit his teeth. She was either an incarnation of Mary Poppins, or a good actress—and his experience of women and the games they played made him favour the latter.

'The woman I was due to marry was *riveted* by the tabloid headlines,' he said sarcastically.

'*Due to marry?* You mean you're *engaged*?'

Athena's stomach swooped. She couldn't explain the hollow sensation she felt inside at Luca's revelation. He had a reputation as a womaniser, and she wondered what kind of woman had finally tamed him.

'Not any more—since Giselle read in the papers that I stole my old school friend's bride from under his nose and, according to at least one overly imaginative tabloid journalist, we spent last night having hot sex at my hotel.'

Luca cast a glowering look at the newspaper photo of him carrying Athena into the hotel lift. He hadn't noticed any photographer in the lobby, but he had been distracted when Athena had pressed her face against his throat and he'd felt her warm breath graze his skin.

It was possible that *she* had been aware of the photographer, he brooded. She might even have arranged for the press to be at the hotel. She'd admitted that she had discovered hours before her wedding that Charlie had cheated on her—perhaps she had decided to pay her errant fiancé back by being photographed apparently on her way to bed with her lover.

'*Oh, no!* That's *terrible* about your fiancée!' Athena's hand flew to her mouth and she dropped the sheet, exposing the sexy push-up bra that was nothing like her usual sensible underwear. Flushing hotly, she snatched the sheet back up to her chin.

'It's too late for modesty,' Luca told her impatiently. 'Last night you were so drunk that I had to take off your dress and put you into bed.'

'I'm sorry I've caused you so much trouble,' she said stiffly.

The idea that he had seen her almost naked body—the thong was *very* revealing—made her feel hot all over. But from Luca's grim expression she guessed he was thinking only about his fiancée's refusal to marry him.

The tense silence was broken by the sound of his phone. He glanced at the caller display and frowned. 'Excuse me—I have to take this,' he muttered, not even glancing at her as he strode out of the room.

Luca could feel his heart beating painfully hard as he walked through the interconnecting sitting room and into his bedroom. Maria never usually called him this early in the morning—unless something was wrong with Rosalie.

His daughter's nurse greeted him calmly, but Luca detected an underlying note of concern in her voice.

'Rosalie had a severe seizure earlier this morning, which lasted for approximately six minutes.'

'That long?' Luca swallowed. 'It must have put a huge strain on her heart. Were you with her when it happened?'

'I had just come on duty and taken over from the night staff. Because of the length of the seizure I called the doctor, and he has just left after checking Rosalie over. She seems fine, Luca. She's asleep now, and later I'll push her wheelchair out into the garden. You know how she loves to sit beneath the weeping willow tree.'

'I wish I had been there,' Luca said heavily. 'I *should* have been with her.'

Guilt clawed inside him that it wasn't always possible for him to be with his disabled daughter. He employed excellent staff to look after her, and Maria, who had been Rosalie's main carer since she had been diagnosed with a degenerative genetic disease ten years ago, adored her.

It would be Rosalie's thirteenth birthday in a few months, but she could not lead a normal life or enjoy the fun of being a teenager. Luca felt a familiar dull ache in his heart. His daughter's world was confined to Villa De Rossi and the rooms that had been adapted for her needs. One of her greatest joys was to spend time in the special garden he had created for her.

It was imperative for Rosalie's health and happiness that she remained living at Villa De Rossi. But unless Luca found a woman who was prepared to marry him before his thirty-fifth birthday he would lose the villa that was the only home his daughter had ever known. He could not imagine the trauma it would cause Rosalie if she had to be moved to a new house, away from familiar surroundings and the things she loved.

A nerve flickered in his jaw as he thought of his grandmother's vindictive last will and testament. His lawyers had picked over the details with a fine-tooth comb and had advised him that there were no grounds for him to challenge the will.

His only hope of keeping Villa De Rossi was to go

crawling to Giselle and agree to pay her whatever she demanded to marry him. Two million pounds was nothing compared to his daughter's wellbeing. It would stick in his craw to pander to a gold-digger like Giselle, but nothing was more important to him than his darling Rosalie, who was unable to walk or talk but whose beautiful smile was priceless.

Luca clenched his hands into fists. *What a mess!* He had been doing a favour for Kadir when he'd helped Athena to escape from her wedding, but in doing so his own marriage plans had been wrecked.

He walked into the sitting room and stopped dead. Athena was wearing her wedding dress—presumably because she had not brought any other clothes with her. And as he stared at her Luca was struck by the thought that fate had presented him with an alternative convenient bride.

He tried to push the crazy idea out of his mind as he strode over to the table where the hotel staff had set out breakfast. A pool of coffee was spreading across the white damask tablecloth and Athena was frantically trying to mop up the mess with a napkin.

'What the hell happened?'

'I'm so sorry. I knocked over the cafetière.' She grabbed another napkin and attempted to stanch the river of coffee, almost knocking over the milk jug. Luca's quick reactions allowed him to snatch it out of the way.

'Perhaps if you put your glasses on you would be able to see better,' he suggested.

'I'm wearing contact lenses. I can see perfectly well. I found a new pack of lenses in my bag. I'd forgotten that I *had* ordered some new ones before the wedding,' Athena explained. 'Charlie used to say that my mind has more holes in it than a Swiss cheese,' she said flatly.

She stared at the mess on the table. The breakfast had

looked so elegant until she'd poured herself a cup of coffee and the handle of the cafetière had slipped in her fingers.

'Charlie found my clumsiness very irritating. He called me hopeless, and he was right.'

'It's just spilt coffee—it doesn't matter,' Luca said, wondering why Athena's dejected voice made him feel strangely protective. 'I remember at school Charlie had as much charm as a pit of vipers. What made you decide to marry him?'

It was impossible for Athena to explain that she had felt unthreatened by the lack of sexual chemistry between her and Charlie. In the early days of their relationship she had been *relieved* that he hadn't pushed for anything more than a simple kiss at the end of the evening. Charlie had never tried to put his hands up her jumper. There had been no fumbling in his car—no need for her to push him away, her heart thumping with anxiety as memories of being assaulted by her Latin tutor made her, in the words of one disappointed ex-boyfriend, 'as frigid as a nun'.

Now, of course, she understood why Charlie had not pressured her for sex. It hadn't been out of respect for her. It had been because he had never been in love with her and had only asked her to marry him so that he could hide his relationship with the person he really loved—Dominic.

It was true she had realised she did not love Charlie either, but she was still hurt that he had intended to use her so callously, and she felt a resurgence of her old feelings of worthlessness.

'I believed that Charlie and I wanted the same things.'

Tears filled her eyes as she remembered how Charlie had said he wanted them to start trying for a baby as soon as they were married. She had never hidden the fact that she loved children and longed for a family. No wonder Charlie had decided she would be an ideal wife.

'He is very ambitious to do well at the bank, and I hoped to support his career and make a home for us.'

In other words Athena had hoped to enjoy a luxurious lifestyle provided by a wealthy husband, Luca thought derisively. She had told him she did not work. Perhaps she was looking tearful again now because she was regretting her decision not to marry Charlie and one day being able to sign her name as Lady Fairfax.

'Luca…' Athena turned away from the ruined breakfast table. It was one more thing to add to her weight of guilt. 'I feel terrible that your fiancée saw the story about us in the newspapers and has refused to marry you. It's partly my fault…'

'So you *admit* you tipped off the press that I'd brought you to my hotel?' Luca's temper soared.

'No!' Athena felt her insides knot with tension at Luca's explosion of anger. She hated confrontation, and whenever she and Charlie had argued she had always been the one to back down—just as she had with her parents. 'I've explained that I didn't tell anyone of our whereabouts. Charlie must have known the name of your hotel. Perhaps he phoned and found out that you had brought me here. But I do feel partly responsible because Kadir asked you to help me. I'm really sorry that your fiancée thinks we spent the night together. If I explained to her what really happened she might still be willing to marry you.'

Oh, Giselle would be willing—for the right price, Luca thought grimly. At the end of their phone conversation, when she'd realised that he wasn't going to concede to her demand for more money and was prepared to walk away, she had turned nasty and threatened to go to the media with the story of their marriage deal. He would be damned if he would allow her to manipulate him. It was bad enough that his grandmother was doing so from her grave.

'My relationship with Giselle is over for good,' he told Athena.

She looked visibly upset, which surprised Luca, for in his experience women rarely cared about anything other than themselves.

'I wish there was something I could do to help put the situation right,' she murmured.

The mellow September sunshine streaming through the window made Athena's hair gleam like silk. The chestnut tones were mixed with shades of gold through to dark auburn, Luca noted absently. He skimmed his gaze over her wedding dress—not with the critical eye of a designer this time, but with a view to fulfilling the terms of his grandmother's will.

'There *is* something you can do,' he said abruptly. '*You* can marry me.'

Athena's breath lodged in her throat. She knew she could not have heard him correctly. Luca De Rossi could *not* have just asked her to marry him. But even though she was certain she had misheard him, her heart was banging against her ribs.

'I'm sorry…could you say that again?'

'I want you to marry me.'

Oh, God! She felt a strange trembling sensation inside. Was it possible that Luca had been unable to forget, as she hadn't, the kiss they had shared in Zenhab nine months ago?

'We…we hardly know each other,' she stammered.

He frowned. 'Obviously I am not suggesting a *real* marriage.'

Obviously! Athena flushed with embarrassment that she had misunderstood him.

Luca's black hair was ruffled, as if he had been running his fingers through it, but the careless style only made him look even sexier. The sunlight highlighted his sharp cheekbones and the sculpted angles and planes of his face. He was the most handsome man Athena had ever seen, and she wondered how she could have been foolish enough to think he might be interested in someone as plain and ordinary looking as her.

'I didn't think you *were* suggesting a real marriage,' she said quickly. 'But I don't think it's a good idea for you to marry on the rebound as a way of paying your fiancée back for rejecting you. I realise you are probably heartbroken over Giselle...'

'I don't have a heart to break,' Luca drawled.

He had once. He had loved Jodie and it had hurt like hell when she had left him. He had no intention of repeating the great mistake of his youth. He did have a heart, but it belonged solely to his daughter.

He gave Athena an assessing look. Earlier, when he had leaned over the bed, he had sensed that she had wanted him to kiss her. A memory of when he had kissed her in Zenhab had stirred his desire, and he had been tempted to kiss her again. But then he had remembered that he suspected her of telling the press that he had helped her to run away from her wedding.

'I need to get married,' he said abruptly. 'But emotions won't be involved.'

He could see that had been the problem with Giselle. She had wanted more from him, and like every woman scorned, she had become spiteful when she'd realised that she meant nothing to him.

He looked into Athena's sapphire-blue eyes and dismissed the brief flicker inside him that he did not understand. 'I'm offering you a business deal. I'll pay you one million pounds if you will be my wife in name only for one year.'

CHAPTER FOUR

'ARE YOU THINKING what you could do with a million pounds?' Luca demanded as the silence stretched and Athena seemed to have been struck dumb.

She shook her head. 'I'm thinking that you are mad. Why do you *need* to get married?' He was wealthy, successful, and seriously gorgeous—it seemed bizarre that he had to pay someone to marry him. 'You have a reputation as a playboy. A lot of women would pay *you* to marry *them*,' she murmured.

'If I asked one of my mistresses I'd run the risk of them becoming emotionally involved.' He swept his gaze over her. 'I need to make it quite clear that there will be no point in you falling in love with me.'

Athena felt a spark of temper flicker inside her. Luca must *really* think she was pathetic if he felt he needed to warn her off him. 'If I was crazy enough to accept your marriage deal—which I'm not—I'm sure I would be able to restrain myself from falling in love with you,' she said curtly.

His brows rose, as if he was surprised by her sarcasm, and that infuriated her even more. She was tired of people walking all over her—but it was her own fault. She had spent her life trying to please people, but however hard she had tried she had never made her parents proud, and Charlie had neither loved nor respected her. It was time she grew a backbone—starting with telling this man who was too sexy for his own good what he could do with his outrageous marriage proposal.

The memory of the dismissive, faintly disdainful glance he had given her made her painfully aware of her shortcomings. At least Charlie had *pretended* he wanted to marry her, she thought dismally. Luca hadn't bothered with niceties when he had offered to buy her as if she was a prize heifer at a cattle market.

'I'm sorry, but I don't—' she began, but he cut her off.

'You asked why I need to be married. The terms of my grandmother's will demand that I must marry before I am thirty-five or I will lose the house which has belonged to the De Rossi family for eight generations. I will also lose my place on the governing board of the family business— despite the fact that I restored the company's fortunes and saved it from bankruptcy,' Luca said harshly.

Athena succumbed to her curiosity. 'Why did your grandmother make such a horrible will? Didn't you get on with her?'

'She disapproved of me—and especially of my lifestyle.' He gave a humourless laugh. 'Although I believe that Violetta would have disapproved of me even if I had become a priest. I could do nothing right in her eyes.'

Athena had half turned away from him, but she caught the faint note of hurt beneath his sardonic tone and hesitated. She knew what it was like never to feel good enough, consistently to fail to meet the expectations of parents.

'What about your parents? Aren't they included in your grandmother's will?'

'My mother is dead.' Luca did not mention his father. He neither knew nor cared if the faceless, nameless man who had fathered him was alive or not. 'I am the only De Rossi heir. But if I don't produce a bride by my birthday, in two weeks' time, I will lose everything I have worked for over the past fifteen years.'

'I'm sorry,' Athena murmured for a second time. She felt guilty that Luca's fiancée had dumped him, but she couldn't marry him just to appease her conscience. 'I understand why you feel an urgency to marry, but what you're suggesting is…well, *wrong*—and immoral. Marriage should happen because of love, not financial gain.'

'So you were going to marry Charlie because you *loved* him, and the fact that the Fairfaxes are one of the richest families in England had nothing to do with your decision?' Luca said sharply.

'I thought I loved him. I didn't care about his money or his title,' Athena insisted, flushing when Luca gave her a disbelieving look. 'It's difficult to explain. My parents were so delighted when Charlie asked me to marry him… I just wanted to do something right, for once, that would make them proud of me. The wedding preparations snowballed and I couldn't bring myself to admit even to myself that I was making a mistake.'

'But the truth is that without a wealthy husband or a job you presumably do not have any means of supporting yourself.'

Luca forced her to face the reality of her situation.

'What would you do with one million pounds? Think about it,' he urged.

His voice softened and his sexy, smoky accent caused the tiny hairs on her body to stand on end.

'What do you wish for more than anything, Athena? Jewellery? Beautiful clothes? A house?'

His words circled in her mind. She wasn't interested in jewellery or designer dresses. But a house… She thought of the dilapidated building situated on an area of scrubland that housed fifty-four orphaned children. Rajasthan was one of the poorest areas of India, and the orphanage in Jaipur, which had been founded twelve years ago by a remarkable American woman called Cara Tanner, was built of crumbling bricks, with a tin roof that leaked during the monsoon season and made the house as hot as an oven in the summer.

The House of Happy Smiles provided food, shelter and hope to children who were utterly destitute. Athena had discovered the orphanage during a holiday to India with her parents, and the contrast between the luxurious hotel where she had been staying and the devastating poverty she'd witnessed in the slums of Jaipur had had a profound effect on her.

Since that day four years ago, when she had met Cara Tanner and learned of the work she was doing running the orphanage, which was dependent on charitable donations, Athena had set up a fundraising campaign in England, and she returned to the House of Happy Smiles to work as a volunteer as often as she could.

Cara had plans for the orphanage, which included building a properly constructed house for the children to live in and also a school, and employing teachers to give the children an education.

'It will cost hundreds of thousands of pounds to turn the Happy House into a proper home and school for abandoned children, and to pay for staff to care for them,' Cara had explained. 'That kind of money will take years of fundraising, but think how it would transform the lives of those kids who have nothing.'

Deep in thought, Athena walked over to the window and stared unseeingly down at the crowd of people standing outside the front of the hotel. Her training as a nursery nurse meant that she could look after the younger children at the orphanage. Her visits to Jaipur and the fundraising she organised back in the UK meant a lot to her, and she felt she was actually doing something worthwhile.

A million pounds could transform the lives of those orphaned children. Her heart gave a jolt as she imagined the plans for the new house that Cara had shown her coming to fruition. There would be six beds in each dormitory, with curtains around each one to give the children a sense of privacy. A nursery for the babies and toddlers would be filled with toys, and there would be colourful murals painted on the walls. And a school would be built, with proper classrooms and desks and books. The children could be taught to read and write and to develop the skills that would enable them to find good jobs.

A million pounds would set the orphaned children free from grinding poverty. And *she* could make that difference with the money Luca was offering her to be his wife in name only for a year.

She swung round to face him. Her brain was telling her she would be mad to accept his proposal, but her heart ached for children like Suresh, a seven-year-old boy who was unable to walk as a result of contracting polio, who had been found begging on the streets. The orphanage was the only home he had ever known.

One million pounds could transform a rundown shack into a true House of Happy Smiles and give Suresh and the other children a future.

'How would this marriage work?' she asked shakily. 'Where would I live?'

'I have a penthouse apartment in Milan, close to the famous shopping precinct, where I am sure you would be very comfortable. I only stay at the apartment occasionally, if business requires me to spend a few days in the city. I live mainly at Villa De Rossi. Occasionally I might need you to come to the villa and act as a hostess at dinner parties.'

She grimaced. 'I'm not very good at organising dinner parties. I always seem to forget something or spill something.'

'My staff will take care of all the arrangements. I don't do a lot of entertaining, but sometimes I have to invite the board members of De Rossi Enterprises to the villa.' Luca stared intently at Athena. 'So, what is your answer?'

She bit her lip, hardly able to believe that she was actually contemplating accepting his proposal. 'When…when would I be paid the money?'

'Five hundred thousand will be paid into your bank account when we marry, and you'll receive the other five hundred thousand after we have been married for a year.'

That would mean work on the new building for the orphanage could begin *soon*. She remembered Luca had said that he had to be married before his birthday in two weeks. But could she go through with a sham marriage?

She glanced at his sculpted features, softened slightly by that lush mouth, and something hot and fierce unfurled inside her.

He walked over to her, and swore when he glanced out of the window and saw the crowd on the street below. 'The damned paparazzi have caused enough trouble.' He glared at Athena. 'And so have you.'

Guilt swamped her. If Luca hadn't helped her escape from her wedding his own wedding to Giselle would still be on. 'I promise I didn't tell the press you brought me here.'

He didn't seem to hear her. 'You owe me, Athena.'

A nerve flickered in Luca's jaw as he thought of how Rosalie loved to watch the weeping willow tree in the garden of Villa De Rossi swaying in the breeze. He could not bear the thought of taking his daughter away from the few simple pleasures she had.

For a moment he considered telling Athena about Rosalie, in the hope of gaining her sympathy. But he still wondered if she had tipped off the press, and he did not trust her not to talk to journalists about his daughter. When Rosalie was younger he had often taken her out to the park or the zoo, but she had been terrified by the paparazzi, who followed him everywhere with their camera flash-bulbs. His global fame as a fashion designer had made him a target for the press's interest.

Nowadays, Rosalie's disabilities meant that she was rarely well enough to leave home. Thankfully the media seemed to have forgotten about his daughter, and Luca was determined to protect Rosalie's privacy.

He pulled Athena away from the window and the prying lenses of the photographers. 'If I am not married two weeks from now I will lose everything I've spent the past fifteen years working for, and it will be *your* fault,' he said harshly.

She had a chance to do something worthwhile—something that mattered. What was a year out of her life if she could improve the lives of the orphaned children of Jaipur?

Athena drew a sharp breath. '*All right*, I'll do it. I'll marry you. But I want the one million pounds to be paid to me on the day of the wedding.'

That way she could give all the money to Cara Tanner to ensure that the project to build a new orphanage and school would be completed.

Luca frowned and she explained. 'If the money is in instalments you might decide not to pay me the full amount at the end of the year.'

'But if I pay you the one million up front how do I know that you won't take the money and disappear?' he said grimly. 'I can only claim the deeds to Villa De Rossi after I have been married for a year.'

'I give you my word that I will be your wife in name for one year.'

Luca's brows lifted. 'You'll understand why I am suspicious of trusting the word of a woman who jilted the man she had promised to marry an hour before the wedding,' he drawled.

Athena blushed guiltily, even though she knew she could not have married Charlie after she had discovered the truth about him. But she was determined to stand her ground. The orphanage project would need to be fully funded before building work began, and she had to have all the money Luca had said he would pay her.

'I want a million pounds on the day I marry you or we don't have a deal.'

Luca's eyes narrowed on her flushed cheeks and resolute chin. 'I think I might have underestimated you. You're not as sweet and innocent as you look—are you, *mia bella*?'

It was lucky he didn't know that her knees had been shaking when she'd insisted that she wanted all the money upfront. It was the first time she had ever stuck up for herself, and Athena's feeling of euphoria was only slightly tempered by the knowledge that Luca would be shocked to know just how innocent she was.

She bit her lip, remembering Charlie's taunt. *'Who will want to marry a twenty-five-year-old virgin with a hang-up about sex?'* It was a good thing that Luca *did* only want her to be his wife in name. He had a reputation as a playboy and no doubt preferred his mistresses to be sexually experienced.

His dark good looks exuded a raw sensuality that both fascinated and repelled her. Briefly she found herself imagining what it would be like if Luca's marriage proposal was real and he wanted her to be his wife not just in name but in *every* way—including sharing his bed. As if that would ever happen, she mocked herself. In the unlikely event that Luca might find her attractive, she would not know how to respond to him, and she was sure he would be turned off by her lack of experience.

He should not be surprised that when it came to money Athena was as hard-nosed as every other woman he knew, Luca told himself. But he had to move fast—before she decided to up her price.

'Fine—you'll get all the money when we marry.'

He punched numbers into his phone and spoke in rapid Italian to his PA.

'My plane is waiting at the airport,' he told Athena when he'd finished the phone call. He frowned as a thought struck him. 'Do you have your passport with you?'

'Yes, but…'

'The hotel manager is arranging for us to leave the hotel through the kitchens, so that we can avoid the paparazzi out the front.'

She glanced down at her wedding dress. 'I need to buy some other clothes.'

'There is no time for you to go on a shopping spree now.'

Luca's jaw hardened. Nothing was going to stop him claiming the Villa De Rossi and everything that was rightfully his. All he had to do was get his ring on Athena's finger and her signature on the marriage certificate as quickly as possible.

It was hard to believe she was on a plane, Athena thought, looking around the cabin, which was more like a room in a house, furnished with cream leather sofas, a polished wood dining table and a widescreen television. She had only ever travelled economy class to India, sitting in a cramped seat for the nine-hour flight to Delhi. Luca's luxurious private jet belonged to another world, but she did not belong there. She belonged in his world even less than she had belonged in Charlie's.

She stared at her reflection in a mirror. Yesterday, when she had put on her wedding dress, she could not have known that she would still be wearing it twenty-four hours later, as she flew on Luca De Rossi's private jet to Italy so that she could marry him. Of course he only wanted her to be his wife in name, and in fact that was all Charlie had wanted, she now realised.

She had been so shocked when she'd found him in bed with Dominic. Her relationship with Charlie had been built on his lies. He hadn't suggested that they wait until their wedding night before they had sex because he'd been mindful of her feelings… No, Charlie had never desired her or loved her. And she had not loved him, she admitted. She had tried to convince herself she did to please her parents—and because she wanted children and Charlie had said he was keen to start a family.

Her wedding dress was a mocking reminder that her life for the past year that she had been engaged to him had been an illusion.

'The sleeves of your dress are wrong,'

Luca's voice broke into Athena's thoughts. Since the plane had taken off from London he had been working on his laptop, but now he stood up and came to stand behind her. He gathered a voluminous puffed sleeve in his hand.

'There's far too much material here,' he told her, studying her reflection in the mirror. 'You are not tall enough to wear big sleeves and a full skirt, and your curves need to be accentuated—not hidden by yards of material.'

'I know I'm short and unfashionably curvy,' she muttered. 'You don't need to point out my defects.'

'I don't consider breasts and hips to be "defects".'

His eyes met hers in the mirror, and something in his enigmatic expression made her heart lurch.

'The truth is that most men prefer women to have curves...' his voice was smoky '...especially Italian men.'

'Including you?' The question sounded too intrusive, and the atmosphere in the cabin suddenly felt too intimate. Athena laughed loudly. 'As you're a fashion designer, I thought you would favour stick-thin women.'

Tall, rangy blondes had always been his preference, Luca mused. He did not know why Athena's diminutive size evoked a primal masculine desire to protect her. She was tougher than she looked, and a sharp negotiator, he reminded himself. But her sapphire-blue eyes were big enough to drown in, and her waist-length chestnut-brown hair smelled of lemons and felt like silk against his skin as he pushed her hair over her shoulder.

Athena released her breath as Luca moved away from her, but moments later he returned to stand behind her.

His eyes met hers in the mirror once again as he ordered, 'Keep still.'

She gasped when she saw a pair of scissors in his hand, but before she could protest he began to cut through the puffed sleeves of her dress. 'Are you mad? Do you know how much this dress cost?'

She flinched as the scissors flashed near to her throat, but it soon became clear why Luca was regarded as one of the world's top designers. Within a few minutes he had cut away the sleeves, leaving narrow shoulder straps, and he had reshaped the neckline of the dress, taking it lower, to reveal just a hint of her cleavage.

'I need pins,' he murmured, although he was so engrossed in what he was doing that Athena was sure he had forgotten that she was not a tailor's dummy.

He opened a cupboard and swung out a table on wheels that held a sewing machine.

'I've created some of my best designs in the air,' he said when he noticed her startled expression. 'I like the fact that no one can disturb me and my imagination can flow. Why did you choose a dress that could double up as a parachute?'

He pulled the skirt against her hips, gathering up the excess material at the back.

'You see how much more flattering the dress looks when it moulds your hips? You have a beautiful body and you should make the most of your feminine figure.'

Her? Beautiful? He wasn't serious, of course, Athena told herself, thinking of her breasts, which were too full in her opinion and usually disguised beneath baggy tops. But Luca was a playboy—no doubt flattering women was second nature to him.

'How…how do you know what my body is like?'

Why was she asking him in that husky voice that was so unlike the way she usually spoke? she wondered. His hands were resting on her hips, and the warmth of his skin was burning through the satin dress. She was aware of him with every atom, every cell of her body, but she was confused by her reaction to him. Why didn't she feel tense, as she usually did when a man stood too close to her? The molten sensation in her pelvis was something she had never experienced before, and yet she understood that the ache between her legs was the ache of desire: primitive, raw, and shockingly intense.

'I took your dress off when I put you to bed last night,' he reminded her. 'Your underwear left little to the imagination—and I have a very good imagination.' His amber eyes glinted with amusement when she blushed.

'You should have been named after the Greek goddess Aphrodite.'

She stiffened, and in split second the warm blood in her veins turned icy cold and a familiar feeling of revulsion churned in her stomach. '*Don't* call me that,' she said sharply.

Come on, Aphrodite, goddess of love. Inside her head she heard the sound of her cotton blouse ripping, and her high-pitched cry as she tried to hold the torn material across her breasts.

'Athena!' Luca's deep voice dispelled the images in her mind. 'Are you feeling ill? You've gone white. Do you suffer from air sickness?' It was the only explanation he could think of for her sudden pallor, but it did not explain the haunted expression in her eyes.

She swallowed. 'I… I feel unwell. I guess I'm still paying for drinking too many cocktails last night.' Somehow she forced a faint smile. 'It was my first hangover, and I'm going to make it my last,' she said ruefully.

She was surprisingly unsophisticated, and Luca once again felt his protective instinct stir. It was that instinct that had caused all his problems, he thought darkly, remembering how he'd offered to help her run away from her wedding.

'You'd be best to sleep it off,' he said abruptly, pressing the buzzer to summon the stewardess. 'Tia will show you to the bedroom, and she will bring you a drink or anything else you want.'

It was becoming a habit to wake up in a strange bedroom, Athena mused when she opened her eyes. The portholes instead of windows were a reminder that she was on Luca De Rossi's plane and that she had agreed to marry him for one million pounds. It had seemed straightforward before she had fallen asleep, but was less so now that her hangover had cleared and her brain was functioning.

It felt like a lifetime ago that she had fled from Woodley Lodge. Guilt surged through her as she wondered what had happened about all the wedding preparations. She pictured her parents explaining to the guests as they arrived that the wedding was cancelled because their daughter had jilted the groom.

Her wedding dress hanging on the back of the door was a painful reminder that she had made a mess of everything. But it was all she had to wear—and it was unrecognisable from the over-the-top dress that had not suited her, she discovered when she put it on.

Luca must have sewn his alterations into the dress while she had been asleep, and his new design, incorporating delicate shoestring shoulder straps instead of those big sleeves, and a fitted fishtail skirt that skimmed her hips and emphasised her narrow waist, flattered her hourglass figure.

There was a knock on the door, and when she opened it Luca stepped into the bedroom. He raked his eyes over her in a brooding appraisal that made her heart beat faster.

'I'm a genius,' he murmured. 'You look stunning in my redesigned dress—and very sexy.'

Athena blushed and stared at herself in the mirror. Luca was right: she *did* look sexy in the figure-hugging dress, with her hair tumbling around her shoulders. It was a long time since she had worn anything faintly revealing. Since the sexual assault when she was eighteen she had deliberately hidden her body beneath shapeless clothes, and she had stopped wearing make-up and experimenting with the way she looked.

She felt angry and sad that she had lost the years of her life that should have been fun. She had never flirted with boys after Uncle Peter had told her she gave off signals that she was hungry for sex.

She turned her head and found Luca was watching her. The predatory gleam in his eyes stirred something deep inside her, and suddenly she wished she was normal and didn't feel that anxious sensation in the pit of her stomach when she was in the company of a man.

Strangely, she did not feel anxious with Luca. She couldn't stop looking at him—as if her brain wanted to absorb every detail of his handsome face: the sharp lines of his slashing cheekbones and the sensual curve of the mouth that had once brushed across her lips when he had kissed her in the palace gardens in Zenhab.

'I'm not sure how long I dozed, but I expect we must be landing in Italy soon,' she said, desperate to shatter the in-explicable tension that she sensed between her and Luca.

'I came to tell you that you will need to wear a seat belt when we land. But we're not in Italy.' He dropped the news casually. 'The plane will make a brief stop-over in New York to refuel before we fly on to Las Vegas.'

CHAPTER FIVE

IT WAS DONE! He was legally married! Luca felt a mixture of triumph and relief as he escorted his new bride down the aisle of the wedding chapel in downtown Las Vegas. He had met the terms of his grandmother's will and nothing could prevent him from claiming his inheritance—which included the right to live at Villa De Rossi with his daughter.

He had felt a brief moment of guilt at Athena's shocked gasp on hearing that they were not on their way to Italy but to Las Vegas, but as soon as the plane had landed at McCarran International airport he had wasted no time and taken her to the Marriage License Bureau so that they could complete the necessary paperwork that would allow them to marry in the State of Nevada.

The next step had been to find a wedding chapel with availability to perform the wedding ceremony. Although it had been heading into the evening, many of the chapels had already been fully booked. Marriage was still a thriving industry in Vegas, Luca thought cynically.

Athena had looked increasingly tense as they had driven along the famous Las Vegas strip, and he had feared that she might change her mind at the last minute and refuse to go through with the wedding. But, although her voice had faltered during the brief ceremony, she had kept her side of the deal and married him.

The seats on either side of the aisle were empty apart from his PA, Sandro, and the stewardess from his plane, who had acted as witnesses at the wedding ceremony. The chapel was small, and its decor could only be described as tacky—the violently patterned carpet was stained and the chairs were made of plastic. At least there were flowers: white roses and lilies, whose sickly sweet perfume filled the air.

A lack of air-conditioning meant that the temperature inside the chapel was stifling—perhaps that was the reason why Athena was so pale. She looked as though she was about to faint.

As if she sensed his scrutiny, she turned her head towards him. Her eyes were huge sapphire pools and her face was white and strained. Something kicked hard in Luca's gut—the same feeling he'd had when he had slid the cheap ring he had bought at the airport onto Athena's finger. Her skin had been icy cold and her hand had trembled in his.

He had been unprepared for the fierce emotion that had gripped him when the wedding officiant had pronounced them man and wife. He had never expected to marry and had had good reason for his decision to remain single all his life. But he had been forced into this sham marriage.

As for his bride—tomorrow he would arrange for one million pounds to be transferred into Athena's bank account. She was his wife in name only and there was no reason why he should feel responsible for her, he told himself.

His wife! A nerve flickered in his jaw. The marriage was simply a formality. It meant nothing to him. Athena was a means to an end, and the only thing he cared about was his daughter's happiness and well-being.

As he led his bride towards the chapel doors, his PA stepped forward and spoke to him in a low voice. Sandro Vincenzi had worked for him for ten years, and the Vincenzi family had served the De Rossi household for generations. Luca trusted his childhood friend as completely as he trusted Sandro's sister Maria, who was Rosalie's nurse.

'Luca, a problem has arisen.'

'What kind of problem?'

'Social media is buzzing with a story that has broken in the English newspapers. The English and European daily papers have just been issued, and several of the tabloids carry headlines about your relationship with Giselle.'

Luca shrugged. 'I assume Giselle has done a kiss-and-tell. It's not the first time an ex-mistress has sold supposed details of an affair with me for cash,' he said sardonically.

'It's rather more serious than that.'

Sandro showed Luca the online edition of one of the newspapers that he had downloaded onto his smartphone.

Bartered Bride!

Luca De Rossi offered me a million pounds to marry him in a cynical bid to cheat the terms of his grandmother's will!

Luca swore beneath his breath as he read the interview Giselle had given, in which she revealed that he had asked her to agree to a sham marriage so that he could claim his inheritance.

But, in a shocking double betrayal, love rat Luca has dumped his faithful girlfriend and run off with his old school friend Charles Fairfax's fiancée.

In a statement, French glamour-model Giselle Mercier sent a message to Luca's latest mistress, warning Athena Howard not to be fooled if her playboy lover proposes marriage.

'Luca isn't looking for love. All he wants is to

con the board of De Rossi Enterprises into mak-
ing him chairman of the company by having a fake
marriage.'

Luca thrust the phone at his PA. '*Dio*, I underestimated
Giselle. But I don't believe it is a problem. The story will
be forgotten in a few days.'

He glanced at Athena. She still looked pale and vulnerable, as if she was in shock, as she twisted the wedding
ring on her finger. Luca felt an uncomfortable twinge of
guilt, although he reassured himself that he had done nothing to feel guilty about.

'Miss Howard is aware of the reasons why I have married her,' he told Sandro in Italian.

'Giselle is only half the problem,' Sandro advised. 'Your
great-uncle Emilio has evidently seen the media coverage
and has released a statement announcing that in light of
Miss Mercier's story, the board of De Rossi Enterprises
will now be suspicious if you should marry before your
thirty-fifth birthday. Emilio is threatening that if you *do*
marry the board will try to prove that the marriage is a
sham, and will take legal steps to prevent you from claiming the chairmanship of the company and ownership of
Villa De Rossi.'

Luca shot another glance at Athena, thankful that she
could not understand Italian. At least he assumed she could
not speak his language. He frowned, realising that he knew
virtually nothing about her. But why should he? Their marriage was a business arrangement and he did not intend to
spend much time with her after he took her to Italy.

He ground his teeth as he thought of his great-uncle.
Luca knew that Emilio would do anything to get his great-
nephew removed from the board of De Rossi Enterprises.

But to have any chance of doing so Emilio would have to *prove* that his marriage to Athena was fraudulent.

'There is one more thing you should know,' Sandro said. 'Some American journalists have heard of the story breaking in the English media and somehow the information has been leaked that you are here in Las Vegas to marry Miss Howard.'

Athena wondered what Luca and his PA were talking about. She was curious about the fierce urgency in Luca's tone. She guessed he was speaking Italian. Perhaps she should try to learn the language, seeing that she would be living in Italy for a year. She grimaced as she remembered that she had not been any good at French at school, and even worse at Latin. But it was supposed to be easier to learn a language if you lived in the country where it was spoken, and if Luca spoke to her in Italian regularly it might help her to pick it up...

Her eyes were drawn to her husband. She could not quite believe that they were married. Luca did not look particularly happy, she noted. His sculpted features looked harder than ever and his mouth was drawn into a thin line, as if he was angry about something. She wondered if he wished he had married Giselle. He must have been devastated when his fiancée had broken off their engagement. And it was *her* fault, Athena thought guiltily. If she hadn't asked Luca to help her escape from her wedding, he could have married the woman whom she assumed he loved.

She tensed as he finished his conversation with his assistant and came to stand beside her. But her tension was not from the anxious feeling she usually experienced when she was around men. Her heart beat faster as she breathed in the spicy scent of Luca's aftershave, and her stomach muscles clenched when she lifted her eyes to his face and absorbed the masculine beauty of his chiselled jaw and above it the lush fullness of his mouth.

'In a moment we will leave the chapel,' he told her. He hesitated. 'When we step outside it will be necessary for me to kiss you.'

She blinked at him. 'Necessary for you to…? Why?'

Athena had the most incredible eyes. The thought came unbidden into Luca's mind. 'There's no time to explain now. The press are outside, and it's vital that we make them believe our marriage is real.'

'Real?' She knew she probably sounded witless, but she couldn't take in what he had said about needing to kiss her.

'All you have to do is kiss me back,' Luca said impatiently when she stared at him as if he had grown a second head. 'It shouldn't be too much of an ordeal. You seemed to enjoy it when I kissed you in Zenhab.'

So he *hadn't* forgotten that kiss. Her mind flew to the palace gardens and she remembered vividly the whisper of the fountains and the silver gleam of the moon, the scent of orange blossom and the gossamer-soft brush of Luca's lips on hers.

He opened the chapel door and Athena's thoughts scattered as she was blinded by an explosion of flashbulbs. Luca slid his arm around her waist and drew her close to his body—so close that she could feel his powerful thigh muscles through her dress, his hard, masculine frame a stark contrast to her softness.

'Remember, this has to look convincing,' he murmured as he lowered his face towards hers.

Athena's heart lurched as she realised that he hadn't been making some bizarre joke and was actually going to kiss her. She was aware of a fluttering sensation in the pit of her stomach, but it wasn't the horrible nervous feeling she'd had when her ex-boyfriends—she could count on one hand the number of men she had briefly dated after the incident with her Latin tutor—had tried to kiss her.

Time seemed to be suspended as she watched Luca's dark head descend. He slanted his mouth over hers and she discovered that the fluttering sensation in her stomach was not apprehension but anticipation.

He claimed her mouth with the supreme confidence of a man who had had more mistresses than he cared to remember. His lips firmly coaxed hers apart in a blatant seduction designed to make her capitulate to his mastery and warn her that resistance was futile. Luca was the ultimate charmer, and he knew exactly how to make a woman melt while he retained complete control.

For a moment Athena felt a familiar sense of panic—especially when he tightened his arms around her so that she could not escape. But the dark shadows in her mind receded as Luca continued to kiss her and she felt his tongue probe between her lips, seeking access to the moist interior of her mouth. She closed her eyes to blot out the flashing bright lights of the photographers' flashbulbs and sank into darkness and the sweet pull of desire that was stirring inside her.

Luca's tongue tangled with hers, and she dissolved, sliding her hands up to his shoulders to cling to him for support as she dismissed her inhibitions and kissed him with unrestrained passion.

He had asked Athena to kiss him convincingly and she was certainly complying, Luca thought. *Dio*, he was almost convinced himself that her passionate response was real and not just an act in front of the paparazzi. Her warm breath filled his mouth as she parted her lips beneath his. He could easily become addicted to the taste of her, he thought, to the softness of her mouth and the sweetness of her kiss that made his gut ache.

He had not expected to be so turned on that his body felt as if it was on fire. Athena was not doing anything more than kissing him. She wasn't running her hands over his body, or whispering artful suggestions in his ear the way he was used to women doing. There was something curiously innocent and unsophisticated in her kiss that he found incredibly erotic. He felt as though he was the first man to have awoken her sensuality, but he knew that could not be true because she had been engaged—and anyway he preferred sexually experienced women, he reminded himself.

He heard someone call out from the crowd of journalists gathered outside the wedding chapel, but did not catch what they said—and he did not care as he pulled Athena against him so that her soft contours were moulded to his taut body. His arousal was unexpected and painfully hard, and he heard her little gasp of shock as he rubbed his pelvis up against hers.

The voices and the camera flashbulbs disappeared and he was conscious only of Athena: the delicate rose scent of her perfume, the silky softness of her hair against his cheek and her incandescent sensuality that captivated him and made him long to remove the barrier of their clothes so that they were skin on skin, a man and a woman poised on the brink of fulfilling their sexual desires.

He drew her closer still, so that he could feel the erratic thud of her heart echoing the unsteady rhythm of his, and deepened the kiss, taking it to a level that was flagrantly erotic.

On the periphery of his mind Luca heard raucous laughter, and a voice called out, 'What do you say to the allegation that your marriage is a sham, Mr De Rossi?'

Someone else said loudly, 'It looks real enough from where I'm standing. Let them get to a hotel room before they combust. Will you and your wife be taking a honeymoon, Mr De Rossi?'

Luca felt a pang of reluctance as he lifted his lips from Athena's and turned his head towards the journalists. 'Of course Signora De Rossi and I will have a honeymoon. We are looking forward to spending a few days in Las Vegas.'

'Did you design your wife's wedding dress?'

'Certainly I wanted to create a gown that complemented Athena's beauty.' He returned Athena's startled look with a bland smile.

'Is it true that you only married Miss Howard to meet the terms of your grandmother's will?' someone called.

'I married Athena because...' Luca looked into Athena's sapphire-blue eyes and thought again how easy it would be to drown in their depths. 'Because she captured my heart when we met in Zenhab nine months ago, and I was determined to make her my wife,' he told the journalists. 'Now, if you will excuse us...?'

Athena was glad of Luca's arm around her waist as he led her towards the waiting limousine and the paparazzi surged around them. The sound of voices shouting questions and the glare of camera flashbulbs was disorientating. The chauffeur held open the door and she fell inelegantly into the car after Luca, almost landing in his lap. Hot-faced, she slid along the seat, and moments later the car pulled away from the kerb, chased by the photographers still snapping pictures.

'Why did you say all that rubbish about me capturing your heart?' she demanded. And why was there a little part of her that wished that what he had said to the journalists was true? Athena wondered. She and Luca were virtually strangers, but since her sister's wedding in Zenhab she had been haunted by the memory of his kiss, she admitted.

'It's important that the press believe our marriage is real,' Luca said tersely.

The man who had played the role of adoring husband outside the wedding chapel had disappeared, and his sculpted features were impossible to read.

'I don't understand.' Shock, jet lag, and the fact that her body clock was out of sync were having a detrimental effect on Athena's ability to think. 'Why would they think our marriage is a sham?'

Luca handed her his phone. 'I've downloaded the online edition of a tabloid newspaper currently being read by people in England while they eat their breakfast.'

She looked at the screen and gasped as she read the interview with Giselle Mercier. 'Why does your fiancée say that you offered her money to marry you?'

'Because it's true.'

'I assumed you were going to marry Giselle because you were in love with her, and that when she broke off your engagement you had to find a wife before your birthday in order to claim your inheritance.'

'I certainly wasn't *in love* with Giselle.' Luca's lips curled into a cynical expression. 'I accept that some people find true love...' he thought of Kadir and Lexi '...but for the majority of people love is simply a romanticised excuse for lust. And whilst I am happy to enjoy the latter, I have no inclination to fall in love.'

Athena felt a flicker of temper at his dismissive tone. 'One of the reasons why I agreed to marry you in name only was because I felt guilty that I had unwittingly been the cause of Giselle breaking up with you. I felt it was partly *my* fault that you would lose your inheritance if you didn't marry before your birthday.'

'Let's not forget the main reason you married me is because I'm paying you a million pounds,' Luca drawled.

Athena might have convinced herself that her motive for agreeing to be his wife was altruistic, but he didn't believe it for a second. She was as much of a gold-digger as Giselle, but the situation resulting from Giselle's story in the press meant that Athena was going to have to work a little harder for her money.

Anger surged through Luca, and with it another emotion —*desperation*. He was so close to achieving his goal. He did not care if he lost the chairmanship of De Rossi Enterprises, but he *had* to have the deeds of Villa De Rossi for Rosalie's sake. The degenerative disease his daughter suffered from was taking her from him, bit by bit, and in perhaps only a few more years it would claim her life. He would *not* allow the time that Rosalie had left to be disrupted by having to move her to a new house, away from the things she loved.

'Why were there journalists outside the wedding chapel?' Athena bit her lip. 'The pictures they took of us won't be printed in the newspapers in England, will they?'

'I hope so.' Luca's jaw hardened. 'After Giselle's stunt, my great-uncle Emilio—my late grandmother's brother— said that he and the board of De Rossi Enterprises will try to prove that my marriage to you is a sham. Their intention is to prevent me from claiming my inheritance. That's why it is vital that we convince the press—no, the world, and especially my great-uncle—that we married for conventional reasons. We are going to have to act like we are in love.'

He sighed impatiently when Athena looked blank.

'Pictures of us kissing on the steps of the wedding chapel will be a good start. For the only time in my life I will be happy to court the paparazzi. The more publicity we can get showing us as adoring newlyweds, the less chance my great-uncle will have to persuade the courts that our marriage is a fake.'

'You said our marriage would be in name only,' Athena said worriedly.

'In private it will be. But in public we must appear to be a blissfully happy couple.'

She shook her head. 'That wasn't part of the deal. I can't imagine what my family will think when they see photos of us and hear that we are married. I wasn't going to tell them that I'd married you. I planned to say that I was working abroad for a year. My parents will be horrified if I tell them about our deal.'

'You *can't* tell them of our financial deal,' Luca said sharply. 'No one can know the truth about our relationship except us. I can't risk the press finding out that we are married in name only. Your parents already think you and I are lovers because Charlie told them so. Convincing them that we are happily married shouldn't be too difficult.'

Athena gnawed on her bottom lip. 'I don't like the idea of lying to my family. You said that we would live quietly at your penthouse in Milan and few people would even know we are married.'

The limousine drew up at the entrance of a famous Las Vegas hotel and immediately a flurry of camera flashbulbs exploded outside the car window.

'Why have we stopped *here*?'

'My PA has booked us into the honeymoon suite. It's all part of the pretence that we are happily married.'

'I can't do this,' she said falteringly. 'I can't pretend to be in love with you.'

'If you want your million pounds, I'm sure you'll manage to give as convincing a performance as you gave outside the wedding chapel,' Luca said grimly. 'Keep thinking of the money, *mia bella*.'

He moved before she had time to register his intention, cupping her chin in his hand and dropping a hard kiss on her mouth that left her lips tingling. He had timed the kiss for the exact moment when the chauffeur opened the car door—much to the delight of the waiting paparazzi.

Athena would have liked to hurry into the hotel with her head down, but Luca clamped his arm around her waist and sauntered up to the front entrance, apparently totally relaxed as he smiled for the photographers.

'Can we have another shot of you kissing your wife, Mr De Rossi?'

He obliged, his eyes gleaming with a silent warning to Athena to play her part as he dipped his head and captured her mouth in a long, slow kiss that earned a few more cat-calls from the journalists.

He had missed out on a career as an actor, she thought dazedly. His performance as an adoring husband was so thorough that she simply melted against him, and her legs were trembling when he escorted her across the hotel lobby.

Her hope that Luca would take her to their suite, for some respite from the attention of the paparazzi and the other hotel guests, who were staring at her wedding dress, was dashed when they were greeted by the hotel manager, who personally showed them into the restaurant and explained that the head chef had prepared a special wedding dinner for them.

The elegant table, set with silver cutlery, crystal glasses and fine china, was a potential minefield for her. She was bound to knock something over or break something, and Athena kept her hands firmly in her lap.

'Would you like oysters, madam?'

'No, thank you.' She stopped the waiter just as he was about to place a plate of the unappealing-looking shellfish arranged on a bed of ice in front of her. Her stomach churned. 'I don't like oysters.'

The hotel manager who was hovering close to their table looked surprised. 'I understood that Mr De Rossi ordered oysters because they are your particular favourite?'

'Yes, darling,' Luca murmured. 'You love oysters, remember?'

'Oh…yes, of course I do, *darling*.' Athena flushed when the manager gave her a strange look. 'I *hate* oysters,' she muttered to Luca when they were alone. 'This is hopeless. How can we convince people that we are…in love when we don't know the first thing about one another?'

'We'll have to take a crash course in learning about each other.'

Luca sipped his wine and, noticing that the hotel manager was still looking at them curiously, reached across the table, clasped Athena's hand and lifted it to his mouth to press his lips against her fingers. He felt a tremor run through her and for a split second imagined that their marriage was real, and that after dinner they would go up to the honeymoon suite and he would remove her dress and the wispy scraps of lace underwear that he had been unable to forget since he had put her to bed in his hotel room in London.

'Tell me about yourself,' he instructed. 'I actually know more about your sister than I do about you. Lexi was an RAF helicopter pilot before she married Kadir, wasn't she? Did you consider joining the armed forces?'

Athena shook her head. 'Even when we were children Lexi was brave and bold, but I'm afraid I'm not. Lexi was adopted, but in fact she is far more like our parents than me. She is clever, and she did well at school, whereas I was an average student. Mum and Dad are both doctors and brilliant academics,' she explained. 'They named me after the Greek goddess of wisdom, but were hugely disappointed when I failed to get the grades to go to university to study medicine.'

'Did you *want* to be a doctor?'

'Not really. I didn't enjoy science, and I was useless at Latin—even though my parents paid for me to have extra lessons.'

Athena's stomach tied itself into a knot as she visualised her Latin tutor: Peter Fitch. He had been the same age as her father, and grey haired. He had worn grey flannel trousers and had had the air of respectability you might expect from a learned university professor.

Years after he had assaulted her she could still remember her absolute shock when he had commented on her breasts. She had felt uncomfortable rather than scared at first—until he had pushed her up against the door and grabbed at her blouse.

'You've gone very quiet.' Luca wondered why she had turned pale. Maybe it was the damned oysters. 'What are you thinking about?'

'I was thinking what a disappointment I've always been to my parents.' It wasn't far from the truth. She did not want to imagine how her parents would feel when they saw in the newspapers that she was married to Luca.

'What subjects were you interested in at school?'

'I loved art—particularly drawing. I would have liked to study fine art at university.'

'So why didn't you?'

'Oh, I wasn't good enough.'

'Did you apply to universities and get turned down?'

'Well, no, but my father said I was wasting my time doing silly drawings.'

She had buried her dream of becoming an illustrator and had revised like mad for her chemistry and biology exams—but she had still failed to get the grades required for medical school.

'How about you?' Athena asked Luca, keen to turn the spotlight away from her mediocre achievements. 'What made you decide to be a fashion designer?'

'Designing is in my blood. My great-grandfather founded De Rossi Enterprises when he began to design shoes for his wife after she complained that she could never find stylish shoes to wear with her evening gowns. Raimondo expanded to design handbags and accessories. To me it seemed a natural step to create clothes which reflected the De Rossi brand of cutting-edge style and exceptional quality.'

Unfortunately his grandparents had not shared his belief that the company needed to move into fashion design, including off-the-peg clothes to be sold on the high street, Luca brooded. He had fought constant battles with Aberto in his bid to expand the company into new global markets. But his instincts had proved right and De Rossi Enterprises, together with DRD, the fashion label he had created, were now in the top ten of Italy's most successful companies.

'Your parents must be proud of your success,' Athena said.

'My mother died when I was fifteen.'

'I'm sorry.'

It was not a throwaway remark. The compassion in her voice and in her eyes was genuine, Luca realised when he looked across the table and saw a gentle expression in her sapphire-blue gaze.

He shrugged. 'I didn't really know her. She had a wild lifestyle and was constantly flitting between her homes in Monaco and New York. Obviously I needed to be in one place to go to school, so she dumped me on my grandparents at Villa De Rossi.'

'I can't imagine your grandparents minded looking after you,' Athena murmured, thinking of the happy visits she had made to *her* grandparents' home when they had been alive. Unlike her parents, they had accepted her for who she was and had not put pressure on her to be cleverer or more studious.

'My grandparents bitterly resented me,' Luca said flatly. The *bastardo* had been a shameful reminder of their daughter's often outrageous lifestyle. He hesitated, wondering why he found it easy to talk to Athena. The only time he really spoke to women was when he made small talk before taking them to bed, but something about the way she quietly listened, as if she was actually interested in what he had to say, made him relax his guard.

'In fact it was because of my mother that I wanted to be a fashion designer. I lived with her when I was younger, although I was mainly cared for by nannies, and I used to watch her getting ready to go out in the evenings. She would allow me to choose what dress she was going to wear, and her shoes and accessories. Even as a small boy I had a good eye for colour, and Mamma trusted my opinion.' He recalled the happiest moments of his childhood, when he had felt close to his mother. 'I felt proud that I had chosen what she wore when she went to grand parties. She was very beautiful.'

In the eyes of a young boy his mother had been like a fairytale princess, Luca mused. But one day she had disappeared out of his life and had gone to live with a lover who had not wanted a small child around. He had been sent to live with his grandparents, who had made it clear that they did not want him either.

His mother's desertion had hit him hard. It had been

an early lesson not to trust his heart—a lesson that had been reinforced years later when he had fallen in love with Jodie. She'd been a backpacker from New Zealand, who had been travelling around Europe and had taken a summer job in a village near to the Villa De Rossi. He had thought that Jodie would stay for ever—that their love would last for ever. But one day she'd disappeared from his life without warning, just as his mother had done, and Luca had realised that only a fool put his faith in love and the promises people made.

But there was another kind of love that he *did* believe in—the unconditional love of a father for his daughter. Jodie had not only deserted him, she had walked away from their daughter when medical tests had revealed the devastating news that Rosalie was suffering from a genetic brain disorder which would affect her development.

Luca's jaw clenched as he thought of his daughter who, since she was two years old, had been denied a normal life, and he felt the familiar, agonising sense of guilt that *he* was to blame for Rosalie's illness. Even though doctors had insisted that he must not feel responsible, he always would.

Despite her severe disabilities, Rosalie's smile lit up Luca's heart. His daughter was the reason why he had married a woman he barely knew, he brooded as he glanced at Athena and wondered how she was planning to spend a million pounds. They both had something to gain from their marriage and everything to lose unless they gave a convincing performance that they had married because they were in love.

CHAPTER SIX

'If I HAVE to keep smiling I think my jaw will snap,' Athena muttered to Luca. 'How much longer are we going to stay in the casino? I want to go to bed.'

'Can you repeat that last statement in a louder voice, so that the paparazzi who have been stalking us all evening can hear you?' His eyes gleamed. 'Your eagerness for our wedding night is just the sort of thing to convince people our marriage is real.'

She was furious with herself for blushing, and with Luca for...well, for being Luca. For being drop-dead handsome and sexy and so charming that she was finding it impossible to resist his charisma.

'I'm sure we must have done enough to convince the press, seeing as you haven't left my side all evening and you keep kissing me,' she said tartly. 'You're like an octopus wrapping its tentacles around me, or in your case your arms, so that I can't escape.'

It was the first time in his nearly thirty-five years that he had been likened to an octopus, and it was not the most flattering comparison, Luca thought with a mixture of amusement and pique.

'I haven't seen much evidence that you've wanted to escape, *mia bella*,' he murmured. 'I have been impressed by your enthusiastic response when I've kissed you.'

He watched a rosy flush spread along her cheekbones

and suddenly felt as tired as Athena clearly was of keeping up the pretence that they were blissfully happy newlyweds in front of the paparazzi. Tomorrow's papers would undoubtedly publish photos of him and his bride staring adoringly into each other's eyes as they played craps and blackjack. The hotel's casino was jam-packed with tourists, which was why he had chosen it as a public arena in which to demonstrate that his marriage was the real deal.

Not that he had a problem with kissing Athena. He had found it surprisingly addictive to angle his mouth over hers and feel her soft, moist lips part, allowing his tongue to probe between them. He had spent the entire evening feeling so turned on that he hurt, and worse still was the knowledge that the only option ahead of him to alleviate the ache in his groin was to take a cold shower once he had escorted his bride up to the honeymoon suite.

'If you're tired we'll call it a night,' he said abruptly. 'You might as well play all your chips on one last spin of the roulette wheel. What are you going to bet on?' he asked as the croupier called for everyone to place their bets.

Athena put her stack of coloured chips on the board. 'I'll put everything on black, thirty-five. It seems to be a significant number, seeing that the reason we married is because you needed a wife by your thirty-fifth birthday.'

'Why don't you shout it out so that everyone in the entire room can hear you?' Luca growled.

'I'm sorry—I didn't think.' She cast a quick glance around and gave a sigh of relief when it appeared that her careless comment had gone unnoticed by the other people crowded around the roulette table.

The croupier spun the wheel and released the ball. Athena watched it half-interestedly. She had never gambled before, and after spending several hours in the casino still couldn't understand the attraction. Luca had teased her that with a million pounds behind her she could afford to place a few bets, but she did not want to risk losing a penny of the money that would pay for the new orphanage and school in Jaipur.

The white ball continued to rattle around the wheel and eventually came to rest—on black, thirty-five.

'You've won,' Luca told her when she stared in surprise at the roulette wheel. 'Thirty-five must be your lucky number.'

At least her winnings meant that she could buy some new clothes, Athena thought as she walked with Luca across the hotel lobby and was conscious of the curious looks her wedding dress still attracted from the other guests.

The honeymoon suite was on the thirty-fifth floor—although she did not believe in lucky numbers, she told herself. It was breathtakingly opulent, and she slipped off her shoes and walked barefoot across the thick velvet carpet as she explored the rooms—and discovered that one vital thing was missing.

'There is only one bedroom,' she told Luca when she went back into the sitting room and found him pouring himself a drink from the bar.

'I imagine there isn't much call for two bedrooms in the honeymoon suite,' he said drily.

'We can't stay here. We'll have to ask at Reception for a different suite, with two bedrooms.'

'And risk one of the hotel staff rushing to sell an exposé about our sleeping arrangements to the press? I think not.'

Luca noted Athena's anxious expression and felt a twinge of guilt for mocking her. She had played the part of his loving wife all evening, and it was not her fault that he had looked at the huge bed and visualised her naked, voluptuous, creamy-skinned body spread on the black silk sheets.

'I'll sleep on the sofa,' he reassured her. 'The suite *does* have his and hers bathrooms. I suggest you go and get ready for bed. You look...' The word *fragile* slid into his mind, and perhaps it was unsurprising considering the events of the past forty-eight hours since he had helped her to escape from her wedding to Charles Fairfax. 'You look tired,' he said flatly.

She did not feel tired, Athena thought twenty minutes later as she stepped into the pink marble sunken bath that was the size of a small swimming pool. She had used nearly the whole bottle of bubble bath provided by the hotel, and she sank into the foaming, scented water with a sigh of pleasure. The clock said it was one a.m. in Las Vegas, which meant it was morning in England, but she had slept for a few hours on the plane and her body felt strangely energised.

There was no mystery about why she felt more alive than she had ever done in her life, she mocked herself. She had spent all evening with Luca's arm wrapped firmly around her waist and his thigh pressed against hers, so that she had been aware of the muscled hardness of his athletic body. She knew that every time he had kissed her it had been a show for the watching paparazzi—so why had she trembled when he had brushed his lips over hers before deepening the kiss and stirring a passionate response that had shocked her?

She hadn't felt the knot of fear in the pit of her stomach that she'd felt in the past, when other men had kissed her. Charlie's chaste kisses had never made her feel apprehensive, she reminded herself. But since she had found him in bed with his best man she understood why there had been a complete lack of sexual chemistry between them. Her awareness of Luca did at least prove that the sexual assault years ago had not destroyed her sensuality. But she had buried normal feelings of passion and desire until Luca had kissed her outside the wedding chapel and awoken a yearning to satisfy the ache of need that throbbed deep in her pelvis.

The overnight bag that she had brought with her when she had escaped from Woodley Lodge contained her toothbrush and other personal toiletries—as well as the black negligee she had planned to wear on her wedding night with Charlie. The sheer black lace baby-doll nightgown barely covered any of her body, but it was all she had to sleep in.

Top of her shopping list tomorrow would be a pair of sensible pyjamas, Athena decided as she walked out of the en-suite bathroom into the bedroom—just as Luca entered the room through another door from the sitting room.

He must have showered, because his hair was damp, and he was wearing a black towelling robe loosely belted at his waist and gaping open over his upper body, so that she could see the whorls of black hairs that covered his chest. The skin visible beneath the mat of hair was dark bronze—the same as the bare legs revealed below the hem of his robe. The idea that he was naked beneath the robe made Athena feel quivery inside, and she could not stop staring at him.

'I came to get a pillow. I knocked but you didn't answer, so I assumed you were still in the bathroom.'

His voice was curiously husky, his accent more pronounced than usual and incredibly sexy, causing the tiny hairs on Athena's body to stand on end. Her heart lurched as he walked towards her and she saw the predatory gleam in his eyes. Her brain told her that he shouldn't be looking at her as he was doing—with a dark intensity, as if he was mentally undressing her.

It would not take him long, she thought ruefully, glancing down at her skimpy negligee and discovering that the darker skin of her nipples showed through the semi-transparent material.

'Luca...'

Did that breathless voice belong to her? She licked her dry lips with the tip of her tongue and watched him swallow convulsively. He was still coming closer, and she backed up until she bumped into the bed and couldn't go any further.

'What do you want?'

She remembered he had said he wanted a pillow, but he did not glance at the head of the bed, just kept his glittering gaze focused on her.

What did he want? Luca almost laughed at Athena's innocent question. As if she did not know, he brooded, noting how her pupils had dilated so that her eyes were almost completely black. The sexual tension shimmering between them was so acute he could almost taste it.

He knew he should not feel like this—as if his body was a tightly coiled spring, thrumming with frustration. It wasn't part of his game plan. When he had asked Athena to be his wife in name only he'd had no idea that he would be more turned on than he could ever remember by her petite but delightfully curvaceous figure, now inadequately covered by a wisp of black lace.

Everything had changed when he had kissed her on the steps of the wedding chapel, he acknowledged. Until that moment he had viewed her only as a means to claim his rightful ownership of the Villa De Rossi, which was so important to his daughter's happiness. But when he had taken Athena in his arms and her soft, voluptuous body had fitted so snugly to his, he had suddenly been aware of her as a desirable woman.

Their evening spent in the casino had been an exquisite form of torture as she had responded to his kisses with a sweet ardency that had driven him crazy—because he had known she was only acting for the benefit of the paparazzi.

But now they were alone in the honeymoon suite, and with no members of the press to impress there was no reason for Athena to catch her breath as he halted in front of her and ran his finger lightly down her cheek. He felt the tremor that ran through her and his body tightened in response as anticipation licked hot and hungry through his veins. There was nothing to stop him changing the rules of his game plan and making Athena his wife in every sense.

'I want you, *mia bella*,' he said softly.

If he had been able to think clearly he would have wondered about the flicker of wariness in her eyes, but Luca's thoughts were distracted by the betraying quiver of her lower lip.

'I want to kiss you,' he murmured as he cradled her cheek in his hand and brought his mouth down on hers.

Luca only wanted to kiss her. The knot of apprehension in Athena's stomach unravelled. That was all right. She did not mind him kissing her—didn't mind at all, in fact, she admitted as his lips gently teased hers apart and he explored their shape with his tongue.

He smelled of soap and spicy cologne, mixed with that subtle scent of maleness that so intoxicated her senses that without being aware of moving she swayed towards him and curled her arms around his neck. It seemed quite natural for him to lift her up and place her on the bed. Even when he knelt above her, his chiselled features accentuated in the golden glow of the bedside lamp, she was so absorbed by the feelings he was stirring in her, so entranced by the sharp, sweet throb of desire between her thighs, that the shadows from her past did not trouble her.

'You have beautiful hair,' Luca told her, threading his fingers through the long chestnut mane that felt like silk against his skin. 'And a beautiful body,' he growled as he trailed his lips down her throat before moving lower to the deep vee between her breasts.

His kisses scalded her skin, and the ache low in her pelvis grew more insistent as he slowly drew the straps of her negligee over her shoulders, peeling the wisp of black lace down so that, inch by heart-jolting inch, he bared her breasts. Athena held her breath as he cupped the pale mounds of firm flesh in his palms. She was not repelled by his touch, she discovered. She *liked* the feel of his hands caressing her.

'You are exquisite,' he said hoarsely.

His eyes blazed with a smouldering intensity and Athena realised that he wasn't joking—he really did think she was beautiful. He made her *feel* beautiful, especially when he rubbed his thumb pads over her nipples so that they instantly swelled to hard peaks and he gave a groan of appreciation. Her breasts felt heavy, and the tingling sensation in her nipples seemed to have a direct connection to the spiralling throbbing sensation between her legs.

Driven by instinct, she moved her hips restlessly, and felt a quiver of excitement as he slid his hand over her stomach and ran his fingers along the edge of the black lace knickers.

'*Mia bella* Aphrodite…' Luca stared down at Athena's creamy, perfect breasts with their rosy tips, and her glorious hair spread like a silken curtain across the pillows, and desire jack-knifed inside him. 'You should have been named after her—the goddess of beauty and pleasure,' he said thickly, anticipating the pleasure-filled night he was sure was ahead.

His words penetrated Athena's mind and the haze of sensual delight Luca had created began to fade as the warm blood in her veins cooled.

'*Don't* call me that.'

'*Let me touch you, Aphrodite. Do you wear low-cut tops to tantalise me with a glimpse of your breasts? Have you any idea how much I want to feel your firm, youthful flesh? Your body was designed for sex, and you're hungry for it, aren't you?*'

She looked up at Luca, but inside her head she heard the sound of her cotton blouse ripping, and her high-pitched cry as she tried to hold the torn material across her breasts. She heard her parents' friend Peter Fitch's panting breaths as he forced his hand inside her bra, his strong fingers pinching her flesh, hurting her, making her feel sick with fear when he shoved his other hand between her legs. This was *Uncle Peter*, whom she had known all her life. He shouldn't be touching her and saying horrible, disgusting things about what he wanted to do to her.

She looked at Luca but it was Peter Fitch's face she saw leering at her, sweat on his brow, his eyes glazed.

'No! Stop!' Panic ripped through her and she pushed frantically against the male chest leaning over her, while in her mind she fought against the hands ripping her blouse.

But it was *Luca's* chest that her hands were splayed flat against, she realised as the images in her head receded and the past turned into the present. It was *Luca* who was staring at her—not Uncle Peter.

She took a shuddering breath.

'No?' Luca drawled.

His voice was deceptively soft, but Athena sensed he was confused and frustrated by her sudden change from being warm and responsive to her curt rejection of him.

'What happened to make you change your mind?'

It was only natural that he wanted an explanation, she acknowledged. But his cynical tone annoyed her. He spoke as if it had been a foregone conclusion that they would have sex, but that had not been her intention when he had started to kiss her, and if anyone had changed their mind about the rules of their relationship it was him.

She could not tell him the real reason why she had pushed him away. The sexual assault had been humiliating, and although logically she knew it had not been her fault she had never forgotten Peter's accusation that she had deliberately led him on. The Latin tutor had insisted that she was wanton and eager for sex and that that was why she had worn a blouse that had revealed a hint of cleavage. Perhaps Luca believed that by wearing a sexy negligee she had sent out a message that she was available.

She bit her lip as logic once again pointed out that there was nothing shameful about a single, twenty-five-year-old woman living in the twenty-first century letting it be known that she was sexually available. The problem was *her* and her hang-ups. She wished she *could* let go of the past and make love with Luca. But now she was on dangerous ground—because Luca was a playboy and all he wanted was casual sex.

'When we made our deal you said our marriage would be in name only,' she reminded him. 'You also told me there would be no point in falling in love with you.'

His eyes narrowed. 'What does *love* have to do with what, up until a few minutes ago, you were as keen as me to enjoy? Why is it wrong to take pleasure in sex for no other reason than that we find each other attractive?'

Athena knew it would be pointless to deny his assertion that she was attracted to him after she had initially responded to him so enthusiastically.

'Sex wasn't included in the deal we made,' she muttered. 'You might be happy to indulge in casual sex, but for me making love is more than simply a physical act— it's a way of expressing the deep emotion of being in love.'

Having never had sex, she didn't know how she could be so certain of her feelings; she just *knew* that, for her, love and the act of making love were inextricably linked.

'Ah…' Luca finally understood.

Presumably if he offered to pay Athena more money she would turn back into the sexually responsive woman he'd thought—*damn it*, he'd *known* had wanted him as much as he had wanted her. The rubbish she'd spouted about sex needing to be an expression of love was ridiculous.

He still wanted her, he admitted as he stood up and looked at her lying on the bed. She had pulled her nightgown back into place, but her plump-as-peaches breasts were in danger of spilling over their lacy constriction and her pebble-hard nipples were clearly visible beneath the sheer material. *Dio*, she was small but perfectly formed—a pint-sized goddess.

He frowned as he remembered that the big freeze had happened after he had called her Aphrodite. He had almost thought she had seemed afraid. But afraid of what? Of *him*…? The idea made him feel uncomfortable. Maybe he *had* come on to her too strongly, but it hadn't been all one-sided, he reminded himself. The sexual awareness between them had been electrifying.

She sat up and pushed her hair back from her face. In the lamplight Luca caught the sparkle of tears on her lashes and something kicked in his gut.

'Athena?' he said softly.

'You said you needed a pillow…' She avoided looking at him as she handed him one.

He hesitated, feeling reluctant to leave her when she was clearly upset. 'What happened just now? Do you want to talk about it?'

And say what? Athena thought miserably. She felt ashamed—not about the sexual assault, but the fact that she had been unable to deal with what had happened to her when she was eighteen. She wished she could move on. At first when Luca had started to undress her and touch her breasts she had enjoyed his caresses—before ugly memories of the assault by her Latin tutor had intruded and her desire had been replaced with the feeling that she was dirty.

'Please go,' she whispered.

She held her breath when he did not move away from the bed, each passing minute stretching her nerves, until he sighed heavily.

'Goodnight, *piccola*. Try to get some sleep.'

The snick of the door closing told her she was alone. She wondered what *piccola* meant.

The unexpected gentleness in Luca's voice proved to be the last straw for her raw emotions, and she could not hold back her tears.

In the sitting room, the makeshift bed Luca had made on the sofa was comfortable enough, but he could not sleep. He wondered how many other bridegrooms had spent their wedding night relegated to the sofa in the honeymoon suite. Not many, he would bet. But this was not a real wedding night—just as his marriage was not real.

He should feel jubilant that he had found a way to meet the terms of his grandmother's will. And of course he was relieved that he would not have to move Rosalie away from Villa De Rossi. But he had barely given a thought to his position as chairman of De Rossi Enterprises, or the fact that his own design company, DRD, could now continue to use the De Rossi name.

His thoughts centred on his new wife. The muffled sound of crying he could hear from the bedroom tugged at his conscience. He remembered it was less than forty-eight hours since Athena had discovered her fiancé had been unfaithful. Perhaps she was heartbroken that her dreams of marrying Charles Fairfax had been shattered and that she was trapped in a sham marriage with *him* for a year.

Muttering a curse, Luca took his frustration out on the pillow and thumped it hard, before rolling onto his side and waiting a long time for sleep to come.

'Athena?' Luca knocked on the bedroom door a second time. After what had happened the previous night, when he had walked in and seen her wearing that sexy little negligee that had sent his blood pressure soaring, he wasn't going to risk entering the room without her permission.

She opened the door and he stared at her in surprise. The pink towelling robe provided by the hotel was at least five sizes too big for her and she looked as soft and sweet as a marshmallow. Without a trace of make-up, and with her glasses perched on her nose, she looked fresh-faced and wholesome. She was the complete opposite of the glamorous socialites Luca usually chose to be his mistresses, and he could not understand the powerful rush of sexual hunger that swept through him.

Last night he had vowed that, apart from having to pretend in public that they could not keep their hands off each other, when they were alone he would keep his hands very much to himself. It was disconcerting to admit that his will power was already being tested.

'I've arranged for some clothes to be sent over to the hotel from the Las Vegas DRD store,' he told her. 'You can't spend another day wearing your wedding dress.'

Athena followed him into the sitting room and looked along the rail of assorted outfits. 'They're not really my style,' she said, holding up a scarlet dress that she could tell would cling to her curvaceous figure. 'I tend to wear clothes that are less fitted and have a higher neckline.' *And preferably are not such an eye-catching colour,* she added silently, thinking of the mainly beige or navy skirts and blouses in her wardrobe in England. She glanced at the price tag on the dress and quickly hung it back on the rail. 'These are definitely *not* in my price range.'

Luca's brows lifted. 'You'll soon have a million pounds in the bank. I assumed you planned to spend a substantial amount of it on designer clothes. But I'll pay for any clothes you choose now.' He held the red dress against her. 'This will look fantastic on you. With your colouring you can carry off bold shades.'

'How do you know it will fit me?' Athena reluctantly took the dress from him.

'I have spent my entire adult life dressing women.' His eyes gleamed wickedly. 'And undressing them. I made a professional guess as to your size.' Helped by the fact that he had run his hands over her body last night and memorised the shape of her narrow waist and full breasts, Luca mused.

Athena had thought of another reason why the clothes Luca had chosen wouldn't be suitable. 'Tight-fitting dresses and skirts are no good for my line of work. I need to wear things that will allow me to move easily and even to roll around on the floor.'

He looked surprised. 'I thought you said you didn't work. What *is* your job anyway? Circus performer?'

She felt a sudden release from the fierce tension that had seized her when she had opened the door to Luca and been swamped by memories of how he had nearly made love to her last night.

Her lips twitched. 'I'm a qualified nursery nurse and I work with young children up to the age of about five years old. A lot of the time the job involves getting down on the floor to play with them. The nursery I worked at closed down a couple of months before I'd planned to marry Charlie. I told you—I used the time to go on cookery courses so that I would be able to give sophisticated dinner parties like the wives of his banker friends. Actually, most of the dishes I cooked were a disaster,' she admitted, thinking of her soufflés that had failed to rise and her mayonnaise that had curdled, whatever she did to it.

'You won't need to work while we are married—or after we divorce, if you invest your million pounds wisely.'

'Of course I'll work.'

She hesitated, wondering if she should tell Luca of her intention to give the money he was paying her to the orphanage project in India. Charles had been uninterested in her fundraising campaign for the street children of Jaipur, she remembered, and although her parents were supportive, Athena knew that they still wished she would focus more on furthering her career rather than her charity work.

But the orphanage meant a lot to her. She felt she was actually doing something worthwhile that could change the lives of homeless children, and she was afraid Luca would not understand her decision to give such a vast sum of money away to charity.

'I love being a nursery nurse,' she told him. 'I realise it may not be easy to find a job at a nursery in Italy, because I can't speak the language, but there might be a family that wants to employ an English-speaking nanny.'

She looked again along the rail of clothes and picked out a couple of dresses.

'I'll try these on, and *I'll* pay for them. You are already paying me a fortune. I won't allow you to buy my clothes.'

Five minutes later she walked back into the sitting room, feeling painfully self-conscious. The scarlet dress moulded her body like a second skin. 'It's too clingy,' she told Luca, 'and the shoes are too high.'

Luca swung round from the window and was powerless to prevent his body's reaction as his gaze encompassed Athena's hourglass figure shown off perfectly by the fitted dress. She was every red-blooded male's fantasy! And where had those legs come from? The three-inch stiletto heels accentuated her slim calves—and gave her a delightful wiggle when she walked, he noticed as she came towards him. She had swapped her glasses for contact lenses, and caught her hair up in a loose knot with stray tendrils framing her delicate face.

He swallowed. 'You look incredible.'

She bit her lip. 'You don't think the dress is a bit too…?'

'Too what?' He was puzzled by her doubtful expression. Hadn't she looked in the mirror and seen how gorgeous she was? How had he ever written her off as the plain Howard sister?

'Too revealing…' Athena mumbled.

'You have a beautiful figure and I think you should absolutely show it off.'

Luca silently acknowledged that the last part of that statement was a lie. He didn't want other men looking at Athena. He had discovered he had caveman tendencies, and would like to lock his wife away where only he could see her. Unfortunately the need to convince the board of De Rossi Enterprises that his marriage was not fake meant that he and Athena must court the attention of the paparazzi. His global fame as a top fashion designer guaranteed that pictures of him and his new bride wearing a sexy red dress would feature in newspapers around the world.

'I have something else for you.' He pulled a small velvet box from his pocket.

Athena frowned when he handed her the box. 'What is it?'

'An engagement ring. I thought you'd better be seen

wearing one at the press conference I've arranged for us to give this morning. Open it,' he bade her.

Her hands shook as she lifted the lid and revealed an exquisite oval sapphire surrounded by white diamonds. 'They're not real stones, are they?' she choked.

'Of course they're real. I didn't get the ring out of a Christmas cracker.'

'It must be worth a fortune.'

Athena did not know much about jewellery, but she had seen a similar ring in the exclusive shop in the hotel's lobby and been astounded by the price tag.

'I'd *rather* have a ring from a Christmas cracker.' She bit her lip. 'It doesn't seem right for me to wear this.'

The engagement ring was beautiful, and she felt that it should be a token of love between a couple who were in a genuine relationship—rather than a stage prop to fool the press and ultimately Luca's great-uncle and the other De Rossi board members that their marriage was real.

'People will expect me to have given you an engagement ring,' Luca said as he slid the ring onto her finger.

It fitted perfectly. Athena could not explain why tears blurred her eyes, making the diamonds that encircled the sapphire glisten.

'I'll return the ring to you at the end of the year, when our marriage is over,' she said huskily.

Luca gave her an intent look. 'It's yours to keep.'

'No.'

He recognised the resolute angle of her jaw and shrugged. In truth, he was puzzled. His assumption that Athena was as much of a gold-digger as Giselle did not fit with her refusal to accept anything from him.

He glanced at his watch. 'I've arranged the press conference for ten o'clock. You can leave most of the talking to me. I'll explain that we fell in love at your sister's wedding in Zenhab, but because we had both promised to marry other people we fought our feelings until we realised that we couldn't live without one another. Hopefully the story will convince my great-uncle *and* satisfy fans of romantic fiction,' he said sardonically.

Luca was a consummate actor, Athena thought later as she sat next to him at the press conference, and forced herself to smile for the paparazzi who had crowded into the room and jostled for a prime position to take photographs.

His reputation as a playboy meant that the press were fascinated by the story of how Luca De Rossi had eloped to Las Vegas to marry the woman who had captured his heart. As he had predicted, there was a great deal of interest in her engagement ring, and Athena lost count of the number of times she'd assured the journalists that she was blissfully happy and in love with her new husband.

'I completely refute the suggestion that my marriage to Athena is a sham,' Luca replied, to a question about the validity of their relationship.

'How about giving your bride a kiss?' someone called out.

'Nothing would give me greater pleasure.'

Luca's smile did not slip as he turned his head slightly towards Athena.

'We'd better keep the paparazzi happy,' he muttered. 'My PA informed me just before the press conference that my great-uncle Emilio has begun legal proceedings to try and stop me claiming my inheritance, and the only way he can do that is if he can prove our marriage is a fake.' He dipped his head closer to her. 'Are you ready?'

He made it sound so clinical. But of course for Luca kissing her was just part of his strategy to show the world that they were in love.

He had not been acting in front of the press when he had kissed her in their honeymoon suite last night, she remembered. When he had walked into the bedroom and seen her wearing a virtually see-through nightgown his eyes had glittered with desire. His hands had explored her body with the skill of a man well practised at seducing women, but his touch had been surprisingly gentle, almost reverent, when he had cradled her bare breasts in his hands and played with her nipples until they'd hardened.

She watched his darkly beautiful face descend and was gripped with panic. It was not the nervous feeling she'd had in the past whenever a man had tried to kiss her—it was a different kind of panic…a sense that she was being drawn ever deeper into a situation that was out of her control.

'I can't,' she whispered.

His face was so close that she could see each individual eyelash, and his lush mouth was a temptation she knew she must resist if she was to survive a year of being married to him.

Luca was puzzled by the fearful expression in Athena's eyes. It was the same expression he had seen on her face last night, when she had called a sudden halt to their love-making. He couldn't think of any reason why she would be afraid of him, but something had happened that had upset her. She had cried for a long time after he had left her.

'Relax, *piccola*. I'm not going to hurt you.'

His softly spoken assurance was whispered across Athena's lips. *Piccola* meant 'little one'—she had looked up the translation last night.

Luca's gentleness was her undoing, and she released her breath on a ragged sigh as he covered her mouth with his and kissed her with heart-stopping passion mixed with an unexpected tenderness that evoked an ache inside her for something elusive and indefinable.

She had no idea how long the kiss lasted. Time was suspended and the journalists with their microphones and cameras disappeared from her consciousness. There was only her and Luca. She heard his low groan as he took the kiss to another level, where there was nothing but the sensations of darkness and velvet softness and the sweet, slow throb of desire stealing through her veins.

When eventually he lifted his head, she could not say a word as she waited for him to make some witty comment to the paparazzi. But he didn't speak. He simply stared into her eyes, and a nerve flickered in his jaw when he saw the tears clinging to her lashes.

'Don't.' His voice sounded strangely rusty as he pressed his lips to each of her eyelids in turn and tasted moisture on his lips. 'You cannot deny the attraction between us any more than I can,' he said in a harsh whisper, to avoid being overheard by the journalists. 'So what was last night about?'

Athena was incapable of answering him—and was spared from having to try when Luca's PA appeared at his shoulder.

'I received a message for you from Villa De Rossi while your phone was switched off during the press conference,' Sandro told Luca quietly. 'Maria has asked you to return home urgently.'

CHAPTER SEVEN

ATHENA'S FOOTSTEPS ECHOED on the black-and-white chequered floor of the entrance hall at Villa De Rossi. Luca's secluded home, set in thirty acres of stunning parkland with views of Lake Como and the surrounding mountains, was a haven of peace and tranquillity after vibrant Las Vegas. Athena had fallen in love with the villa at first sight, and after three days of exploring the house and beautiful gardens she felt incredibly lucky that she would be able to spend time here for the year while she was married to Luca.

But if the past few days were anything to go by she would not be spending much time with her husband. She hadn't seen him since the evening they had arrived at the villa and he had shown her to a suite of rooms: a large bedroom, en-suite bathroom and a charming sitting room overlooking the lake.

She had eaten dinner in splendid isolation in the wooden-panelled dining room, and when she'd asked the affable butler, Geomar, if the Conte—she had been shocked to discover that Luca had a title—would be joining her, she had been informed that he was very busy.

Whatever it was that occupied him, it wasn't to do with his work.

His design studio, on the second floor of the villa, was a huge space, which must have been created by knocking through several rooms. Athena had taken a quick look inside, and had been amazed by the dozens of sketches pinned to the walls. Luca's designs. He was obviously a gifted artist, who used bold pencil or charcoal strokes on his drawings, and she had thought how fussy her own drawings were in comparison.

Luca had not been in his studio or in his study when she'd looked. The villa was huge, and she remembered he had said they would be able to keep out of each other's way most of the time.

At least the staff were friendly—and Geomar and his wife Elizavetta, who was the cook and housekeeper, spoke reasonably fluent English. She would have to find someone to give her Italian lessons, Athena thought. The two nurseries in nearby villages where she had made enquiries about a possible job both required her to be able to speak at least basic Italian.

The late summer sunshine pouring through the front windows filled the entrance hall with golden light and danced across the portraits of the De Rossi family lining the walls. Luca's ancestors shared his classically sculpted, rather haughty features, but she noticed that none had his curious amber-coloured eyes. The two most recent portraits were of a stern-faced couple who Athena guessed must be Luca's grandparents and, in contrast, a last picture of a smiling woman wearing an eye-catching orange dress. She was very beautiful, with long black hair and slanting eyes, and she looked so vividly alive that Athena almost expected her to spring out from the canvas.

'My mother—Beatriz.'

Luca's gravelly voice sent a ripple of reaction through Athena and she spun round to see him walking into the hall through a door which was usually kept locked.

'I see you can't take your eyes off her. She had that effect on most people—particularly men,' he said sardonically.

Athena noticed that he could not seem to tear his own gaze from his mother. 'What happened to her?'

'She had an addiction to cocaine and vodka. A maid found her body at the bottom of the stairs in her apartment in Monte Carlo. It was supposed at the inquest that she had fallen and broken her neck, which resulted in her accidental death.' Luca's voice was emotionless but a nerve flickered in his jaw.

Athena drew a sharp breath. 'What a terrible thing to have happened—for her and also for you,' she said gently. Intuitively she realised that Luca had been deeply and irrevocably affected by his mother's death. 'She looks so full of life in the painting…as if she was determined to live her life to the maximum.'

'My mother was the most selfish, self-obsessed woman I have ever known—and I've known quite a few,' Luca said cynically. 'When she was a child my grandparents gave her everything she desired, and as an adult she carried on taking what she wanted without giving a thought to anyone else.'

'When did you come to live with your grandparents?'

'Just before my eighth birthday.' It had been a week before, and in the upheaval of dumping him on her parents, his mother had forgotten his birthday. His grandparents did not even know the date of his birth, and Luca had never told them. 'My mother moved in with a lover who didn't want me around. I rarely saw her after I came to live here.'

Athena looked along the row of portraits. 'There isn't a picture of your father here.'

Luca hesitated. He had long ago stopped feeling ashamed of his illegitimacy, but memories of being teased by the other boys at school about his mother's outrageous lifestyle and very public affairs with a string of men meant that he rarely discussed his background.

'That's because his identity was unknown—even to my mother.' He shrugged. 'She had a vague idea he might have been a croupier she'd had a fling with in Monte Carlo, but she told me she couldn't be sure who had fathered me.'

He grimaced when he saw Athena's shocked expression.

'My grandparents were appalled that my mother had given birth to a bastard. They believed—with some justification—that Beatriz's wild lifestyle of drugs, drink and careless sex would bring the De Rossi brand name into disrepute. And I was the living proof that they had gone badly wrong when they brought up my mother. Rather than spoiling me, they went to the other end of the spectrum,' he said grimly. 'I loved being at boarding school, because at least during term time I had some respite from Aberto and Violetta's constant attempts to suppress any source of happiness or enjoyment in my life.'

He gave a harsh laugh.

'Perhaps it was natural that when I grew older I rebelled against my grandparents' strict ways. They regarded my playboy reputation as proof that I had inherited my mother's irresponsibility—especially when…'

'When what?' Athena asked, puzzled by his abrupt halt.

'It's not important.'

Luca's jaw clenched as he remembered his grandparents' anger when he had brought his illegitimate daughter to live at Villa De Rossi.

'You continue to heap shame on the family with your immoral behaviour,' Nonna Violetta had accused him.

Even when Rosalie's illness had been diagnosed, his grandparents had been uninterested in the *bastardo's* bastard child.

The situation he now found himself in was difficult,

Luca brooded. When he had married Athena he had intended for her to live at his penthouse in Milan, as he had originally planned for Giselle. But since Emilio had threatened to try and prove that his marriage was a sham, he had been forced to bring his bride to live at the villa.

He realised he could not keep his daughter a secret from Athena for a year, but he could not forget his concern that she might talk to the press about Rosalie's medical condition. He was determined to guard his daughter's privacy, and he certainly did not want journalists hanging around the villa—or, even worse, the local hospital. Rosalie was frequently admitted there for treatment, and she had been there for the past couple of days, receiving treatment for a chest infection.

Sufferers of Rett Syndrome were prone to developing pneumonia—which was why Maria had urgently called him home from Las Vegas when Rosalie had shown signs of breathing problems. But, thank God, his daughter was okay after a course of antibiotics to treat the infection.

Relief that Rosalie was recovering from her latest bout of illness was replaced with frustration as Luca acknowledged that he had no option but to tell Athena about his daughter—sooner rather than later.

He turned his back on his mother's portrait and skimmed his gaze over his wife. She had obviously spent time outside in the garden since arriving at the villa, and the mellow September sunshine had given her bare arms a light golden tan and encouraged a sprinkling of freckles on her nose.

'You are sensible to wear a hat. The sun at this time of the year can still be very hot, and although your hair is dark you have fair skin, which would burn easily.'

The light blue cotton sundress Athena was wearing was not at all glamorous, but the square-cut neckline showed off the upper slopes of her breasts and Luca found her natural, wholesome beauty incredibly sexy. He tried to ignore the tug of desire in his gut.

'Are you settling in at the Villa De Rossi? If there is anything you need just ask Geomar.'

'I'm fine now that my luggage has arrived from England,' Athena assured him.

The villa felt more like home since her parents had sent over her clothes and personal belongings. The phone conversation she'd had with her mother about her shock marriage to Luca had been extremely tense, but now her parents were on a Caribbean cruise, and she hoped they would soon come to terms with her decision not to marry Charlie—although it sounded as if he still had not told the truth about his relationship with his best man.

She looked at Luca's darkly handsome face and her stomach twisted. She had missed his company these past few days—missed his kisses, she acknowledged.

'Where have you been? Geomar said you were busy. Was it to do with your work?'

'I had matters to attend to.'

Luca stiffened as he watched Athena lift her straw hat from her head so that her hair tumbled down her back like a river of silk. It was all he could do not to reach out and run his fingers through the glossy chestnut mane. *Dio*, she was going to be a distraction he did not need at the villa.

'Did you go to Milan?' Geomar had told Athena that Luca often went to the city. The head offices of his design company DRD and also De Rossi Enterprises were there. 'You told me you have an apartment in the city.'

He sidestepped her first question. 'My penthouse is close to Galleria Vittorio Emanuele II—Milan's famous shopping gallery. You are welcome to go and stay there if you are bored at Villa De Rossi.'

'I can't imagine ever being bored here—the house and grounds are so beautiful. But there *is* something I'm curious about. What is behind the wall that runs along the side of the house? There's a door in the wall, but it's locked.'

Luca frowned. 'The area beyond the wall is out of bounds. There's nothing much there,' he said, seeing the curiosity on Athena's face.

She wanted to ask him *why* the place was out of bounds, if there was nothing there, but he was striding across the hall towards the library. She followed him, puzzled by his secrecy about the locked door. What *was* beyond the garden wall? Luca clearly did not want her to find out.

Perhaps it had something to do with the mystery of the disappearing women!

She thought of the attractive dark-haired woman she had seen arriving at the villa early every morning, and another woman of whom she hadn't managed to get a good glimpse because she arrived in the evening, as it was getting dark. Both the women parked their cars at the back of the house.

When Athena had asked Geomar about these regular visitors to the villa he had made out that he hadn't understood her—although usually he had an excellent grasp of English.

Were the two women Luca's mistresses? Athena's imagination went into overdrive. Now that she thought about it, he *did* look tired. Perhaps he had been 'busy' entertaining his lady friends.

Her thoughts scattered when she stepped into the library and found Luca flicking through the sketchpad she had left on the table.

'Are these your drawings?'

'Yes, but please don't look at them.'

In an agony of embarrassment, she tried to snatch the sketchbook out of his hands.

'They're very good.' Luca put the pad back on the table, but continued to turn the pages. 'Your drawings of animals are incredibly detailed. Have you ever thought about becoming an illustrator?'

Some of Athena's tension eased when she realised that Luca wasn't mocking her. 'I'd love to illustrate children's storybooks.' She hesitated. 'Actually, I've written a few books for children in the five to eight age group, and illustrated the stories.'

'Have any been published?'

'No, I've never sent my work to a publisher. My father...' Athena bit her lip as she remembered her father's irritation with what he had called her time-wasting. 'He used to get annoyed if he found me scribbling childish drawings instead of studying for my exams. I really don't believe my drawings are good enough to be saleable,' she said ruefully.

'It sounds like your parents did a good job of destroying your confidence.'

Luca could sympathise with how Athena must have felt when she had failed to meet her parents' expectations. He had never fitted the mould his grandparents had tried to force him into.

'I think you should send your work off to some publishing houses. What have you got to lose?'

'Do you *really* think my drawings are good enough for a publisher to be interested in them?'

Her shy smile transformed her from pretty to beautiful, Luca brooded.

She straightened up and tilted her head to meet his gaze. 'Thanks for being so encouraging.'

'You're welcome.'

Luca knew he was staring at her—but then, she was staring at him. He watched a soft flush of colour run under her skin, suffusing her cheeks and throat and spreading down to the upper slopes of her breasts. The tip of her tongue darted out to lick her lips and desire corkscrewed inside him.

He wanted to kiss her as he had done in Vegas. Hell, he wanted to tumble her down onto the sofa and make love to her hard and fast, and then take the slow, leisurely route and satisfy the hunger that he was convinced she felt as strongly as he did.

But all *he* wanted was to spend an afternoon enjoying sex with no strings attached, and he remembered Athena had told him that she regarded making love as a physical expression of being in love. It was enough to make any sensible man run a mile.

Maybe some people *did* find happy-ever-after—Luca thought of Kadir and Lexi in Zenhab. But even if he *had* wanted a relationship with a woman that involved spending time with her on both sides of the bedroom door, it wasn't possible. He was committed to caring for his daughter, whose life was slowly being destroyed by a terrible disease, and just as important as his devotion to Rosalie was the terrible secret he carried, along with the gut-wrenching sense of guilt, which had led to his decision to remain single.

The ticking clock sounded unnaturally loud in the quiet library. Athena could hardly breathe as she recognised the gleam of desire in Luca's eyes, and she found she was mentally urging him to pull her into his arms and kiss her.

He moved towards her, but at that moment Geomar appeared in the doorway and spoke to Luca in Italian. Athena could not understand anything of the conversation between the two men, but she stiffened when she heard the name Maria.

In Las Vegas, Luca's PA had mentioned Maria. Was

she one of the women who drove up to the villa and then disappeared?

Athena would have liked to ask Luca, but he took no more notice of her as he finished talking to the butler and strode out of the library.

Ominous purple clouds obscured the mountaintops, and the air in the courtyard at the front of the villa was so hot and still that it felt as if there was no air at all. Geomar had told Athena he thought a storm was brewing when she had passed him in the hall on her way outside. She wondered if it would be cooler down by the lake and started to walk in that direction.

Her route took her along a path next to the high wall that had the locked door in it. There was probably no mystery on the other side, she told herself, just as there was probably a simple explanation for the women who arrived at the villa but she had never met. She was allowing her imagination to run away with her.

But she was sure she hadn't imagined the faint sound of a child crying during the night. And she definitely wasn't imagining the sound of Luca's voice coming from the other side of the wall.

Athena stopped and strained her ears. She recognised Luca's gravelly tones, but not the woman's voice. Laughter drifted over the wall. Luca and his companion were speaking in Italian, and again he said the name Maria. Athena felt a spurt of anger. It was true that her marriage to Luca was in name only, but it wasn't right for him to entertain his lover—perhaps *lovers*—under the same roof as his wife.

She shielded her eyes from the sun with her hand and looked up at the wall. From the ground it did not look terribly high, and the missing bricks in places would provide hand and footholds if she was mad enough to decide to climb to the top—which of course she wasn't.

She heard another peal of laughter. The mystery woman was evidently enjoying Luca's company. Damn it! What was going on behind the wall? Athena's curiosity got the better of her dislike of heights and, fuelled by temper and bravado, she began to climb.

It was surprisingly easy. The old bricks were worn, giving her plenty of places to grip while she hauled herself up. Determined to see what was on the other side, she continued to climb until she was almost at the top, and then she managed to hook one leg over so that she was straddling the wall.

Below her was a pretty garden with wide paths bordered by lavender hedges. The spires of purple flowers were fading in late summer, but even from her high vantage point Athena could smell their sweet scent. In the centre of the garden was a pond and next to it a beautiful weeping willow tree, with sweeping branches that reached down to the water.

There was no sign of Luca or the woman in the garden. Athena looked towards the house just as a woman appeared at the window. She recognised her as the pretty dark-haired woman she had seen arriving at the villa every morning. The woman looked shocked when she stared up at the wall, and quickly drew the curtains across the window.

'*Santa Madonna!* You crazy woman! What the devil are you doing?'

Luca's furious voice caused Athena to jerk her head round, and she realised that he had unlocked the door and walked through to the opposite side of the wall—where she had been standing when she had first heard his voice. She stared down at him—which was a mistake, because now she was aware of just how high up she was, and immediately felt dizzy.

'Sit still while I go and find a ladder,' he commanded.

She wanted to assure him that she had no intention of *not* sitting still, but her vocal cords, like every muscle in her body, had seized up with fear. Her head started to spin, and she gave a cry as she toppled from the top of the wall...

Luca was staring down at her when Athena's lashes fluttered open.

'This is becoming a habit,' Luca growled, reminding her of when he had caught her after she had climbed out of the window at the Fairfaxes' home, Woodley Lodge, on her wedding day.

Instead of marrying Charlie, she had married Luca— and swapped one unfaithful husband for another, she thought with a rush of temper.

'I *told* you that the area beyond the wall was out of bounds.' Luca felt a fresh surge of anger as he set Athena down on her feet. Thank God he had managed to catch her. 'Your stupid actions could have resulted in you breaking your neck.'

The word *stupid* acted like a red rag to a bull for Athena. Just because she wasn't a brilliant academic, like her parents, she had spent her whole life feeling a failure, and had meekly allowed herself to be bossed around by Charlie. It was time she stood up for herself.

'I wanted to find out *why* the other side of the wall was out of bounds, and now I know,' she told Luca hotly. 'It's where you entertain your mistresses. I suppose the room I saw is your harem?'

'*My harem?*'

Luca looked so astounded that Athena felt a tiny flicker of doubt.

'Yes,' she ploughed on. 'I've seen the women who arrive at the villa every morning and evening.'

She thought of the attractive dark-haired woman who had shut the curtains, and jealousy fizzed like corrosive acid in her stomach.

'I know you have a reputation as a playboy, but do you *really* need your girlfriends to work a double shift? No wonder I haven't seen you since we arrived at Villa De Rossi. I suppose you've been in *there*—' she pointed at the door in the wall, which led to the garden and the rooms beyond '—with your women.'

Various thoughts circled in Luca's mind—one being that Athena was incredibly sexy when she was angry. He forced his gaze up from the swift rise and fall of her breasts and narrowed his eyes on her flushed face. The slight tremor of her bottom lip touched something inside him.

'You're right,' he said coolly. 'I *have* spent the past few days in a part of the house that Geomar would not have taken you to when he showed you around.' He frowned. 'But I do *not* have a harem, and the women you have seen are *not* my mistresses.'

Athena stubbornly refused to back down. 'Well, who are they, then?'

Luca came to a decision. He was fairly certain Athena was not a hard-nosed gold-digger like Giselle—although she *had* married him for a million pounds, he reminded himself. He frowned again. He could not keep his daughter a secret for a year, he acknowledged.

'You had better come and meet Maria and Rosalie,' he said abruptly.

Athena's heart was thumping as she followed Luca through the door in the wall. He had insisted that Maria and the other woman he had called Rosalie were not his mistresses—so who were they?

Unlike the gravel paths in other areas of the villa's grounds, the paths in the garden were made of smooth stone, and the garden's beds were planted with lavender and other fragrant herbs—rosemary, basil and thyme—which released their scent as she brushed past them.

Luca led her through big glass doors into a room that she instantly realised was unlike any other room in the villa. It was like a hospital room, with a bed that could be raised and lowered, and there were oxygen tanks stacked against one wall.

Against another wall was a huge fish tank filled with brightly coloured fish, but Athena barely noticed it for her attention was focused on a young girl—it was difficult to guess her age—who was sitting in a wheelchair. Standing next to the wheelchair was the dark-haired woman, who was even prettier close up than Athena had realised when she had seen her from a distance.

Luca introduced the woman. 'This is Maria. She is one of Rosalie's carers.' He crouched down in front of the girl in the wheelchair. 'Athena, I'd like you to meet my daughter—Rosalie.'

At the sound of his voice, his daughter smiled. She was extraordinarily beautiful, with black curly hair and Luca's amber-coloured eyes, Athena noticed dazedly. But it was obvious that Rosalie had severe disabilities, which meant that she was confined to the wheelchair.

'Rosalie suffers from a rare degenerative illness called Rett Syndrome,' Luca explained quietly. 'The condition affects mainly girls, and is incurable.' He gently stroked his daughter's cheek and his voice deepened with emotion as he continued. 'A few years ago Rosalie could walk and talk. Sadly she can't do those things now. But she loves listening to music and watching her fish, and she especially loves to sit beneath the weeping willow tree in the garden.'

Acting instinctively, Athena knelt down beside Luca so that her face was level with his daughter's. 'Hello, Rosalie. I'm pleased to meet you,' she said softly. She gave Luca a rueful look. 'I don't suppose she can understand me? I wish I knew some Italian.'

'It doesn't matter. We are not sure how much she understands, but she will like hearing your voice.' He stood up as Maria came back into the room.

'I give Rosalie a drink?' the nurse said in hesitant English. She gave Athena a friendly smile. 'The weather— he is very hot. I think a storm will come.'

'You could be right.' Luca glanced outside at the sullen clouds that had covered up the sun. 'I'll give Rosalie her drink.' He looked at Athena. 'You don't mind if we stay for a while?'

'Of course not,' she assured him quickly.

It took a good ten minutes for Luca to help his daughter drink from a special feeding cup, and afterwards he lifted her onto his lap and read to her. His voice was softer than Athena had ever heard it, and tears pricked her eyes when she saw his obvious devotion to Rosalie.

They stayed for half an hour or so, before Luca tenderly kissed his daughter's brow. 'I'll come and see you later, *mio angelo.*' Turning to Athena, he said, 'Rosalie will probably have a nap, so we'll go now.'

Her mind was swimming with questions as she walked with him through the lavender garden. She was struggling to equate Luca, the world-famous fashion designer dubbed a playboy by the paparazzi, with the deeply caring father of a disabled child she had seen just now.

'Where is Rosalie's mother?'

'Jodie lives in New Zealand and by her own choice has no contact with her daughter. She couldn't cope when Rosalie was diagnosed with Rett's at two years old,' he said, in answer to Athena's look of surprise. 'It's a cruel disease.'

Luca's jaw clenched.

'You don't know what it's like to watch your child slip away from you bit by bit and be unable to help. All I can do for Rosalie is spend as much time as I possibly can with her and make sure she has the best medical care. She has frequent seizures, which means that she can never be left alone. A nurse looks after her night and day, and Maria often brings her own children to the villa, so that Rosalie has company even though she can never play or run around and do all the normal things children enjoy,' he said heavily.

He looked around the garden.

'I believe she is happy here. She loves the weeping willow tree. *This is my daughter's home*,' His voice had suddenly become fierce. 'When my grandmother wrote her damned will she did not think about how Rosalie would be affected if I was denied ownership of Villa De Rossi and had to move her to a new house away from familiar surroundings.'

Athena swallowed the lump in her throat caused by Luca's emotive outburst. 'Is that why you were so determined to marry and comply with the terms of your grandmother's will?' she said softly.

He nodded. 'Being chairman of De Rossi Enterprises is not a huge deal for me, and even if I had lost the right to use the De Rossi name for my fashion label I would have continued the company under a different name. My grandmother used my love for my daughter to manipulate me,' he said bitterly.

'Why *did* your grandmother want you to marry?'

'She disapproved of my reputation as a playboy—a reputation that has been exaggerated by the press, by the way. But mainly Nonna Violetta disapproved of me, the *bas-*

tardo, and I think she wrote that will because she liked to make trouble.'

Luca fell silent, clearly lost in his thoughts. Athena wanted to ask him if he had been married to Rosalie's mother. She also wondered why he had not told her about his daughter when he had proposed his marriage deal. More than anything else she felt guilty for her curiosity and the awful accusations she had made.

'I'm sorry for the things I said,' she murmured as she followed him through the door in the wall. 'All that stuff about you having a harem.' She flushed beneath his cool stare. 'My mother always says that I act first and think afterwards,' she said ruefully.

'Why were you jealous when you thought I had a mistress?'

Luca watched in fascination as rosy colour spread from Athena's cheeks, down her throat and across the creamy slopes of her breasts showing above her dress.

'I was not *jealous*. That would be ridiculous,' she muttered, 'when our marriage is in name only.'

A low rumble of thunder rolled down from the distant mountains, and the air prickled with the approaching electrical storm.

'It doesn't have to be,' Luca said quietly.

'What do you mean?'

She swallowed when she saw his wolf's eyes gleam with a predatory hunger. Suddenly the atmosphere between her and Luca was electrifying, making the tiny hairs on her body stand on end.

'You know I want you. I made it obvious in Las Vegas. And you want me, *mia bella*. You can shake your head to deny it all you like, but your body is sending out a very different signal.'

Following the direction of his gaze, Athena glanced

down and saw the outline of her nipples pushing provocatively beneath her lightweight cotton dress. Her breasts felt heavy, and the warmth in Luca's eyes was eliciting a molten heat between her legs. Half of her wanted him to take her in his arms and kiss her senseless, but the other half wanted to run away from the powerful undercurrents she sensed swirling between them.

'I don't...' she whispered.

'Yes, you do.'

Luca saw the indecision in her eyes and decided it was time for him to take charge. She was driving him to distraction, and without giving her time to debate the issue of their mutual desire he claimed her mouth with his, intent on kissing her into willing submission.

He felt her lips open, and her sweetly ardent response had a predictable effect on his body, so that he was instantly massively aroused.

'Your body was made for pleasure,' he told her thickly as he roamed his hands over her, shaping the gentle curve of her hips, the dip of her waist and the firm fullness of her breasts. 'I can't stop thinking about you in that sexy scrap of see-through lace you wore in Vegas.'

'Your body was designed for sex and you're hungry for it, aren't you?'

Athena tried to block out Peter Fitch's voice, but he was there inside her head, saying those awful things and accusing her of teasing him just because she had left the top couple of buttons on her blouse undone. She didn't want to remember. She *wanted* Luca to kiss her and touch her breasts. But as he slid his hand into the top of her dress and inside her bra she froze.

'What's the matter?'

He lifted his mouth from hers and stared down at her,

frustration at her sudden transformation from soft and pliant to stiff and unresponsive evident in his taut features.

'*Dio!*'

Luca raked a hand through his hair and was surprised to find it was wet. He had no idea when it had started raining. A loud clap of thunder shook the ground and when he looked up he saw that the sky was as black as night. The rain fell harder, flattening Athena's hair to her head and running down her face. Luca had the strange idea that they were tears he could see on her cheeks.

'You were with me all the way,' he said harshly. 'What brought about the change?' His jaw hardened. 'Or do you get a kick out of leading men on and playing hard to get?'

'*No!* Of course not!'

Athena's teeth were chattering as she tried to hold herself together. Raindrops the size of coins stung her bare arms and Luca's accusation lashed her heart. She could not blame him for thinking she was a sexual tease. She *hated* herself for her inability to escape from the past.

'I can't,' she choked. 'I just *can't.*'

She couldn't deal with his questions. And she could see from his determined expression that he was going to demand answers. In panic, she whirled away from him—but tripped on a tree root and went sprawling down onto the gravel path. For a few seconds she was winded, and then she felt stinging pain from her grazed hands and knees. She heard the crunch of Luca's footsteps on the gravel, and the bizarre thought went through her head that his handmade leather shoes would be ruined by the rain.

She tensed as he gripped her arms and lifted her onto her feet, expecting his anger. But his voice was heartbreakingly gentle.

'I can't pretend to understand what's wrong. But you have to stop running away, Athena.'

CHAPTER EIGHT

'ARE YOU AFRAID of me?'

'No…' It was a thread of sound. Her voice would not work properly. Athena looked up at Luca and saw not anger but concern in his eyes. 'No,' she said more firmly, 'I'm not afraid of you.'

'But you are, or have been in the past, afraid of *someone*?' He had seen fear on her face moments ago when she had pulled out of his arms—the same look he had seen when he had kissed her in their hotel room in Las Vegas.

'It was years ago.' Her voice cracked. 'I don't know why I can't forget about what happened.'

Luca stared at the tears mingled with rain running down her face and felt a strange sensation, as if a hand was squeezing his heart. 'What *did* happen?' He thought of her fearful expression. 'Did someone hurt you?'

Silence, and then she whispered, 'Yes…'

Athena remembered the livid purple fingerprints that Peter Fitch had left on her breasts. The bruises had eventually faded, but the memory of his assault was like a festering wound in her mind.

Blood was running down her legs from her grazed knees. Luca wanted to find out who had hurt her—and where he could find the person so that he could mete out retribution—but first and foremost he needed to take Athena inside, away from the storm.

He scooped her up into his arms, ignoring her startled protest as he carried her into the house. His steps did not falter as he strode across the entrance hall and up the stairs, giving instructions in Italian to Geomar, who had not been able to hide his surprise when he had seen Athena, wet, dishevelled and bleeding.

Twenty minutes later her grazes had been washed and bandaged and she was sitting in an armchair in her bedroom, sipping hot, very sweet tea. Luca had dropped four sugar cubes into her cup, but she didn't tell him the tea tasted like syrup when he was being so kind and taking care of her.

Outside, the storm had passed, and the air felt fresher as a soft breeze drifted into the room through the open window. Luca was relieved to see that Athena had regained some colour in her cheeks. Her wet hair had dried into loose waves, and not for the first time he felt as though he could drown in her sapphire-blue eyes.

'Do you want to talk about what happened to you?' he murmured.

No, if she was honest, Athena thought. But not talking about it for all these years since Peter Fitch had assaulted her hadn't helped her to get over it. Perhaps if she had been closer to her parents she might have confided in them, but instead she had kept the assault a secret that had festered inside her.

Luca had a right to know why she had blown hot and cold with him. She looked at him, standing by the window. He had changed into dry jeans, and the denim moulded his powerful thighs. His shirt was open at the throat to reveal his dark bronze skin and a sprinkling of black chest hair. Even casually dressed, he was effortlessly elegant—and so utterly gorgeous that Athena quickly glanced away, her heart thudding.

She took another sip of tea and searched for courage. 'When I was eighteen I was assaulted…sexually…by a friend of my parents.'

Luca said nothing, but she knew from his intent gaze that he was listening.

'He was a university professor and my parents had arranged for him to give me private Latin tuition so that I might stand a chance of passing my exams to get into medical school.'

In her mind she was back in Peter's study. She could see the dark mahogany furniture and the brown leather sofa, see herself sitting opposite Peter at his desk, trying to concentrate on Latin verbs that might have been Greek to her.

'You look hot, my dear. Why don't you undo a few more buttons on your blouse? In fact, why don't you take your blouse off, and your bra, and let me see your breasts?'

Athena remembered her sense of shock at Uncle Peter's suggestion.

'One day Peter asked me to take my blouse off and show him my breasts,' she told Luca in a low voice. 'At first I thought he was joking. But he carried on saying awful things—calling me *Aphrodite* and telling me how much he liked my body and what he wanted to do to me.' She swallowed. 'He said he knew I would enjoy him touching me because…because I looked hungry for sex, and I obviously wore low-cut tops because I liked to tease him.'

She twisted her fingers together.

'My clothes were not particularly revealing, but I was eighteen and I was starting to experiment with fashion. I suppose a couple of my tops *were* a bit daring…'

'Just because you wore a low-cut top that did *not* give your tutor the right to assault you,' Luca said grimly.

'He said my body sent out signals that I wanted sex. I was scared,' Athena admitted. 'This was a man I had known for most of my life. I called him Uncle Peter, and his wife was Auntie Jean. I tried to run out of his study but he had locked the door.'

Luca cursed softly. 'What happened, *carissima*?'

'He ripped my blouse and forced his hand into my bra,' she said tonelessly. 'He kept squeezing my breasts and saying I would like what he was going to do next. And then he…he…'

Luca's heart stopped. '*Dio*—did he *rape* you?'

She shook her head. 'He put his hand up my skirt… between my legs. I believed he was going to rape me and I felt sick. I didn't know how to stop him.'

She drew a shuddering breath.

'It was like an answer to a prayer when Peter's wife knocked on the study door. It was so bizarre. Uncle Peter was trying to force himself on me and Auntie Jean was asking if we wanted a cup of tea. Hearing her voice must have brought him to his senses. He asked Jean to go and make tea, and when he heard her go downstairs he unlocked the study door and let me go. I put my cardigan on over my torn blouse and ran out.'

'Presumably you went straight to the police?'

Luca frowned when she shook her head.

'Why didn't you? You were subjected to a serious and terrifying sexual assault.'

'Before I escaped from his study Peter warned me that no one would believe me if I reported what had happened— because he was a highly respected university professor and I was a silly, over-imaginative girl.'

'Your parents would have believed you, surely?'

'Peter was my father's best friend from school. He was vice chancellor of the university. Everyone liked and respected him. I didn't know how to tell my parents,' she said miserably. 'I tried to forget about the assault, but I couldn't—especially when I went on a few dates with guys and they tried to kiss me. I felt...*dirty*.'

Luca said something under his breath in Italian. '*You were not to blame for what this man did, piccola*—of course you weren't.'

Somehow he controlled the white-hot anger that had surged through him when Athena had told him the details of the assault. What she needed from him was sympathy and understanding. He imagined how terrified she must have been during the attack and once again felt a strange sensation—as if his heart was being squeezed in a vice.

He crossed the room and hunkered down in front of her. 'You were the victim of a dreadful crime, and the perpetrator should not have got away with it just because he is a friend of your parents.'

'That's what Lexi said when I told her about the assault a few years after it happened. She persuaded me to report Peter to the police, but before I could do so he died suddenly of a heart attack.'

Athena had been left in limbo, without the sense of closure she might have gained if her tutor had been brought to justice, Luca realised. The sight of tears rolling down her cheeks moved him unbearably and stirred his protective instincts, so he scooped her into his arms and sat down in the chair with her on his lap, just as he had done with his daughter an hour earlier.

A thought occurred to him. 'Did you tell Charlie about the assault?'

She shook her head. 'I couldn't bear to talk about it, even though we were meant to be getting married. I suppose that should have made me realise I didn't love him,' she said ruefully.

It felt good to rest her head on Luca's shoulder. Athena did not know how long she sat in the safe circle of his arms, only knew that she *did* feel safe with him. Seeing his gentle patience with his daughter had shown her a different side of him from his playboy image. She had dreaded speaking about the sexual assault, but now she felt lighter somehow—as if by bringing it out into the open it was no longer a shameful secret from her past.

They had both learned something about each other today, she mused, her thoughts turning to Rosalie. The realisation that Luca had been prepared to pay her a million pounds to marry him so that he could keep his disabled daughter in the home where she was happy had altered Athena's perception of him.

But her awareness of him hadn't changed—if anything it was fiercer than ever, and she felt desire unfurl in the pit of her stomach as their eyes met and his gaze burned into hers.

He dropped a gentle kiss on the tip of her nose. It was no more than a butterfly caress, but it evoked a yearning inside her for more. Her lower lip trembled as he traced his thumb pad over it. Suddenly she did not want to think about the past or the future, but simply live for the present and enjoy the anticipation of knowing that Luca was about to kiss her.

They both jumped when the house phone rang, and he cursed softly as he reached towards the bedside table to pick up the handset.

'That was Geomar, saying he needs to see me,' he told Athena. 'He also said that Elizavetta is about to serve dinner. Do you feel you can eat something? Good,' he said when she nodded. His eyes held hers and his smile stole her breath. 'I'll meet you downstairs in five minutes.'

Her dress had a streak of mud down the front from when she had tripped and landed on the garden path, and her knees were grazed. Athena was about to put on her jeans, but then she changed her mind and searched through the clothes Luca had bought her, finally selecting a pair of beautifully tailored cream trousers and a pink silk shirt that showed off her curves.

For too long she had allowed the memory of Peter Fitch to dictate how she lived her life, and she had worn clothes that disguised her hourglass figure. But Luca had made her see that taking pride in her appearance and wearing sexy clothes was *not* an invitation to be sexually assaulted, as Peter had told her.

As she walked down the stairs, Luca came out of his study. His unsmiling face filled her with unease.

'I've had a call from Kadir,' he said abruptly. 'Lexi gave birth to a baby boy earlier today.'

'That's wonderful news…' Athena's swift burst of delight faded and her feeling of foreboding turned to dread. 'Luca…what's wrong?'

'Apparently there is a problem with the baby's heart. It's possible he will need surgery to correct the fault.'

'Oh, God—Lexi must be out of her mind with worry.' In an instant Athena's priorities changed. Nothing was important compared to the health of her sister's newborn son. 'I have to go to Zenhab and be with Lexi,' she said frantically.

'I have already instructed my pilot to prepare the jet for our flight.' Luca ushered her into his study and handed her the phone. 'Kadir is on the line. He will be able to tell you more about the baby's condition.'

Kadir's deep voice was taut with concern. 'We have named the baby Faisal,' he told Athena. 'He is beautiful, and he has a strong cry. I'm sure he will be as feisty as his mother.'

'How is Lexi?'

'Holding up.'

Athena heard her brother-in-law swallow hard before he continued.

'She's tired after a long labour, and she is worried about our son—we both are,' he said huskily. 'Lexi has asked if you will visit…'

'Luca is arranging a flight to Zenhab.'

'What is going on, Athena? I've heard reports that you and Luca are *married*. Lexi is worried about you, too.'

That was the last thing Athena wanted. Her sister had enough to worry about. 'It's true that Luca and I got married in Las Vegas,' she told Kadir. 'I know it sounds crazy, but…' she glanced at Luca '…we realised we had fallen in love with each other when we met at your wedding, and we decided to marry in secret and tell everyone afterwards.'

Kadir laughed. 'I always suspected that Luca was a romantic at heart. Lexi will want to hear all the details of your wedding when you get here.'

As Athena replaced the phone she was conscious of Luca's eyes boring into her.

'I couldn't tell Kadir the real reason for our marriage.' She bit her lip. 'Kadir is putting on a brave front, but I know he and my sister will be distraught about the baby's health problems and I don't want Lexi to worry about me as well. While we are at the royal palace we'll have to keep up the same pretence that we married because we are madly in love.'

Luca had suggested that Athena should try to sleep on the flight to Zenhab, but she found it impossible to relax when she was so concerned about her new nephew.

A limousine was waiting at the airport to take them to the palace. The last time Athena had driven though the capital city, Mezeira, the streets had been decorated with white-and-gold ribbons for the wedding procession of the Sultan and his bride. But today she did not feel any sense of excitement from the Zenhabian people, and knew that Kadir had delayed announcing the birth of his son and heir until baby Faisal had been examined by the world-renowned heart specialist who was flying in from America.

'I know it's hard, but try not to worry,' Luca murmured. He wrapped his hand around hers to stop her unconsciously twisting her fingers together. 'Your sister will need you to be strong.'

She glanced at him, and it struck her that he must know exactly what it was like to be worried about a child's health. 'It must have been a terrible time when Rosalie became ill and was diagnosed with her illness.'

'Ironically, I only knew I *had* a daughter because Rosalie became ill.'

'What do you mean?'

'I was not with Rosalie's mother during her pregnancy.' Luca exhaled heavily. 'Do you want to know the whole story?'

Athena nodded. 'Were you married to Rosalie's mother?'

'No. Jodie describes herself as a free spirit. She's from New Zealand, and I met her when she was travelling around Europe and came to stay in a village near Villa De Rossi. I was a young man, and life at the villa with my grandparents was tense and frankly unbearable. Jodie was a breath of fresh air.'

He shrugged.

'I fell for her hard and I thought she shared my feelings. I hoped we would stay together for ever. But she grew bored and wanted to continue exploring the world. I couldn't go with her because my grandfather had named me as heir of De Rossi Enterprises, and I was also trying to establish my own fashion label.'

He hadn't thought about Jodie for a long time, Luca mused. Sure, he had been hurt when she'd left him—but he had got over it. So much for everlasting love, he thought cynically.

'Jodie cleared off while I was at a business meeting in Milan, without saying where she was going or how I could contact her. She effectively disappeared out of my life, and I had no idea that she was pregnant with my child when she left. She later admitted that she had decided to bring up our daughter on her own and not tell me I was a father. She only came back to find me when Rosalie started to show early signs of Rett's.'

Athena remembered that Luca had told her Rosalie's mother had been unable to cope with the news that their daughter had an incurable degenerative disease. 'So Jodie left you to care for Rosalie alone?' she murmured.

She thought of the two women Luca had loved in his life. His mother and Jodie. They had both abandoned him, and in Jodie's case she had also abandoned her sick child. It was small wonder that Luca was so scathing about love.

The car drove through the palace gates into a huge courtyard where the helicopter that Lexi had often piloted before her pregnancy was parked. Kadir descended the palace steps to greet them.

Similar in height and build to Luca, his swarthy skin and jet-black hair made a stark contrast to his white robe and headdress. Athena adored her ruggedly handsome brother-in-law, who had made her sister so happy, and she flew into his arms.

'How is baby Faisal?' she asked urgently.

'He's okay.' Kadir gave a strained smile. 'The heart specialist has seen him and things are better than was first thought. I won't go into too many medical details, but Faisal has what is known as a hole in the heart. It might require surgery to repair it in a few months, but there is a chance that the hole will heal on its own.'

They had been walking through the palace while Kadir explained the situation. He hesitated now, outside the nursery.

'Lexi is trying to hide it, but I know she was terrified we could lose Faisal. I want to keep her as calm and unworried as possible.' He glanced from Athena to Luca. 'I must admit we were both shocked when we heard that you two had got married.'

Athena felt herself blush, and she did not know what to say as Luca slipped an arm around her waist.

'I know our decision was sudden,' he said smoothly.

He looked down at Athena's and his sexy smile made her toes curl.

'But once we realised that we felt the same way about each other we didn't want to wait for months while we planned a big wedding—did we, *carissima*?'

Luca was back in performance mode, as he had been in front of the paparazzi in Las Vegas, she reminded herself. The tender expression in his eyes was not real but for Kadir's benefit.

Kadir opened the door, and Athena hurried across the room and flung her arms around her sister. No words were necessary. The bond of love they shared was so strong that they simply held each other. But when they finally drew apart Athena was shocked to see her usually strong-willed, fiery sister looking pale and infinitely fragile.

'Kadir says the specialist thinks the baby will be all right,' she said jerkily, desperate to try and reassure Lexi.

'The situation looks a lot more hopeful,' Lexi said, and

exchanged a look of intense love and trust with her husband that brought tears to Athena's eyes.

This was how marriage should be, she thought. Lexi and Kadir were soulmates, and their love for each other was a bright flame that would never be extinguished.

Lexi leaned over the crib and handed Athena a small bundle. 'Meet your nephew—Faisal Khalif Al Sulaimar.'

Athena's heart turned over as she stared at the baby's tiny screwed-up face and mop of black hair. 'He's beautiful,' she said softly. And deep inside her she felt an ache of maternal longing.

'I *knew* you would go gooey over him,' her sister said. Lexi looked over at Luca. 'I expect you know that Athena is mad about babies? I don't suppose it will be long before you start a family.'

Athena stiffened, and then breathed a sigh of relief when Luca made a comment about them just wanting to enjoy married life for now. She glanced up and wondered why Kadir was frowning—but just then Faisal decided to demonstrate his strong cry, and she forgot about the puzzling expression she had noticed on her brother-in-law's face.

'As you're newlyweds, we've put you and Luca in the tower room,' Lexi had told Athena. But she didn't understand the significance of that, or why her sister had winked at her, until that evening, when a servant escorted them to their room.

'It looks like a sultan's harem…' she said faintly as she looked around the circular room.

The walls were covered in richly coloured silks that matched the satin sheets on a huge circular bed set on a platform in the centre of the room.

'I wonder why there are mirrors on the ceiling…'

Luca's eyes glinted with amusement. 'You *can't* be that

naive.' But perhaps she was, he thought. He could not imagine her ex-fiancé Charlie Fairfax had been an adventurous lover. 'Some people find it erotic to watch themselves making love,' he explained patiently, when she looked at him blankly.

'Oh!' Athena felt hot colour flood her face. She grabbed her suitcase. 'I…um…I think I'll go and take a shower.'

She could not forget the mirrors—or what Luca had said. Had he ever watched himself making love to one of his mistresses? A tremor ran through her as she imagined looking up to see a reflection of herself and Luca on the circular bed, their naked limbs entwined, his body poised above hers. *Sweet heaven!* She covered her scalding cheeks with her hands, shocked by the visions in her mind that had elicited a fierce throb of need deep in her pelvis.

The sense of relief she felt that baby Faisal's heart problem was not life-threatening, together with the relief she'd gained from telling Luca about the sexual assault, meant that she was now able to relax—and focus on the new feelings stirring inside her.

She spent ages drying her hair, conscious of her heart thudding painfully hard in her chest. But she could not put off returning to the bedroom for ever. A decision had to be made. She opened her suitcase and stared at her pink cotton pyjamas sprigged with a daisy motif that she had packed next to the black lace negligee Luca had admired in Las Vegas…

'Stand still,' he ordered when she walked from the en-suite bathroom into the bedroom. He was sitting on the bed, his legs stretched out in front of him and a sketchpad in his hands. 'Hold that pose for two more minutes.'

'What are you doing?'

'Designing a new dress for you.' He glanced at her briefly, before looking back down at the sketch pad as his pen flew across the paper. 'I've decided to make you some-thing special to wear for when we hold a dinner party at Villa De Rossi for my uncle and the other board members of De Rossi Enterprises. I've been inspired by this Ara-bian Nights room,' he added.

Athena's brows lifted. 'Does that mean I'll be wearing a belly dancer's outfit?'

He laughed softly. 'Only in my dreams, *mia bella*.'

Luca finished his drawing and dropped the sketch pad onto the floor.

'Can I ask you something? How are you planning to spend a million pounds? I'm curious,' he said when she looked surprised, 'because you seem uninterested in clothes and jewellery and the usual things that most women consider important.'

She hesitated. During dinner Lexi had asked her about the fund-raising campaign she'd organised for the orphan-age in Jaipur. Athena had felt flustered as she'd replied that the campaign's funds had been boosted by an anonymous donation. In fact the million pounds Luca had paid into her bank account had already been transferred to Cara Tanner, who had arranged for building work on the new orphan-age house and school to begin immediately.

The conversation had led to Luca talking about the char-ity he was patron of, which raised money for research into Rett Syndrome and other genetic illnesses. But, even knowing his charity work, Athena still wondered how Luca would react if she admitted that she had given the entire one million pounds to the orphanage project.

'I...I'm planning to spend the money on a house.'

'That's a good idea. Investing in the property market is a wise investment.'

Keen to change the subject, she glanced around at the silk-lined walls. 'This room is amazing, isn't it? Although we have the same problem we had at the hotel in Las Vegas—only one bed. I wonder which end you're meant to sleep in a circular bed.'

'I don't think the bed is designed to be *slept* in,' Luca said drily.

Her eyes strayed to the mirrored ceiling above the bed. 'Probably not…' she murmured.

'Don't worry.' Luca took pity on her in her obvious embarrassment. 'I'll sleep on the sofa.'

He stood up and stretched his arms above his head, drawing Athena's eyes to his superb musculature. She took a deep breath.

'You don't have to.'

'I suppose it *is* a big bed…' He considered her statement. 'Are you suggesting we sleep on opposite sides of the mattress?'

'Actually…I'm suggesting that we don't sleep at all.'

CHAPTER NINE

THE SILENCE THAT followed Athena's statement was profound. Luca jerked his eyes in her direction and she saw his startled expression change to one of burning intensity as he watched her untie the belt of her silk robe. It slithered to the floor, leaving her in the wisp of a sheer black lace negligee that had definitely not been designed to sleep in.

His eyes narrowed. 'You had better be clear about what you are suggesting,' he said tensely.

She pushed her long hair over her shoulders and felt a tingle of anticipation as Luca stared at her breasts, with their swollen nipples visible through the semi-transparent negligee.

'I want you,' she told him simply. He frowned, and she said quickly, 'I won't change my mind, or freeze on you like before. I've allowed what happened when I was eighteen to affect the way I live my life for too long.'

She met his gaze, and her voice was steady.

'I'm determined to put the past behind me. I have tried to deny the chemistry that exists between us, but…but I'm done with fighting a battle I can't win,' she admitted.

'Athena…' Luca's voice was unsteady, and he could feel his heart beating faster than normal beneath his breastbone.

How ironic was it that the man dubbed by the paparazzi the 'Italian Stallion' had been reduced to the state of a hormone-fuelled youth by the most unsophisticated, unassuming woman he had ever met? he brooded. Somehow he needed to regain control of himself, but the almost painful hardness of his arousal was an indication of how turned on he was by the sight of Athena's gorgeous, ripe breasts which were in danger of bursting out of her nightgown.

'Come here, *piccola*.'

Luca's husky endearment dismissed Athena's last lingering doubts about what she was doing. What she was about to do, she silently amended as she took the few steps required to reach where he was standing next to the bed.

She had thought she would feel shy, or nervous, but she felt neither of those things as he put his arms around her and drew her towards him. The spicy tang of his aftershave intoxicated her senses, and with a low moan she pressed herself against him and tilted her head as he angled his mouth over hers and claimed her lips with a bone-shaking passion mixed with a tenderness that enchanted her heart.

Luca lifted her onto the bed without breaking the kiss and lay down next to her, running his hands over her body and leaving a trail of fire wherever he touched her.

'I have fantasised about doing this since Las Vegas.' He traced his lips down her throat to the edge of her negligee, where the dark pink tips of her nipples were clearly visible through the sheer material. *'Bella...'* he murmured, before he closed his mouth around one hard peak and suckled her through the black lace.

Athena gave a gasp of pleasure when he peeled the damp material away and bared her breasts to his glittering gaze. For the first time in her life she did not hate her breasts for being too big. Luca's appreciation of her body and his respect for her, shown by the almost reverent way he caressed her, made her glad of her curvy figure.

The realisation that Peter Fitch no longer had power over

her and she was finally free of the dark memories of the past gave her confidence to touch Luca as he was touching her. She swiftly undid his shirt buttons, as if she'd had plenty of practice undressing a man, and pushed the material aside so that she could run her hands over his naked chest.

His bronze skin was warm and silken, with a covering of dark hair that arrowed down over his abdomen. Athena traced the fuzz of hair down to the waistband of his trousers and drew a startled breath when she felt the huge bulge of his arousal.

'Now you know what you do to me,' he said thickly. He lifted his head and looked into her eyes. 'I could die with wanting you. I've never felt like this before.'

It was the truth, Luca thought. His desire for Athena was beyond anything he had felt for any other woman. Her courage in facing up to the traumatic incident in her past filled him with admiration and he knew he must not rush her, even though his blood was on fire and he was desperate to appease his hunger for her.

He stroked his hand over her sheer lace knickers and almost forgot his good intentions when he felt the dampness of her arousal.

'We'll take things slowly,' he promised—as much to himself as to Athena. 'You're trembling.' He frowned. 'You are not afraid of me, are you *carissima*?'

He assumed that as a consequence of the sexual assault when she was younger it would take her a while to relax with a lover.

'No,' she assured him, 'it's just that this is all new.'

Luca lowered his head and flicked his tongue into her navel. Her soft moan of pleasure urged him to trail his mouth lower, but his brain questioned her curious statement.

'What do you mean, new?'

Athena wished he would continue, would slip his hand inside her knickers and touch her where she longed to be touched, but Luca propped himself on one elbow and looked down at her with a puzzled expression in his eyes. She knew it was only fair to tell him the truth.

'The way you are touching me is new,' she admitted.

'Do you mean that Charlie never spent time on foreplay before making love to you?'

'I've never slept with Charlie...or anyone else.' She swallowed as she watched shocked comprehension slowly cross his face. 'I'm a virgin.'

The only other time in his life that Luca had been rendered speechless was when he had read his grandmother's will. 'But you're...'

'Twenty-five. Yes, I'm aware that I'm an oddity,' Athena muttered.

She had half assumed, half hoped, that Luca would have guessed she was inexperienced when she told him about the sexual assault. But he rolled away from her, and in the mirror above the bed she watched his expression change from shock to something she could not read as his chiselled features hardened.

'You were engaged to Charlie for a year. How the *hell* are you still a virgin?'

'He was happy to wait until we were married before we had sex.' She bit her lip.

'He must have had the patience of a saint to resist his desire for you for a year.' A thought occurred to Luca. 'You told me you discovered on your wedding day that Charlie had been unfaithful. Did he turn to another woman because he had agreed to wait until you were his wife before you had sex?'

'Sort of...'

Athena felt embarrassed by her nakedness now it was

evident that Luca was turned off by her lack of experience. She sat up and pulled the purple satin sheet around
her body, wishing she could crawl away and hide.

'Charlie never desired me,' she said in a low voice. 'On
the morning of the wedding I found him in bed with his
best man, Dominic. He admitted he had asked me to marry
him to conceal the fact that he's gay.'

'Why didn't you *say* anything—instead of allowing
Charlie to blame you for calling off the wedding and accusing you of having an affair with me?'

'I had realised that I didn't love him, but I couldn't betray his secret relationship with Dominic. Lord Fairfax is
an ex-Royal Marine, and Charlie has spent his life trying
to live up to his father's expectations. It was one thing we
had in common. I've always been a disappointment to *my*
parents,' she said ruefully.

'*Santa Madre*, what a mess.'

Luca rolled onto his back and stared up at the mirrored
ceiling at the image of himself and Athena lying on the
circular bed. The knowledge that she was naked beneath
the sheet she had covered herself with evoked a sharp tug
of desire in his groin. But, *Dio*, she was a *virgin*—and he
was in dangerous territory.

'What were you were hoping for when you decided that
you wanted me to be your first lover?' His eyes narrowed
on her pink cheeks. 'Because if you were hoping for hearts
and flowers and for me to fall in love with you, then you
chose the wrong man,' he said bluntly.

She flushed. 'I don't—'

'In Vegas you said that you believe the act of making
love should be a physical demonstration of being *in* love.'

'I think I felt that at the time because Peter Fitch had
made me feel sex was somehow dirty. In my mind I thought
that if I only slept with a man I loved it couldn't be wrong.

But now I understand how I had been affected by the past. You pointed out that there is nothing wrong with two people who are attracted to each other taking pleasure in sex. I'm not in love with you,' she told Luca earnestly. 'I chose you to give me my first sexual experience because I trust you, and because I...I think you are an honourable man.'

An honourable man! For the second time in the space of ten minutes Luca did not know what to say. He had earned many accolades—a great lover, a gifted designer, a brilliant businessman—but people had always admired him for his achievements in the fashion industry, or for his wealth. Athena did not care about those things. She had said that she trusted him.

His mother had abandoned him, his grandmother had told him he was worthless so often that he'd believed her, and Jodie had thrown his love back in his face. But Athena believed he was an honourable man, and to Luca it felt like the greatest accolade of all.

Luca seemed lost in his thoughts, and as silence stretched between them Athena remembered Charlie's taunt: *'Who do you think will want a twenty-five-year-old virgin?'*

'I suppose you're put off by my inexperience,' she said dully.

She sensed him shoot her a sharp glance.

'I'm not *put off* by you.' But if he had known she was a virgin he would not have married her, Luca thought silently. 'When our marriage ends in a year's time you deserve to fall in love with a man who loves you and will propose a proper marriage.'

She grimaced. 'After running away from my society wedding and then having a quickie wedding in Las Vegas I won't be in any rush to plan another wedding.'

Her eyes kept straying to the mirror above the bed and

to the reflection of Luca, looking sinfully sexy sprawled on the satin sheets. She wondered if he was wishing he was here in this Arabian Nights room with one of his sophisticated, sexually experienced mistresses instead of her. *Of course he is*, taunted a voice in her head.

'You're too tall for the sofa, so I'll sleep on it,' she muttered, keeping the sheet wrapped around her as she wriggled over to the edge of the mattress.

He watched her awkward progress across the bed with amusement. 'You look like a caterpillar.'

'It's okay, Luca. I *know* I have the sex appeal of a creature you'd find crawling out from under a stone,' she choked.

The wobble in her voice got to him.

'You know I didn't mean it literally.'

He caught hold of the edge of the sheet she was clutching to her like a security blanket and gave a hard tug. She gave a cry of surprise as the slippery satin was jerked from her hands and unravelled from around her body.

'You know I find you incredibly sexy,' Luca told her in a fierce voice as he pushed her flat on her back and knelt over her.

His brain was insisting that this was a bad idea, that he should walk away and leave Athena to give her innocence to a man who would love her in the future. But he'd caught the glint of tears in her sapphire-blue eyes and he hated himself because he knew he had hurt her feelings.

Her self-confidence had been destroyed by the vile monster who had sexually assaulted her. Athena must have dug deep to find the courage to ask him to make love to her and now she was mortified, believing he had rejected her because he did not desire her, when the truth was very different.

He lay down next to her and skimmed his hand over

her stomach and up to her breasts. 'See how beautiful you are…' he murmured, directing her gaze to the mirrored ceiling above the bed.

The contrast of her milky-skinned body against the purple satin sheets was intensely erotic. She reminded him of a Renaissance painting by one of the great masters, with her glorious hair spilling over her shoulders and her ripe, curvaceous body so utterly perfect that a saint would be tempted by her.

And he was no saint, Luca thought with wry self-derision.

In the mirror he watched his dark fingers stroke her white breasts with their rosy-tipped nipples. He watched her eyes darken as he rolled first one nipple and then its twin between his thumb and forefinger until each peak was pebble hard.

'Luca…' she whispered.

Her breathing quickened as he bent his head and anointed one nipple with feather-soft kisses before drawing the nub into his mouth and suckling her until she gave a thin cry and he transferred his mouth to her other breast.

Athena's gaze was riveted on the twin reflections in the mirror of her and Luca. Her dark nipples stood out against her pale breasts and were swollen and reddened from where he had sucked them. She looked wanton and shameless, her near-naked body sprawled on the satin sheet for his delectation—*and hers*, she thought with a shiver of excitement as she watched him trail his fingers over her stomach and hook them into the waistband of her knickers. The sheer black lace afforded little protection from his predatory gaze, but when he slowly pulled her panties down her thighs she felt suddenly vulnerable—because Luca was the first man to see her naked.

Perhaps he sensed her slight hesitation, because he lowered his mouth to hers and kissed her deeply, demandingly, until she relaxed and parted her lips to allow him to explore her with his tongue.

He lifted his head and his eyes burned into hers. 'Watch me touching you,' he said huskily. 'Sex isn't shameful, *carissima*. It's beautiful—just as you are.'

She stared up at the mirror and her heart jolted against her ribs as she watched Luca push her thighs apart and slip his hand between them. She felt him press his finger against her moist opening, and gently, oh, so gently, push forward until the tip of his digit was inside her.

'Good?' he queried softly.

She nodded, unable to find the words to describe the sensuous pleasure that swept through her as Luca slid his finger deeper into her. She felt herself relax as her body opened for him like the petals of a flower unfurling.

'You see how your body is ready for me?' he murmured.

Athena found it incredibly erotic to watch her reflection as Luca caressed her, to see her face flush with sexual heat as he swirled his finger inside her in an exquisite dance that evoked a trembling sensation deep in her pelvis. And as she watched her body's response to his touch and saw *his* reaction—the sudden tautness of his features and the streaks of colour that winged along his cheekbones—she no longer felt shy or nervous.

Luca made her feel beautiful and powerful. There was no shame in admitting that she wanted him—no shame in showing him how much she desired him and how impatient she felt for him to make love to her.

She cupped his face in her hands and pulled his mouth down on hers, kissing him with a passion that made him groan.

'*Mia bella*, we need to take things slowly. I want to make it perfect for you.'

So much for his assumption that he would be in control,

Luca thought ruefully. Athena's eagerness was testing his self-control to its limit, and his fingers were all thumbs as he fumbled with his zip and finally managed to remove his trousers without any of his usual finesse. He pulled off his boxer shorts and, hearing her swift intake of breath when she saw the hard length of him, reinforced his determination to concentrate on making Athena's first sexual experience as pleasurable as he could.

He kissed her mouth, and something fleeting and indefinable tugged on his insides when he felt the sweet sensuality of her response. He moved lower and kissed her breasts, before trailing his lips over her stomach and lower, to the triangle of neatly trimmed brown curls between her thighs.

'Luca...'

Uncertainty edged into Athena's voice as she stared up at the mirror and watched Luca's dark head move down her body. His mouth left a trail of fire across her skin and her thighs trembled as he pushed them apart. She realised with a mixture of shock and excitement what he was about to do.

'I don't think...' she protested faintly, but he stopped her frantic attempt to close her legs by sliding his hands beneath her bottom and angling her to his satisfaction.

'Don't think...just feel,' he ordered, before he lowered his head.

The first stroke of his tongue over her sensitised flesh caused Athena to gasp and jerk her hips. But Luca held her firmly as he proceeded to use his mouth and tongue to devastating effect, decimating her inhibitions as he bestowed upon her the most intimate caresses of all and brought her closer and closer to the edge of somewhere that remained frustratingly just out of reach.

The flick of his tongue across her clitoris drove her

higher, and she twisted her fingers in the satin sheet as she tried to hold on to her sanity.

He lifted his head and she gave a choked cry as her body quivered like an overstrung bow. 'Watch and see how beautiful you are when you climax,' he said thickly.

In the mirror she saw his dark head nestled between her pale thighs. It was shockingly intimate, but she could not stop watching him making love to her with his tongue and his fingers. The pressure inside her was building, and the need for fulfilment was so urgent that she arched her hips, seeking the heat of his mouth.

And then suddenly she was there, poised on the tip of a wave's crest, before the wave broke and she was swept into a maelstrom of exquisite sensations that she was sure nothing could surpass.

She was wrong. As Luca moved over her and she felt his naked body pressing down on hers she realised that the journey had not finished—it was only just beginning.

He positioned himself so that the swollen tip of his arousal pressed against her, and then he slowly eased forward and entered her with tender care, taking his time so that her tight muscles stretched to accommodate him.

Athena found the sensation of him filling her new and wondrous. There was a brief moment of discomfort as her body tried to resist him. He immediately stilled and looked into her eyes, his own dark with remorse.

'Did I hurt you? Do you want me to stop?'

'No!' She wrapped her arms around his back to prevent him from withdrawing. 'Don't you dare stop,' she whispered.

The delicious spasms that had racked her body when Luca had brought her to orgasm with his mouth were beginning again—little ripples that intensified as he began to move inside her. She soon learned the rhythm he set as he thrust into her, gently at first, and then harder and faster, as their breathing quickened and their hearts thundered in unison.

Luca rolled onto his back, taking Athena with him so that now she was on top. She braced her hands on his shoulders and he moved her so that she was sitting astride him. Their new position allowed him access to her breasts, and he heard her gasps of pleasure as he sucked one hard pink nipple and then the other while he held her hips and showed her how to ride him.

'See how beautiful sex is…how beautiful you are,' he said hoarsely, directing her gaze once more to the mirror above them.

Her body was peaches and cream, her full breasts ripe for his mouth, and she tasted of honey and nectar. She was a goddess, and Luca was entranced by her as she moved her body in perfect accord with his and the fire inside him burned hotter and fiercer. He was losing his mind— certainly he was losing control. He wrapped a strand of her silky chestnut hair around his fingers and tugged her forward so that he could kiss her mouth endlessly, hungrily, wishing these moments could last for ever but at the same time desperate to climax inside her until he was utterly sated.

She reared above him and tipped her head back, her long hair swirling around her shoulders. In the mirror Luca watched her expression change from startled surprise to wondrous amazement at the moment she climaxed. He felt her body convulse as her muscles contracted around his shaft, and the pressure inside him exploded like a volcanic eruption.

Through the waves of his own pleasure he was determined to extend hers, and he rubbed his finger over her clitoris until she trembled and came again, sobbing his name in the throes of her orgasm until at last she slumped onto his chest and he enfolded her in his arms and held her tightly against his heart.

Was it because it had been new for her that sex with Athena had felt like a uniquely special experience for him? Luca wondered. He had found her untutored responses a thousand times more exciting than the honed skills of his sexually experienced mistresses.

But the idea that she somehow belonged to him made him realise he was on dangerous ground. He had no right to feel possessive of her because one day, without a shadow of a doubt, he would set her free from their marriage deal. That was the way it was, the way it had to be, and there was no point wishing for something that could never be his, Luca told himself firmly.

Yet he could not resist threading his fingers through her silky hair, and he felt a deep reluctance to withdraw from her when it felt so right, so complete, for their bodies to be joined. He could have stayed like that for ever, but at last she lifted her head and smiled at him, and for a split second he felt an iron fist squeeze the lifeblood out of his heart.

Athena loved the sensuous drift of Luca's hand stroking up and down her spine almost as much as she had loved the sensation of being filled and possessed by him when he had made love to her. She felt utterly relaxed and at the same time incredibly alive—as if every cell on her body was fizzing like champagne.

When he shifted position she thought he would move away from her, but instead he pulled her close, so that her face was pressed against his chest, and she fell asleep listening to the steady thud of his heart.

CHAPTER TEN

'YOU MUST TELL Athena the truth, Luca.'

Athena opened her eyes to find the tower room flooded with sunlight, and a glance at her watch revealed that it was mid-morning. For a moment she thought she had dreamed that she'd heard a man speaking, but now she heard two muffled voices and recognised Luca's sexy, husky accent and the deep tones of her brother-in-law. The two men must be in the sitting room which adjoined the bedroom where she and Luca had slept.

Not that they had done much sleeping! She felt hot all over as she recalled that Luca had made love to her twice more after the first time, and had combined fierce passion with unexpected tenderness. It had been an incredible night, but the fact that she was alone in the circular bed this morning seeded doubts in her head.

She frowned as she tried to make sense of Kadir's words. What was the truth that Luca had to tell her?

She sat up and pushed her hair out of her eyes, puzzling over the muffled conversation she had overheard, but at that moment the door opened and Luca walked into the bedroom. Athena's heart missed a beat. He looked gorgeous in black jeans and a polo shirt, his dark hair ruffled and his eyes glinting with sensual heat as his gaze dropped to her bare breasts.

It was ridiculous to feel shy after he had seen and kissed

every centimetre of her body last night, she told herself. But she still pulled the sheet up to her neck and heard Luca give a soft laugh.

'It's too late to try to hide yourself from me, *mia bella*, after the amazing sex we enjoyed last night.' He leaned over the bed and tilted her chin so that she was forced to look at him. 'And I *know* you enjoyed the night as much as I did,' he stated, with enviable self-confidence.

'If you enjoyed it so much why did you get up this morning without waking me?'

'At dinner last night you heard me arrange to go riding with Kadir this morning. We had to leave at dawn—before the desert sun was too hot for the horses.'

She did remember now, and her tension dissolved with the realisation that Luca had not left her because he regretted making love to her.

'I heard you and Kadir talking a few minutes ago.' She remembered the strange comment she thought she had heard her brother-in-law make. 'What were you talking about?'

He shrugged. 'Nothing important.'

Athena did not need to know the details of his conversation with Kadir, Luca assured himself. He understood Kadir's concerns, but Kadir was unaware that his marriage to Athena was not real.

On the other hand, he mused, there was no reason *not* to tell her the truth about himself—especially as she had met his daughter and knew about Rosalie's illness. But he had only revealed his situation to a few trusted friends, Kadir being one of them. It was surprisingly difficult to discuss a matter that was so deeply personal to him, but as he looked into Athena's sapphire-blue eyes Luca acknowledged that she was the only woman he had ever known whom he trusted implicitly.

'To spare your sister further worry while she is worried about baby Faisal we have kept up the pretence that our marriage is real while we are in Zenhab. But that has given Kadir cause for concern.'

'Concern about what, exactly?'

Luca wondered why his heart was beating painfully hard. 'There is something about me that I haven't told you—something that *if* our marriage was real I *should* have told you.'

Athena said nothing, simply stared at him, and after a moment Luca continued.

'I explained previously that Rosalie's illness, Rett Syndrome, is a genetic disorder. Most cases are sporadic, meaning that there is no reason why children—mainly girls—develop the disease apart from bad luck. Rett's usually strikes randomly, but studies have proved that in very rare circumstances a man can carry the gene mutation responsible for the disease, and he will *always* pass that mutation on to his female offspring.'

A nerve flickered in Luca's jaw.

'After Rosalie was diagnosed I had tests which showed that I carry the gene mutation for Rett's in my DNA.' He heard Athena's swiftly indrawn breath and saw the shock on her face that she could not hide. 'It is because of *me* that Rosalie's life is slowly being destroyed by a terrible illness,' he said harshly.

Athena's reaction of stunned silence exacerbated his familiar feelings of pain and guilt.

'Obviously if I had known I was a carrier, with the potential to pass a dreadful debilitating disease to my daughter, I would not have risked having a child.'

'But you didn't know. How could you have done?' Athena said gently. 'You said Jodie hadn't even told you she was pregnant when she left you and went back to

New Zealand. It must have been devastating when Rosalie's illness was diagnosed, but you can't blame yourself, Luca.'

He *did* blame himself, though, she realised as she stared at his hard-boned face and the rigid line of his jaw.

Her heart ached for him. She had seen how much he adored Rosalie. And not only did Luca have to watch his daughter's health deteriorate, but he also felt responsible for her illness. There must be implications for any more children in the future, too. Rett Syndrome was incurable, and she could understand why he would not want to risk passing on the mutated gene he carried to another child.

'Whether or not I blame myself, it doesn't help Rosalie,' Luca said grimly.

He looked away from Athena, rejecting the sympathy he could see in her eyes. His emotions felt raw, and he was in danger of admitting to her that sometimes he cried when he saw his daughter suffering—that sometimes, deep in his heart, he wondered if he *was* as worthless as his grandmother had told him he was as a boy, and that Rosalie's illness was punishment for his sins.

'All I can do is ensure that Rosalie's life is as good as it can be in the circumstances, and that she is as comfortable and happy as possible.'

He strode back over to the bed, and his eyes were hard as he stared down at Athena. 'That's the reason I married you—the reason I paid you to be my wife. To keep Villa De Rossi so that Rosalie can live the rest of her life in the home she loves.'

Their marriage was a business deal with certain rules attached. There was no harm in reminding Athena of those rules, Luca decided.

'Last night was fun.' He looked into her sapphire-blue eyes and remembered how they had darkened with desire when he had made love to her. 'But that's all it was,' he warned.

'Do you mean it was a one-night stand?'

Athena bit her lip. Perhaps, despite Luca's insistence that he had enjoyed having sex with her, he had found her lack of sexual experience boring.

He looked surprised. 'No, what I mean is that just because we've slept together it doesn't change the fact that our marriage is temporary and in a year from now we will divorce, as agreed. What I'm trying to say is that I would like to have a sexual relationship with you, but there is no chance I will fall in love with you.'

'No hearts and flowers?'

She remembered what he had said when she had asked him to be her first lover. From the very beginning, when he had proposed his outrageous marriage deal, Luca had been completely honest with her, Athena acknowledged. If she chose not to sleep with him again she knew he would respect her decision.

But why deny them what they both wanted? she asked herself. Luca had proved last night how much he desired her, and he had helped her to bury the ghosts from her past for good. He had shown her that sex was not shameful but beautiful—and he made her *feel* beautiful...especially when his eyes gleamed with a predatory hunger, as they were doing now when he looked at her.

A heady sense of power swept through her as she let go of the satin sheet so that it slid down her breasts and Luca gave a low growl of appreciation.

'I need a shower—and I need you,' he told her as he scooped her into his arms and strode into the en-suite bathroom.

She helped him strip off his clothes and he pulled her into the shower cubicle with him and turned on the tap, so that they were deluged by a powerful jet of water. They took turns to slide a bar of soap over each other's bodies—although Athena breathlessly pointed out that he did not need to lavish *quite* so much time on washing her breasts.

His low rumble of laughter turned to a groan when she took the soap and traced it over his abdomen, before circling his arousal with her hand and caressing him until he muttered an oath and lifted her against him.

'Wrap your legs around me,' he commanded, even while he slid his fingers inside her and brought her to the edge.

She cried out as he suckled her nipples, setting her body alight, and when he entered her with one smooth, powerful thrust, she dug her nails into his shoulders and clung on for dear life.

He took her hard and fast. She should have been shocked by his primal passion, but she loved how hungry he was for her, loved each deep stroke he made inside her.

They reached the pinnacle together and climaxed simultaneously in a glorious explosion of pleasure. And Athena told herself she must have *imagined* it had felt as though their souls as well as their bodies were joined.

Autumn was slipping inexorably into winter, and the last few leaves falling from the trees looked like orange-and-gold confetti, while the mountain peaks beyond Lake Como were wearing their first snowy overcoats.

Luca parked his car outside the front of Villa De Rossi and tightened his mouth with frustration when he glanced at his watch and realised that the dinner party he was hosting for his great-uncle Emilio and the other board members was due to start in less than an hour.

After a week of tense negotiations and boardroom battles in Japan in his role as chairman of De Rossi Enterprises, all he wanted to do now that he was home was spend some time with his daughter, and then a enjoy a quiet dinner with Athena before he took her to bed.

In truth, he was impatient to take his wife to bed and satisfy his hunger for her before he even thought about dinner. Five nights was the longest time they had spent apart since the first time they had slept together in Zenhab, and he had missed Athena more than he would have believed possible. And he hadn't only missed making love to her, Luca acknowledged, although he *had* found himself thinking about her gorgeous, curvaceous body at the most inappropriate times while he had been away.

It had been a new experience for him to be distracted by thoughts of a woman—but Athena was not *any* woman. During the past weeks that they had been living together properly as man and wife at the Villa De Rossi he had learned that her sweet nature hid a surprisingly strong will, and her newfound self-confidence meant that she was not afraid to argue with him—which he found a novelty, because he had only known women who either sulked or sobbed in order to get their own way.

And their few arguments had been resolved by mind-blowing sex that had left him feeling as if he had conquered Mount Everest, as if he was king of the world—because he had never forgotten that Athena had said she believed he was an honourable man, and her words had finally banished the memories of his grandmother telling him he was worthless, a *bastardo*, and not a true De Rossi.

Luca walked into the villa and was surprised to see a stunning floral arrangement on the hall table.

'Geomar.' He greeted the butler, who was hurrying across the hall towards him. 'Did you manage to book another catering company to organise tonight's dinner party?'

'Unfortunately not—and, as you know, the company I *had* booked cancelled at the last minute,' Geomar explained. 'But Signora De Rossi has organised everything. She made the decorative flower arrangements herself, Elizavetta is cooking the menu Signora De Rossi planned for dinner, and some girls from the village will be waitresses for the evening—including my own daughter.'

The butler looked rueful as a door opened and a small boy came into the hall, followed by his baby sister, who toddled after him.

'I'm afraid my daughter has also brought her children,' Geomar said. 'I have tried to persuade them to stay in the kitchen, but Signora Rossi has allowed them to play in the house. She loves to see the *bambini*.'

'I know she does,' Luca said, in a non-committal tone intended to disguise his sudden tension.

Geomar smiled. 'Perhaps before long you and the *signora* will be blessed with a family.'

A nerve flickered in Luca's jaw. The staff did not know that his marriage was temporary and that he had paid Athena a million pounds to be his wife. But it was important that he reminded *himself* of that fact, he thought grimly. Maybe he also needed to remind Athena that the reason they had married had nothing to do with love, or planning to spend a lifetime together—all the usual reasons why people got married. And definitely not because they hoped to have a family.

He had made it clear that all he could give Athena was sex and that was all he wanted from her. But lately he had caught her looking at him in a certain way that sounded alarm bells in his head. He had seen that hopeful look on women's faces before. Past experience had taught him that it always ended in tears, recriminations and hurt—and he really did not want to hurt Athena.

She was sweet and kind to everyone, and the staff loved her. And she was caring and endlessly patient with his daughter, often spending hours during the day with Rosalie, reading to her and pushing her wheelchair round the garden.

For the past few weeks Luca had felt increasingly aware that Athena deserved so much more than a sham marriage—and she definitely deserved to marry a better man than him.

He glanced towards the top of the stairs, and his breath became lodged beneath his breastbone when he saw her. The blue velvet gown he had designed for her matched the sapphire-blue of her eyes. The dress was maxi-length, with a full skirt, and had a tight-fitting bodice that displayed her slender waist and full breasts to perfection. Her chestnut hair fell almost to her waist in a silken curtain, and she looked so breathtakingly lovely that Luca felt a curious ache in his chest.

The ache intensified when she walked down the stairs, as graceful and elegant as a princess. 'I've missed you,' she greeted him softly.

He felt a sudden spurt of anger. She had no right to miss him. Their marriage was not like that and it never would be. She had no right to look at him with a dreamy expression in her eyes that was a sure sign she was weaving fantasies about him and their relationship.

Plenty of women had done the same thing in the past and he hadn't cared. The realisation that he cared enough about Athena to want to protect her from losing her pride and, even worse, her heart over him showed him that he must take action now. And if he felt a twist of regret in his gut it was *his* problem and he would get over it, Luca assured himself.

'Geomar tells me you have taken charge of organising the dinner party. Thank you.'

'It was no problem. Elizavetta is working wonders in the

kitchen, and everything else is under control. You might just want to check the wine I had brought up from the cellar. I *think* the wines I've chosen will suit the food...'

The wine appreciation-course she had gone on before her wedding to Charlie had been useful after all, Athena mused. She was surprised by how much she remembered, and felt fairly confident of her choice of wine to serve at the dinner party. It was funny how she no longer felt daunted by organising a dinner party for twenty guests, and yet it had been such an ordeal when she had been engaged to Charlie and desperate to impress his sophisticated friends.

She was a different person from the awkward, accident-prone virgin with a bucketload of hang-ups she had been a few months ago, she acknowledged. And she had Luca to thank for her transformation.

When she had first met him she had believed the image of him portrayed by the paparazzi of an irresponsible playboy. But she had learned that Luca took his responsibilities for his work with his fashion label, for his role with the De Rossi company established by his great-grandfather, and most of all for his disabled daughter, very seriously. His devotion to Rosalie was one reason why Athena was convinced that beneath his seemingly impenetrable steel shell he *did* have a heart—despite the fact that he had once told her he lacked that crucial piece of his anatomy.

Her wasn't always cool and reserved, she reminded herself. Mostly when he made love to her he was in control, and he brought her to numerous orgasms before he took his own pleasure. But sometimes his iron control slipped and she glimpsed emotions in his eyes that filled her with hope for their marriage which had begun so inauspiciously.

She smiled at him, unable to keep the news she had

received earlier in the day to herself any longer. 'I have something exciting to tell you. You remember I sent the children's books I wrote to an agent? Well, the agent phoned today and she said she has sold my stories to a major publishing company—and they have offered me a contract for more books!'

'That's wonderful.' Luca dipped his head and brushed his lips over her cheek.

She gave a playful pout. 'I was hoping for a *proper* kiss.'

Athena was disappointed when he stepped away from her.

'I've been travelling all day in this suit,' he murmured. 'I'll quickly shower and change before the guests arrive.'

'Your great-uncle Emilio is already here. He said you had asked for a meeting with him before dinner. He's waiting in the library—'

Athena's voice broke off as she watched Geomar's grandchildren run across the hall towards her. Marco and his little sister Mia were adorable, and she scooped the toddler up in her arms with practised ease after working for several years as a nursery nurse.

'Let's go and find your *mamma*.'

'You will be a good mother when you have your own *bambini*,' Geomar commented.

Luca watched Athena blush, and she darted him a quick glance that revealed more of her hopes and dreams than perhaps she realised.

It could not go on, he realised as he turned and strode up the stairs, his jaw and his mind implacably set on the course he was convinced he must follow.

The dinner party had been a great success, Athena thought later that evening, after the last guests had departed. The food and wine had been excellent, and the long table in the dining room had looked beautiful set with silverware, crystal glasses and the centrepiece of red roses and trailing ivy that she had arranged. Her only concern was Luca, who had barely spoken to her all evening.

He had emerged from the library grim-faced after the private meeting with his great-uncle. During dinner she had been aware of his amber gaze burning into her, but every time she had smiled at him he hadn't smiled back, and his hard features had been indecipherable.

At least now that the guests had gone she and Luca could be alone—perhaps she would discover what his problem was.

She frowned when she noticed a light shining from beneath the door of his study.

'I thought you had gone up to bed,' she said, after she had knocked and he'd curtly told her to come in. Her eyes flew to the suitcase by his desk. 'Are you going somewhere?'

He was standing in front of a fire that had burned down to glowing embers in the grate, and did not turn his head as he answered her.

'I'm driving to Milan tonight because I have an early meeting in the morning.'

'But you've only just come back from a trip.'

Athena's stomach muscles tightened with tension, and she wished he would turn around so that she could see his face.

'Luca, what's wrong?' she said softly. 'Was there something wrong with the dinner party?'

'No, it was perfect—thanks to you.'

She bit her lip and forced herself to ask the question that had filled her with sick dread all evening, since she had started to wonder if he had grown tired of her. 'Do you have a mistress in Milan who you are going to see?'

Luca hesitated, tempted to lie so that Athena would leave him without further discussion. But when he glanced at her and saw her scared expression he couldn't do it. One way or another he knew it was inevitable that he was going to hurt her—but he had no wish to shatter her self-confidence, and he could not forget that she had called him an honourable man.

'No.' He watched the ripple of relief cross her expressive features and hardened his jaw. 'But why would you care if I *did* have a mistress? Our marriage is not real. We made a deal.'

'I know we did.'

Athena did not know how to handle this new dark and dangerously unpredictable Luca. She acknowledged that it would probably be better if she went up to bed and left him alone, but she sensed that his black mood had something to do with their relationship.

'But I thought over the past weeks we had grown... close,' she ventured.

'We've had a lot of sex,' he said tersely. 'And it was fun. But I warned you not to hope for hearts and flowers.'

He walked across to the table, where Geomar had earlier left a tray with a bottle of Scotch for his meeting with his uncle, and poured a generous measure into a glass.

'Tonight I made a new deal with my great-uncle Emilio.' He took a mouthful of whisky and savoured its fire at the back of his throat before he looked over at Athena. 'Emilio has always been desperate for the chairmanship of De Rossi Enterprises, which is why he hoped I would fail to meet the terms of my grandmother's will, and why he wanted to prove that my marriage to you is a sham.'

'You must have given him all the evidence he needs—you virtually ignored me all evening,' she muttered.

'It is no longer necessary for us to continue the pretence that we are happily married. I have agreed to hand over the role of chairman to Emilio. In return he will not seek to prevent me from using the De Rossi name for my fashion label, and more importantly he won't challenge my right to inherit Villa De Rossi. My lawyers have managed to overturn the clause in Nonna Violetta's will which stipulated that I must be married for one year before I can inherit. The villa is mine from now, and Rosalie can live here for the rest of her life. I have got everything I wanted.'

Luca said all this in an unemotional voice, and it felt like nails being driven into Athena's heart.

'And you have one million pounds, as we agreed. You don't have to pretend to be my loving wife any more. You are free to leave and get on with your life.'

Athena tried to swallow past the boulder that had formed in her throat. She couldn't believe that Luca was sending her away. She had not just *imagined* they had been happy since he had brought her to live at Villa De Rossi, and she *had* sensed a developing closeness between them—even though he insisted that they had only been having sex.

Her pride urged her to walk away, as he seemed to want her to do. And it was what the old Athena would have done. But she had changed from the nervous mouse who had never stood up for herself, and she wasn't prepared to give up without a fight.

'I haven't *pretended* to be your loving wife,' she said huskily. 'It's the truth. I…I love you, Luca. I know you warned me not to fall in love with you, but I couldn't help it. You helped me to step out of the past and leave behind my memories of being assaulted. You showed me that it didn't matter if I failed to meet my parents' expectations as long as I met my own. You gave me the confidence to be *me*,' she said simply, 'and it is because of your confidence in me that I have been offered a publishing contract for my children's books.'

She took a step towards him, but halted when he turned away to stare back at the dying fire.

'Don't make me out as a hero, Athena, because I am certainly not one,' Luca said with savage self-contempt. 'I can't be the man you want me to be—or the husband you deserve.'

'How do you know what I want?'

'I know you want a family…children of your own. I saw the wistful expression on your face when you held your sister's baby, and I've watched you with Geomar's grandchildren. You were born to be a mother. But I can't give you children. After I found out that I am a carrier of Rett Syndrome I had a vasectomy, so that I would never have to watch another child of mine suffer as Rosalie suffers.'

He swung round to face her.

'You're shocked. Don't deny it. I can see it in your eyes. I couldn't risk having another child. Now I'm setting you free so that you can fall in love with a man who loves you and who can give you children.'

'What if I don't *want* to be set free?' she said stubbornly. 'I'm not shocked by the news that you can't have more children. I guessed as much when you told me you carry the mutant gene which caused Rosalie's illness.'

Athena plucked up her courage and walked over to him.

'I have had time to think about the fact that we wouldn't be able to have children of our own, and it doesn't change how I feel about you. There are other ways we could have a family. I also have an idea why you shy away from commitment. It doesn't take a genius to work out that, having been rejected by your mother, your grandmother and

Jodie, you in turn have rejected love.' She put a tentative hand on his arm. 'You are the only husband I want, Luca. I love you. And if you love me—'

'But I *don't*—that's the point.'

The fire in the grate had died completely, leaving behind a pile of black ash. Luca stirred the debris with the tip of his shoe, and did not, *could not* bring himself to turn his head and look at Athena.

'I appreciate your theory about the reason for my supposed emotional retardation,' he said sardonically, 'but the truth is that I preferred my life without the addition of a wife and I'm ending our marriage deal.'

Snow lay thick on the ground, and the roofs of the houses around Lake Como looked as though they were covered in a layer of white icing. People said it was the harshest winter they could remember, and Luca knew he had never felt such bitter, biting cold. It had turned his heart into a lump of ice in his chest.

Even the roaring fire in his study at Villa De Rossi that Geomar so assiduously tended failed to warm him. He felt dead inside, and brutally alone—as if Athena had ripped his soul from him when she had left that same evening he had told her he intended to end their marriage. And as the days slipped into weeks, and the ache inside became unbearable, Luca faced the truth: without Athena he would never be whole again.

Reminding himself that he had acted in her best interests when he had sent her away did not help. Being noble was highly overrated, he'd discovered. Missing her felt as agonising as if one of his limbs had been severed, and now, two weeks before Christmas, as he trudged through the crowded streets in Milan past brightly lit shop windows and the huge Christmas tree in front of the Duomo, he realised that he had to do something to try to ease the pain that overwhelmed him.

But what could he do? As much as he might wish it, Luca could not change the man he was—and he could not give Athena the family he was sure she wanted.

He remembered Athena's accusation that he shied away from commitment because he was afraid of rejection after his mother and his grandmother and Jodie had rejected him, and he admitted there was some truth in her words. He was scared of being happy with Athena in case he lost her and his happiness ended.

He was a coward, Luca told himself disgustedly, but that was something he could and would change—if he hadn't left it too late.

CHAPTER ELEVEN

THE STREETS IN the centre of Jaipur, capital city of Rajasthan, were a chaotic mix of buses and bikes, rickshaws and camels—who often added to the mayhem by lying down in the road and refusing to budge.

Luca observed the confusion of traffic and people from the back seat of a taxi. Ordinarily the sights and sounds of a new city would have enchanted him: the colourful silks in the bazaar and the astounding architecture of the majestic City Palace. But he stared unseeingly out of the window as the car joined the highway and headed out to the suburbs, where the houses became progressively more dilapidated and the sides of the road were filled with fruit stalls and bread stalls, with children running, dogs barking and the occasional cow ambling.

After what seemed like an eternity of driving along roads with potholes as big as craters, and nothing on the horizon but dry-as-dust land and a few sparse trees, the taxi driver spoke over his shoulder to Luca.

'The House of Happy Smiles is over there.'

For the first time in days, in *weeks*, Luca felt interest. He felt alive instead of feeling the dull nothingness that had plagued him day and night. And he felt a lurch of fear in his gut, so that he actually had to stop himself from retching when he remembered how he had dismissed Athena's love and sent her away from Villa De Rossi.

He looked at the square modern building. Half of it was apparently an orphanage and the other half was a school—or it would be when it was finished. Next to the new house was a ramshackle old building, with crumbling walls and a tin roof.

'What is that place?' he asked the taxi driver.

'That's the old orphanage—before the American and the English *memsahibs* came together with some Indian businessmen and raised the money to build the new one.'

Two contrasting images flashed into Luca's mind: his Christmas fashion show, attended by the wealthiest women of Milan's high society, and the waste tip the taxi had driven past further back along the road, where he had seen children crawling over the rubbish—searching, as he had been informed by the driver, for anything of minuscule value to sell so that they could buy food.

In his mind he heard Athena telling him she was going to build a house with the million pounds he had paid her to be his wife. He had assumed she meant a house for her to live in, but no.

As the taxi drove up to the House of Happy Smiles, a swarm of children ran into the compound, laughing and chattering, their big eyes wide with curiosity when they saw their visitor.

Athena was somewhere here—in this house she had built for the orphaned children of Jaipur.

'*I love you, Luca.*'

Dio! Luca ran his hand across his eyes. What had he done?

Athena finished feeding the two youngest residents of the orphanage and settled them next to each other in a cot. The twins, a girl and a boy, had been discovered abandoned in a cardboard box in the city. It was thought that Jaya and

Vijay were about six weeks old, and caring for them had helped a little to ease the ache in Athena's heart, which had splintered when Luca had announced he was ending their marriage.

She had left the villa and Italy immediately, and flown to India. Working at the orphanage gave her some solace, and a reason to get up every morning, but at night she could not hold back her tears. She had to accept that Luca did not love her, but she wondered if her broken heart would ever mend.

Cara Tanner put her head round the nursery door. 'Athena, you've got a visitor in your office.'

A visitor? No one apart from her sister and brother-in-law even knew she was in India.

The door to her office had fallen off its hinges a long time ago. Now that the new building was finished, Athena was looking forward to moving in to her own private flat at the orphanage. Her thoughts scattered as she pushed past the old sheet pinned across the doorway— and her stomach bottomed out as she stared in disbelief at Luca.

'What…?' Her voice was a thread of sound. She swallowed and kept on staring at him, sure he could not be real.

He looked even more gorgeous than her memories of him, his body leaner, harder beneath a white silk shirt and beige chinos. But when she looked closely at his face she saw fine lines around his eyes, as if his nights were as sleepless as hers, and his hair was longer, so that he had to rake it back from his brow with a hand that she noticed shook slightly.

'How did you find me?'

'I went to Zenhab and pleaded with Lexi until she gave in and told me about this place.' His eyes moved to the window and its view of the crisp white new building. 'I like the house you've built,' he said huskily. 'Why didn't you tell me about your involvement with the orphanage?'

She bit her lip. 'I thought you might not approve of how I had spent your money.'

'It was your money to spend as you liked. But, for what it's worth, I think what you have done here is amazing.'

His smile caused a shaft of pain to slice through Athena. 'Why are you here?' she said abruptly. She froze as a thought struck her. 'Rosalie…?'

'She's okay. Her condition will never get better, but thankfully she is no worse.' He hesitated. 'She can't say the words, but I know she misses you.'

'I miss her, too.' This was agonising. 'Luca…'

He strode towards her, but then stopped. There was no sign now of his usual effortless grace. His amber eyes sought hers, and seeing his emotions unguarded for once made Athena catch her breath.

'I came to ask you to come back to Villa De Rossi and be my wife again,' he said tautly.

Athena swiftly quashed her leap of hope. 'Is your great-uncle making problems again? Do you need to convince him that our marriage is not a sham?'

He shook his head. 'Emilio is out of the picture. The other board members refused to vote him in as chairman of De Rossi Enterprises and instead unanimously voted for me. My great-uncle has retired to his vineyards in Sicily.'

She frowned. 'Then why…?'

'I miss you.'

Luca saw shock in her eyes and knew he only had himself to blame. Because—as he could see she was about to remind him—he had sent her away. He had done it for the best of reasons. He would always feel guilty that he had unwittingly been the cause of his daughter's illness, and he could not live with yet more guilt knowing that he could not give Athena children. But he did not know if she would understand or if he had hurt her too much.

'I miss you,' he repeated, his voice rasping as if he had swallowed metal filings. 'I'm asking you to come back to me.' He swallowed. 'Not for ever...' He did not have the right to ask her to sacrifice her dreams of having a child. 'But for a little while...until you decide you want to move on and meet a man who can give you...give you what you want. A family...children,' he qualified roughly when she looked mystified.

Athena ignored the violent pounding of her heart. Every night after she had cried herself to sleep she dreamed of Luca coming back to her, but now it actually seemed to be happening she felt angry—and scared that she was mis-reading the message in his eyes.

'*Why* do you miss me?'

The whirr of the ceiling fan above the desk suddenly seemed to fill the room. *Whump-whump*. Luca's mouth felt dry and the palms of his hands were wet. *Man up*, demanded a voice inside his head. But for moment he was eight years old, sitting on his mother's bed, holding a silk scarf that smelled of her perfume, wondering why she had left him.

His grandmother had told him his mother hadn't loved him, that no one ever would—a dirty *bastardo*. His grandmother had been right. Jodie hadn't loved him, and she had left him alone to bring up their poor, damaged little girl.

But Athena wasn't like Jodie. He had to keep telling himself that.

'I love you.' The words felt unfamiliar on his tongue.

Something hot and fierce poured through Athena's veins. It was temper, she realised with surprise. All her life she had been meek and mild, but right at this moment she felt furious.

She marched over to Luca and pulled off her wide-brimmed hat so that she could see his face clearly. The gleam in his eyes as he watched her hair unravel and slide down her back evoked an ache in her belly—but sex was easy. She wanted so much more.

'Let me get this straight. You want me to be your wife again—but not for ever. Just until I meet another man who presumably will have a medical certificate to prove that his genes are perfect.'

She saw Luca's gaze drop to the jerky rise and fall of her breasts beneath her thin cotton dress and folded her arms over her chest.

'How am I supposed to meet this man? Will I live with you during the week and go on dates with other guys at weekends?'

He raked an unsteady hand through his hair. 'I haven't thought out the details. If you want the truth, I can't bear the idea of you with some other guy,' he said grimly. 'But I have to think what is best for *you*. I'm trying to do the right thing. I won't allow you to sacrifice your desire for children.'

Athena shook her head. 'I don't want a half-hearted relationship—*or* your half-hearted love.' Tears stung her eyes. 'If you really love me, *say it like you mean it, Luca.* I want everything…or nothing.'

He caught hold of her arms to prevent her from turning away.

'I can't give you everything,' he said hoarsely. 'You know I can't give you babies. I love you with all my heart—more than I knew it was possible to love someone—and because I love you I want you to be happy. That's why I sent you away from Villa De Rossi, away from me. I felt like my heart had been ripped out when I watched you drive away, but I wanted you to have the chance to fall in love—to be wooed, to have a fairytale wedding and plan the colour scheme of your nursery. I know how much you love children.'

'*I love you more.*'

She could not see him properly through her tears, so she stood on tiptoe and reached up to cradle his face between her hands, feeling the rough stubble on his jaw scrape her skin.

'You *are* everything, Luca. You are my one love, and there can never be anyone else for me because you are all I want and I will love you until I die.'

She stared into his eyes.

'If we had fallen in love and married in the conventional way, and then discovered that for some reason I couldn't have children, would you have ended our marriage and looked for another wife?'

'*No*, of course not. I want to spend the rest of my life with you and only you.' Luca felt as if iron bands were squeezing his lungs. 'I love you, Athena—more than I can say in words. I didn't expect to, or want to, if I'm honest,' he said rawly, 'but it crept up on me bit by bit. I wanted to hurt anyone who hurt you, to keep you safe and see your beautiful smile every day.'

He kissed her damp eyelashes.

'Don't cry, *piccola*,' he whispered.

But his own tears mingled with hers as he wrapped his arms around her and kissed her face, her lips, in a silent avowal of his love that would last a lifetime.

He reached into his pocket. 'I bought this the day after I'd lied and told you I didn't love you. But for weeks I was afraid to come and find you because I was sure you'd tell me to get lost.'

Athena smiled when she saw the gold heart-shaped locket inscribed with tiny flowers on the front. 'You said you wouldn't give me hearts and flowers,' she remembered.

Luca's amber eyes blazed with emotion. 'I said a lot of things I didn't mean, but I couldn't say the words that come from the bottom of my heart. *Ti amo.* I love you, *piccola.* Will you be my wife and the love of my life for ever?'

'I will,' she promised. 'Let me show you.'

She led him by the hand into the bedroom behind her office—which luckily did have a door.

Luca glanced around the sparsely furnished room and thought that Athena asked for so little and gave so much.

'It looks like a nun's cell,' he murmured as he sat down on the narrow bed and pulled her onto his lap.

'But you *know* I'm not an innocent virgin.'

Her eyes darkened with anticipation as he removed her dress and bra and cupped her breasts in his hands, bending his dark head to anoint each rosy pink nipple with tender kisses until she moaned with pleasure. She helped him strip out of his clothes and gave a contented sigh when he covered her naked body with his and she felt the hardness of his arousal push between her thighs.

'I wish there were mirrors on the ceiling... You've corrupted my body and captured my heart, and now I am yours for ever.'

'As I am yours,' Luca vowed. 'For ever.'

EPILOGUE

THE WEEPING WILLOW tree provided shade from the Italian summer sun, and the lavender bushes in full bloom hummed with the sound of industrious bees. Luca pushed his daughter's wheelchair along the wide paths, pausing often so that Rosalie could smell the mingled scents from the herb garden.

Following him toddled a sturdy little boy with a mop of black hair and a determined chin. Faisal Al Sulaimar, heir to the desert kingdom of Zenhab, showed no sign of the slight heart problem he had been born with, and Kadir had told Luca that Faisal had recently been given the all-clear by his specialist.

'My nephew is as daring as his mother,' Athena said as she ran along the path and stopped Faisal from trying to climb into the raised garden bed. 'I think Lexi is hoping the new baby doesn't turn out as adventurous as his or her older brother.'

She glanced at her heavily pregnant sister, and back to Luca, and her smile lifted his heart as it always did.

'We're going to have our work cut out when Jaya and Vijay learn to walk. The drawback with twins is that they do everything at roughly the same time. They're double trouble.'

Luca knelt down on the rug spread on the grass and scooped his adopted baby son and daughter into his arms.

'Double the joy,' he said softly. 'Double the fun and laughter and love.'

'Oh, yes, we're doubly lucky,' Athena agreed.

A few weeks after she and Luca had had their marriage blessed in a beautiful ceremony in the local village church in Jaipur they had become the proud adoptive parents of Jaya and Vijay. They were determined to bring their children up with an understanding of their Indian culture, and planned to spend as much time as possible at the orphanage in Jaipur, helping to care for the abandoned children who called the House of Happy Smiles home.

She knelt down beside Luca and her heart missed a beat when she saw his love for her blazing in his eyes. 'Most of all we are lucky to have each other,' she whispered. 'I couldn't ask for more.'

His eyes took on a wicked glint. 'Actually, there *was* one thing missing from our lives—but a mirrored ceiling above our bed is being fitted today. I think we should have a very early night, *mia bella*...'

* * * * *